# CRITICAL PRAISE
# FOR HILLARY FIELDS

## MARRYING JEZEBEL

"Fresh, fun, and romantic! *Marrying Jezebel* is an irresistible blend of passion and adventure—a reader's delight! Hillary Fields is fantastic!"
  —Tina St. John, author of *Lady of Valor*

"Hillary Fields delivers a humorous tale of adventure and mayhem. Beautifully written and sinfully clever. In short, simply wonderful."
  —Kinley MacGregor, author of *Master of Seduction*

## THE MAIDEN'S REVENGE

"Who wouldn't like a good, swashbuckling pirate story? Especially when the pirate is a woman! Hillary Fields takes us on a grand adventure."
  —Kat Martin, author of *Perfect Sin*

"Captain Lynnette Blackthorne ranks right up there with Emerald and Serena as the boldest women pirates in romance. Readers who like their romance with a sea breeze, sexual tension on high, and rapier-sharp dialogue will adore *The Maiden's Revenge*. Hillary Fields makes her mark with an unforgettable debut."
  —*Romantic Times*, 4½ Stars

"What a fabulous read! . . . Tender, spicy, thoroughly entertaining from the laugh-provoking opening pages to the utterly delightful epilogue, *The Maiden's Revenge* is a must-read-today book."
  —*Under the Covers Book Reviews*

ST. MARTIN'S PAPERBACKS TITLES
BY HILLARY FIELDS

*The Maiden's Revenge*
*Marrying Jezebel*

# MARRYING JEZEBEL

## HILLARY FIELDS

St. Martin's Paperbacks

MARRYING JEZEBEL

Copyright © 2000 by Hillary Fields.

All rights reserved. No part of this book may be used or reproduced in any manner whatsoever without written permission except in the case of brief quotations embodied in critical articles or reviews. For information address St. Martin's Press, 175 Fifth Avenue, New York, N.Y. 10010.

ISBN: 0-312-97567-8

Printed in the United States of America

St. Martin's Paperbacks edition / October 2000

St. Martin's Paperbacks are published by St. Martin's Press, 175 Fifth Avenue, New York, N.Y. 10010.

10  9  8  7  6  5  4  3  2  1

# *Acknowledgments*

*This* book could not have been completed without the kindness and infinite patience of my lovely editor at St. Martin's, Kristen Macnamara. Kristen, thank you for Lucinda and so much more!

As well, I'd like to thank Jane Dystel, Miriam Goderich, and Stacey Glick over at Jane Dystel Literary Management. You guys are absolutely the best at what you do!

To the folks at The HealthCare Chaplaincy, thank you for letting me write while I was supposed to be working.

And to my friends and my family . . . well, you know.

# MARRYING JEZEBEL

# Chapter One

~

*A* droplet of rainwater clung annoyingly from the tip of Raphael Sunderland's patrician nose, cold rivulets following the lines of his scowl as he glared across the wharf.

Still no sign of the girl.

Most of the other passengers had already disembarked from the ship he was watching, but so far the young lady he'd come to meet had yet to show her face, and Rafe was getting tired of waiting. He was the bloody duke of Ravenhurst, for God's sake. His family had owned most of the counties of Derby, Middlebury, and even parts of Somerset since the fifteenth century—and as the seventh duke to inherit title to these estates, he was indubitably one of the largest landowners in all of England. He was also sole proprietor of enough profitable business ventures, including various coal mines, textile factories, and shipping concerns, to employ a small army of clerks. He'd long ago been crowned the best catch of any Season by society's ever-hopeful matrons.

He did *not* cool his heels at the pleasure of little girls.

Impatient, aggravated, he'd left his carriage to pace the docks of London Harbor, watching as the passengers filed down the gangway of the clipper ship one after another. *What on earth is the holdup?* he growled to himself. Then he saw. One of the passengers was being carried down the plank on a stretcher, obviously too weak to walk. Could it be she? he wondered. The pang of concern he felt belied his earlier annoyance. Then, as two sailors tilted the

stretcher down to begin the descent to the pier, he saw that
the sick passenger was an elderly gentleman, and Rafe relaxed with a sense of guilty relief. He might not have much
information about the young person who was to become
his new ward, but he doubted Miss Jezebel Montclair, niece
of the late earl of Clifton, looked much like this unfortunate
old man.

God knew what the girl *would* look like, Rafe thought
with a snort. All he knew was what he'd learned two nights
ago, when his country retreat in Derbyshire had been interrupted late in the evening by an unannounced visitor.

*A*knock on the library door shattered Rafe's meditative
musings. He'd just been reflecting on how quiet things
were, how orderly, and he had even managed to convince
himself that he liked it. *All is exactly as it should be,* he'd
been telling himself firmly only seconds before the insistent
rapping began. After he heard it, he mentally amended the
statement. *All except that infernal banging.*

Ensconced in his favorite hunter-green leather chair, sipping a finely aged brandy, he had, as a matter of fact, just
been on the verge of nodding off. Wedged deeply into another overstuffed library chair, his best friend in the world
was dozing nearby in the cozy firelit chamber, sharing his
repose, if not his thoughts.

At the sound of the knock, Damien Marksley, titled marquis of Rutledge (named less formally a profligate wastrel
with a propensity for practical jokes), shifted, scratched,
and belched good-naturedly from the confines of his own
wing-backed seat before the hearth. Damien owned lands
adjacent to Rafe's own, and the two close friends often
passed a winter evening drinking or playing chess compan-
ionably by the fire.

After a day of stag hunting in the parklands and an afternoon celebrating their catch with some rather appreciative maids down at the village tavern, both were worn and
sated this evening. Neither one felt the need to speak, the
late hour and the soporifics they'd consumed making them
very somnolent gentlemen indeed.

The fire was crackling merrily in Rafe's library, sending mellow light to caress the book-lined walls and rich mahogany furnishings. Outside the mullioned windows, the weather had turned wretched, rain and hail intermingling in the bluster of late December, but in that bastion of masculine warmth and comfort, Rafe and his friend had basked like lazy lizards until the loud knocking startled them into alertness.

*Who could be calling at such an hour,* Rafe wondered, *and in such inclement weather?*

A moment later his country butler, Smythe, called from outside the heavy wooden panels of the library's double doors to announce the arrival of a visitor. *Odd,* Rafe thought, just a bit disturbed. *I wasn't expecting anyone.* It was past one o'clock in the morning. He and Damien exchanged startled glances. "Who the devil could that be?" muttered Rafe. The marquis, apparently mystified but already getting a sly gleam of curiosity in the merry gray eyes for which he was famed among the *ton,* simply shrugged. "This had better not be one of your practical jokes, Damien. I'm in no mood to be picking toads out of my Hessians again, 1lI warn you . . ."

But Smythe, well trained in the art of butlery, knew better than to disturb his master's pleasures unless the matter was urgent, so Rafe assumed he couldn't safely ignore the knock and return to the happy doze that it had shattered. Irritated, he called to the old retainer to allow his visitor entrance, growling grumpily to himself, "This had *better* be good."

In a subdued rush, Mr. Aldous P. Chumley, Esquire, Rafe's solicitor and loyal man of business for more than a decade, entered the room, shaking off a deluge of raindrops and apologizing profusely for the late hour. The duke sat up straighter in his chair, waking up a little as his interest was piqued. Midnight meetings were definitely not among Chumley's ordinary business practices, and Rafe's curiosity, always keen, grew by leaps and bounds. Thankfully, he did not have to wait long to satisfy it. After bowing deeply to both peers, the man leapt right in to the subject at hand.

"Your Grace, I would not have dreamed of interrupting

Your Lordships at such an hour, but a matter of the utmost importance has come to my attention, and I am sure it cannot be properly settled by anyone except yourself. . . ." The man trailed off, looking flustered and wringing his hands. A silence followed his words as the solicitor shuffled uncomfortably. The duke had not offered him a seat, and he clearly dared not presume enough to take one of his own accord. Raindrops plopped dolefully onto the dark plum and gold-accented Aubusson carpet as he waited.

Realizing this, Rafe impatiently waved Chumley to the chaise lounge set at a right angle to the two men's chairs along one wall of the room. He tried not to wince at the thought of the antique gold silk sofa absorbing Chumley's excess moisture. The man sat hurriedly before the peers, fidgeting a little under Rafe's steady gaze and the marquis's avid one. With one eyebrow quirked, Rafe drawled, "And that matter might be . . . ?"

"Your Grace." The solicitor removed some papers from his greatcoat pocket and adjusted his spectacles as he squinted to read what was written on the crumpled page. "I am sorry to inform you that Jonathan Montclair, the late earl of Clifton, has passed on." He looked up worriedly, as if expecting the news to be a devastating blow to his employer.

"Montclair," Rafe murmured. "The archaeologist?" At the solicitor's nod, he frowned. "I remember him vaguely. . . . Hasn't he been in the Far East for the past several years?"

"Egypt, Your Grace. I've just received word of his untimely demise this night by special courier."

The duke stared steadily at his solicitor. *Untimely? But Jonathan Montclair couldn't have been a day under seventy,* he thought. *And why,* he wondered, *would Lord Clifton possibly want to arrange for me to have word of his death?* The two men had not been close for ages; in fact, had shared only a rather brief acquaintance years ago when Rafe had, on a whim, joined one of the many societies in London devoted to cultural exploration and the study of antiquities.

"Perhaps," he said softly, "you will care to explain why

this news has warranted a visit so late at night, and in such an agitated state?"

The rebuke in the duke's voice was gentle, but was felt nonetheless by his unfortunate man of business. Lord Ravenhurst was not a man one cared to disappoint, as Chumley was well aware. The time had come to get to the heart of the matter. He swallowed.

"Well, Your Grace, it seems he has left you a rather unusual inheritance." He did not continue, looking vaguely ill at being the bearer of such bad tidings.

"Good God, man, what could be so awful? What has he left me?"

"His niece, Your Grace."

Rafe choked on his brandy.

Through watering eyes, he shot Damien an alarmed glance, but when the marquis seemed filled with as much disbelief as himself, he turned his incredulous attention back to the unhappy solicitor for an explanation. One look at Damien's dumbfounded expression was enough to assure the duke his friend hadn't put the humorless attorney up to this very poor joke.

"Surely you are mistaken; this must be some sort of jest," Rafe gasped when he could breathe again. "What man in his right mind would make *me* his niece's guardian? I assume I *am* to be the chit's guardian?" Chumley nodded shamefacedly. It was clear to Rafe that his rather tarnished reputation with the ladies was as well-known to the solicitor as it was to every gossipmonger in town.

"Your Grace, the matter was apparently settled some years ago when the earl wrote out his will. His instructions were quite explicit. In the event of his demise," he quoted, reading from his handful of documents again, " 'Lord Ravenhurst is to have the guardianship of my dearest niece until she reaches her majority at the age of twenty-five, or until her marriage, whichever shall occur first.' " Chumley drew in his breath, having rushed through the unpleasant reading. "I believe the girl can claim but twenty years of age as yet." Seeing his employer's scowl grow thunderous as he realized just how long this proposed guardianship would last, he added lamely, "The earl mentions in his letter that this arrangement is per a discussion between Your Lordship and himself and has met with your agreement."

"What! I would never have agreed to such a farcical arrangement. . . ." Rafe trailed off, a sudden memory flickering through his somewhat drink-hazed mind. Six or seven years ago, in an attempt to alleviate a period of restlessness he couldn't seem to shake through the usual outlets of whiskey, women, and cards, Rafe had taken an interest in antiquities and exploration. Having joined the well-known Society of Antiquaries, he had met several times with Lord Clifton while that old worthy was on a rare return visit to his homeland. The earl had been taking care of estate business between sojourns abroad, where Rafe understood Lord Clifton spent most of his time.

On one such occasion, he recalled now, they'd shared a rather muddled, rambling discussion about the perils and pitfalls of a life spent adventuring. He remembered sitting with Jonathan Montclair in a corner of the club's comfortably masculine trophy room, raising a healthy glass of spirits to the noble concepts of "exploring the world" and "getting a little excitement out of life."

After an hour or two of this, the two men had grown quite as chummy as any father and son. And at one point during that long afternoon, Lord Clifton had somehow managed to solicit Rafe's promise to see to his "affairs" should the older man run across some bad luck in the wilds of Africa or wherever he was headed next. These affairs, Rafe now gathered, included the man's niece. A niece he'd conveniently never mentioned to the duke.

*Wily old bastard, sticking it to me that way,* Rafe thought, equal measures of outrage and wry humor warring inside him. It was well-known in society that no matter what he might do with his leisure time, however scandalous his affairs, the duke of Ravenhurst *always* lived up to his responsibilities. Being as good as his word was his greatest weakness, he often thought. Far too many people tried to take advantage.

He felt his pulse speed up with what he told himself was righteous indignation, but his more honest side suspected his rapid heartbeat might have more to do with the prospect of the first real challenge to enter his life in some time. Lately, he couldn't help feeling that things had been going far too smoothly, that even the pleasures of his life had grown routine, though he had never let his dissatisfaction show to anyone else—not even his closest friends. The duke of Ravenhurst had a reputation to uphold, after all.

What did it matter if he sometimes felt he was slowly sinking beneath the weight of his title and all that went with it? This was the life he'd been born into, a life most could only dream of, and he must always keep up appearances. That much Rafe's father had drilled into his head before succumbing to a massive attack of apoplexy at the ripe old age of forty-five. Rafe, then only sixteen, had never forgotten the lesson—neither the admonition to duty *nor* the fact that this same awesome responsibility had taken his father's life long before his time.

In light of his father's example, Rafe had long ago determined to take his pleasures where he found them, to exploit the privileges of his position to the fullest in a way the elder Lord Ravenhurst never had. He'd resolved never to become a man such as his father had been: dour, humorless, devoted to his work to the exclusion of his family. Yet Rafe feared that sooner or later, this was exactly what he would become despite all his declarations, for he knew he could never simply walk away from the obligations to which he'd been born. Too much rested on his actions, too many people depended on him to make the right decisions. In his twelve-year tenure as duke, he'd never truly crossed the line, never let his diversions get in the way of his obligation to the Ravenhurst dynasty. And now it seemed he had yet another burden waiting for him.

"Mr. Chumley," the duke murmured, "you still have not managed to explain why this news could not wait until the morning." His tone was ever so slightly impatient, though perfectly civilized. Raphael Sunderland never raised his voice. It wasn't necessary. He stated what he wanted, and it appeared before him. Should that tactic fail, and it rarely did, one cold glance usually took care of whatever the problem was.

Ravenhurst was simply not a man one wanted to tangle with. At three inches above six feet, he towered over most people, and his impressive build, combined with his great height, served to make other men appear puny in comparison. Even his big, quick-spreading grin could seem somewhat threatening to those who were easily intimidated. His golden bronze skin, short-cropped, curling blond hair, massively broad shoulders, and vividly, impossibly blue eyes had often caused women to sigh that it was as if Apollo, the ancient Greek god of the sun, had stepped right down off his chariot and into London's fashionable West End. Certainly, these women didn't seem worried about being burned by his fire.

But it was none of these things—not his remarkable good looks, his life of privilege, or his nearly unfathomable wealth—that made people defer to the duke of Ravenhurst so much as it was the man's sheer presence. Rafe, purely and simply, emanated an overpowering sense of being *alive*. He strode through any gathering like a virile lion carving a swath through a herd of timid antelope. People made way for him instinctively. When you were with him, his friends had decided among themselves, you felt positive that he was just more intelligent, more aware, and more *awake* than everyone else in the group.

Faced with more than six feet of this overpowering, irritated aristocrat, Chumley wilted immediately. It was time to come out with the rest of the awful truth. "The girl is scheduled to arrive in London in two days' time, Your Grace," he choked out.

There was a small, unpleasant silence. The sound of sleet hitting the leaded-glass window casings was suddenly very loud. "Two days, you say?" the duke inquired faintly. He quickly calculated the time and distances involved. That would barely give him enough time to meet her ship, even if he rousted the servants out of bed right now to start packing for town.

But what other choice did he have? Rafe asked himself. He could hardly leave a young girl, who'd recently lost her only relative, standing on the pier with no one to greet her, and he couldn't send someone else to fetch her in his stead either. As her new guardian, it wouldn't be right not to come for her personally.

Chumley echoed the duke's affront at the forthcoming arrival of such unwanted baggage. "Indeed, Your Grace! The very messenger who brought me word of her uncle's death informed me that Lord Clifton had also arranged for the girl to take passage on a clipper for England." He paused, noting Sunderland's thunderous scowl. "I thought it best to leave the matter in Your Grace's more capable hands as quickly as possible, knowing you would want to deal with Miss Montclair yourself." The solicitor looked mightily relieved to be passing off his burden into the hands of the proper authority.

Lord Ravénhurst reflected wryly that it was always his duty to take care of the most unpleasant business, whilst his employees turned over their problems to him to fix, ducking behind their own lack of authority. But perhaps he too could fob the girl off.

"Deal with her?" Rafe scoffed. "Chumley, I don't want to deal with her. I want to be *rid* of her."

Just thinking of hosting some schoolroom chit, all aflutter about her first trip to London and hopelessly naïve, made him long for another brandy. He poured himself one, took a swift gulp. The girl was probably hideous and completely dowdy, if her uncle was anything to go by. Of the many things Jonathan Montclair had been, the word *handsome* did not even make the list. Doubtless, she would be a total ninny as well. Women younger than thirty almost invariably were, and some of them never got better with age. By God, the whole notion of him playing guardian was preposterous! How the *ton* would laugh to hear of the rakish Ravenhurst taking on a ward.

"Is there no way to avoid this situation altogether, Chumley? No one else with whom she might stay, no relations who would take her in and take over guardianship? I would be willing to pay a handsome stipend for the girl's upkeep if that's at issue. Surely she can't remain here under my protection."

"There is no one else who might take her in, Your Grace. I took the liberty of inquiring before I troubled Your Lordship tonight. It seems the girl is entirely alone in the world, though hardly penniless. Her fortune, when she comes into it, will be quite considerable."

Rafe shook off that negligible concern. "You're saying I'm stuck with her no matter what."

"I'm afraid that is so, Your Grace." Chumley looked so woebegone that Rafe almost began to feel sorry for him. It was quite obvious to everyone in the room how ridiculous was the very notion of Rafe Sunderland as anyone's guardian. His sensual reputation, well earned, said he was more likely to play seducer than protector to any young lady who resided under his roof. But Rafe could see Chumley was far too prudent to make mention of this fact. Instead, the man huddled into his sodden greatcoat and simply waited while his two betters began to discuss the bad news.

"What are you going to do, Rafe?" Damien asked, knowing he sounded unusually concerned for someone who had made an art of appearing languid in any and all situations, but finding languor rather difficult to achieve just at the moment. After all, his best friend was in imminent danger of becoming mother hen to a green girl! This could put one hell of a damper on their enjoyment of the Season.

Both men had planned to depart from their sprawling estates in the country early this spring in order to enjoy some of London's less seemly pleasures, to have their bachelor fun before the marriage-minded mamas and their flocks of insipid darlings descended on the town. Both knew they'd have only weeks before they would have to put in polite appearances at an endless series of mind-numbingly dull masques, soirees, routs, and balls. While hunting and weekend parties—staples of country life—had indeed paled rather quickly this year, Damien and Rafe had both been dreading the true beginning of the Season. Much more fun to duck the dowagers and go trolling the stews and slums of London for sport while they could. But Rafe hadn't planned on leaving quite *this* soon! Why, the massive Christmastide Yule log had barely burned to ashes in the great hall. London would be deserted for months yet—what would he do with the chit until then?

"Well, I . . ." Rafe stuttered for a moment. He couldn't think of a single solution and he began to feel the first threads of anxiety winding through his consciousness. Had he been looking for distraction, and had someone "up there" decided to play a cruel joke on him for questioning his perfect life? A fitting punishment, surely, but one he must avoid at all costs. *Think!* Rafe told himself. *There must be a way to salvage the situation.* Then his eyes narrowed and a triumphant expression spread across his face.

"I'm going to marry her off, of course! To the first available suitor! We'll be rid of the chit within a fortnight," he predicted with sudden confidence.

Damien laughed outright. "How on earth are you going to accomplish *that* minor miracle? You're hardly much of a matchmaker, Rafe. Indeed, I thought the very word *marriage* made you ill."

"Only when it's *my* potential marriage being discussed. Besides, I'm not the duke of Ravenhurst for nothing, man! If I want her married off, I'll damn well get her married off. I know plenty of available gentlemen whose greatest desire in life is to remain firmly on my good side. How hard can it be?"

"But what if she's entirely homely, or lacks the social graces?" Damien wanted to know. He didn't like this notion of forcing available gents to pay court to Clifton's niece. After all, he himself was an available gent!

"My guess is she's quite ill-favored, judging by the uncle's looks. He was a warty old fellow, to be sure." Rafe chuckled with restored good humor. "I imagine she's got no polish either. The man was as absentminded as an Oxford don, never took thought to anything beyond whatever blasted antiquity he was studying at the time." Rafe was grinning now. "What a challenge, eh? Take the girl in and send her right out again into the hands of some unsuspecting, utterly worthy old peer."

"*Worthy* being the operative word, I am to understand?" Damien surmised. "You're not simply intending to wed her to the first out-of-pocket scoundrel who comes sniffing about her skirts, are you?" The Rafe he knew was too much of a gentleman to even consider such a tactic.

"Of course not, Marksley. That's half the fun of it. Naturally the man we choose for my little ward will be a stellar

example of English manhood, containing all the virtues a
lady could want—decent and upstanding, surely, but vari-
ously tall or short; skinny or portly; aged or stripling; mel-
ancholic, bilious, phlegmatic, or apoplectic—all depending,
of course, on her own character, disposition, and appearance. Whoever the poor man is, he'll be firmly and inex-
tricably wed to the girl before he ever figures out what's
become of his salad days."

Damien began to see some of the possibilities. Squiring
a young lady about might not be as much fun as living it
up among the gaming hells and brothels of London, but at
least it would prove a novelty. Undeniably, the old amusements were beginning to pall for all of them. Fun was at a
premium these days. "You're a cruel fellow, Rafe, am-
bushing some poor unsuspecting bachelor like that. Worse
than anything I could come up with!" The marquis was
grinning. "I assume you've got a plan in mind to accomplish this Herculean feat, my friend?"

The solicitor was completely forgotten as the two friends
began to plot. "Indeed," Rafe mused aloud, sipping more
brandy. "We'll need a chaperone, of course; first thing.
Clifton's niece can't be known to be staying in a bachelor
residence without proper supervision. Then tutors, dancing
masters, etiquette instructors. We can't afford to take any
chances on the girl's education. She might prove a veritable
savage, growing up with that batty old earl. Luckily, we'll
have some time before the high Season starts to give her
some town polish. Then, when we're sure of her skills,
there'll be her formal presentation and her introduction into
society, as soon as we may arrange them—"

"Wait a minute here, Rafe," Damien protested. "Rein in
that galloping mind of yours. First of all, what reputable
lady could you conceivably get to come live here in this
den of iniquity with you and your new ward? No self-
respecting matron would dare set foot in your townhouse—
or any of your other residences, for that matter—for fear
of corrupting her immortal soul in perpetuity."

"Lady Allison would do it. She is, after all, my dear,
dear cousin." Rafe's eyes twinkled with mischief.

Damien broke into astounded laughter. "Lady Allison!

Mayfair's Merry Widow, you mean? Why, she can scarcely even be considered your cousin, unless you count cousins ten times removed by marriage. And she is not at *all* respectable, my friend."

"Yes, well, no one in society knows that. She's very discreet among the *ton*, as you ought to remember. Why, even Lady Jersey receives her. Which means everybody receives her. And we are indeed cousins of a sort—kissing cousins, if you like." He smiled wryly. "And anyway, close enough that no one will question the propriety of her residing in my household to chaperone my little ward.

"You and I," he concluded with a widening grin, "along with perhaps a very few other discreet gentlemen, are the only ones who know Lady Allison Mayhew is not the stronghold of moral fortitude she pretends to the world. She would do quite nicely, I think." He paused. "More to the point, she *will* do. The lady owes me a favor or two, and besides, she'll see the fun of it all. She loves to take a lost lamb under her wing now and again, and she's no great plans for the Season beyond her latest affair."

"The M.P., you mean?"

"So she's told you? I didn't want to spill the beans if she hadn't. Indeed, we two may be the only ones who know about it. Our dear Allison's got that poor parliamentary bastard wrapped right 'round her dainty little finger. Of course, the minister can't afford the scandal it would cause should anything get out, so he's keeping it all very hush-hush. Just as Allison prefers . . . smart woman, that."

The two seemed prepared to go on at length gossiping about Lady Mayhew's *affaires du coeur,* had not Chumley's uncomfortable throat-clearing drawn them back to the present.

Rafe drew himself back to the matter at hand. "That's the least of our worries, I believe. Allison will surely come to our aid in this noble quest, and we shall have the girl right as rain and ready to go in no time. It's the details of the entrapment we must plan, old friend. And I'll need your help for that. Are you up for it?"

"I wouldn't miss it, Rafe. When have *I* ever skipped an opportunity to shake things up?"

"Then it's settled. As of tomorrow, the campaign to marry off . . . marry off . . ." He stopped, realizing he didn't have so much as an appellation for the object of all his scheming. He turned on the shivering solicitor once more, eyes bright.

"Well, what is the chit called, Chumley? The girl must have a name."

Chumley swallowed hard as he answered. "Jezebel, Your Grace. The unfortunate child's name is Jezebel."

There was a moment of silence after that pronouncement. Then Rafe shrugged, caught Damien's bemused expression with an adventurous look of his own. He raised his brandy snifter. "To marrying Jezebel!"

Caught up in his own plotting and scheming, it didn't once cross the arrogant duke's mind that his new ward might have other, entirely nonnegotiable plans for her future.

None of them, he would soon discover, included bowing meekly to Raphael Sunderland's high-handed meddling.

*M*iss Montclair, as Rafe found out after another interminable half hour of waiting on the dank, smelly wharves, was not on the ship. She'd never *been* on the ship, according to the captain, whose blunt seaman's manner and open, honest face made the duke believe he was telling the truth. Still, Rafe questioned the man closely, concern mounting to actual fear for the girl as the bluff captain explained what he knew.

There'd been a passage booked for a Miss J. M. Montclair, all right, the man averred. He had it on his manifest. Some older gent, a lawyer by the look of him, had seen to the arrangements a few days before the ship was to sail. He'd set her up with a first-rate cabin even on such short notice as he'd been given, the ship's master declared. She'd just never claimed her berth. But when Rafe asked if that meant he'd sailed without ever meeting the girl, without making inquiries as to why she had not showed up, the man corrected him.

"Didn't say I never saw her," he replied laconically. "Said she didn't get on the ship." The captain remembered Miss Montclair clearly. "Dark-haired girl, arrived early at the dock, stayed to talk with some of the other passengers on the day we were to sail. Thought she was on board, bless me, until we gathered for dinner that very night!" He'd asked after her, he said, but none of the paying passengers knew anything about the girl. "Well, none as came to dinner, at any rate. Lots 'a folks down the cabins that night, pukin', ye know. Bit of a squall blew up. Worst of 'em was that fella ye just saw there." He nodded toward the elderly man who, on shaky legs, was being helped from his stretcher into a carriage. "Doubt that poor bloke kept a thing in 'is stomach the whole way here." He shook his head in pity at these hopeless landlubbers. "Questioned ev'rybody 'bout the girl, nobody knew. Guess she changed her mind 'bout comin'."

*Had she?* the duke wondered anxiously. *Or had someone perhaps changed it for her?* Any number of things could have happened to a naive young lady between boarding time and departure, waiting among the riffraff on the Cairo wharves for her turn to embark. It seemed highly improbable to Rafe that she would have chosen to remain in Egypt of her own accord. *After all,* he asked himself, *what would make a young girl like Miss Montclair, alone in the world for the first time, miss the very ship that promised to take her to a safe, secure new home and protector?*

Rafe thanked the captain absently, pressing a gold guinea into his callused hand as he shook it in farewell. His mind was already engaged in planning for the days ahead of him. So much for quiet evenings in the country toasting the Yuletide with his friends and romping with his hounds, he thought ruefully. Life was about to get a whole lot more complicated.

The duke, it seemed, was off to Egypt. And if the Honorable Miss Jezebel Montclair wasn't in trouble now, she damn well would be when he got there.

# Chapter Two

CAIRO, FEBRUARY 1818

Six weeks later as the ship edged its way into port along the banks of the Nile, Rafe was even less amused by the situation old Clifton's death had left him in than he had been when he first learned of it. The heat in Cairo, even in February, was like standing before an open oven door in the middle of Sunday baking. Only the smell hitting him from the docks wasn't the wholesome, yeasty scent of bread. It was the stink of harbors everywhere, of dead fish combined with offal and human sweat, compounded by the scorching effect of the sun to an intense miasma.

Flies buzzed around Rafe's head and he swiped irritably at the pests. His white cambric shirt clung wetly to the muscles of his back, and his trousers felt like a second skin. He'd discarded his jacket already, a breach of etiquette, perhaps, but one that could not be helped until his valet was able to purchase clothing more suited to the climate. Then again, he hadn't exactly had the luxury of planning his wardrobe for this trip, Rafe thought irately.

Wallace Perkins, his valet for many years, had accompanied Rafe on this trip as he did everywhere else. The fussy, middle-aged gentleman's gentleman had warned the duke in the direst tones that he'd surely live to regret such a hasty, ill-planned departure, but he'd paid the servant little heed at the time. Fear for the girl whose guardianship he'd so reluctantly accepted had made Rafe decide he must leave for Egypt as quickly as possible.

A few quick inquiries back in London that day had informed him there was only one ship leaving for Cairo so late in the sailing season, and it was scheduled to leave the harbor within days. With almost no time to prepare, there'd been many arrangements to make, and packing had been the least of his concerns. For a trip of this magnitude, a man of Ravenhurst's many responsibilities must make detailed plans. There were estate managers to alert, business partners to contact, and underlings of all kinds to instruct on how to carry on in his absence.

Dukes didn't just hare off into the hinterlands—Rafe, as master of the Ravenhurst dynasty, was responsible for the lives and livelihoods of scores of people all across Great Britain. He felt a grim certainty that while he was gone, his affairs would probably go all to hell despite his careful instructions. But it couldn't be helped, now, could it? He accepted the inevitable with a brief sigh. He might not have asked to be saddled with looking after the inconvenient Miss Montclair, but once obliged, he simply couldn't turn his back on the girl. And with her life very possibly in danger, there was no way he could have trusted someone else to search for her. No, he'd had no choice but to leave everything behind and come dashing off to this sweltering backwater to find out what had happened to Clifton's missing niece.

Still, it was a fascinating place he'd come to, he saw as the ship sailed slowly toward land, having floated tranquilly along the Canopic branch of the Nile from Alexandria. They'd passed through that famous port with its fabled lighthouse and the enormous standing obelisk called Cleopatra's Needle the day before, but, by means of a discreet liberal palm-greasing at the outset of the voyage, Rafe had yet persuaded the ship's captain not to dock there. Though he would have liked to see the many wonders of that storied city by the sea, without knowing Jezebel Montclair's fate, he couldn't take the time to dally simply for the sake of sightseeing.

But Cairo was enough to distract him from his disappointment, for it was very different from the sleepy farming villages they'd passed on their way up the river so far. Despite the discomforts of the heat and his concern for the loose ends he had left behind in England, Rafe also couldn't help feeling a surge of excitement as he stared around him at the city that was even now coming into view.

He'd always wanted to travel abroad, but ever since he'd inherited the duchy at the tender age of sixteen, his responsibilities had forced him to remain close to home. Aside from a brief tour of the continent and infrequent business trips to see his estates in Scotland and thoroughbred racing stables in Ireland, Rafe had seldom had occasion to sojourn away from England. His natural urge to explore had always been stifled by the many commitments he had back home. Now, however, one of those commitments had finally taken him to an exotic destination, and he was taking everything in with avid eyes. Cairo was like another world.

Men in light-colored cotton robes and loosely wrapped turbans carried bundles of goods on their backs ranging from huge cords of dried reeds to woven baskets easily twice the men's size and whose contents he couldn't begin to guess. Sheep and goats ran loose in the streets, young boys with sticks driving them onto odd-shaped barges at the water's edge for transport to villages upriver. Women swathed in black veils from head to foot, only their eyes showing between the layers of fabric, hurried along on their errands in the narrow alleys between tan and white mud-brick buildings. Striped awnings stretched between the thatched roofs kept the sun away and provided marginally cooler spaces, which the city's merchants took advantage of by filling every doorway and alcove with makeshift stalls full of goods.

The whole city, as far as Rafe could see from the vantage of the tall ship's height, looked like one overflowing, constantly moving bazaar. The cacophony of voices—haggling shoppers, merchants shouting out their wares, laborers singing rhythmic chants as they unloaded cargo from the ships, all augmented by the distinctive earsplitting bray of a donkey coming from somewhere just out of Rafe's sight—fairly inundated his hearing. *Fascinating, indeed,* his sense of adventure whispered, and his blood stirred in his veins for the first time in a long while. If the duke hadn't been so concerned with finding his ward immediately and ensuring the girl's safety, he might even have said he was enjoying himself.

But the reminder of his reason for being in Egypt brought Rafe back down to earth quickly. First things first. He would go to the hotel recommended to him by several of the other British passengers whom he had gotten to know during the voyage. Everyone, from high-ranking diplomats to East India Company men to small independent traders, stayed at Shepheard's Hotel, these seasoned travelers assured him. Someone there was bound to know the whereabouts of his missing ward—or know someone who did. Rafe would check into this hotel, he'd decided, and make it the center of his investigations. From there he would be able to hire men to help him search the city, inquire of the locals if they'd seen her, even drag the river if that turned out to be necessary.

He hoped it would not be necessary.

Perhaps the girl was alive and well in Cairo and had simply been delayed in some unforeseen manner from coming to meet him. There had to be a reasonable explanation for why she had not flown gratefully into the arms of her new protector after her uncle had died, leaving her to fend for herself in a foreign land. Such a situation had to have been a nightmare for a young lady to endure, Rafe thought, suffering a pang of sympathy despite the annoyance he'd been feeling earlier.

Perhaps, in her shock and distress, Miss Montclair had decided against making another sea change so soon and had opted to stay among friends. That was the scenario he was hoping for, anyway, though Rafe couldn't come up with a reason why the girl would not at least have sent him word in that event. Neither could he explain the captain's report of her mysterious appearance on the Cairo docks on the day she'd been scheduled to sail. Well, he would soon find out the answers to all these questions.

After their ship had tied up to its slip and the crew had made her ready for disembarking, Rafe, followed by his valet with their baggage, quickly made his way into the hustle and bustle that was the city's harbor. Within moments the resourceful Perkins had hired a rickshaw carriage, a kind of human-drawn cart that seemed to be the primary means of transportation around the streets, at least for European visitors with money to spend. Their driver, a wild-eyed young man with dusty bare feet and a grin that said he'd been out in the sun too long hauling foreigners around, took off into the traffic with a jolt. The quest to find his ward had begun.

$\mathcal{R}$afe accomplished his mission much faster than he'd ever thought possible.

Needless to say, when he ran into the elusive Miss Montclair within an hour of his arrival, it came as quite a surprise. Yet when he found the woman, it was not simply a relief. It was also a revelation.

After stopping just long enough to deposit his belongings and his valet in one of the Shepheard's better suites, he'd headed for the hotel's bar, expecting the inquiries he made there to be only the first in a protracted investigation into the girl's whereabouts. Instead, the very first group of gentlemen Rafe questioned held all the answers he sought.

The men looked at him as though he'd gone out of his mind when he asked if they'd heard anything about Clifton's missing niece. Though deferential to his rank and stature, the circle of British, Italian, German, and French Egyptologists he introduced himself to clearly thought he was daft. It was not a reaction the duke was used to inducing in people.

"You're looking for crazy old Clifton's niece, you say?" one muttonchopped fellow repeated quizzically. "Why, she's not lost, man. She's right over there." The other men in the circle met Rafe's incredulous gaze with nods and pointing fingers. "Just there, Your Grace, at the table by the window, sitting with those two gents."

Rafe squinted against the sunlight coming in horizontally through the slatted blinds, at first not perceiving what they were talking about. He didn't see any skirts foaming among the sea of both Western- and Turkish-style masculine attire, saw no one sporting a reticule or lace gloves.

However, once he got his eyes pointed in the right direction, he did see the most beautiful woman he'd ever beheld in his life.

Huddled in a tête-à-tête with two very intent-looking men—one a young European and the other a middle-aged Arab—it was her hair that first gave the woman away. Skeins of coal-black locks escaped from a knot at the back of her head and tumbled in a riot of glossy curls around her shoulders. A white gauze head scarf had fallen from its place, draping itself across her slender neck and back and covering the top portion of the man's shirt she wore beneath.

For she was indeed wearing men's clothes, Rafe saw. His eyes had not deceived him while he scanned the room. Even from the sideways angle he had toward her table, he registered the incredible fact that in addition to the shirt, the girl was also wearing men's pantaloons. And men's boots. Over all this, she had layered a long, loose open robe of striped Egyptian cotton, belted at her small waist with a sash of saffron wool. She looked like a desert nomad.

An incredibly beautiful, utterly feminine desert nomad. The costume did nothing to hide the magnificence of the slender figure it draped, or the vital energy Jezebel radiated. He couldn't believe he hadn't noticed her sooner. Even disguised in men's clothes, she drew him with a magnetism he couldn't deny. Rafe's feet took him forward for a closer look, though his mind seemed to have stopped functioning entirely. He wanted to see her face more clearly. He *needed* to see it. And then she laughed, turning her face to the light, and his breath caught.

Jezebel glowed like a youthful siren, filling Rafe's eyes with a picture of all that was good and desirable about women. Her eyes, beneath perfectly arched, winglike brows, were a shade of darkest blue so deeply saturated they might truly be called sapphire. Certainly they shone in her stunning visage like rare jewels set in the face of a pagan idol. Her skin was polished ivory, tinged with coral pink at her high, almost Slavic cheekbones, and tinted a delicate, slightly darker shade at her full, rosy lips. When she laughed, she revealed her even white teeth in a win-

some smile that made her lips turn up at the corners in a
most intriguing way. Those lips had been born knowing the
art of kissing, Rafe thought with a stab of desire. She
looked as untamed as a hot-blooded Gypsy maid, full of
passion and zest for life—and ripe for the pleasures of the
flesh. Her very posture screamed of sensual freedom.

*This is Clifton's niece?* he thought incredulously. It
didn't seem possible. If this was Jezebel Montclair, she was
not remotely the ward he had been expecting. She was not
the ward any man might have expected, except perhaps in
his wildest, most sinful fantasies. He could envision her
coming to him in the dark of some heated desert night, the
wind in her hair and promises of pleasure in her slumberous
eyes. He could imagine her gloriously naked, bathed in
moonlight, her sweet face turned up to receive his kisses.
But he could not imagine her as his ward.

The irony of the situation was not lost on Lord Ravenhurst.

As her guardian, honor demanded she remain well beyond his lustful reach, no matter what his loins might decree. But one thing was certain, Rafe thought in that
moment. If she *hadn't* been under his protection, he'd have
sealed Miss Montclair's fate this very day. He'd have made
her his mistress so fast she'd have been lying beneath him,
crying his name out in pleasure before she even knew what
had happened to her. He'd have used every persuasion in
his power to coax the girl into giving him what he wanted,
teaching her in return all the many lessons of passion he'd
learned over the years, filling her so full of pleasure she
would beg for the release only he could give her. And oh,
how he wanted to give her that release, for he instinctively
sensed she'd respond beautifully. . . . He had to cut off that
line of thought before it became too painful.

*This has to be some sort of cruel hoax,* Rafe thought
miserably. He couldn't believe he was having such an overwhelming reaction to this ravishing creature. Perhaps, like
the Phoenician princess for whom she'd been named, Jezebel had bewitched him with her beauty in order to lead
him to destruction.

All Rafe knew for sure, staring at the woman from

across the busy hotel lounge, was that being her guardian was going to be hell on earth.

*J*ezebel had to laugh. "What kind of rank amateur do you take me for?" she asked the richly robed Egyptian merchant who'd sat down with them for a cup of the strong local coffee at the hotel bar. She lifted her tiny ceramic cup and sipped delicately at the thick, overwhelmingly sweet brew. Relaxed, very much at her ease, she sat back in her woven-cane chair and puffed meditatively at the hookah pipe a servant kept filled and smoldering with fragrant tobacco for the patrons' convenience.

It was a little after four in the afternoon—tea time for the European guests, who usually tended to consume far more spirituous beverages than tea in this bar, truth be known. Slanting rays of sunlight made stripes across the marble-tiled floor of the crowded room, and on all sides silent, sweating native boys in starched livery and powdered wigs worked to keep the fans attached to the ceilings pushing the stale air around. The Shepheard's lounge was indeed the height of luxury for foreigners staying in Egypt, but Jezebel would much rather have been elsewhere.

This meeting had come at her friend Gunther's invitation. The eager young German had assured her this man had a rare papyrus in his possession, one whose extraordinary contents she might have a special interest in. He had also been led to believe that the trader might be willing to part with it for a reasonable sum. Reluctantly, Jezebel had agreed to meet the fellow, mostly to spare her companion's feelings, but now she saw that, as she'd suspected, the merchant was merely a huckster like so many who preyed on gullible tourists' desire for Egyptian souvenirs. He did not have the information she needed—far from it.

The "rare papyrus" that the man claimed would help prove her uncle's theory was no more than a sloppily painted, sixpence-a-dozen treasure map of the sort that generally sported a large, lurid X over the pertinent portion of geography depicted. Jezebel rolled up the "ancient inscrip-

tion" he'd handed her so reverently a moment ago and
tossed it back to him with little respect for its apparent age
and fragility. Impatient with the waste of her time, she
quickly put to rest any notion on the charlatan's part that
she was as easily fooled as most Europeans, addressing the
man in his own language. "The inks are scarcely dry on
this paper, and the papyrus itself is so freshly pressed and
green, the reeds it's made from are barely a week out of
the river! By what definition of the word *antiquity* do you
call this piece old?"

The man's eyes widened briefly at hearing her flawless
Arabic. Then he frowned angrily, clearly not liking to have
his honesty called into question by this impudent foreign
woman. But he was an experienced trader, trained from
birth in the craft of bargaining. The papyrus disappeared
into one of his voluminous sleeves, and his frown was replaced with a bland, obsequious smile. "The missy has a
very discerning eye," he flattered, speaking English so that
both Europeans would understand. "Perhaps she would like
to see something a little more . . . special?" He began digging among his many pockets. "I reserve this only for the
finest of my customers. . . ."

Jezebel rolled her eyes in amusement, smiling wryly at
the crestfallen young man who had been trying to follow
the turn of their conversation, but who had not understood
more than a few words of the Arabic she'd spoken. Only
now was he beginning to catch on, and from the look in
his hazel eyes, Gunther was still ready to believe another
tall story at a moment's notice. Poor boy, to be so easily
taken in, she thought.

Gunther Morgenstern had arrived from his homeland in
the Teutonic north to study with her uncle less than a month
earlier, only to find upon his arrival that his prospective
mentor had recently passed away. When he'd shown up at
her doorstep, claiming to have discussed, through correspondence, the earl's unique beliefs concerning certain
newly emerging Egyptological studies, and asking to join
Lord Clifton in his quest to prove them, Jezebel had been
reluctantly persuaded to take the young man under her wing
in her uncle's stead.

She had agreed to teach him what she knew of archaeology and introduce him around to the society of explorers and amateur antiquarians who flocked in ever-increasing numbers nowadays to the land of the pharaohs. Though she doubted this naive young man would do much to further her uncle's interrupted investigation, there was always plenty of innocuous translation and research work to keep the eager young cub busy.

Indeed, that was how Jezebel herself spent most of her time. One rarely got to enjoy the excitement of discovering a new tomb or unearthing a rare artifact these days, too many other explorers having gone over this desert country already with a fine-toothed comb, though she'd had a hard time convincing the idealistic German of that fact. He had much to learn, she'd decided at the time, and it wouldn't hurt to let him benefit from her experience for a little while.

And keeping up with his inept antics kept Jezebel from dwelling too much on her sorrow over Clifton's death. Watching over Gunther was a full-time occupation, for if he wasn't offending the Mamluk city guards with his ignorance of their customs or getting his toes snapped at by irritable crocs for bathing his feet in the pools once sacred to the cult of the crocodile god Sobek, he was spending his family's fortune on a piece of junk that could be bought by a wiser shopper for mere pocket change.

Even now, she saw, the merchant had again managed to divert the would-be scholar's attention with a carved wooden Ushabti he'd drawn out of his pocket. This was a small statue of the gentle goddess whose purpose it was to watch over a pharaoh in death. He was claiming to have unearthed it, at great risk to his own life, in the tomb of a great king. The earnest blond-haired youth was absorbing every word with rapt attention. Had she ever been that innocent? Jezebel wondered silently. She doubted it, for Lord Clifton had trained her well from an early age how to spot a fraud. How he would have chuckled to see this young pup in action.

He'd taught her so many things, Jezebel thought, a lump catching in her throat. A love of knowledge, first and foremost; a deep and abiding hunger to learn as much as the world had to show her. Especially, he'd given her a respect for history, for the traditions of cultures other than her own. Over the years he'd given her the tools she needed to begin her own investigation into the origins of mankind's many civilizations, not least of which was that of the ancient Egyptians.

The earl had always encouraged her to pursue her studies, to follow in his footsteps despite the fact that she was female and most of his compatriots thought he was daft to raise his only niece in such a fashion. And she had loved her life with Jonathan Montclair. Some had called him scatterbrained, others even worse, but in his absence Jezebel missed his humor and wisdom keenly.

Since he'd gone, nothing had been quite the same. The idyllic existence she'd enjoyed with her uncle was no more, the fulfilling life of intellectual debates and stimulating study replaced by a sort of tense facsimile of the original. Nothing had really changed, and yet everything had. Jezebel continued her researches as she always had, but where once she'd enjoyed a respectable position in Cairo's expatriate European community, working along with Lord Clifton and the other scholars, artists, engineers, and architects who'd come here to unravel the linguistic mysteries of the hieroglyphic language, or journeying to one of the great ruins to explore a tomb rarely seen by Western eyes, now she struggled simply to be allowed to join these expeditions.

It had started when the earl, toward the end of his life, had begun to espouse some rather revolutionary views of which his colleagues had not approved. Rather than keeping them quiet, however, the earl had grown more adamant about his theories each time they were called into question, and Jezebel, who believed in her uncle wholeheartedly, had stood by him through the ensuing firestorm of academic condemnation and scorn. When he had died, pushing the limits of his increasingly fragile health too hard in the process of trying to prove his correctness to these erstwhile cronies, Jezebel had become determined to protect his reputation by continuing his work. Yet after Clifton's death, working and living among the newly dubbed Egyptologists had grown even harder than it had been when the controversial old earl was alive.

The very men who'd once thought nothing—or at least *said* nothing—about having her along on their digs or sharing her archaeological discoveries, now brushed her aside more and more often, made excuses to exclude her from their ranks. No one had yet had the nerve to come forward and declare her unwelcome, but Jezebel feared it was only a matter of time before that would happen. Her tenure in Egypt was precarious indeed, Jezebel thought. But what other choice did she have?

None, she told herself, though apparently the earl himself, the very man who had raised her to follow in his footsteps and become an antiquarian, had had a change of heart at some point before his death. As she'd learned shortly after he'd passed away, it seemed that, rather than remaining here and continuing his work, Lord Clifton had had a very different opinion about what she should do with her future once he was gone—an opinion he'd never once discussed with her during his life.

Jezebel vividly remembered the night she'd first heard of his plans.

An old friend of the earl's, a retired barrister by the name of Sir Artemus Barclay, had come to see her after the funeral to read out the will, and he'd stunned the explorer's niece when he informed Jezebel of the provision the earl had made in it for her. Even now she couldn't help wondering if Clifton had been in his right wits when he'd written up the papers.

Without so much as a word of discussion or debate, Jonathan Montclair had arranged, in the event of his death, to have his niece shipped off back to England. It seemed he'd decided she was to become the ward of a complete stranger, a man named Lord Ravenhurst whom she'd never even heard her uncle mention in conversation before. Quite possibly he'd simply forgotten to mention his decision to Jezebel, or perhaps he had put off telling her, expecting not to need to discuss such depressing matters for many years yet. Regardless of why he'd been so high-handed with her

fate, the earl had grievously misjudged Jezebel's own
wishes for her future.

The will stipulated that for her own protection, and in
order to collect her inheritance (a rather considerable sum
that included the bulk of the Montclair fortune, though the
estate itself was entailed and would go to a distant cousin),
she was to remain dependent on this stranger for another
five years—or until the day she married! To Jezebel, who
had no intention of marrying anytime soon, the notion of
spending up to five years under the "protection" of this
English lord was beyond anything she was willing to endure. But as per Clifton's written request in the will, word
had already been sent to her guardian to alert him to his
newly active status. Money had been provided for the trip,
and Jezebel was expected to arrive at this stranger's dwelling in London as quickly as possible.

*As if I were reporting for duty!* she'd fumed. Whatever
misguided notion of caring Lord Clifton had been ruled by
when he'd made out his will, the results were intolerable.
Jezebel had been taking care of herself—and the earl too—
for most of her life. She wasn't about to surrender her autonomy to some foppish aristocrat who had probably never
set foot beyond the front lawn of his own estates! What
could this man do for her that she could not do for herself?
And who knew what arbitrary rules this Lord Ravenhurst
would try to make her abide by if she did go?

Saddled with her care, he would probably try to fob her
off on the marriage mart as quickly as possible. Certainly,
no matter what sort of man he was, he would never allow
her the freedoms she was used to enjoying without question
now—the freedom to travel, to study, to answer to no one
but herself. She couldn't tolerate that. Society might put
limits on what she could achieve as a woman (a fact she
reluctantly acknowledged without accepting its validity),
but *no one* would ever tell her whom to marry, how to
conduct every moment of her life. No piece of paper could
give this Lord Ravenhurst the right to order her around.

Besides, even if she had wanted to return to England
(and Jezebel had to admit to harboring a certain longing to
visit London, the so-called "most modern city in the

world"), she wouldn't dream of doing so now, when she was coming so close to achieving the vindication she'd hoped to gain for Lord Clifton. Certain vital pieces of information had been coming to her attention recently, fraudulent peddlers notwithstanding, and she felt strongly that she was on the verge of a breakthrough. No, now was not the time to leave Egypt, will or no will, guardian or no guardian.

Jezebel had decided she simply wouldn't go. She might be throwing away a fortune by not returning to England as her uncle had wished—at the very least she would be deferring her ability to touch her money until she reached her majority—but staying here was worth the price, for the sake of her personal freedom as well as her uncle's good name. Besides, she had a little money left to her from her mother, and she managed to earn a small sum with her work in the Cairo antiquities trade.

She'd carved out a niche here for herself, no matter that some of her fellow scholars thought her an eccentric bluestocking and others even a crackpot. The truth was, she'd rather be considered a crackpot with *some* profession here in Egypt than return home to England as her uncle had stipulated and have no profession at all but to obey her new keeper.

In the months since she'd made her choice to remain in Egypt, Jezebel had not had cause to regret it, as difficult as it had become to continue on without Lord Clifton by her side. Whatever possessed the earl to make such a strange provision in his will? she wondered now, for the thousandth time. He'd never expressed any doubts about her ability to take care of herself before. What was so unique about this Lord Ravenhurst that the earl would take the drastic step of making her legally beholden to him?

Lost in this reverie, it was a moment before Jezebel noticed the hush that had fallen over their table, where the two men, merchant and neophyte, had been dickering over the price of the Ushabti for some time now.

When she looked up at last, she thought the mid-afternoon heat must have lulled her from mere daydream to full-fledged fantasy, for the man who stood before her

was far too perfect to be real. Maybe it was that text on
Greek mythology she'd fallen asleep over last night, but
the stranger appeared to Jezebel as a vision of pure, undi-
luted Hellènic beauty. He could have been one of Signore
Michelangelo's statues come to life. But no art could ever
imitate the glorious life that faced her now.

The stranger towered over her, six feet and more of the
most exquisitely sculpted male she'd ever hoped to see.
Beneath a damp, clinging white shirt, his chest and shoulders had the kind of breadth that surely must make young
maidens picture him effortlessly sweeping them up in his
arms. His waist and hips had the leanness of a marathon
runner, and his backside. . . . Without volition, she found
herself craning her neck just a little, wishing he'd turn
around so she could get a better view, for it looked to be
quite stunning. Jezebel flushed as soon as she realized what
she was doing, her embarrassed gaze flying to the man's
face to see if he had noticed the improper direction of her
stare. But looking there only flustered her more.

Beneath a short cap of attractively curling burnished
gold hair lay a face of such astonishing masculine beauty
that she had to blink in disbelief. The immediate strength
of that face, the power of it, leapt out at her from every
chiseled plane, every rugged surface. It was a sensual,
pleasure-loving face, one that radiated a certain cynicism
and worldliness, but it was also a face made for laughing.
Even from this distance, Jezebel could see the little lines
that mirth had carved around his eyes and mouth. And what
a mouth! His lips were lush and firm, wide enough to accommodate what was sure to be a stunning smile.

Jezebel noticed he wasn't smiling now, however. . . .
Startled by the intense degree of emotion in his features,
she looked up into his eyes and tried to read their expression. Jezebel felt her breath catch then, for those magnificent orbs captured and held her prisoner in a way that the
mere physical perfection of his body could not. They were
bluer than the ocean, drowning-deep and full of turbulence
like storm-tossed waters. Full, she realized, of anger. The
direction of his gaze gave no doubt about the object of his

displeasure—for whatever reason, this gloriously handsome stranger was furious at *her*.

She shivered, trapped by the power of his stare. Who was this man? And why did he look as if he wanted to strangle her with his bare hands?

## Chapter Three

〜

*W*ould you care for a drink?" the newcomer asked in a deep, well-rounded baritone. The slim archaeologist found the warm dark-honey timbre of that voice reverberating disturbingly inside her, penetrating to the very bones. He spoke politely enough, she noticed, but the hot look in his eyes utterly belied the civility of the question. Jezebel fancied she could smell the masculine heat rising from the stranger—a scent of sandalwood and leather, and beneath that a pure, somehow less tangible odor that was the underlying essence of the man himself. Her gut clenched in an unfamiliar, instinctive reaction to his presence, and she felt a shiver of trepidation slide down her spine.

Instantly she could see that this man wasn't merely stopping at her table to exchange pleasantries. No, he wanted something specific from her, and she was pretty damn sure it wasn't the pleasure of her company for a drink. Jezebel had the feeling she wasn't going to like whatever it was. However, instead of letting on how rattled his sudden appearance and overwhelming good looks were making her, she merely stared back at him coolly, not backing down from his intense stare.

"I don't accept refreshments from strangers, thanks," she replied dismissively. She glanced away in deliberate insult, gesturing for the waiting servant to bring the hookah back over. Her table companions shifted restlessly, waiting to see if the stranger would accept this cut direct or stay and explain what business kept him there. Gunther looked as though he might protest the man's intrusion, but after glancing over at Jezebel and seeing her almost imperceptible head-shake, he subsided, letting her handle the situation as she would.

And Jezebel really thought she had the matter well in hand. Taking the curved silver-capped stem between her lips and slowly drawing a breath of smoke into her mouth, she let it stream out of her nostrils, shifting her gaze back to the man insolently only after a long, drawn-out exhalation. Her look mutely asked why he was still standing there when he was clearly not welcome.

The man refused to be dismissed. "How about from your guardian?" he asked, a fine edge of sarcasm limning his voice. "Is that an acceptable degree of relationship for you to partake?"

Jezebel's eyes widened in disbelief. Her *guardian*? Had she heard aright? Could this truly be the nobleman under whose protection her uncle had left her? Staring up at the imposing man before her, she could easily believe he was a duke—from the instant she'd laid her eyes upon him, his commanding presence had had her fighting the urge to rise from her chair and curtsy. Since she had not chosen to wear skirts today, it was a damn good thing she was able to control these visceral impulses, she thought with a tiny spurt of humor.

"Lord Ravenhurst?" she hazarded.

"Very good, Miss Montclair," the man intoned with heavy irony. His generous mouth twisted. "Now let us see if that stunningly quick mind of yours can guess what I am doing here."

That was a very good question. What *was* he doing here, for heaven's sake? She quickly worked out the length of time and the distance involved in her head. Why, to get here this fast, the man would practically have had to jump aboard the first ship bound for Egypt after learning she hadn't arrived in England as she'd been scheduled to do. Jezebel eyed the duke more closely, this time taking in the hot, disheveled look of him, the woolen trousers and closely woven shirt that would have been perfectly suitable for a February day in England, but which must have him sweltering here in Cairo, even without the waistcoat, cravat, and jacket that should complete any proper gentleman's attire. Why on earth had he come chasing her all this way? she wondered, though she'd no intention of showing her curi-

osity to the duke—not when the man was madder than
blazes and looking ready to blame her for whatever was
causing the upset.

"You've come to tour the pyramids?" she shot back,
responding to his patronizing tone with hostility of her own.

"Hardly," he replied repressively.

"Well, if it's to be a game of questions, Your Grace,
perhaps you'd care to sit down and take your ease with my
friends here and myself?" She waved casually toward the
empty fourth chair across from her, ignoring the unease of
the two men who witnessed their confrontation, trapped in
the awkward situation by the lack of a polite opportunity
to escape. But Jezebel, occupied with her new adversary,
couldn't take the time to free them just yet. "The coffee is
quite good this afternoon, and Hamad's cakes are actually
edible for once," she continued, referring to the hotel's pas-
try chef as though Lord Ravenhurst gave a damn about
seedcakes and coffee.

Jezebel did not want Lord Ravenhurst looming over her
a single moment more, and offering to share their repast
was the only idea that had come to mind to get him to stop
glaring down at her from his great height. In all honesty,
she didn't want this man anywhere near her, for his phys-
icality was having a rather disturbing effect on her senses.
Still, she knew that now that he was here, the issues that
lay between them would not be resolved quickly without
further communication. Better to invite him down to her
own level, where she could deal with him eye to eye. Face-
to-face. But oh, that *face* . . . Jezebel had to shake herself
out of the spell his looks cast upon her once again.

For a moment, the duke scowled as if he might tell her
to go bugger the cakes, and the coffee as well, but then he
relented, seating himself stiffly in the unoccupied cane-
backed chair. Gunther and the merchant, sensing their moment, flicked a glance at each other and both hastily rose
to leave. "I will call on you later, if I may, Fräulein Montclair?" Gunther asked.

"Please do," she replied, her expression indicating that
she would explain this interruption to him when she could.
Gunther bowed to both Jezebel and the duke, then made

his way toward the door. The Arab merchant merely inclined his head a fraction before taking off for more lucrative climes, obviously disappointed by the return on his afternoon's efforts. Jezebel thought she heard him mutter, "Cheap *ferenghi* woman . . ." as he left.

"Close friend of yours?" Rafe inquired silkily, nodding to indicate the handsome young German, whom his eyes were tracking across the length of the crowded bar. His tone made the question an insult.

Jezebel caught the insinuation immediately. Because she wore men's clothes, many seemed to think she had donned their morals as well, she'd found over the years. It seemed Ravenhurst was no different, disapproving of her from the outset as he so obviously did.

"Yes, as a matter of fact," she exhaled around a mouthful of sweet tobacco smoke. "A very close friend." Let him think what he would. It was no concern of hers what this man believed, guardian or no. She owed nothing to Raphael Sunderland! Jezebel reminded herself, getting angrier by the minute. He might have come nearly three thousand miles to look for her, and she supposed some might have thought that was noble of him, but it didn't give him the right to question her behavior. No one had that right. He must be made to understand that from the start. "Gunther very often assists me with my research and linguistics work," she added, stretching the truth somewhat.

Rafe appeared to be reining himself in once again. "Well, I'm glad *someone* is getting work done," he replied with patently false cheer. "Since I've been forced to neglect my own affairs these past six weeks just to come and find you." It was clear he was finished with his charade of civility and intended to get to the heart of the matter.

"Yes, and why did you do such an extraordinary thing?" Jezebel got to the point for him—she wanted answers just as much as the duke did.

"To see that you were safe, of course," he snapped as though that should have been obvious to her. "And to bring you back."

"Back?" She didn't catch his meaning.

"To England."

Jezebel choked on a laugh, a lungful of smoke getting caught on its way up her windpipe. "You must be joking," she wheezed.

"My dear Miss Montclair, I can assure you I do not make it my habit to travel six weeks out of my way just to exchange jests with recalcitrant young ladies. I came here because you did not arrive as you were supposed to in London this December. Now I would like an explanation, if you don't very much mind."

"But didn't you get my letter?" she asked in all innocence.

"What letter?"

"The one I entrusted to Mr. Rigby to give Your Grace upon docking in London Harbor. He was a passenger aboard the clipper I was to sail on, and a very reliable gentleman. The letter I gave him explains everything."

Rafe frowned as if he doubted her veracity, but then his brow slowly began to clear. "This Mr. Rigby wouldn't happen to be an elderly gentleman, particularly prone to seasickness?"

Jezebel's hand flew to her mouth in dismay. "Oh, heavens!" she gasped, beginning to feel a bit more charitably inclined toward the duke as realization set in. "He never gave it to you?" It was a rhetorical question, for clearly, she realized now, Ravenhurst had never received any word from her. The duke must have assumed the very worst when she didn't arrive, she thought with a pang of sudden sympathy.

It was actually rather endearing. The man had come all this way just to be sure of her safety! Jezebel couldn't remember the last time anyone had made such an effort on her behalf—and particularly not a stranger. She commiserated as kindly as she knew how.

"The letter would have saved you *so* much trouble, Your Grace. In it, I wrote to release you from this awkward commitment into which my uncle has inveigled you. I meant you to know immediately that I was in no need of your assistance, and that you should feel at liberty to remain in England without concern, since I would be staying to continue with my uncle's work here in Cairo indefinitely."

She paused, eyes full of sincere gratitude. "I am deeply sorry the letter's courier was waylaid, but I'm afraid you've come all this way for nothing, after all. As you can see, I am not in need of any rescuing just at the moment." She gestured to indicate her obvious state of well-being, her control over her circumstances. But Jezebel's insouciant manner only seemed to anger the duke further.

"Perhaps you think not, Miss Montclair, but I shall be the judge of that from now on," Rafe growled, his anger breaking through the facade of calm at last. "Whatever you may have believed, Miss Montclair, you do not have the right to simply decide when the term of your wardship is complete, and you *certainly* do not have the right to go about living here in this colonial backwater without a proper chaperone or a legal custodian!"

His aquamarine eyes raked her up and down appraisingly. "I believe I have arrived just in time, as a matter of fact, if not too late altogether to save you from yourself." Rafe paused for a moment to let his words sink in, then continued despite her huff of outrage. "Your manners are appalling, and you most certainly need a lesson or two in how to dress like a lady. I shall give you the benefit of the doubt and assume that it is your uncle's death that has left you without the strict guidance you so desperately need, and shall provide such guidance myself from now on. For when we are back in England, I give you fair warning, this outlandish behavior you've adopted will *not* be permitted."

Very deliberately, as if afraid it might shatter in her grasp, Jezebel set aside the smoldering hookah pipe and pressed her hands flat against the surface of the table. All trace of her former charitable sentiments flew out the window. She didn't know which of these outrageous pronouncements to address first!

"Now, look here, Your Grace," she said carefully, before her temper got the better of her. "If you honestly think you are going to come breezing in here—into *my* territory— and start ordering me around like some medieval tyrant, insulting my behavior and my character as well with your filthy insinuations, well, you've got another think coming!" Jezebel's voice rose as her anger began to slip its leash.

"And as for returning with you to England, you can forget that misbegotten idea right now. I'm not going anywhere with you, you arrogant booby! What makes you think you have any right to dictate to me in this intolerable manner?"

"I have every right, according to your uncle's will and the laws of England," the duke responded shortly.

"Ah, but we are not in England now, are we?" Jezebel crowed triumphantly. "You've no power over me here."

"You're a fool if you think His Majesty's laws don't apply to you in Egypt. When it comes to your care, I have the final say in all matters that pertain to your welfare wherever you go, and no one here, loyal subject of the crown or not, would dream of stopping me from enforcing my will." He waved to indicate the curious onlookers. In response, the gentlemen collected in the Shepheard's lounge, some of Europe's finest gentry transplanted here to the farthest reaches of His Majesty's empire, discreetly turned their eyes away—their eyes, but not their ears.

Jezebel leapt to her feet. "*I* shall stop you!" she cried, ignoring the attention their increasingly loud argument was attracting. Her temper was well and truly gone now, along with all semblance of her control. "You're mad if you think I'm coming back with you," she swore, actually shaking her fist at him in her agitation. "I'm not going anywhere, Your Grace, except as far away from your odious presence as I can get!"

With a crash that could be heard all across the marble lobby, she knocked over her tall, fan-shaped chair in her haste to remove herself from the table, hissing with rage as she stormed from the lounge.

*R*afe merely watched Jezebel go, making no effort to stop her. Somehow he knew she would not be going far. No, this fiery young woman would not tuck tail and run so easily. She would fight him every step of the way. The duke found he was already looking forward to their next meeting.

*So this is Clifton's niece, eh?* he mused, a grin tugging at one corner of his sensual mouth. Their encounter had filled him with a strange mixture of admiration for Miss Montclair's daring and anger at her impudence. He spent a long moment pensively staring after her, wondering at the strength of the reaction she'd induced, not at all sure he liked the feelings he was experiencing.

Well, his first few hours in Egypt had certainly been *unusual,* to say the very least, Rafe reflected at last. Clearly, he would have to rethink a number of the assumptions he'd made about little Miss Montclair if he was going to succeed in his original mission to bring her back to England. Indeed, there were a number of adjustments he thought he might make, now that their initial confrontation had given him a chance to assess the facts of the situation more closely.

What was that old saying again? Ah, yes. When in Rome . . .

# Chapter Four

*Jezebel* absently pushed aside a mummified hand from the pile of crumpled stationery that lay strewn in front of her, too lost in thought to pay it much mind. The blackened, desiccated thing had served for years as a paperweight on her uncle's curio-cluttered desk, just one of many bizarre little treasures he'd collected. Even though it had been several months since his death, she still hadn't had the heart to get rid of his things. Yet now, because of the incredible developments of the past twenty-four hours, she knew she might soon have to discard it, along with many other mementos.

With the advent of Raphael Sunderland into her world, the life she had known with her uncle was in serious jeopardy. The thought saddened her.

Jonathan Montclair had raised her completely on his own from the day her father had been killed, along with several other reckless adventurers, in a mountaineering accident when she was only eleven. Before that, life had been much more chaotic for the young Jezebel. Usually, she preferred not to think back on the days of her early childhood, for the memories still haunted her, but on this day, during which everything in her life might well change irrevocably before noon, it seemed inevitable that she reminisce about the events that had brought her to this point.

Jezebel couldn't remember ever having had a normal upbringing. She had only a fractured recollection of the days she'd once spent together with her mother in England, the two of them living amid the eerie beauty of the windswept, desolate moorlands of the family's estate in the North Country. It should have been an idyllic youth, filled with long romps in the heather and kite-flying expeditions on the heath, but that was far from the case for little Jezebel Montclair. In contrast, she remembered those days with her mother as frightening, chaotic times.

According to Jezebel's uncle, who had told her what he knew about her mother when Jezebel grew old enough to understand, no one had known precisely what ailed the fragile Russian beauty his brother Martin had married against the family's wishes. Right from the beginning, she'd been a fey creature, a woman of great passion and quick emotion, but also one whose charm and beauty had captivated every man she met.

As time went on, however, her wild spells of chaotic laughter, her raging anger, her unusually fierce energy, and her crushing periods of despondency had grown worse and worse. The glowing, passionate diplomat's daughter with whom Martin Montclair had so precipitously fallen in love during the heady days of his youth soon turned out to be dangerously unstable. Little Jezebel, growing up under the pall of her mother's strange malady, had never known whether she'd receive kisses when she approached her mother, or curses.

Martin Montclair had been no source of comfort to his daughter in her earliest years. By nature a reserved, unemotional man, when his wife's growing madness became apparent, he hadn't known how to handle the consequences of his hasty marriage. After Jezebel's birth, he'd begun traveling with his brother, staying away as often as possible, until word of his estranged wife's death had finally brought him home to claim their long-neglected offspring. Jezebel had been eight years old when her father returned for her; a solemn, grief-ravaged child barely able to recognize the man who called her his daughter.

Unwilling to face his unpleasant memories of home, Martin had once again fled as far as he could go, this time returning to his brother's side with his young daughter in tow. Jezebel had had no choice but to accompany her father on his journeys, as Martin more willingly followed his footloose older sibling around the globe. Indeed, the man had seemed driven to keep moving constantly. Whether searching out some new vista or attempting a dangerous feat never accomplished by man before, he had always sought a sense of satisfaction that eluded him. Or perhaps, his daughter thought now, he had been fleeing some demon of guilt he could not shake.

Jezebel hadn't understood what compelled him back then, however, and she hadn't cared to ask. At the time, she'd simply been grateful to her father for taking her with him on his travels, taking her away from the turmoil of her former life and showing her one where the only passions involved were reserved for stone statues and centuries-old secrets found deep within the earth. And she had loved her much older uncle from the first moment her father introduced them, had quickly learned to look up to him as a wise, scholarly man.

There had been no formal discussion about Clifton's taking her in. After her father's death, Jezebel's uncle had simply kept her by his side. She sometimes thought this was because he had honestly forgotten to send her home to England. The earl of Clifton was notoriously absentminded, tending to neglect anything unrelated to his current objects of study unless specifically reminded—including his niece. But the young Jezebel had been tired of being passed around among relatives, lonely and in need of constancy after a childhood fraught with upheavals.

She'd wanted to remain steadily with one person, if not in one place, and so she had consciously chosen not to remind Lord Clifton that he should really send her home to receive the benefit of a proper English upbringing. Instead, she'd made herself indispensable to the man, making sure he had the right maps at hand before he asked for them, arranging with local guides for supplies, and learning to handle disputes among their bearers from the time she was still a young girl.

Though Clifton had seemed not to notice her taking over responsibility for their day-to-day affairs, she knew he'd been grateful for the way she'd freed him to concentrate on his studies. And she'd been happy to care for her uncle rather than return home to the uncertainty of living with distant cousins or being shipped off to languish in some drafty old girls' school.

She'd preferred instead to trek alongside her uncle and share the wonder of each new discovery as he made it, and since he didn't seem to mind, she'd made the most of her adventures. At his side she'd learned Greek and Latin by reading from the very monuments they were inscribed upon, practiced astronomy and mathematics while studying the perfection of the Mayan pyramids' construction, and absorbed history everywhere she looked. As long as she had a secure place in each of his expeditions, Jezebel had been willing to endure the discomforts and disadvantages of her odd upbringing, and indeed very often felt herself privileged to come along on these fantastical journeys of exploration.

As she saw it, having to fend off a llama with a peculiar penchant for chewing on her hair was a small price to pay for seeing the sun set crimson and purple over the Andes, as was sleeping on a prickly bed of crushed ferns in the jungles of Ecuador when one woke up to the brilliant rainbow flash of a dozen screeching parrots rising from the trees for their morning feeding.

The strange little family of two had thus wandered—contentedly, for the most part—through parts of the world that most people back home in England had never even heard of. They hadn't settled down in any one place until fairly recently, when new discoveries by Lord Clifton's fellow explorers concerning Egypt's mysteries had begun to intrigue the old archaeologist so strongly that he'd been convinced to remain there indefinitely. He'd decided to give up his other historical and anthropological studies to concentrate all of his attention on the fascinating civilization of the ancient Egyptians. In the last several years, Cairo had become their home away from home, a base camp from which they'd only occasionally set off for other adventures.

Of late, it had become all the rage among European scholars to discover and chart Egypt's many treasures—and, for the more unscrupulous, to steal as many as they could smuggle home to sell. Clifton himself had been far more interested in the newly emerging study of the ancient Egyptians' hieroglyphic language and culture than in what he disdainfully declared to be mere grave-robbing. Most of the earl's researches, in fact, had revolved around the unglamorous and quite painstaking process of unraveling tiny inscriptions chipped long ago into basalt or granite obelisks and crumbling statuary. These cryptic writings had recently led Jonathan Montclair to some very exciting conclusions—conclusions he'd become obsessed with proving to his highly skeptical colleagues. Unfortunately, he had passed away before managing to do so, and his niece now felt the pressure to fulfill this last goal for him.

Jezebel had helped him catalog his discoveries here as she had everywhere else they journeyed, and both had worked closely with a number of the other amateur archaeologists so rife in Egypt. Both were excellent linguists, as well as meticulous draft artists and chroniclers of their findings. Without ever pausing to think about her choice, she had decided to follow in Clifton's footsteps, leading the peculiarly specialized life of an amateur archaeologist.

But with her uncle's death, and the arrival of her new so-called guardian, Jezebel now wondered how much longer she would be able to continue living here in Cairo. And in truth, she thought, once she had completed her last act of duty to Lord Clifton by proving his theory as she'd sworn to do, she wasn't even sure she *wanted* to stay.

Jezebel had truly loved Egypt, loved its massive monuments, its fertile river valleys, and its arid desert plains. She'd loved its colorful people, steeped in a centuries-old tradition of which she'd felt privileged even to scratch the surface. But there had been many such places in her life, and no single one of them called to her above the others. None of them was home. She didn't know if she belonged here anymore, or if the time had come to move on to some other avenue of study, some other part of the world entirely.

Where should she go if she left? Jezebel asked herself now, staring blindly at the reminders of her uncle's lifelong passion tumbled so carelessly atop the worktable they had shared. And what options could she reasonably pursue now that Clifton was gone and her fortune lay in the hands of a man she intended to avoid for the next five years?

The most obvious solution—simply to return home to England, with or without Lord Ravenhurst—was no solution at all when she thought it through. Though she'd long harbored a desire to visit London and savor its many modern wonders, take part in any number of the famed intellectual societies that proliferated there, she had no great urge to join the ranks of the gentry, as would be expected of a woman in her position, and as the duke would almost certainly require.

How could she even pretend to return to the rarefied world she'd been born into after everything she'd seen, everywhere she'd been? Jezebel might not have had the usual rearing, but she knew enough about the good women of British society to realize she could never be content living according to their strictures. She'd tasted the pleasures of freedom, and it was far too heady a draught to give up now.

She did not want to reside among a bunch of soulless society piranhas whose only goals were to marry well and then spend the rest of their lives feeding their husband's ambitions, all the while tearing down their rivals in their efforts to succeed. But she knew that such would be her fate should she return to England. No one there would tolerate her so-called eccentricities as they did here in Cairo. In England, the way of life she'd spurned long ago would finally catch up to her, and she would be forced to become part of a culture she considered wholly abhorrent. Living among them day by day, Jezebel wondered, how long would it be before she began to resemble these women in every respect? As a student of human nature, she'd seen how the society one chose to live in affected one's behavior, whether the subject changed willingly or not.

It was not that she didn't think she could learn to survive in such a world, but rather that she didn't like to think what might happen to her if she did. The archaeologist's niece had never had trouble blending in with her peers, much as she disliked doing it. Jezebel hadn't entirely lacked for schooling in the traditional feminine arts, her unusual upbringing notwithstanding. Whenever she and her uncle had stayed for a long period in a well-established hotel, or in any region with a large European population, as they did in Cairo, there had always been a number of what the earl sardonically liked to call "our own kind" in residence. Invariably some well-meaning lady or other would take Jezebel in, as adorable as the black-haired, blue-eyed urchin was, and try to make of her a "proper" little girl.

She'd hated the lessons from these women—she'd found the hours of sitting straight-backed and silent with a book upon her head, perfecting her posture or some other nonsense, to be unbearable torture. No fool, Jezebel soon learned that the best way to avoid their well-meaning interference was to appear to have already learned everything these bastions of occidental virtue had to teach. A natural mimic, as well as possessed of an extraordinarily quick mind, Jezebel had no trouble in that area.

Thus, by the time she would normally be preparing to come out of short frocks and pinafores (had she ever deigned to wear the undignified things), young Jezebel Montclair had mastered proper etiquette, along with deportment, dress, dancing, and the womanly arts of sewing, needlework, and watercolors. She could converse in several languages without giving offense, sharing spirited debate with anyone from the highest-ranking foreign diplomat to the lowliest parlor maid. Now, at twenty, Jezebel possessed all the arts of attraction any matchmaking mama could want, along with the rare, stunning good looks to put them into play.

When she chose to play the game, she played it exceptionally well.

The Honorable Miss Montclair could charm the stockings off a Prussian prince or make the most dour East India Company man laugh out loud at her witticisms, lighting up the dullest reception with her unique flair and charming presence. Indeed, she was every bit the proper scion of society when she chose to be. But that was, of course, only *when* she chose to be, which was not very often. Though Jezebel had the ability to mix with any company among whom she might find herself, she hated the charade, the falseness of her pretense. She wasn't like these people, and she knew it—in fact, she took pride in her difference.

So. Going "home" to England was not an option for Jezebel. But what about Lord Ravenhurst? she wondered anxiously. If he had his way, that's exactly where she would end up—will she, nil she.

She'd fled from him yesterday at the hotel, plain and simple. Her dramatic exit had been little better than an admission of defeat, and she was sure the duke knew it every bit as well as she. He might be many things—an arrogant, presumptuous dictator foremost among them—but he was no fool. And he held all the cards.

Lord Ravenhurst, she had discovered as of late yesterday, had the power to turn the local society against her with little more than a wave of one negligent hand. She'd done her research on him last night, accepting a number of the many late-afternoon calls she'd received once it became known that she was linked to the handsome duke who had just gotten off the boat from "home." It was almost comical how quickly word of his arrival and their subsequent confrontation had gotten around to Cairo's gossip-starved matrons and their marriageable daughters. Some of those old buzzards could smell fresh blood a mile away, she swore.

Seeing no point in lying, as the duke would no doubt soon spread the news himself, Jezebel had admitted he was her guardian—and had seen her social status among the women rocket from barely tolerated bluestocking to most sought-out member of the European community in an instant. It wasn't a position she relished, but it did allow her to put forth some discreetly worded questions about the duke.

What she'd learned yesterday had not reassured Jezebel. That he was a known rake and a libertine, she was not surprised to hear from the tittering ladies who'd dropped by her uncle's small bungalow all afternoon and into the evening on one pretext after another. She might have guessed as much about the man just from his virile good looks. But to her dismay, she'd also discovered that Rafe Sunderland was considered a very powerful man back in England.

"Where have you been that you haven't heard of him?" one scandalized lady had asked. Jezebel had ignored that rhetorical question, trying not to flush at the woman's censuring tone. Everyone here knew her history, knew she

hadn't been back to England since she was eight years old.
And she rarely read the papers—usually months out of date
and shipped overseas at great cost—that the rest of them
pored over with such diligence. The society pages, along
with letters faithfully exchanged with friends back home,
were very often these women's only connections to the
world they'd left behind. Jezebel, however, had no such
ties to that world. Still, she bade the ladies tell her more,
pretending suitable awe and admiration for the man who
had come to "rescue" her.

"Apparently, he likes to spread his influence around,"
one flush-faced matron had confided conspiratorially to Jezebel, fanning herself with a habitually languid air. The
breeze created by the motion carried a faint whiff of spirits
in Jezebel's direction, causing the young archaeologist to
think cynically that it was not the "blasted savage heat" of
this "uncivilized clime" but a healthy dose of good English
gin which had caused the high color on the woman's face.
Still, she had seemed to have good information on the duke,
so Jezebel had quelled the urge to make an unkind comment, and simply listened instead.

"From what *I've* heard, he's always gadding about back
in England, whether debating matters of policy in Parlia-
ment or personally looking after his widespread business
ventures," the woman had continued, "an unheard-of activity for a member of his class, of course, and one that my
dear Mortimer"—(here she referred to her chicken-necked
husband, whom Jezebel liked, if possible, less than the lady
herself)—"says we should frown upon. If those unorthodox
business practices of his had not secured Ravenhurst such
phenomenal wealth, and if our poor, sweet, lovely daughters had better prospects in this godforsaken backwater, I
would agree, of course. But faced with these unfortunate
circumstances, who can afford to be such a stickler as to
shun the man for being in trade?"

Jezebel had tried hard not to snicker, with some difficulty pasting an innocuous expression on her face instead.
Glancing over at her own threadbare sofa, where along with
several other of her uninvited guests, the woman's two

daughters had artfully arranged themselves, she could not
help noting that they had inherited the worst features of
both parents—and long, scrawny necks and overly ruddy
cheeks were the least of their problems. Both preened and
simpered grotesquely at their mother's flattery. *As if either
of them had a chance with such a man as the duke!* she
had thought incredulously. *Ravenhurst would not deign so
much as to dance with those two nitwits if they were the
last marriageable females in Christendom.* But she'd shared
none of these thoughts, merely murmuring encouragingly
to keep their mother speaking. The lady had required little
urging, seeing that the rest of those gathered in Lord Clifton's little drawing room were equally eager for her gossip.

"Lord Ravenhurst is even, I've been told, a proponent
of the new reforms, one of those Whig liberals arguing for
newfangled farming methods, child labor laws, political and
judicial responsibility. The man's a real crusader when it
comes to his causes," she'd concluded. A thoughtful pause
among Jezebel's guests had followed this statement. Reformers were looked down upon as a rule, but rich, powerful reformers were another matter—and apparently, they
didn't come any richer or more powerful than Rafe Sunderland.

"He's known for stirring things up, dangerous to cross
but a good man to have on one's side," another lady concluded, and the rest, pleased at this summation, had begun
nodding like a gaggle of overdressed geese. When Jezebel
asked if his somewhat rakish reputation should not give
them pause, the ladies were more than happy to disregard
that little issue.

"Ravenhurst," one fat squire's wife divulged knowledge-
ably as she helped herself to the last of Jezebel's tea cakes,
"is well known for his honorable streak. He might take his
own amusements freely and involve himself in scandal
more often than our own dear Prince Regent, but he would
never expose a young lady under his aegis to impropriety."

"You might soon wish the duke were a little *less* honorable," a tittering older woman had insinuated slyly.
"Why, if I were the one with that gorgeous specimen of

manhood so eager to 'protect' me, I'd find occasion to need 'assistance' with great frequency!"

Another aging matron had snorted at this point. "Face it, Regina dear, *you're* more likely to need a nurse to see to your vital functions than a guardian to watch over your virtue at this stage of your life."

The lady called Regina had sputtered in outrage, but by that time, Jezebel had begun to tune the women out, her mind picturing Raphael Sunderland's remarkable face and impressive physique instead of their gossiping chatter.

She'd hated to agree with those harpies on principle, but she could understand their sentiments! Why, if she were the kind of female who needed a man to care for her, she couldn't have picked a more dashing example of domineering maleness had she tried. But she wasn't that kind of woman, and she hadn't picked this man—for any purpose.

The common consensus was that Jezebel should be thanking her lucky stars Lord Ravenhurst had stepped in to see to her care. In Jezebel's judgment, however, the women's willingness to overlook the duke's faults had more to do with his status as one of England's wealthiest bachelors than any real assurance of his good character. Why, she thought cynically, they'd probably sacrifice their offspring to the devil himself if he owned half of Derbyshire.

Though Jezebel told herself that she didn't fear Lord Ravenhurst, that the worst he could do was make her life uncomfortable, there was a tiny part of her—just the tiniest part—that feared he might actually drag her back to England by main force. And the worst part of it was that everyone here expected her to be grateful for his interference! But she wasn't grateful. She was furious.

Perhaps the rest of the world wanted something from His High and Mighty Lordship. Perhaps they needed him for the things he could do for them, but *she* did not! Jezebel had never taken orders from a single other person as long as she'd lived, and she wasn't about to start now, just because some great arrogant boor told her to pack her bags. There was no way she was going back to England with the egotistical Lord Ravenhurst. Whatever she must do to avoid that fate, the explorer's niece determined, she *would* do.

Jezebel comforted herself with the knowledge that if he tried to abduct her against her will, she still had a few tricks up her sleeve with which to avoid his grasp. Should it prove necessary to use them, she had contacts in the city who would hide her for a day or a week if the duke came after her, and there were river traders who owed her favors, men who would take her up the Nile to whatever destination she wished without revealing her identity.

But sooner or later, she admitted to herself realistically, a man with as many resources as Ravenhurst had would probably find her. There just weren't that many places in this country where a European woman could travel safely, no matter how experienced or intrepid she was. These were dangerous times, after all, in a land with a highly unstable government. If Lord Ravenhurst was determined to come after her, to bribe any number of beys, pashas, and kaichifs for news of her whereabouts, he would eventually ferret her out. And after yesterday's confrontation, she did not doubt him on that score. He was plenty determined, all right.

If she couldn't manage to reach a compromise that would send the duke back to England without her, she might even have to abandon Egypt and start over somewhere else—perhaps before completing her sworn mission. Without much money, without connections, running from Raphael Sunderland would be no easy task. Therefore, Jezebel had decided, no matter how she despised his arrogance, it didn't make sense to alienate the duke or to flee him unless there was no other recourse left to her.

And already she thought she had come up with an idea that might work. A rather ingenious plan had come to mind—one that, if she was lucky, might even kill two birds with one stone. . . .

Once again Jezebel fingered the blackened artifact on the desk, staring off into the distance and chewing thoughtfully on the end of a pen. After a moment she scratched out what she had written on her current sheet of paper and started over with yet another fresh page.

Deciding to write this very difficult, humbling message

to her guardian in the first place had been hard enough.
Deciding exactly *what* to write was even harder. Since
dawn's light had first crept across the warm terra-cotta tiles
of her uncle's study floor, Jezebel had been trying to compose a missive that would strike the perfect note of concil-
iation and sweet reason with the rotten bastard who'd put
her in this deucedly awkward situation. Figuring out the
phrases that would sway the duke to agree with the decep-
tive proposition she intended to lay out for him was no
easy task.

In the end, however, she settled for brevity, a night spent
in a state of sleep-deprived agitation leaving her at a loss
for eloquence.

> *Miss Jezebel Marie Montclair requests the honor of
> your presence at a breakfast to be served on the pri-
> vate terrace of Shepheard's Hotel at ten o'clock this
> morning.*
>
> *Several matters of import to be discussed.*

She'd probably have a better chance of success if she
explained her position to the duke in person anyway, Jezebel decided—she'd always been at her most persuasive
face-to-face. Hastily sanding and sealing the short letter,
she went downstairs and handed it to the cook's son, a fleet-
footed lad well used to running messages over to the hotel.
As the sound of his steps faded down the lane, Jezebel
gnawed nervously on a fingernail, then shook herself out
of her inactivity.

It was time to get busy, for she had much to do in just
a short while!

# Chapter Five

~

*W*hen Rafe arrived at the sunny, palm-wreathed private veranda promptly at ten that morning, he found himself enclosed in an enchanting bower more suited to romantic rendezvous than the kind of highly charged confrontation he'd expected to encounter.

The terrace had a splendid view, through a screen of waving palm fronds, of the ever-impressive Nile. Though he'd come in on that same watercourse, somehow here, in a bend of the riverbank more tranquil and less trafficked by oceangoing ships, the mighty river looked more as he'd always imagined it. Wide and placid, the waters shone a vibrant green in the sunlight. Rafe had never seen any color to match it. *I suppose that's why they named the color "Nile Green" after it,* he thought wryly.

Off to his left, he glimpsed a small fleet of boatmen poling across the water, their papyrus vessels decorated with elongated eyes painted on the tall, curving prows. Tiny iridescent birds rustled in the foliage surrounding the veranda, while larger black and white kingfishers hunted the waters below, and locusts hummed their morning song all around. It was an enchanting, secluded little hideaway, an oasis of quiet and charm in the bustling city.

The girl who waited for the duke in the midst of this leafy bower completed the picture of genteel elegance. Rafe had to look twice before he recognized his ward.

No less lovely today dressed in a white muslin gown trimmed with rows of tiny embroidered strawberries at neck, waist, sleeves, and hem, her dark hair caught up softly beneath a broad-brimmed hat of stiffened white organdy, Jezebel's whole demeanor appeared far more demure than when he'd last seen her sweeping furiously from the hotel lounge. Fresh as a daisy in the morning's relative cool, smiling cordially as he entered, she looked anything but the fiery vixen he'd expected.

Something about the winning smile she offered made Rafe's hackles rise with suspicion, even as his loins clenched in involuntary appreciation of her beauty. The girl was even more dangerous to his equilibrium decked out in feminine fripperies than she'd been in her outlandish desert gear, but he was ready for her today. He must maintain tight control around her at all times, for he did not like to think what might happen should that control slip. He vowed that no matter what inflammatory comments she might make, whatever brazen things she did, he wouldn't rise to her bait again.

But she merely offered him pleasantries, a distinct change from her prickly manner of the day before. "Good morning, Your Grace. You are very kind to agree to join me on such short notice."

Definitely cause for suspicion—but then, Rafe was beginning to suspect that nothing was quite as it seemed with Jezebel Montclair. "Well, my dear," he replied mildly enough, "you are, after all, the whole reason for my visit to this fine country. Consider me available and at your service at all times." He smiled, and his eyes crinkled with genuine warmth.

"Please, come and share my repast," Jezebel invited. She indicated the silver chafing dishes that lined a small buffet table by the filigreed stone railing of the balcony. She had already served herself, filling her plate with a selection of fresh figs, dates, and apricots, sweet rolls and honey.

Rafe strolled over and lifted the lid off one dish. One sandy brow quirked in bemusement when he saw what was under it. "What on earth is that?" he asked with a startled laugh. A precariously towering pyramid of tiny egg halves filled with a violently orange-colored substance was arranged before him on a bed of wilted greenery.

"The general consensus," Jezebel drawled from her seat at the table, "is that the staff believes they're providing the guests with a taste of home in the form of deviled eggs. No one's managed to convince them that neither quail's eggs nor an excess of saffron for spice are in the recipe. I wouldn't eat them, if I were you," she warned. "Try the fruit mélange, Your Grace, or the scones if you prefer traditional English fare. The cooks have been practicing those with somewhat greater success."

Rafe obeyed. Soon, plate filled with innocuous edibles, he seated himself opposite Jezebel in his own cushioned, cane-backed chair. It was good to know that the girl was as willing to start over as he was, he thought—or at least he assumed she was, given her newfound charm and amiability. Yet when he studied her demeanor more closely, he decided that despite the warmth she was trying to project, Jezebel was nervous. She fiddled with her flatware intermittently, and Rafe noticed she was twisting her linen napkin on her lap. But the duke hadn't any intention of making their meeting any easier for her. She didn't need encouragement to take advantage, he judged. He figured she'd try any tactic in her considerable arsenal to gain what she wanted—and it wasn't too hard to guess it was freedom Jezebel desired. He waited for her to speak.

"Your Grace—" she began.

"Please, call me Rafe," he interrupted. "It seems absurdly formal to ask you to use the title, given the circumstances of our acquaintance. Besides, all of my friends call me Rafe, and I do hope that despite the awkward start we shall indeed become good friends." Let her wonder at his sudden kindness, just as he wondered at her uncharacteristic docility.

*At least he seems a good deal more friendly today,* Jezebel thought nervously. That was a positive sign. Perhaps the duke did have a reasonable side to him after all. Perhaps it had been only the strain of his journey or the shock of finding her alive and unharmed after expecting the worst that had made him behave with such unnecessary rigor yesterday. He was far more relaxed this morning, she judged, and it was vexing to note just how devastatingly attractive the man was when he wasn't scowling or ordering people about. She had to stop staring before he guessed the sort of indecent fantasies his virile good looks were bringing to mind . . . fantasies of him with his arms locked around her, his lips, those lush, knowing lips, arcing down to brush her own. . . . Jezebel's senses were flooded suddenly with a warmth that had nothing to do with the steamy climate.

Though she was certainly no prude, having witnessed mating acts between men and women during her travels that would have had most young ladies swooning in distress, Jezebel herself had never before been the victim of carnal desire. But ever since he'd confronted her yesterday, she'd been positively swamped with the strange new sensation. That it should strike her now, with this man, was not only inconvenient, it was a complete disaster! She had to stop this madness right away, Jezebel thought urgently. If she couldn't focus on why she'd brought him here, then everything she'd worked for was lost.

"Rafe, then." She said the name hesitantly, but then shook herself for her foolishness. She'd faced far more nerve-wracking situations than this in the past and never made such a ninny of herself before! Why, hadn't she once faced down a Bengal tiger with nothing but a jammed rifle and a prayer? She could deal with one little duke. Well, maybe not so little. . . . Regardless, she must remember why she was so angry with him and forget how damnably attractive she found this man. *Down to business, then,* she ordered herself sternly.

"I've asked you here this morning firstly to apologize for my poor behavior yesterday," Jezebel began, making an effort to sound contrite when she was anything but. She'd had every right to defend herself against the duke's bullying, but that didn't matter now. What mattered was placating him. After she'd lulled him into a state of complacency, once he believed she'd been cowed by his authority, she'd have a far better chance of getting her own way in the matter of her wardship. And so she swallowed her pride. "I am very sorry I was so rude, Your—Rafe," she amended. "It was only that you caught me so off guard."

He just bet he had. The little minx was trying to bamboozle him! Wearing her modest little outfit, whispering her coy little apology, when he'd no doubt she'd rather be spitting in his eye and storming off to exchange her frilly gown for the nearest pair of trousers. Oh, he'd heard plenty about

Miss Montclair, all right. Last night Cairo's menfolk had gathered to welcome Lord Ravenhurst to their number, and they'd given him an earful about his new ward's wayward ways.

The gentlemen who'd invited him out for whiskey and conversation last night had claimed to be relieved that someone would finally be taking this spirited minx in hand, but Rafe rather got the impression that no few of them would miss her lively style even more than the excellent professional abilities they'd reluctantly conceded her to have.

Letting the duke see just how much work he had in store for him in taking on such a ward, Cairo's self-proclaimed Egyptologists had spun quite a number of yarns about Jezebel's past, completing Rafe's picture of his new ward with some astonishing revelations about her habits and general deportment.

Jezebel rarely ever wore skirts, he'd learned, and it wasn't just a foible on her part. The explorer's niece adopted men's clothing because she'd also adopted their pursuits. It seemed the girl, both before and after her uncle's passing, had often joined her fellow archaeologists out in the field on digs, climbing with as much vigor as any man (and a good deal more than some, said one grinning fellow, elbowing his stout companion in the gut) over piles of rubble and broken statuary to get to the treasures beneath.

She'd been known to wriggle her way into dangerously unstable stone passages too narrow for anyone else to push through, determined to be the first to investigate a newly opened tomb. She'd been known to look a cranky camel in the eye and make the beast accept the halter after it had chased its own handlers away with snapping, vicious yellow teeth. She'd been known to ride as swiftly as the desert wind itself, shoot a cobra in the eye at twenty paces, outdrink river pirates, and outbargain Cairo's most cunning peddlers.

Jezebel Montclair, it seemed, was known for many things, but she was *not* known for begging anyone's pardon.

Rafe knew full well the girl's contrition was anything but honest. Still, he decided to allow her to play out the charade. Knowing Jezebel was having to throttle back her anger and speak politely made watching her performance very entertaining indeed. His own anger had mellowed somewhat overnight, his usual good humor inevitably reasserting itself after he'd had time to relax and take in the day's events a bit. He'd even managed to chuckle a bit at some of the chit's more outrageous comments.

"Come to tour the pyramids, indeed," he'd snorted. What gall! No one, man or woman, had ever dared speak to Raphael Alexander Sunderland in such a manner. And yet, strangely enough, he found he liked it very much. A part of him wanted to take delight in her every outlandish act, encourage her wit and saucy repartee, but duty reminded him that he couldn't give Miss Montclair that luxury. Instead, he found himself in the paradoxical position of having to play the dictator with her. He must be the voice of discipline for this brash girl, force her to accept society's codes, just as he himself was constrained to do.

It was for her own good in the end, Rafe told himself. Brave-hearted though she was, magnificent in her daring, he clearly couldn't allow her to keep on with her masculine games any longer. Anything could happen to her without a protector to see to her safety. It was only a matter of luck that no harm had so far befallen her, he thought, feeling an inward shiver for all that could have occurred before he'd arrived. A woman as beautiful as Jezebel would always be a target, and in a land where slavery was not only still accepted but a major source of income for the Ottoman Turks, her days of roaming freely were most certainly numbered. He would have to take her in hand.

But just because he was providing guidance and supervision for her, that didn't mean he had to behave like an ogre to his new ward if it could be avoided.

"I accept your apology, Miss Montclair, and hereby tender one of my own. It was unconscionable of me to behave with such a boorish lack of consideration. I only hope you will allow us to begin anew."

Rafe found he meant his words sincerely. Jezebel Montclair was someone he wanted to get to know better, despite the dangerous temptation of her beauty. She might be a sly minx with an agenda of her own, she might want nothing to do with him, and she might have a wild streak a mile wide, but Rafe was beginning to like the girl! He offered his hand to her across the table.

Startled by the gesture, Jezebel had to put down her fork before she could accept the clasp of his warm hand around her own. The touch of the duke's palm felt like a miniature bolt of lightning.

It was a moment before she could breathe normally.

"Your Grace, you are too kind," she said, carefully extricating her hand from his firm grip. She wondered if his callused fingers had left imprints on her skin, or if the burning she felt was just in her imagination. "After coming all this way, it must have been exceedingly unpleasant having me shriek at you like a harpy when your only object was to assist me in my hour of need—quite a heroic gesture, I should say." Jezebel ladled out a heavy dose of charm, wondering if she ought to bat her eyelashes to complete the picture of witless, grateful damsel.

Rafe slung one arm casually over the back in his chair as he reclined, eyeing her shrewdly. The girl was unbelievable! One day she was howling at him like an avenging fury, the next begging his pardon like the veriest angel. Of the two, the fury was probably more in character for Jezebel, he guessed. He wondered how she would react if he called her bluff, and decided to find out.

"Come, now, Miss Montclair." He chuckled. "Really, this brand of insipid flattery doesn't suit you at all, and it certainly doesn't affect *me*. So why don't you drop the facade and get to what's really brought you here today?"

She didn't blink. "How did you know I was being insincere?" Jezebel asked curiously, not bothering to be offended.

"My dear, I've seen better performances from the street mummers who entertain *outside* Drury Lane's theaters."

She laughed. "All right, I admit I *was* being a tad obsequious. I just wanted you to see how obliging I can be—and that, contrary to what you seem to think, I do know how to act like a proper lady when the occasion warrants."

"You believe all ladies use such wiles to secure what they want?"

Jezebel looked at him askance. "Don't you?"

"Perhaps. At one time or another," he admitted.

"Then perhaps you can also see why I prefer not to fulfill society's expectation of a proper lady, Your Grace. As you say, these feminine affectations really do not suit me well." Jezebel shrugged, not seeming overly distressed over her shortcoming. "And yet I manage to get along quite well regardless, as I intend to prove to you."

"And just how do you intend to accomplish such a prodigious task, if I might ask?" Rafe responded with interest.

"Well, for one thing, I've come here today to issue more than just an invitation to breakfast." She paused. "I would also like to invite you into my world."

What an intriguing offer. Still, there were other invitations Rafe would rather hear emerging from Jezebel's lips. An invitation to her bed, specifically. He had a feeling that offer wasn't on the table, however, and it wasn't one he could accept in any case, due to this damnable trust of her uncle's. But by all the saints, it wasn't fair that he should have to sit across from possibly the most enticing woman he'd ever met and make no move to seduce her! Though he knew he should be quelling her outspoken behavior before she got them both into trouble, he wanted to hear more. "What precisely did you have in mind?"

"Well, Your Grace—Rafe," she quickly corrected herself again. "I thought perhaps I might lead you on a tour of some of Egypt's many historical sites, if you have time to sojourn awhile in the land of the pharaohs. The wonders of this country are not to be missed," she assured him earnestly. *And the ancient secrets my uncle died to uncover must be revealed,* she thought privately.

"Don't tell me your only desire in making this gesture is to ensure I do not miss out on any 'marvels' whilst I am here," he chided gently. "I thought we were through with dishonesty, Jezebel." He found her given name rolled off his tongue easily, though he saw her flush at his use of the familiarity.

Indeed, she had very little desire to play tour leader to this overprivileged aristocrat as he oohed and ahhed over the customary sights displayed like some cheap spectacle before every Englishman who came to see great mother Egypt. No, taking the duke along on this sightseeing journey—its route carefully planned to coincide with certain sites Jezebel had planned to visit on her own—was only the cover for the scheme she'd come up with overnight. The plan she'd developed was risky, but it might be her best hope of fulfilling her obligation to her uncle while simultaneously fighting for her own precious independence.

"Of course not," Jezebel said, truthfully enough. "Simply playing tour guide would hardly be beneficial to me, not when I've so many more important matters to attend to in my researches at the moment. And while I've no doubt you will find the sights pleasurable, I'm sure a man of your, um . . . reputation . . . has pastimes he would rather pursue than tromping about the desert to gaze at old stones and inscriptions. No doubt you normally prefer a more sophisticated sort of . . ."—she paused briefly, mentally flailing for a polite description of what rakish dukes might do with their free time—"ah . . . diversion . . . to occupy your attention."

Seeing his sudden scowl, she hurried on, laying out the convoluted reasoning she prayed he would believe. "Actually, what I hope to accomplish is to show you a little of what I do here, and thus to convince you that I am capable of seeing to my own care. By the end of our time together, I expect you will be completely assured you need no longer concern yourself with me."

All of this was true, to a point. However, Jezebel saw no reason to inform her overbearing new guardian that this was only the first portion of her dual agenda. He need never know that she was pursuing a vital new avenue of research while she simultaneously shuttled him around. Her desire to see her uncle vindicated before his peers was none of Lord Ravenhurst's business. He could not be of help to her in this regard—or in any other, for that matter, she reminded herself—so why should she share her plans with him? The duke could only get in her way, Jezebel thought. Her job, her duty to her uncle's memory, was to get rid of this hindrance as quickly as possible. To that end, she would cheerfully lie to this man—and do much worse, if she had to.

"Will you undertake this journey with me?" she asked. She wasn't sure she had been convincing enough, whether her offer would appeal to the dictatorial duke. But she had to try.

Rafe tried not to be annoyed by the way Jezebel had just casually categorized him as less important to her than a bunch of moldy old remains. He also tried to be sanguine about her clearly low opinion of his character, the insulting way she assumed he would happily leave her unprotected at the first opportunity. Neither effort was entirely successful. After a few rounds of deep breathing, he still found himself with an urge to smother the girl, though whether he wanted to cover her luscious mouth with kisses or with a stout gag, he wasn't yet sure. But if he was going to be spending the next several weeks in close contact with this chit, he knew he'd better learn some less provocative methods of dealing with her blunt manner of speaking.

For no matter what else happened, they *would* be spending a good deal of time together. Rafe had made a few decisions of his own last night. The first was that they were both going to remain in Egypt for a few weeks—a decision he was sure Miss Montclair would be delighted to hear, since it meant she'd have a short reprieve from the fate she so obviously wished to avoid. He was determined Jezebel must be made to face the reality of her position—but he'd also decided that perhaps she need not face it right away. After all, he was here to watch over her now. He could afford to be generous, to allow her just a little more time to enjoy the world she had created here for herself.

And Rafe would be enjoying it with her, it seemed. Even if he'd wanted to depart immediately, he'd discovered it would be impossible to leave right away. Had he been such a barbarian as to consider hauling Jezebel over his shoulder kicking and screaming aboard a ship, it would have done him no good, for there simply *was* no ship available to haul her aboard. The clipper he'd arrived on was headed to India for its next stop, and the first vessel leaving for England would not be departing for several weeks, as he'd learned upon making inquiries at the docks. In any case, he'd decided there were better ways to deal with the spirited explorer's niece than by brute force, ways that would not have her storming out on him every time they met. He knew he'd have a much easier time handling the chit if he led her to believe he was willing to consider letting her staying behind.

For the meanwhile, he'd gladly let her lead him around the monuments Egypt offered up so abundantly from her sands—or at least let her *think* she was leading him around. Rafe would watch the explorer's niece with a steady eye at every moment to make sure the girl was as good as her boasts and knew the country well. And in the process, he too would learn new skills. He felt an absurd wash of pleasure at the prospect of touring the ruins. He'd always wanted to explore this fascinating land, and for once, duty and pleasure were coinciding, allowing that to happen. Rafe intended to make the most of the opportunity, seeing all he could see before his responsibilities called him home.

"All right," he agreed.

"But Your Grace, I'm sure I can persuade you if you'll only—What did you just say?"

"I said all right," he repeated mildly.

Jezebel felt the steam she'd been building up for this argument rush out of her all at once. "Oh. Well, then." She couldn't believe she'd won so easily. She'd expected the duke to prove far more difficult to persuade.

"I'm sure you'll soon see why your presence here is unnecessary—appreciated, of course, but unnecessary," she reassured. "Why, in no time you'll have seen the best sights that Egypt has to offer—from one of the best antiquarians she has to offer," she boasted cheerfully. *And, in the meanwhile, I hope to have gathered all the proof I need to make those bombastic old fools who sneered at my uncle eat their words.* "I'm certain you'll come 'round to my point of view very quickly." Jezebel smiled in clear relief.

Rafe was equally sure he would not. However, though he knew there was no good reason to disrupt the newly fledged peace between them by saying so, some devil of perversity made him want to needle her just a little bit, to test her mettle when he really should be doing his best to discourage it.

"Would you care to stake your certainty on a wager, Miss Montclair?" Rafe's tone had the same easy, in-control cadence he'd employed all along, but his eyes were suddenly glowing with the blue flames of mischief.

"A . . . a wager?" Jezebel faltered. Her smile faded into wariness. *Damn,* she thought. *I knew he was accepting this too easily.*

"Yes, a wager. Surely you are familiar with the concept."

She scowled at his patronizing tone, hesitation forgotten. "Indeed, Your Grace," she clipped off shortly. "I understand the principles—created, I believe, by men such as yourself with a good deal of spare time and cash on their hands, and an urge to squander both. So do tell me, what are the terms of this bet you propose?"

"No money need change hands in this instance, if that's what you're worried about. I simply thought it might prove interesting to raise the stakes of our little agreement just a bit. But if you are not up to the challenge . . ." Rafe let the sentence drop off, goading her. He wanted to see if Jezebel's fiery temperament would resurface.

It did.

"My Lord Ravenhurst, I am *more* than a match for any piddling challenge you could think to throw out. Now, what are these terms you speak of?" she demanded again, her eyes glittering with recklessness. Jezebel wasn't about to let this dandified aristocrat get the best of her!

"They're very simple, my dear." He smiled slowly, eyeing her speculatively. "*You* are determined to prove your independence. I do not believe you can handle such liberty without getting yourself into trouble. *I* will wager that you cannot, in the space of the next few weeks, prove to my satisfaction that giving you the autonomy you crave is in your best interests. Should you win, I will allow you to choose the course of your own future, even remaining alone here in Cairo if you desire—and I will release your uncle's fortune to you immediately, to do with as you will. It will be as if you never had a guardian.

"Should you fail, however," Rafe paused significantly, "you must accompany me back to England without further protest. There, you will quietly live out the terms of your uncle's will, and we both know what they are—five years with me as your protector, or marriage to a suitor I must first approve."

Rafe could see the sly thoughts going on behind Jezebel's lapis-blue eyes, and he knew she didn't trust his offer. He himself was having trouble believing he'd just made it— this hasty wager certainly hadn't been in his original plans! But then the chances she'd win were so slim, it really didn't matter, Rafe reassured himself. Even Jezebel must know it. He could tell she was already planning ahead for her inevitable loss, and he decided to disabuse her of any notions she might have of running from him.

"Should you refuse to accompany me quietly, I shall take it as within my rights to instruct the British consul here in Cairo to revoke all of your papers. He won't extend permission for you to travel so much as across the *street* in this town, let alone allow you to roam freely all over the country as you do now. If you choose to run, he will instruct anyone who comes across your path to report your whereabouts to his agents, who will be dispatched at once to collect you.

"As a matter of fact," the duke continued, leaning back in his chair and considering his words as he went on, "I believe I will have the consul call out the guard and have you hauled aboard my ship in chains if you refuse to come along peaceably. Very embarrassing, I'm sure you'll agree. But no matter what you do, make no mistake, your life here will be over." All the time he spoke, Rafe's tone was quietly implacable, as was the look in his eyes as his gaze bored into hers.

Jezebel wilted back into her chair, all the breath escaping her. These were high stakes indeed! Though Henry Salt, the British consul-general and an influential Egyptologist in his own right, usually turned a blind eye to her unfeminine pursuits, and had even, in the past, helped to expedite the processing of the travel passes she required, the man retained the power to effectively cripple her activities in

Egypt. Should he suddenly be reminded of his responsibility to "protect" this member of the British expatriate society from herself, Jezebel would find herself in quite a bind. Given the proper incentive from her influential guardian, Jezebel had no doubt the normally lax Mr. Salt would instantly become a model of patriarchal concern. And if he called the guard . . . Jezebel would be forced to flee forthwith.

"But how can I trust your honesty in such a subjective wager?" she asked shrewdly. "You have only to claim yourself dissatisfied in order to win your bet," she pointed out.

Rafe grinned broadly at his ward, shifting as he did so to an even more relaxed position in his chair. "My dear girl, you fail to see the point entirely." At her uncomprehending stare, he sighed softly and explained. "I shall be just as happy to lose this bet as to win it, of course—happier, if you want to know the truth. With this wager, I'm giving you a chance to get us *both* out of this mess, though quite honestly I don't hold out much hope you can do it."

His gaze raked her appraisingly. "Nothing personal, you understand. But in truth I don't wish to be saddled with the responsibility of a ward any more than you seem to like being one," he said, echoing Jezebel's own earlier thoughts. Rafe continued with a mocking twist of his lips, "As you suggested so delicately before, there are other . . . pursuits . . . I find more enjoyable than seeing to the welfare of one overbold young lady who is foolish enough to think she needs no one's assistance. However, if you think that means I shall allow you to go gallivanting off all over God's creation without first being absolutely sure of your safety, then you much malign my honor. Now, do you accept the wager, or will you call it quits and concede?"

Jezebel found herself flushing from the reproof in the duke's words—an odd reaction when this was what she'd wanted all along! Ravenhurst was handing her the chance to prove her competence, practically begging her to give him a way out of the farcical situation engendered by her uncle's will. And she had no doubt she could do it, if only he proved open-minded enough to concede the truth. The risks of this bet might be high, but the rewards were even greater if she won. Why, not only would she be rid of this nuisance of a man, whose very presence threatened her equilibrium, but she'd also earn the bulk of her inheritance in the same act. . . .

That money could cushion her lifestyle for years to come; finance her travels and her researches, even let her hire men to form her own expeditions one day. It was a prospect so tantalizing, Jezebel hardly dared dream of it. So why then did the duke's obvious rejection still sting?

It was only her pride that was wounded, she told herself staunchly. No one liked to be told they were unwanted baggage—especially not when the implication was that the baggage in question was also an incompetent nincompoop. But she couldn't deny she felt an element of disappointment in the duke as well, strange as the emotion was under the circumstances. Though the duke was not disreputable enough to abandon her outright, she noted he still sought ways to avoid responsibility for her.

Why it should surprise her, Jezebel couldn't imagine. Why it should *bother* her was even more of a mystery. *For heaven's sake,* she told herself roughly. *The man's giving you a chance to get exactly what you want. You should be thanking him, not angry at him for being overeager to do your will!* Still, she couldn't help the somewhat bitter thought that Ravenhurst had shown himself to be no different than any other man she'd known in the past. She would never let herself forget he saw her only as a duty, one he wanted to dispose of quickly so that he could go back to the licentious pleasures of his life back home.

*Well,* she told herself. *I have a life of my own to return to, don't I? And one way or another, that's exactly what I'll do within the next few weeks. If Ravenhurst plays fair, there's no doubt that I'll win this wager. But if the scoundrel claims I've lost, then I see no reason to uphold my end of the deal, for he'd have to be either blind or lying not to concede my competence. Either way, I lose nothing by agreeing to it.*

So determined, Jezebel smiled falsely at the duke. "I

shall certainly consent to your wager, Your Grace." She paused then with a sudden thought. "But I have a condition of my own to add."

"Oh?" Rafe's brow rose in its habitual gesture of amusement. "And what would that be?"

Jezebel wanted nothing more than to pierce that smug superiority of his. "My condition is this: If at any time before your scheduled return to England you should prove yourself to be less than a proper guardian—if your 'supervision' should prove detrimental to my welfare rather than beneficial, then you will agree to end this farce, turn my inheritance over to me unconditionally, and be on your way, never to darken my doorstep again."

Rafe ignored the drama of her statement, but found himself disturbed by its content. "And how will I trust to *your* honesty in judging this detriment, Jezebel? I can hardly depend on your opinion of my protection to guide me."

Jezebel thought for a moment, eyeing the duke as though judging his worth by his countenance alone. She sighed, coming to her decision after a moment's scrutiny. "You can trust the honesty of the judgment because *you* will be the one to make it, Your Grace. I shall trust you, on your honor as a *gentleman*"—she stressed the last word with wry emphasis—"to own up to your own failings."

"How very generous," Rafe murmured, but he could not see a reason to deny her this codicil to the bet between them. He couldn't imagine how he could fail to do a better job of seeing to Jezebel than the reckless girl could do on her own—and as for actually *causing* his ward some form of harm, well, there was only one action on his part that he could envision doing *that* . . . but surely the chit couldn't be suggesting what he was thinking! Worldly-wise as she might appear, Rafe doubted Miss Montclair would wager so easily with her virtue. Besides, he'd been seduced by women with far more skill and experience, if not with greater beauty, than this young lady. She couldn't make him break his vow to watch over her chastely—could she?

Rafe dismissed the possibility as unworthy of them both. "Agreed, Miss Montclair. Should I prove an inferior guardian, I shall bow out of your life quite happily."

Jezebel released the long-pent-up breath she'd been holding, whether in excitement or anxiety she didn't know. She wasn't sure exactly what she was getting into, but it was highly stimulating!

Jezebel rose to leave the table, dabbing her lips unnecessarily with her napkin as she prepared to take her leave. "Very well, then." She thought for a minute. "If I may suggest, I believe a trip to the Giza plateau to view the Sphinx and the Great Pyramids would be an excellent place to start." Though there was nothing there of interest to Jezebel this time around, she could hardly skip showing the duke the most famous monuments in all of Egypt! Besides, according to her calculations, the stop in Giza would take them no more than a day out of their way as they headed south.

Rafe shrugged his wide shoulders in an easy gesture of acceptance. "I shall leave myself entirely in your hands, my dear."

She flushed, briefly overwhelmed by a startlingly vivid vision of what it would be like to have Raphael Sunderland "in her hands." Images such as she'd never entertained before flooded her mind and sent a shiver of unwanted delight down her spine. If he considered her behavior inappropriate already, what would he think if he knew the thoughts she was having about him right now? It didn't bear considering.

"Good, then I shall make all the arrangements today. We should be able to set out first thing tomorrow." She started toward the terrace door.

"Where are you going, my dear?" the duke asked.

Jezebel paused warily. "Why, to make the needed preparations, of course. I must arrange for a dahabeah to take us up the river, and provisions. . . ."

The duke rose as well, reminding her of his great height. His head blocked out the sunlight and cast his face in shadow so that she could not see his expression. "Then I shall accompany you."

She protested instantly. "That's really not necessary." Jezebel told herself that the last thing she wanted was Ravenhurst trailing around behind her in the bazaar while she bargained with her limited funds for the things they would need. But while it was true that the sight of the blond, blue-eyed foreigner would probably drive most merchants' prices up a good three hundred percent, that wasn't the real reason she wanted to be alone. In truth, Jezebel needed time away from the magnetic Lord Ravenhurst just to clear her head!

However, Rafe wasn't having any of her excuses. "I believe you said you wanted me to observe your survival skills," he replied. "Therefore I will accompany you whilst you demonstrate them."

Somehow Jezebel knew this was not negotiable. Though the duke's tone was perfectly genial, it nevertheless managed to indicate his absolute immovability on the issue. Why push it? She'd already accomplished much more than she'd hoped to today, and so she reluctantly decided to concede this minor battle. If she couldn't get rid of Ravenhurst, she'd just have to shake off his heady effect on her as they went along.

"I shall just go change out of this overfrilled getup, then," she said, gesturing at her demure white gown, "and we can meet in the lobby in an hour, if that suits you." At the duke's nod, Jezebel curtsied with mocking grace, then took her leave most gratefully.

*Well*, the young Egyptologist told herself once she'd reached the safe confines of the hotel's cool, dim corridors. *I'll just focus on marshaling this little expedition from now on. With any luck, it'll keep the duke so busy gawking at the scenery that he won't notice me gawking at* him!

If she stayed in command of herself and the situation at all times, she might even be able to restrain the untoward direction of her thoughts long enough to impress the man with her competency rather than her girlish fascination with his magnificent physique.

Maybe this adventure wouldn't be so bad, after all.

But probably it would.

# *Chapter Six*

*~*

*E*h, princess!" an Italian-accented voice shouted. Curious as to the source of the booming call, Rafe glanced around just as Jezebel did, turning from the oiled-canvas tents they'd been examining at a vendor's outdoor stall. For a moment, the sheer number of people packed into the small square housing Cairo's dry-goods market blocked his view, but his ward seemed to know the significance of that odd hail well enough.

"Belzoni."

Rafe heard Jezebel sigh the name with a mixture of resignation and good humor. A second later he saw an immense bald-headed gentleman with bristling black mustachios and biceps that strained the very fabric of his shirt come barreling toward them out of the crowd. Alarmed, Rafe was about to step between his ward and the bullish man when he saw the welcoming smile growing upon Jezebel's luminous features. He checked the action, waiting to see what Miss Montclair found to smile about with such an apparition bearing down on her. After all, he had promised to observe her life, not interfere—and he knew next to nothing about the sort of companions she favored. He might see Lord Clifton's niece cavorting with a lot of unacceptable characters before he discovered the worst of the behavior with which her unusual upbringing had left her.

Indeed, Rafe found what happened next quite beyond the pale. The fellow hefted Jezebel, now clad once more in loose layers of Turkish-style cotton robes, up in his arms, tossing her skyward as though she weighed no more than a feather. He began to swing her around and around without much regard for the dozens of others packed into the

square, who scattered to avoid her flying feet and swinging
ebony hair. Jezebel was laughing, Rafe noticed, and slapping merrily at the stranger's arms and shoulders in mock
protest. He felt the beginning of some ugly, unfamiliar
emotion welling up inside him as he witnessed the scene.

"Down, Belzoni!" she was saying. "Put me down, you
monstrous behemoth! Yes, yes, it's good to see you too,
but the ground's as good a place to meet as the air, now,
isn't it?"

"Ah, *mi bella donna,* you never let me have any fun!"
the burly man roared, but he set her back on her feet
quickly enough. Jezebel, winded with laughter and scraping
strands of silky black hair from her eyes, turned back to
Rafe as soon as she regained terra firma.

"Your Grace, may I present Giovanni Belzoni, one of
the best explorers and excavators in all of Egypt. Belzoni,
this is Raphael Sunderland, the duke of Ravenhurst." She
smiled fondly at the gargantuan Italian.

Rafe made a conscious effort to smooth out the scowl
that had overtaken his features at the sight of his ward in
the arms of this overgrown ape. There was no reason for
the instant animosity he felt toward the man, he told himself. He instincts told him there was no improper relationship between his ward and the Italian—unless one counted
exuberant public displays of friendship improper, as Rafe
was beginning to think he did. He allowed his hand to be
crushed briefly by the beaming Belzoni. "A pleasure to
make your acquaintance, signore," he replied fluently in
Italian, his tone as cordial as he could make it.

"Oh, Giovanni's quite comfortable with English, my
lord," Jezebel answered for him. "Don't let that heavy accent fool you—he actually spent much of his youth in England, ah . . ."—Jezebel grinned mischievously as she
sought the proper euphemism—"studying. I think he just
plays up his Italian heritage for effect," she joked with a
secretive wink at her friend. It was clear she didn't expect
the duke to understand the cause of her amusement.

But Rafe was quicker than she gave him credit for. "You
aren't 'Belzoni the Strong-Man' of London theatrical fame,
by any chance?" he asked incredulously. He looked closer

into the leathery, sun-darkened features. The face did resemble somewhat the caricatures he'd seen years before on leaflets dispersed around London's cobbled streets, advertising the virtues of the actor-cum-carnival-performer.

"Ah, an admirer!" cried the man, abruptly losing his exaggerated accent. He curled a bicep roughly the size of Rafe's entire head to demonstrate. "The great Belzoni hasn't lost a bit of his old skill, am I right?" He laughed. "Only now, instead of lightening the pocketbooks of you swells back in London, these days I use my astonishing prowess to carry the weight of kings!" he boasted.

"Giovanni is an expert engineer, Your Grace," Jezebel explained. "Currently he is assisting Henry Salt in his excavations at the Valley of the Kings."

"Valley of the Kings?" Rafe queried.

"That is what we are calling the mountainous area a ways up the Nile on the western bank across from Thebes. It's a part of the desert that's more rock than sand, and in recent years, several promising tombs have been unearthed in that region, though none intact to date." Jezebel looked mournful. "There is so much we could learn about the mysterious rituals of the ancient Egyptians if only we could discover one of their burial sites undisturbed."

"Ah, that would be fine indeed," agreed the Italian. From the avaricious light in his brown eyes, Rafe felt safe in assuming his motives were not purely scholarly.

"Much gold in that, is there?" He asked the question idly, directing it equally at either antiquarian.

"Presumably, Your Grace, since we know the Egyptians believed in burying their dead with all of their earthly possessions, and they were a wealthy people at the height of their empire," Jezebel replied. "But the real treasures will come when, as linguists such as Champollion and Young are striving to do even now, we finally decode the hieroglyphics they've left so copiously upon their monuments. Then we will begin to understand how people lived in the time of the pharaohs."

"You take part in this effort, Miss Montclair, do you not?" Rafe's tone held a sort of noncommittal interest, as though he was reserving judgment on what a young woman such as herself could contribute to such an arcane realm of study. "It is an odd interest for a lady of your breeding and station," he commented.

"Not so odd, Your Grace. I only do what I can to further our understanding of this fascinating culture, just as my uncle taught me to do. I do not consider it at all strange to want to continue his life's work," Jezebel replied. From the degree of defensiveness in her voice, Rafe felt sure this was not the first time she'd been so questioned.

"Plenty of hieroglyphs to decipher at the Kings' Valley since we found that new tomb—though no gold, sadly," Belzoni interjected, seeming to sense the building tension between the two. "Perhaps you will come to visit us there again soon, *cara mia?*" he asked hopefully. "We have a great bunch of fellows down in the valley now, a veritable tent city, with dozens of us gents digging and chipping away all day long among the rocks. I'm only up in Cairo now to supervise the shipment of some heavy pieces back through Alexandria to our paying friends in England. Once I see the boat off tomorrow, I intend to head back south. I know you've been interested in some of those inscriptions we found in the new tomb. Do say you'll come along," he pleaded with cumbersome grace.

Rafe scowled at this blatant piece of flirtation, but Jezebel didn't appear to notice it. "As a matter of fact, I may indeed pay you and your companions a visit soon. You see, I am promised to show Lord Ravenhurst his fill of our adopted nation for the next fortnight or so, and that is certainly one sight we will not want to miss. Still, I think if it meets with His Grace's approval we shall push on farther south first to view that marvelous temple from which you cleared the sands at Abu Simbel."

She paused significantly, knowing that Belzoni had heard of her uncle's interest in the place and knew of her own recent determination to investigate the unique hieroglyphics said to be found there. "As you know, I have a great desire to see it before the vultures descend and disturb all the artifacts from their original sites, as they will inevitably do. We'll sail back down the Nile afterward at a more leisurely pace and meet up with you on our return journey, if we may." Her tone was conversational, but Jezebel's eyes, flicking warningly between the tall men who hemmed her in like two gigantic gateposts, told a more serious story.

Belzoni had clearly gotten the message. His little princess didn't want any questions asked in front of Lord Ravenhurst. The veteran engineer took it in stride, merely glancing skeptically at the sweating duke. "You are taking him that far into the heat upriver?" he asked dubiously. "Well, then you had best make sure the man buys some proper clothes before you set out. . . . Don't want to fry in the sun, now, do you?" he said to Rafe jovially.

The duke clenched his teeth against an ungracious reply. The man was only trying to be friendly, but it was obvious he thought Rafe a tyro at best, a complete dandy at worst. Much as it grated on his nerves, he had to admit that he was a newcomer here, and he had much to learn—about Jezebel and her companions, at any rate.

"And speaking of sunshine, what's happened to that little shadow you'd developed last I saw you?" Belzoni continued.

Jezebel looked blank for a moment, then realized what he meant. "Gunther!" she exclaimed. "Oh, I'm so glad you reminded me of him. Something must be done with that poor boy while we're gone."

"I see no need for you to concern yourself with his activities, Miss Montclair," Rafe interrupted sourly. "Indeed, I do not think it at all proper for you to be sharing your company so freely with him. That 'poor boy,' as you call him, seemed well grown enough to be ogling your charms quite openly when I saw him yesterday." For some reason he could not fathom, the subject of the young German was a sore one with him.

Jezebel was embarrassed that Lord Ravenhurst would bring such a topic up in front of her friend Belzoni, and she immediately tried to play it down. "Gunther *Morgenstern*? Ogling? Don't be ridiculous," she dismissed. Then, seeing that her guardian's concerns would not be dealt with so easily, she sighed. "Gunther is one of my uncle's remnants," Jezebel explained, deciding it wasn't wise to provoke the duke any further with hints that the young man might mean something more to her. "He came from Germany to study with Lord Clifton by prior arrangement, but arrived too late. My uncle had already passed away," she told him tightly. "After that I promised Gunther I'd help him learn his way around in Egypt. He's a bit wide-eyed, I'll admit, but I'm sure he has never been known to 'ogle' anyone."

Rafe was still ready to protest her having any involvement with the handsome young pup when Jezebel suddenly brightened with an idea. She turned her dazzling smile on her large friend once more.

"*You* could take him, Belzoni!"

"What?" the strongman looked alarmed.

"Oh, come, be a darling, won't you? It's the perfect solution. You could take him back south with you and introduce him around the camp there. I know he seems a bit, well, inept at times, but he's sure to find something he's good at among that crew of tomb-robbing old pirates you're leading."

Belzoni was shaking his head, not so much saying no as pleading with her not to ask this of him. She persisted regardless.

"It wouldn't be so bad. I know Gunther's still somewhat naive, but he needs to get some seasoning sooner or later if he intends to remain here. Who better to give it to him than a collection of the finest, most rough-and-tumble adventurers this side of the Sudan? Especially one led by such a fine strapping gentleman as yourself." She laid on the flattery shamelessly, smiling up winsomely into the bald man's reddening countenance until he could not help but bend beneath the weight of so much gamine charm.

"All right! All right!" He threw up his hands helplessly. "Send the boy to me. I'll set him to work on something he couldn't bungle with a thirty-pound sledgehammer in one hand and a two-foot pickaxe in the other. I'll make a man of him, just as you ask," Belzoni promised, some of his boastfulness returning. "After all, he can't help learning something about the subject, just by sharing my company day by day."

"You are a pharaoh's treasure yourself, Giovanni," Jezebel cried. She blew Belzoni a kiss, the man's face too far up for her to reach. "Excellent! Then we shall see you again in a couple of weeks."

She held out her arm for Rafe to take, and, impressed with the neat way she'd maneuvered the engineer into doing her will, he allowed her to lead him away to the next row of shops.

Score one for Miss Montclair on the side of competence, the duke thought with a reluctant smile. She'd certainly handled *that* poor bloke without a trace of difficulty.

*J*ezebel was admiring the sight of the pink and violet dawn that had just begun to touch the sky the next morning. Having been unable to sleep well that night after the day spent shopping in the bazaar with the duke, she'd arrived early for today's meeting with Lord Ravenhurst. She had been waiting for him near the side entrance of the hotel, which was usually deserted at this hour of the morning, and silently wondering how she was going to manage staying with the man long enough to win the wager she'd made with him when just one morning of walking in his company had left her feeling restless and disturbed in ways she still didn't fully understand.

Maybe, she thought, it was the alert, protective way he'd walked beside her as she led him through the bazaar to make their purchases, the wakeful readiness he displayed that still, somehow, had managed not to make Jezebel feel smothered. Though he was a newcomer, Lord Ravenhurst nevertheless gave off an impression of total confidence, of ease with his circumstances. She had the feeling very little could rattle Rafe Sunderland, no matter where he went.

As good as his word, the duke had not interfered in her dealings, though it was clear at times that he wanted to step in. But even when the bargaining got heavy and heated words were exchanged before him in a language he did not understand, Ravenhurst had done no more than inquire as to the price of her purchases. His only insistence that day was that he pay for the supplies they bought. "They are, after all, being bought for my benefit, are they not?" he'd asked. And Jezebel had been more than happy to let him take responsibility for paying for their trip. What was a guardian for if not to dole out one's inheritance? She'd been forced to economize long enough, in her opinion.

All in all, Rafe Sunderland had impressed her a great deal yesterday. She'd had the strangest sense, even as he sat back and allowed her to take the lead, that he was every bit in control of the situation. Certainly, he'd seemed quite ready to leap to her aid should anything go amiss. No one, she realized with a dawning sense of wonder, had ever made her feel protected in that way in her entire life.

Jezebel didn't like the feeling. She didn't want to feel the warm glow that his presence evoked—not when, as she'd had to remind herself sharply several times that day, it was his *absence* she desired. And, as she'd promised herself yesterday when she'd agreed to the wager, Jezebel was determined to achieve that absence no matter what she had to do to get it. There was no way in hell she was going to surrender herself into Ravenhurst's hands if he declared she'd lost their bet.

Quashing the remnants of shame that nagged at her brain, she told herself firmly she was doing the right thing, the only thing she could do under the circumstances. While *he* might think it vital to honor the terms they'd agreed upon—and she wasn't sure yet whether he did—*she* could not afford to be encumbered with such nice scruples. She had a higher purpose to fulfill.

Had the stakes been anything less than her uncle's very reputation and the disposition of her own future, she might have been content to let the chips fall where they would, but Jezebel was taking no chances in this case. She could not afford to let the duke declare himself the winner of their wager—something, she knew, that could only happen should the man prove to be a dishonorable cheat. At the first sign of foul play on Rafe's part, she would take off running, she resolved. In fact, she'd already arranged for a secret store of money and extra survival gear to be cached among their supplies in that event. It was the only prudent thing to do.

Distracted by the plans running through her mind, Jezebel didn't notice the man coming toward her down the alley until it was almost too late. One more reason, she told herself, to get away from the duke as soon as possible. He was playing havoc with her normally sharp defenses!

She'd been leaning with one shoulder tucked up against the stucco wall, but upon seeing the figure striding toward her out of the dimness, she immediately straightened, prepared to defend herself from whoever was approaching. Her hand went to her dagger, a wickedly curved Turkish blade that was just one of several weapons she carried at her belt. She might be overreacting, but one never knew friend from foe in Cairo and it was always best to be cautious.

Jezebel relaxed when she saw who it was.

"*Guten Morgen,*" she offered to the red-faced young German confronting her. She slid her hands up inside the flowing sleeves of her djellaba and eyed him expectantly, knowing he would have words for her today.

It was a moment before Gunther could speak.

"How could you do it?" he asked finally. The words, spoken in agitation, were heavily accented.

"Do what?"

"You have practically foisted me off on that lunkheaded Italian, while you take this—this duke of yours—a man whose conduct and reputation I do not approve of, by the way—to view the very ruins which I have come so far abroad to study! Why can I not also accompany you on this expedition?" His sullen tone came perilously close to whining.

"Firstly, Herr Morgenstern, I am not 'foisting' you off," she returned tartly, using his surname to indicate her displeasure. Privately, however, Jezebel admitted that this was almost exactly what she was doing. "I am providing you with a valuable educational experience—one which anyone who professes an interest in antiquities should be eager to exploit. Secondly, Lord Ravenhurst knows nothing about our special area of study—a blissful state of ignorance I intend he shall remain in for as long as he resides in Egypt. Whilst he sojourns here, I shall lead His Grace upon what amounts to no more than a mere sightseeing tour. I doubt

we shall do more than visit the most popular ruins, which
have already been studied thoroughly, and from which there
can be little to learn."

"But I have heard that you intend to take him to Abu Simbel." Gunther's accent made the word sound like *Zimbel*. "Is
that not where your uncle believed he would find—"

Jezebel cut him off hastily. "Yes, yes," she shushed him,
looking around as if to spot prying eyes peeking out from
the dark, shuttered windows of the hotel above. "That is
the site where I shall look for the next clue, but as you
know, even should I find it, that will merely be the beginning of a larger search. All I can hope to find in Abu Simbel
is a certain inscription, and you can be of no assistance to
me there, since you cannot recognize one hieroglyph yet
from another."

Gunther flushed at this pointed reminder, but Jezebel had
no time to spare his feelings. None of them could truly
claim to understand the mysterious language of the ancient
Egyptians, but at least most serious scholars could tell the
difference between the symbol for a snake and the symbol
for water! "We shan't stay there long before heading back
north to view the more popular ruins in any case—hardly
long enough for me to do any research at all. If you want
to help, you will do much more good exploring the new
tombs in the Kings' Valley with Belzoni and the others.

"Don't let them know what we are after while you are
there," the cunning archaeologist said conspiratorially, "but
keep a sharp lookout at all times. Perhaps"—and she dangled the prospect before the prickly young man like a
sweetmeat—"you will even make an important new
discovery of your own, and you'll earn your reputation in
the field. It's quite a coup for a young man your age to be
invited into such a distinguished company of explorers."
Jezebel knew how sorely Gunther wanted to earn his stripes
as an archaeologist, and how little respect he had so far
managed to engender. He'd certainly picked the wrong
mentor, she thought wryly, if he wanted his colleagues'
esteem!

"Young man my age!" Gunther huffed. "Why, I am

older than you, Fräulein Montclair! You are no more than
a young girl yourself, and yet you think it wise to go off
alone with this man whom you know so little about? Even
if, as you say, this is no more than a pleasure excursion,
you will still be spending a great deal of time unprotected
in his company. I do not think you should go. I think Lord
Ravenhurst is dangerous."

She *knew* Lord Ravenhurst was dangerous. That much
was undeniable, but Jezebel didn't like the sudden propri-
etary air Gunther was adopting. He'd been happy enough
to let this "young girl" provide the contacts he needed in
the city, to follow her about and learn from her, but the
instant she made a move he disapproved of, he was suddenly reminded of propriety. It shouldn't surprise her, she
thought to herself with a twinge of bitterness. Men always
seemed to think they had a right to tell a woman what she
could and could not do, especially when, as now, what she
*planned* to do did not agree with their own agenda. Indeed,
Jezebel was beginning to suspect the young German's mo-
tivation was not simply the selfless concern for her welfare
that he claimed.

Since she'd agreed to ease his way into Cairo's society
of antiquarians, he'd been an agreeable companion, if a
trifle eager to please, but now Jezebel began to suspect that
Lord Ravenhurst had been right about Gunther. His pos-
sessive behavior suggested he'd developed stronger feelings
for her than mere friendship. How awkward! She felt a
twinge of sympathy for her friend even through her anger.
Despite his greater chronological age, Gunther had not yet
completely left the comforts of childhood behind as she had
long ago. Some people were raised with the luxury of taking their time to grow up, Jezebel thought philosophically.
Others led lives that forced them to mature earlier on. Gunther just needed some reassurance.

"Don't worry over me, my friend," she soothed. "We
shall catch up to you before you know it. I will be as safe
as can be with His Grace. After all, he *is* the man my uncle
chose to be my guardian—a mistake I intend to rectify as
soon as possible." Jezebel didn't intend to confide her plans
for disposing of her unwanted protector to Gunther. She

certainly wouldn't tell him that she might not be returning from this journey, for she couldn't trust him to keep his reaction to the news quiet. Better that he not know anything, if questioned later about her whereabouts.

So instead she merely said, "Men like Lord Ravenhurst only need to be shown a temple or two, and that is enough to bore them to tears. That and a few weeks in this heat will convince His Grace that a swift return to England is the most *capital* idea he's ever had." Jezebel mocked a dandy's inflection. "I assure you, I know just how to handle this," she predicted confidently, although she knew no such thing.

Before Gunther could ask how she planned to avoid accompanying the duke on this return trip, they were interrupted.

"Handle what, my dear?" asked an amused voice from behind her. Jezebel whipped around to see Lord Ravenhurst, now dressed very similarly to herself in light desert robes, standing at the hotel's entrance.

"Why, the provisioning for our journey, of course," she replied smoothly, trying to steady her heart after the leap it had taken at the sight of her guardian. He looked . . . well, *dashing* was the only word that came to mind. Tall and commanding in the traditional Egyptian garments, a rifle slung casually across one broad shoulder, Rafe Sunderland appeared ready to take on anything the desert had to offer. He couldn't have heard them discussing her plans, could he? she wondered. "Gunther was just wishing us a safe trip and inquiring as to the state of our supplies."

"Was he, now?" Rafe looked the stripling over. "It's very kind of you to be concerned, Herr Morgenstern," he drawled. It was clear he didn't believe he'd interrupted any such innocuous conversation.

Gunther, meanwhile, was obviously struggling for the courage to challenge the bigger man, and his mouth worked for several seconds as he chose and discarded replies. At last, however, he gave it up, intimidated by Lord Ravenhurst's air of baiting confidence, and merely bowed with stiff grace. "I shall take my leave of you both, then," he said through frozen lips. "I must be going if I am to meet

Herr Belzoni at his barge." With these words he threw a darkling glare in Jezebel's direction. "I wish you both a pleasant journey."

"And you as well," Rafe replied to the young man's back as he stalked off toward the river.

There was a moment of silence as the two, ward and warden, sized each other up. Jezebel could tell the duke was not best pleased at finding her alone this morning with the man he was so sure had designs on her. But there was little she could do to correct that impression now, and she thought it best to turn the topic quickly in another direction.

"That's quite an ensemble you are sporting, Your Grace," she sallied with a nervous smile.

"Do you like it? I assure you, had my valet not been heaving what little is left of his guts up in the garderobe this morning, he would not have allowed me to venture out the door wearing it. As it was, I believe poor Perkins may have burst into tears of despair upon my departure." Rafe sighed dramatically. "I suppose I shall just have to do without the poor man's services while he recuperates. The hotel's manager tells me it is a common malady among newcomers who partake unwisely of the waters, and can take a few weeks to overcome. What I shall do until then, I cannot guess," he said, eyes twinkling.

"I cannot imagine the hardship," she murmured with equal seriousness.

"Well"—Rafe sighed again—"I shall endeavor to push on." Then he stopped teasing, rubbing his hands together as though preparing to take on some great project. "Right, then. What is our first order of business?"

"The rest of our party awaits us by the river with our gear already loaded on the dahabeah." At Rafe's blank look, she explained. "A dahabeah is a kind of boat with a large triangular sail and a wide keel, built for pleasure cruising on the river—very commodious. However, we shall only be sailing a short distance aboard it today before we put in on the west bank and continue overland across the desert. From there it's only a short ride by camel to reach the Giza plateau."

*Camels!* thought Rafe with a surge of boyish excitement. He'd yet to see this mythical beast during his short tenure in Egypt, and he was looking forward to the novel experience.

Novelty, he was soon to find out, wore thin rather quickly.

## Chapter Seven

~

*B*ackside firmly planted in the dirt, the seventh duke of Ravenhurst glared up at the unrepentant face of the animal who'd just tossed him into this undignified sprawl in which he found himself. He did his best to ignore the laughter that was pealing forth from the girl who had put him on the camel in the first place. At any other time, he would have found her throaty sounds of mirth engaging, but just at the moment there was nothing funny to Rafe about Jezebel's amusement.

"Ha, ha, ha, ha. Your face!" she gasped. "You should see—" more choked levity, "the look—" uncontrollable giggling, "on your face!" From where she perched, completely at home atop her own more placid camel, Jezebel pointed rudely with one hand, her other hand clutching her stomach in an attempt to keep her guts in place.

The duke's camel bellowed in agreement, the long face with its stained yellow teeth seeming to grin at him in victory. Rafe forced his fingers to unclench from around the lump of sod they were gripping. He would *not* sink so low as to lob a clump of dirt at this humped monstrosity, he told himself. He really would not . . .

Jezebel's giggles had become strangled gasps of hilarity. "Oh, my lord, I truly am sorry, but that was quite a sight to behold."

Raphael Alexander Sunderland was not used to being laughed at. No one had let loose so much as a snicker in his presence since he was six years old—and certainly no one had ever *pointed* at him while they did it. Well, today was a day for new experiences, he thought with a mental shrug. A spark of matching humor stole through Rafe as he picked himself off the ground and dusted off his abused

posterior. Jezebel had such an infectious laugh, it was hard
to stay mad at her. And he supposed he *had* looked a bit
ridiculous when the contrary beast had shrugged him off
its back. He started to chuckle, picturing the fall from her
standpoint. Running his hands through his short curls to
remove any lingering grit, he laughed even harder when he
found a reed from the nearby river sticking straight up out
of his hair. What would his friends back home say if they
could see him now?

A grin still stretched unwillingly across his handsome
features, Rafe furrowed his brows and growled, "All right,
missy. That will be quite enough impertinence for now,
thank you. Someone really ought to have taught you by
now that it's not polite to mock your elders. I'm going to
count that disrespect a mark against you in our wager. Now,
why don't you come over here and show an old man how
to climb aboard this fractious creature you've so kindly
supplied for our journey? He seems to have developed a
dislike for me."

"*She,* Your Grace. The camel is female." Still chuckling,
Jezebel used a stick and a soft-spoken command to make
her own camel kneel, front feet first and then hindquarters
dipping in an exaggerated rolling motion. She hopped off
lightly and approached. "Here, Your Grace, let me demonstrate. The females can be a might touchy, and you have
to handle them just right."

"And here I thought I'd learned the secret of handling
females quite thoroughly years ago," he quipped. "You
seem intent on proving me wrong, don't you, Jezebel?"
Rafe lost his smile then as she reached his side, his aquamarine eyes searching her darker ones with a strange solemnity.

Jezebel found herself suddenly breathless, and far too
close to the duke for comfort. She fancied she could feel
heat radiating from his large frame; heat that had nothing
to do with the Egyptian sun. It wrapped around her, making
her feel dizzy, unable to think straight. She wanted to back
away from Lord Ravenhurst, but instead found herself leaning in closer, drowning in his gaze. "Some females require
more delicate handling than others, Your Grace," Jezebel

managed. She swallowed against the sudden knot in her throat.

"You don't say?" he murmured, wondering what sort of handling Jezebel herself preferred—delicacy, or a more hands-on approach? "Why don't you call me by my given name, as I asked you yesterday?" Rafe questioned. He wanted to hear her say it in that husky way she had of speaking. Even more so, he wanted to hear her moan it in the throes of passion.

"I don't tend to take suggestions well, as you may already have realized," Jezebel whispered, eyes downcast. Things were getting warmer between them by the moment, their faces closer together as they stood in the shade of the camel that was the ostensible source of their quandary. Just thinking about using the duke's name made her blush. It seemed far too intimate a gesture—though he did not seem to have the same difficulty using hers.

"I've noticed that about you," he replied, a tiny, sensual smile playing about his mouth. "Nevertheless, allow me to make another." He leaned even closer, his lips a breath away from her sensitive ear.

"What would that be?" she asked breathlessly, the tingles created by his rich baritone sliding down her spine.

Rafe was suddenly all business, straightening up and allowing her room to breathe. "I *suggest* that you help me onto this camel before those porters you brought along begin to wonder what the crazy foreigners are doing spending the entire day hanging about in the shade of this one-humped demon."

He gestured over at the riverbank, where three men were surreptitiously casting glances their way while loading up the pack animals Jezebel had arranged to have waiting here for them with the gear they'd brought along in the dahabeah. One man, the pilot, had been assigned to remain behind to guard the boat from thieves during their day trips and overnight jaunts, keeping the craft ready for them to use as often as they wanted for the continued journey south. The other two porters would accompany them with their baggage and set up camp in the evenings.

"Oh," said Jezebel in a small voice. Confusion etched

her delicate features for a moment before she was able to shake off the strange spell the duke had created around them. Clearly, he was not having the same trouble, and it stung her to realize she had been such a fool. She couldn't permit herself to grow soft in the head over this man—not when he held her very fate in his hands! And not when he himself felt no such attraction in return, as his polite, faintly inquiring expression now led her to believe.

The duke looked at her as if he were wondering if she was quite right in the head, and though Jezebel was feeling anything but all right after their little *tête-à-tête*, she was determined that he should see none of it. She could not afford to let this glib, handsome man use her own often volatile emotions against her. He had enough power over her as it was, she judged. Damn him for being so unaffected by her!

But though his ward did not know it, it had been the hardest thing Rafe had ever done to pull away from Jezebel instead of breaching those last few inches of distance between them with a kiss that would have had them both melting in the scorching heat of passion. His *original* suggestion, the one he'd stifled, had had nothing to do with camels, and everything to do with kissing the wits out of the girl. And he wouldn't have stopped there. Though Rafe knew full well the licentiousness of wanting Jezebel in this way, the temptation to taste her ripe charms was nearly overwhelming. He couldn't imagine how he'd forced the words that would push them apart out of his throat, but he had. And he'd seen the flash of disappointment in her eyes. The girl had wanted his touch as much as he wanted to give it. God! If only she were not his ward. . . .

Jezebel forced herself to recover from the moment. "Right you are, my lord," she said with feigned heartiness. "We don't want to be lollygaging around here all day and miss sunset over the pyramids, do we?" She pasted a tight smile across her compressed lips. "Here, let me demonstrate the technique."

The spell was broken, and as she gave instructions on mounting the tall creature, both were able to pretend no awkwardness had occurred. And when the normally agile duke finally managed, by dint of much scrambling and swearing, to keep his seat aboard the beast after it rose to its full height, the tension had eased considerably.

"I suppose I'm ready to go now." He grinned, mopping his brow with one sleeve of his cotton robe.

And go he did.

The duke's alarmed yells drifted back to the riverbank and echoed across the water as Jezebel stood, one hand covering her mouth to hold back gales of laughter. She'd just remembered something Abdul, the lead porter, had told her when they met up with him this morning after their short sail along the Nile. He'd told her to take special care with one of their camels, who had a nasty temper. The beast in question had once been a champion racer—and apparently she thought she was being taken out of retirement!

Though the porter hadn't specified which camel had the problem disposition, Jezebel had assumed that, knowing their circumstances, he would have given her the more difficult one to ride. And under that assumption, she'd asked the bearers to load the tempermental camel with her extra supplies—the ones she would need if escape from Lord Ravenhurst became a necessity. But apparently Abdul had decided it was more appropriate for the man of the party to take the more fractious animal, even though he knew Jezebel had been riding camels for years and the duke had never so much as seen one before today. Thus, Rafe had just unwittingly taken off with her secret stash of gear.

Well, she supposed it would not be too much trouble to switch the packs later, when the duke was otherwise occupied. The only difficulty would be in making sure her new guardian did not break his neck before she had the chance! Because of Abdul's decision to ignore sense in favor of his patriarchal values, that was a very real possibility.

Men *would* be men, she thought with a sigh. And women would deal with their foolishness.

Jezebel quickly remounted her own camel and took off to rescue her guardian.

# Chapter Eight

$\sim$

$\mathcal{M}$atters between the duke and his ward seemed to cool to comfort even as the sun rose hotter over the ancient land through which they rode. Rafe had never seen a desert, and his eyes darted to and fro to capture every image, from the endless waves of golden sand shimmering in the midday sun, to the towering, strangely carved monuments (mastabas, as Jezebel identified them) that marked their path at intervals. He wanted to remember everything, for he knew it would be a long time before he ever again experienced such an exotic adventure as this he shared with his ward.

Already he regretted that he'd missed catching more than a brief glimpse of the sudden transition between fertile farmland and rocky desert that marked the boundary of the Nile's influence, having been too busy at the time reining in his contrary camel to take in the scenery. Still, once he'd subdued the beast and his ward had caught up to him, he'd refused Jezebel's offer to switch mounts, smoothly claiming to be developing a real fondness for the creature. In truth, however, he kept hold of the bawling, rank-smelling camel solely because he would rather deal with its vicissitudes himself than expose Jezebel to them. In a moment of facetiousness, he'd even decided to name his new mount Lucinda, in honor of one of his old mistresses. The animal reminded Rafe of the spoiled beauty from his past in her behavior, though not, thankfully, in her looks.

At least, he thought ruefully, he'd managed to salvage some of his dignity by managing to get the runaway beast under control before his delectable ward had arrived to help. He didn't know if he could have borne her smirking assistance, especially when he'd been riding everything from the short, shaggy ponies of the Scottish highlands to the swiftest of high-strung thoroughbreds with matchless skill since his boyhood. Now, seemingly content to plod sedately in the direction of the sun, Lucinda had settled down for the nonce, though he continued to trust the camel's good humor about as far as he did his ward's.

Rafe's gaze canvassed Jezebel's face. Partly covered by the keffiyeh she wore to protect her fair skin from wind and sun, it was nevertheless a stirring sight, the faraway look in her jewellike eyes and the timeless beauty of her features strikingly framed against the barren desert. A strand of silken black hair had escaped the headdress, and she brushed it back with absent grace. He wondered again how he'd had the strength to push her away with his words this morning, when all he'd wanted was to lay the minx down in front of God and everyone and have his way with her. She'd done nothing to discourage him—had seemed more than willing to participate at the time. Yet he had sworn to protect her from any man displaying the very same animal behavior he'd been contemplating himself.

Rafe couldn't help dwelling on the meaning behind the mysterious clause she'd added to their wager yesterday. Was she trying to seduce him in the hopes that, having caused him to behave disreputably, she could claim to have won their bet? No, he hadn't seen deception in her eyes— only the honest awakening of desire. He wondered if he was the first man ever to stir such passions in her heart, or if she had had others in her past—a thought that gave him a strange twinge to entertain. His intuition, which rarely failed him, said that both men he'd seen her with so far might have shared her confidence, but they'd shared no more than that. She had not been gifting them with her favors.

If nothing else, he should give her uncle credit for sheltering her from such carnal knowledge, even if in most other respects Rafe guessed the earl had allowed Miss Montclair a shocking degree of liberty. His new ward didn't strike him as immodest, in all truth. No, it was more that she simply seemed to have no interest at all in conforming to society's conventions. Jezebel didn't flaunt them, she just ignored them; as though the rules and regulations created expressly for her protection had, in her mind, no relevance to her whatsoever. She didn't have to *try* to shock him with her behavior. Everything she instinctively did, everything she naturally was, came as a complete change from the sort of ladies Rafe had known all of his life. No. Regardless of the images her name might conjure, Jezebel wasn't a calculating wanton. She was, purely and simply, an original.

Besides, he admitted, feeling ashamed of himself, he'd been aroused enough on his own this morning. Jezebel hadn't had to make any special effort to get him excited—but God help him if she ever did!

And then even that tantalizing line of thought was forgotten for the moment, for rising up at him over the sands was a sight unlike anything he'd ever seen before. Too regularly shaped to be mountains, the three large peaks coming into view still seemed far too tall to be structures built by human hands. And yet they could be nothing else. Even the camel paused in awe.

Rafe had arrived at the great pyramids of Giza.

"It's incredible," he said, voice hushed. Jezebel, who'd ridden up beside him and halted with her knee almost touching his, agreed. A smile of understanding lit her features.

"Isn't it? It's hard to believe these are the work of human labor—slave labor, actually, if the biblical accounts are to be believed."

Rafe narrowed his eyes against the afternoon sun slanting over the tops of the three enormous pyramids. He saw that the top of the greatest one, the one in the middle of the cluster, appeared to have a cap of smoother stone adorning its top, as a mountain peak collects snow. The others were farther away and harder to study.

Seeming to read his mind, Jezebel commented, "The great one in the middle has a covering of polished limestone on top of the granite it's built from, as we think the others must once have had, but the rest of the covering has all either crumbled or been salvaged for other uses." She touched his hand briefly with her own to gain his attention. "Come, let us go in closer, Your Grace, and have a better look."

As if in a dream, Rafe followed.

\*   \*   \*

*W*hile the porters set up a shelter from the sun on the edge of the plateau, Rafe and Jezebel circled the enormous tombs they'd come to view. In the distance, they could see only a few other visitors touring the vast monument today, and it almost seemed to Jezebel that they had the entire site to themselves.

Most visitors she'd seen here were content to gaze at the grandiose stone pyramids silently, overawed and marveling at the great endeavor it must have taken to create them, and Jezebel still felt the same respect herself, though she'd come here many times in the past few years with her uncle. The sight of the pyramids, along with the nearby Sphinx, which had not yet come into their view today, always inspired Jezebel as nothing else could. She shared what she knew of their history with her companion.

"We think the pyramids were built many hundreds, perhaps even thousands of years ago, by a great king named Cheops, or Khufu, as his name is sometimes pronounced. This pyramid"—and she indicated the largest—"is his tomb, and the ones around it were made for his descendants. Along with several smaller ones in the vicinity called the queens' pyramids, which were meant for royal wives and concubines, the great mausoleums in this area were the work of many generations of master builders and architects. Though the ancient Egyptians had only stone tools and used no mortar to secure the blocks, the structures have still outlasted almost every Western monument ever created."

"It's unbelievable," Rafe commented, feeling his words were grossly inadequate. "Look at how smoothly the blocks fit together, and how huge each individual piece is. It's a wonder they ever managed to lift even one."

"No one knows exactly how they did it. And there are many other mysteries associated with King Cheops's burial site—such as, was he truly ever buried in the pyramid at all?"

"What, all that work and he's not even resting here?" Rafe laughed.

"It's possible, Your Grace. Though several rooms have been excavated, we have not yet found a burial chamber that truly seems to befit a building of this grandeur. There are so many tunnels riddling the pyramid—air shafts, secret passages—that no one knows how extensive they may be, and there is much debate still going on over whether the entrance we've found so far is even the main one."

"Really?" The duke was fascinated. He couldn't get enough of gazing at this monument. Just the sheer audacity of that long-ago ruler, that overwhelming determination to leave behind a lasting legacy, boggled his mind. Was there no limit to the ambitions of the human imagination? Rafe thought he could understand the sentiment, though personally, he hoped he didn't share it to quite this degree.

His father would have appreciated a burial site like this, he reflected—would have liked knowing that when he left the world, his name would never be forgotten. Rafe doubted anything much less than this remarkable piece of work would ever have satisfied the elder Ravenhurst's need. Certainly, nothing Rafe had ever done while his father was alive had been enough. "There must be a great deal of excavation work being carried out among these buildings if men still hope to find more royal chambers."

"Yes," she confirmed. "Although what appears to be a burial chamber was found deep inside the heart of the structure of the main pyramid, no body was ever found in it, no sarcophagus, and none of the king's treasures. The other two large ones have been even less fully explored. I believe all of the pyramids were looted long ago by grave robbers, perhaps even in the time of the pharaohs themselves. Others believe that chamber is only a decoy, and the real final resting place of the great king still remains to be found."

"Others like your friend Belzoni?"

She laughed. "Yes, you have the right of it there. I think Giovanni would like nothing more than to drape himself with all the weight of a pharaoh's gold and parade about for the world to see."

"There are many who feel the same. You do not?"

"What would I do with all that gold?" Jezebel asked sincerely. "I believe knowledge is the greatest treasure man can possess, not material wealth. As did my uncle." Her voice wavered for a moment as she thought about Clifton's lifelong quest for knowledge, his sometimes radical, but always brilliant, hypotheses. "He believed that all history holds a lesson for the wise to study, and that only by understanding the past can the future be bettered. He'd hoped that uncovering the secrets of the ancient Egyptians might prove a means of enhancing our own culture with their knowledge one day. It is my wish that my uncle's hopes will be borne out, in some small fashion." This was as close to telling Rafe the truth as she could come. Afraid she sounded foolish, Jezebel looked away. "And yet the very men who claim to be the makers of history continue to wantonly destroy the monuments that could benefit future generations in untold ways."

"What do you mean?" Rafe asked. As he spoke, they rounded the far corner of the middle pyramid.

"Look there, Your Grace." She pointed. "That is the Great Sphinx." She touched her stick to her camel's withers, and the beast loped ahead toward the long rectangular stone figure. Rafe followed, and was soon confronted by the massive, lion-bodied, human-headed statue that had been the source of so much fable and fiction for centuries. They stopped in the shadow of its huge outstretched paws and gazed up solemnly.

"Do you see how the face is disfigured?" Jezebel asked.

"Yes. Is it not the work of natural erosion? I've seen many Greek and Roman statues that have suffered a similar loss of features."

"No, the damage is recent. Napoleon's fusiliers, the fools, used it for target practice during the 1798 invasion."

The duke shook his head in disbelief. "All those hundreds of years it stood unchallenged, and then a bunch of French buffoons knock the nose right off it for a laugh? Those cretins. It's to the good that we've taken Egypt back from those scoundrels before they could destroy it all."

"Ah, but we're no better, really," she sighed. "Most of the treasures looted by the French during their occupation have been stolen right out of their hands by the British and taken home as spoils of war. Even now I understand Par-

liament has voted to expand the British Museum just to
house all of the antiquities we've taken from the Egyptians."

"True. I will not argue the rape of the Nile goes on even
to this day, for I've seen a number of the pieces you speak
of in that very museum. But do you not worry that your
own efforts will eventually only aid these tomb robbers?"
he asked curiously. "The more you unearth, the likelier it
is that others more greedy than yourself will want to possess your findings."

"It is troubling," she admitted. "I sometimes think it
would be best if all of us foreigners simply left the Egyptians to their own devices, to reclaim their heritage or destroy it in their own right." Jezebel couldn't continue, for
at that moment it came to her again strongly how little she
understood her own purpose here, how unsure she was of
her avocation since her uncle's passing. Her only real goal
now was to vindicate Lord Clifton's beliefs before his
peers. After that, she had no solid plans of her own. Sudden
tears stung Jezebel's eyes, surprising her, and she was
forced to look up into the dazzling sunlight for a moment
to hide their cause. Then she shook off the feeling. She had
no choice, now, did she? She had made a promise, and she
would keep it. She could worry about the future later, Jezebel told herself.

"Would you like to climb up inside the Great Pyramid?"
she asked. Changing the subject seemed like a good idea.
"I warn you, it's even hotter and more stifling inside the
passage than it is out here, but I believe it is worth the trip
if one is only going to visit Giza once."

"Certainly, Miss Montclair. I am eager to see everything
your expertise can disclose," Rafe agreed, silently wondering. He'd seen her sudden hesitation, and he wanted to ask
her about it. But now did not seem like the best time to
press his ward.

Rafe was learning more about Jezebel with every minute
they spent together, and he did not want to put her back on
her guard just yet with any uncomfortable questions. They
had plenty of time to get to know one another, he reminded
himself—more time than he could handle, if he was going

to be enjoying himself this much. Damn it! He hadn't expected to *like* Jezebel the way he was fast discovering he did. Already he couldn't deny that she was more spirited, more charming, more intelligent than practically any other female he'd ever met. Her presence at his side was making this unplanned but welcome adventure in Egypt even more savory—quite shocking when he considered that a few days ago, his only desire had been to get rid of her with all due dispatch. Why, when he'd first learned of his ward's existence, he'd expected to have no more to do with her than would be required to get the chit married off. But now . . .

*Now nothing,* he growled sharply to himself. Nothing had changed. Just because the woman was a thousand times more personable—not to mention more attractive—than he'd anticipated, just because every hour he spent with her made him look forward to a dozen more, didn't mean anything had changed. He was still saddled with an unwanted responsibility, and, once he got her back to England, he'd make short work of discharging his duty. He'd find her a husband as soon as could be arranged, and then he would think no more about the inconvenient Miss Montclair.

Rafe ignored the inner voice that shouted, *Liar!* and followed Jezebel back across the sandy wastes to the pyramids.

$\mathcal{S}$he hadn't exaggerated. The tunnel, reached only after first climbing several levels of exterior five- and six-foot blocks of ocher-colored granite, was a narrow flight of roughly hewn steps leading endlessly upward into the body of the pyramid, tight and excruciatingly hot. It sloped up steeply into the humid darkness, and the smoke from the torch Jezebel had procured them did little to alleviate the stifling conditions. Nevertheless, they pushed on. The duke went first, in truth mostly because in his present state he didn't think he could bear a protracted view of his ward's derriere going up the ramp before him. All Rafe said, however, was that as the taller of them, he deemed it best that he should hold the torch and light their path.

Jezebel didn't argue, since if one of them got stuck in the low-ceilinged tunnel, it would be her rangy guardian, and she knew it was best if they did not bottle up their only escape route. Besides, she thought mischievously, letting him go first gave her the perfect opportunity to observe the duke's firm, rounded buttocks without his notice.

If possible, Jezebel felt the temperature grew a few degrees warmer in the passage.

Getting to know the duke a little better today had come as a surprisingly enjoyable experience. Instead of the citified dandy she'd half expected, or the usual insular, bigoted British aristocrat disinterested in anything beyond his own borders, Rafe Sunderland had an unexpected curiosity for everything around him. It was in his keen, intelligent eyes, his rapid-fire, well-informed questions, his general air of being extremely pleased to learn something new, even if he had to learn it from a woman.

Jezebel found the quality of the duke's intellectual curiosity to be a rare one, even among many of the men of her acquaintance who were professional scholars. So many came here with an agenda, stubbornly advancing their own theories regardless of the facts that presented themselves at every turn. So many refused to look at the truth. Rafe, however, had no preconceived ideas about Egypt, she thought. He just absorbed all there was to see, processing it in his quicksilver mind without judgment—though not without understanding. He was possessed of an impressive amount of information about this land already, she'd discovered.

She'd asked how he came to be so knowledgeable about Egypt (a subject not many English found worthy of intensive study) and had been impressed by his answer. The duke had spent a great portion of his voyage aboard the clipper ship reading everything he could lay his hands on regarding the country he was to visit. As he laughingly admitted, Rafe had spent more time ensuring his stock of reading material would not run out aboard ship than his linens.

Like the emperor Napoleon, who was said to have read and made notations in the margins of almost every book contained in the French national archives on *"L'Egypte"* before beginning his campaign at the end of the last century, Lord Ravenhurst had studied most of the accepted modern works on the country. His intentions here, however, seemed a good deal more peaceful than those of his Corsican predecessor. Rafe's only conceivable adversary at the moment was Jezebel herself, and he no longer appeared in the least disposed to pugnacity in his dealings with her, she'd noticed.

Over the course of the day, they'd engaged in a lively discussion of Egypt's turbulent recent past, as well as the educated guesses that were being advanced by current scholars and linguists about her more distant history. Indeed, they'd shared such an enjoyable conversation that Jezebel had almost forgotten the disturbing incident that had so nearly occurred this morning. Now, however, alone with the man in the small passage, having told the porters to remain outside so as not to deplete the already limited store of oxygen in the tunnel, she felt the strange discomfort that wasn't quite discomfort rise again. Much as she wished to attribute her faintness to the sweltering conditions in the passageway, Jezebel knew that wasn't the problem.

*Dear lord,* she thought as she watched him climb the ramp, *he really does have the most delicious—*

Not looking where she was going, Jezebel stumbled over a loose stone on the uneven footpath. Instantly Rafe was there with a hand to steady her and a murmured, "Are you quite right?" that left her even less steady than before.

"I'm fine," she muttered, then made a lie of that statement as she tripped again. Unfortunately, she was still holding his large hand in her own and she ended up yanking the duke toward her. She felt her ankle twist as she windmilled frantically, and her legs started to go out from under her. Jezebel hissed in pained humiliation, sure she was about to land in a heap at her guardian's feet.

But the duke grasped her bodily this time, and in his embrace Jezebel felt every last trace of balance disappear. Still managing to keep the torch aloft in one hand somehow, Rafe swept her up into his arms and swiftly carried her forth the last few steps up the passage and into the large rectangular room at its summit. She hadn't even noticed they were reaching the tunnel's end, Jezebel thought dimly before he spun her world around once again, setting her down on a stone block and dropping to his knees before her.

Rafe wedged the torch upright in a crack in the wall to illuminate the space directly around them, but neither of them used the flaring light to look around the nearly barren chamber. They were far too absorbed in one another.

"Have you hurt yourself badly?" The duke asked the question rhetorically, for he was already examining her lower limbs in an effort to answer the question for himself. His hands pushed gently at the loose, flowing fabric of her baggy trousers, searching for swelling or breakage at her ankles.

"I'm . . ." Jezebel swallowed, then gasped sharply as his warm fingers circled the tender flesh of her right ankle. "Fine." Her voice cracked embarrassingly.

"You injured this ankle when you tripped?" he asked in his low voice, disregarding her protestation of wellness.

"The other one, actually," she confessed, then blushed furiously. Oh, why had she said that? Now he would know how much even his casual touch could affect her.

Rafe caught Jezebel's embarrassed glance as she tried to look away. His own gaze, at first sparkling with humor at her admission, abruptly sobered. The orange torchlight lovingly caressed the austere planes of his Romanesque features, deepening the blue of his eyes.

*He is beautiful,* she thought, a lump in her throat making it hard to swallow. *So very, very beautiful.* Like a priceless treasure unearthed from the depths of time, he called to her, and Jezebel knew she had to touch him. She didn't even know why, could not have explained her compulsion under pain of torture. All she knew was that *not* touching him was a torment she couldn't bear a moment longer. She reached down, as if in a trance, and cupped the strong curve of his jaw in the palm of one hand.

"God help me," Rafe groaned. His tenuous control snapped, and his own hands left her ankles to take Jezebel's face between strong, callused palms. A heartbeat later, his lips captured hers in a kiss he couldn't have stopped himself from delivering were she a thousand times his ward.

## Chapter Nine

*R*afe swallowed Jezebel in tenderness, the lush heat of his mouth possessing hers with insistent gentleness and raging want. His hunger was like a living thing, consuming all reason as his sensitive lips tasted and touched and took over her body. Jezebel moaned softly, whether in shock or with pleasure he didn't know at first, but then her arms wrapped themselves tighter about the column of his neck and she inched closer to the edge of the granite block upon which she sat. Another little bit farther and she would be in his lap. That was fine, he thought hazily. Just fine. Nothing had ever felt so right, so immediate and necessary.

Rafe hadn't meant for this to happen, but once their kiss began—and he still wasn't sure who'd truly begun it, she or he—he was powerless to deny the force of his desire. He'd never craved a woman the way he craved Jezebel. Even in the short time he'd known her, she'd made him angrier, caused him to laugh harder, and fascinated him in ways that no other female in his past had ever done. The force of her personality drew him no less than her enthusiastic, untutored kisses—and those kisses, just now, were driving him to the brink of madness.

But it was the very innocent fire of her response that finally recalled Rafe to his senses. It was when his hand boldly, instinctively went to cup her soft breast, and when she cried out in unexpected pleasure and leaned helplessly into his touch, that the iniquity of his actions came home to the duke like a cold-water plunge.

Jezebel did not have the wherewithal or the sophistication to stop this. He knew it, damn it, could sense it with each blissful caress of her tongue against his own, each incredible, erotic melding of their mouths. Jezebel had never done this before—never mind that her kisses inflamed him more than the practiced caresses of the most skillful courtesan in England ever could—and he was the worst kind of cad for taking advantage of her naïveté.

He pulled back, panting, but the sight of her dewy, kiss-swollen lips conquered his will once more and he had to return briefly for more of her nectar. With nipping kisses, he took Jezebel's mouth again and again, laving and suckling her lower lip, tracing the bowed curve of her upper lip, plunging inside her honeyed depths for taste upon taste. All the while Rafe told himself he must pull back, must stop before he committed an unforgivable offense against this girl's fragile honor—and his own.

But Jezebel wasn't making it easy. Her throaty, sighing moans, her trembling, cool fingers lying against his neck, and the natural sensuality of her kiss all combined explosively, making her a temptation every bit as powerful as her namesake. She learned from his own caresses how to give him pleasure, ably following where he led, trading strokes of her tongue and stinging, playful nips from her sharp white teeth. She seemed lost in this world of his making, unable to surface.

And Jezebel was, indeed, quite lost to all but the kiss they shared. Never before had she been so completely taken over by her emotions, never before had sensation so thoroughly swamped her, drowning reason and caution and everything else beneath a tide of liquid ecstasy that felt like honeyed hot lava running through her veins. The taste of her guardian's lips as they shaped her own so masterfully, the sweeping caress of his strong, elegant hands over her untouched flesh, had sent Jezebel over the edge of sanity the instant she first felt them upon her. Each moment their embrace continued sent her further from any thought of stopping it. She was as helpless to protest as a newborn babe.

She *was* newborn, thought Jezebel with the tiny corner of her mind that remained lucid. Until just now she had not known that losing control could be so wonderful, that surrender to a force more powerful than herself could feel so right. Whether that force was Raphael Sunderland or passion itself, she didn't know and didn't care. The only thing that mattered was touching him in this moment.

His hair curled crisply beneath her questing fingers as she wrapped her hand about the back of his head, mapping the regular shape of his skull, absorbing the slight sweat-dampness of his scalp. It was odd, yet terribly exciting, to feel a man's skin against her own; the beard-stubble roughness of a square jaw, the warm sweet breath against her neck, the tensile velvet of masculine lips commanding her body to obey their teachings. But it wasn't just any man she wanted. No, Jezebel wanted only *this* man; this brilliant, smiling, demanding near-stranger with his aqua-colored eyes and his hearty, booming laugh; this man whom she already felt she knew in some fundamental, elemental, and completely inexplicable way; this man whom she dared not trust with her secrets or her future.

Though she knew she should fear him, loathe him for his autocratic ways, Jezebel responded to the tenderness, the innate chivalry and kindness, and to the vital, incredible life energy that she sensed in Rafe instead. With each kiss he taught her a world of knowledge about passion, about giving, and the miraculous magic that could be created between the right man and woman. Had she not already been sitting, Jezebel thought her legs would surely have given way beneath the power of it. Though earlier she had been distrustful and wary around the duke, now she could deny him nothing. Jezebel moaned deep in her throat and kissed him yet more deeply.

Rafe had to stop them before they both drowned. "Jezebel," he whispered raggedly in a pause between their kisses. His hands pressed gently at her shoulders, pushing her back more solidly upon her stone seat. She whimpered in frustration and craned forward to take his lips again, a touch he cravenly allowed for a long moment before cursing and leaning back on his heels. Her hands remained draped loosely about his neck, playing softly with the curls at his nape as she smiled dreamily. Jezebel's eyes were closed, dark lashes fanned against her porcelain cheeks, as if she wished only for him to return to her.

God, how he wanted to grant that wish. Rafe's breath

came in shallow, rapid gasps, and his blood pounded. Sanity returned only slowly as he closed his own eyes, determined to fight the raging desire in his veins. He had never kissed a woman who had so much unfettered passion within her, who gave of herself and gave *up* herself so completely. His mind reeled as the lower regions of his anatomy clambered for attention and he forced himself to ignore their demands. He knelt in the dark, heated chamber inside the Great Pyramid for a long while, fists clenched, trying to retake control. It was only his ashamed awareness of the impropriety of his actions that finally allowed Rafe to regain command of his rebellious flesh.

He had just almost ravaged his ward, only days after meeting the girl for the very first time! Dear Lord, he was everything the gossips claimed, a rake of the worst sort. Rafe felt his gut clench in remorse. What had become of the disciplined, dependable man he had always thought himself to be? He'd made a lie of that man, disgraced himself thoroughly. He knew what his father would have said had he been able to see his son today. He deserved to be horsewhipped! Jezebel might win their wager after all, only days into the contest. Rafe was even tempted to let her have the victory, to let her go her own way, for he feared continued contact might do them both lasting damage. But he knew he could not.

As lucky as Jezebel had been in the months since Clifton's death, as knowledgeable as she clearly was about archaeology in general and about Egypt specifically, Rafe was well aware she could not be allowed to traipse off on her own, potential prey to any man (like himself, he admitted with a sting of guilt) who wanted to take her for his own. She needed watching over, and she needed guidance—today only proved how much.

Jezebel needed a chaperone here as much as she would in England. She should not be traveling about freely, visiting other so-called Egyptologists and living like a man in this wild, unsafe country. She should not be living alone in a makeshift old bungalow and wending her way through the souks and coffeehouses of Ottoman-controlled Egypt. It was only a matter of time before this innocent, intrepid young lady discovered the darker side of men. And he had better not be the one to show it to her, Rafe castigated himself, for there was no one else now to protect her should he give up the responsibility.

Things had been different while her uncle was alive. No matter how much credit Jezebel could take for seeing to their day-to-day affairs, no matter how hard she'd worked by his side, it was clear to Rafe that it had been Lord Clifton's presence backing her up that had made it permissible for the young explorer's niece to pursue her unconventional lifestyle. During the earl's life, a kind of invisible shadow had hovered over Jezebel wherever she went, a silent warning to those who might take advantage that she was not alone. To the world at large, and to Cairo society in particular, the shadow cast by the wealthy earl had given her license to do as she pleased, as long as it was clear that he approved of and was monitoring her behavior. It might only be an illusion—Ravenhurst doubted the absentminded old earl had done much in the way of watching over his niece—but it had served the purpose.

Now, however, with Clifton gone, there was no longer any barrier, no longer any perception that the girl was under protection—unless it was Ravenhurst's own. Rafe knew this was a responsibility he could not shirk, no matter how much he wanted to tell the world to go to hell and take what Jezebel offered so sweetly. When it came right down to it, the truth was that Jezebel didn't deserve that kind of treatment, even if right now she thought she wanted it. It was just this sort of thing Rafe was supposed to ward her away from, and he was letting her down.

He had to ensure this never happened again, for he was not at all sure that if ever they found themselves in each other's arms in the future, he could bear to deny them both a second time. And so when the duke spoke, his tone was remote, polite but seemingly unaffected by the passion they'd shared only moments before. For her own benefit, she must never know how much the effort cost him.

"Jezebel—Miss Montclair—stop." He gently, reluctantly untangled her fingers from his hair. "This must cease right now." As he rose to his feet and reached for the torch,

he saw her eyes begin to clear, the dawning horror in them
that made him cringe mentally at what he'd done to her.

"Let me carry you out of this place so I may see to your
ankle, Miss Montclair," Rafe said with brisk kindness. "We
really should not leave it to swell in this heat." He deliberately looked away so as not to see the hurt and accusation
that was building in her eyes. "Come, I'll take your
weight." Rafe, taking a deep breath and, bracing himself to
ignore the contact, reached to gather her into his arms.

"Don't!" she screeched, pulling away sharply. "Don't
touch me!" Confusion and horror tumbled through Jezebel's passion-soaked brain. What had she done? How had
this happened? And why was the duke looking at her now
with that pained, embarrassed expression? He looked, she
thought sickly, as if he were facing some deluded country
wench who, after a night's tumble in the local coaching
inn, expected His Exalted Grace to propose to her on the
spot.

The situation was moving far too rapidly for her to adjust. One moment they'd been sharing the most incredible
sensations Jezebel had ever experienced in her life, both of
them (or so she'd thought) overcome with intense carnal
pleasure such as she'd never imagined possible; the next,
they were once again two total strangers sharing nothing
but the overheated air of the pharaoh's burial chamber. It
seemed the duke had not been partaking of the experience
with her, as she'd thought. No, she realized with a sick
sensation in her gut. From the way he was acting now, he
must have found her kisses quite repellent. Just as he had
earlier in the day when they'd found themselves so nearly
touching, he'd once again wrapped her in his sensual spell,
then refused her. Jezebel couldn't bear the humiliation.

· The only thing she could think to do was flee to safer
ground—ground not already occupied by the overwhelming
masculinity of Rafe Sunderland. And, roiling in hurt and
confusion, the best way she could think to clear the way
for her escape was by lashing out at the one who had
caused her distress. Yet she did not want him to sense that
distress. No, she wanted him to think what had just happened between them meant no more to her than it obviously

had to him. She took a deep breath, striving for a calm to match that of her so-called guardian's.

"I assure you my ankle is perfectly fine, Your Grace," the explorer's niece said frostily. As she gathered herself to rise from the granite block, she shot him a venomous glare and an even more poisonous parting dig. "Indeed, the only thing bothering me at this moment is *you*." She rose to her feet unsteadily and forced herself to take a step forward on her left ankle. It really *was* beginning to hurt now, but she'd be damned if she'd admit it to Lord Ravenhurst!

Dear Lord in heaven, she had never been so mortified. It wasn't the so-called impropriety of what they'd just done—though she might be a novice in passion, Jezebel wasn't a prude and she didn't hold to the ridiculous values of British society that would have her feel shame for such "lewdness." No, the shame she felt right now came from Ravenhurst's obvious rejection of their kiss. How could she have misread his signals so dreadfully—not once now, but twice? And what must he think of her?

True, the duke had responded at first to her advance—and that response still sang a dizzying melody in her blood—but her boldness must have repulsed him at some point. Most likely, the women he was used to would never dream of behaving with such brash wantonness. Why else would a man with a reputation for womanizing like Ravenhurst's push her away like that? The women in his world probably communicated their desires with coy flutters of their eyelashes or sidelong glances over the top of a waving fan. She, on the other hand, had practically leapt into his lap!

Jezebel sent up a silent prayer of thanks for the dimness and heat of the chamber. At least in these conditions, her guardian would never guess the real reason behind the flush in her cheeks. She swore she wouldn't let him see how deeply he had shamed her, and she cursed herself for ever having had the foolish idea of bringing the man up here in the first place. Well, she vowed, if she could only get out of this damnable little room now, she'd take care never to be alone with him again!

Abruptly, in one of the mercurial shifts of mood that

sometimes overcame her, Jezebel decided that she'd had enough of this ridiculous, doomed-from-the-start arrangement, enough of the duke, and enough of playing tour guide while he held her fate like an axe over her head. She wasn't staying here to be humiliated and treated like a child by this man. No matter what she had to do, she was leaving her guardian today, and damn the consequences. She had to get out of here!

But Rafe wasn't moving out of her way. Jezebel took another determined step forward, one that was clearly intended to force him to move aside and let her pass. Despite her militant stance, however, the duke stood his ground. If she took one more pace she would bash straight into his broad, muscle-banded chest. As appealing as that prospect had seemed only moments before, now the only thing Jezebel could think of was getting as far from him as possible. "Get out of my way, you towering bully," she gritted.

"Jezebel—" He tried again for kindness.

"Either get out of the way of your own accord, or I will *make* you get out of the way whether you like it or not." And suddenly, out of nowhere, the dull metallic gleam of a pistol's barrel stretched its length between them.

Rafe went very, very still.

*Good,* she thought. *That's got his attention. He'll never try to overwhelm me bodily like that again.* Jezebel was filled with a blazing-hot anger, trembling a bit from the strength of her emotions and the close confines of the space they shared. If she didn't get away from him and from the site of her own humiliation soon, she didn't know what she'd do! She clutched the comforting weight of the gun butt in her sweating fist.

"Well, well. You are full of surprises, aren't you, Jezebel? Where did that nasty little weapon come from?" he asked.

"Don't think for a second that I'll hesitate to use it," she warned. "I believe I have told you more than once that I am capable of protecting myself from anyone or anything that threatens me, Your Grace. If you make that number include you, I shall not lose sleep over doing what I must." Jezebel saw the duke make a move as if to come closer, and steadied the heavy Royal Navy–issue pistol so that it was aimed directly at his heart. "You'd best believe I'm serious, if you don't wish to be the first to be buried in this tomb since Cheops!"

"Oh, never fear. I've no doubt you are one hundred percent serious, Jezebel." The duke's tone was mild, but somehow not reassuring. Ravenhurst didn't seem very impressed by the weapon pointed at his heart. What if he wouldn't give way? Could she really shoot him?

Jezebel stepped back unconsciously while her few options raced through her mind. Thankfully, Rafe was keeping his distance for now, though Jezebel herself continued to back farther and farther away into the dark recesses of the burial chamber. The light of the torch only covered so much ground, and the far walls were completely shrouded in shadow. Jezebel began a slow merge with that darkness, never taking her eyes off her guardian, illuminated by the guttering torch at his side.

Heavy as it was, she did not allow her grasp on the pistol to tremble. Her heart was beating frantically in her chest and her breath came in ragged gasps. Despite the heat, her skin grew cold and gooseflesh rose on her arms and back as though a breeze fanned her perspiring flesh. And then Jezebel realized that her senses were not playing tricks with her. There really *was* a draft coming from directly behind her. Of course! Sudden memory swamped her.

Several years ago—the first time she'd been in this chamber, in fact—she'd been killing time with the son of one of her uncle's tomb diggers while Lord Clifton explored the other tunnels nearby, when she and the boy had discovered an air shaft near the back of the room. A square-cut hole camouflaged behind a pile of rubble that reached about halfway up the wall, it led sharply downward into the black unknown depths of the pyramid. The boy had dared Jezebel, then only in her teens, to go down that shaft and see where it led. She hadn't wanted to go—oh, Lord, how she hadn't wanted to go!—but even less had she wished to face her companion's taunting grin when he accused her of being a mere cowardly *girl*.

Jezebel had gone feet first down that shaft, dragging and

scraping her agile young body down the interminable twists and turns for what had seemed like forever, her only assurance that there was indeed a way out at the end the occasional whiff of fresher air that blew up the tunnel. Thank God she hadn't been deceived, for the climb back up to the burial chamber would have been next to impossible.

Would she still fit in the shaft now? she wondered desperately. And would the darkness at the edges of the chamber be enough to hide her while she climbed inside? Though the torch was dying down in the oxygen-poor atmosphere and the light it shed flared only unevenly to illuminate her trembling form in her guardian's sight, Jezebel didn't yet dare glance back at the partially hidden crevice that was her objective. If she could just keep Ravenhurst far enough away so that he couldn't see her for a few moments, she thought, she might well have the chance she needed. But he didn't look ready to grant her that grace period.

"I *was* going to apologize for my poor behavior in taking advantage of you a few moments ago, Miss Montclair," he said mildly. Rafe stood with his arms folded, the soul of patience and reason. Yet she knew better than to take that casual posture for granted. The steely, uncompromising note that came into his voice as he continued told her that he was furious. "But now I believe we have more important matters to discuss first—such as how you may extricate yourself from this mess you've created without further annoying me."

"Annoying you! Why, you arrogant bastard," she seethed, half in real outrage and half to keep him talking instead of walking toward her. Little more than ten feet separated them, and though the torch was dying, the pitch hissing and fizzling now, she could still make out the anger on his set features. Jezebel eased back another couple of paces. She'd bet she'd make him far angrier before she was through! she thought with a surge of manic glee. "You'll find annoyance is the least of your worries if you don't back away right now." She cocked the pistol, the click of the hammer echoing loudly in the otherwise still chamber.

Rafe ran a hand through his hair in a gesture that was beginning to be habitual with him, if only since Jezebel's stormy entrance into his life.

"Miss Montclair," he tried, still not taking his eyes from the weapon maintaining the space between them, though it was a mere glint of light in the shadows now and he could barely make out his ward's slender outline behind it. "I suggest we begin again, before we wind up doing anything else we'll both regret."

Jezebel snorted. She still couldn't believe she'd really pulled the pistol she carried in the back of her sash (usually worn as protection against bandits and snakes) to threaten her guardian. But she was committed, and she wouldn't back down. She was close to the hole now, could feel the cooler air teasing the exposed nape of her neck and the sweaty hair piled atop her head. "As I believe I've mentioned more than once already, I do not take suggestions well, Your Grace. I prefer to give them. So, instead, here is what *I* propose: *You* leave me alone, whilst I take my leave of your less-than-agreeable company—permanently. We're through with this 'guardian' charade," she pronounced.

"We are not through unless I say we are through," the duke shot back uncompromisingly, peering through the dark toward the place where Jezebel had disappeared. "And I see no reason to think we are."

"No reason!" She laughed disbelievingly, a disembodied voice in the pitch-blackness. Jezebel felt behind her and her fingertips brushed the uneven lip of the roughly square air shaft. A number of loose blocks lay below it—thank God no one had removed the rubble in the interim—and Jezebel began the agonizing process of wedging her body up backward into the tight space. It was nearly impossible not to make noise as she climbed blindly, one hand still wrapped in a death grip around her gun. She knew she must continue to distract the duke, lest he hear some slight sound and realize she wasn't just cowering away from him. A desperate prayer ran nonstop through her mind as she eased herself one leg at a time into the small passage.

"No *reason!*" she growled again. "If you want a reason,

how about the fact that you've just bloody well lost the wager?"

"How do you figure that?" he asked patiently. Rafe seemed ready to wait her out all day if necessary, the condescending rotter. Of course, he thought he had her cornered. The duke had every reason to believe he held the upper hand, after all. But Jezebel would soon show him he didn't!

"Your *care*—and I use the term loosely—was proven to be highly detrimental to my well-being not five minutes ago. Or don't you consider kissing your ward half out of her wits to be a breach of duty?"

"No, you have the right of it there," he said quietly.

She almost didn't hear him, with her heart pounding so heavily in her ears. Only her shoulders were left to go, and then she would be free. Thank God she was still slim enough to attempt this crazy stunt! But the duke was still talking, and she made an effort to listen, more to guess his location from the sound of his voice than because she wanted to hear what he would say.

"I apologize more profoundly for my actions than words can express, Miss Montclair. I have wronged your honor, but I assure you, it will not happen again."

Jezebel wasn't buying any of it. The cad would say anything to get the gun from her hands. She must not listen to these honeyed words—not when she was so close to freedom! "Damned right it won't. Not with you on one side of the ocean and me on the other!"

With that, she pulled her head into the opening and felt the tight passage widen to more comfortable dimensions around her lower body as she slid deeper inside. She inched backward soundlessly until she was dangling by her fingertips from the sloping shaft. And then she let go.

# Chapter Ten

*~*

*R*afe sighed. He really did not want to have to go over there and wrest the gun out of his ward's impulsive grip, but the girl seemed to be leaving him little choice. This was ridiculous! He couldn't believe he was standing here in the dark interior of one of the world's greatest monuments, arguing with a woman whose honor he'd just very nearly besmirched, while she held him off handily with a pistol almost as big as her own forearm. He would try one more time to be conciliatory before he was forced to put his foot down.

"Please listen to me, Miss Montclair, and let us try to conclude this absurd standoff peaceably." Rafe paused, then after a moment's consideration said, "Your behavior and mine have both been unfortunate, but I am willing—for now—to chalk it up to our difficulties adjusting to this unusual situation. I have never played guardian to a young lady, and you have never had your activities curtailed by anyone but your uncle, who appears to have been rather lax about certain issues. It is not easy for either of us to accommodate the other, but we must strive to do so—for your benefit much more so than mine."

There. That sounded reasonable, didn't it? Once again Rafe ran his hand through his hair as he finished his thought. "So let's say no more about the matter, and go on in future as though today had never happened. Now, no more foolish protests. Allow me to unburden you of that extremely weighty pistol you're carrying, and then we'll see to your sore ankle, shall we?"

He waited, listening for the sound of Jezebel's acquiescence.

Rafe waited for quite some time before he realized she wasn't in the room.

*J*ezebel added a sore bottom as well as her sore ankle to the list of grievances to be dropped at her guardian's doorstep—a list that began with his very existence and ended with his infuriating persistence in tracking her all the way to Egypt. But it was this latest outrage of his that had precipitated her hasty, ill-planned escape.

When she'd agreed to their wager, agreed to accompany her guardian on this tour, she'd never anticipated a situation like the one that had just occurred between them. Though she couldn't say she hadn't fantasized about kissing the duke from the moment she'd first encountered his too-handsome visage, those fantasies had never included Rafe pushing her aside afterward like a veritable leper! Like some wanton hussy, she had inexplicably lost all control, and he had quite rightly despised her for it.

How could she continue on with him after something like that? It was impossible, she thought. No, there was no choice, no two ways about it. She must leave him now rather than later. And truthfully, while Jezebel hadn't planned on reneging on their bet quite so soon, she could feel no guilt about doing so now, for she was sure that fleeing him was the only way to ensure her continued safety, both mental and physical.

As the archaeologist's niece dusted herself off and checked for further bruises, she looked around at the secluded area of tumbled rock and debris into which the air shaft had dumped her. She didn't have much time, she knew. Soon enough Rafe would figure out what had happened to her, and it wouldn't take long after that to discover where the tunnel she'd used to escape Cheops's tomb let out. Jezebel didn't imagine he'd be too pleased if he found her.

*Well, then, he'd best not find me at all*, she resolved, half fearful still, but already feeling a rush of triumph at the neat way she'd evaded her guardian. *I'll bet he wasn't expecting that!* she thought, even laughing to herself a little. Jezebel, mindful that she wanted the pleasure of her escape to last more than a few precious moments, hid herself behind a cluster of loose blocks, scanning the plateau before her for some means of prolonging her freedom.

The dahabeah was too far for her to risk, she reluctantly decided, though it contained most of their supplies. And even the spot where they'd left their camels picketed under the care of their bearers was a good distance from where she crouched, and far too exposed for Jezebel's liking. Besides, she didn't know if she could trust the men not to betray her to the duke—even Abdul, with whom she'd worked before, might give away the direction in which she'd fled, either for money or because his Eastern sensibilities disapproved of a woman trying to flee her male protectors.

But flee she must, Jezebel knew. Still shaky from the stunning contact of Rafe's lips upon her own, even more shocked by her own uncontrolled reaction to the touch, Jezebel knew that something dangerous had happened today between herself and this mercurial, unpredictable man who was her guardian. He had tapped into a part of her that she had thought safely buried, an instability she'd prayed she'd conquered long ago. She could not allow him to do such a thing again. Even if, by remaining in hiding for a time, she must delay her search for the missing link that could restore her uncle's reputation, it was a sacrifice she was willing to make to guard herself from the unwelcome and overpowering sensations Rafe Sunderland had brought about in her heart.

When he'd kissed her, so tender and sweet with hunger, he'd exposed a vulnerability that Jezebel never, *ever* allowed herself to indulge. His touch had made her feel a terrible urge to surrender everything she had: her body, her mind, even her very autonomy. She'd been willing, in those few moments of madness, to lay everything within herself utterly at his disposition. The duke had somehow awakened that madness inside her, Jezebel thought—feelings such as she'd hoped would never surface from the secret depths within her. He must have some sort of sorcery in his lips, to beguile her so. Why, with just one touch, he'd unraveled years of cautious resolve and made her a slave to his passion, a wanton offering him everything she had to give.

And then he had spurned what she'd offered! She'd never before allowed anyone to rule her will in such a fashion, and she certainly had never opened herself to the humiliation of being rejected as Rafe had done to her. Now Jezebel knew why. The sting of it was almost more than she could bear.

*I am not the sort of woman who stands for that kind of treatment,* she told herself bracingly, *and I would do well to remember that now. No man has the right to treat me with such casual disregard. That arrogant cad can go stuff his head down a cobra's nest, for all I care. I'm not going to stick around and let him play merry hell with my emotions or my future!*

No, indeed. Instead, Jezebel would leave him and his intolerable guardianship far behind her. She had sworn to fulfill a vow, and she could not afford to let Lord Ravenhurst distract her from that purpose with his kisses or his commands. Jezebel had a life to live, and she intended to get on with it—without the damnable duke!

But how to accomplish that worthy goal? By now Rafe had probably discovered her escape route, and though she doubted he'd be able to fit those brawny shoulders of his into the narrow crawlspace, he had only to come back down from the pyramid the way they'd entered and circle the base until he found her. If she took a chance on reaching their camels by dashing across the open sands, he'd more than likely catch her.

*Damn!* Jezebel cursed to herself. *Am I going to be stuck in this rockpile forever?* She couldn't see a way out, though she scanned the desert hopefully. The first flush of giddy triumph began to fade, and Jezebel started to worry in earnest. She must make a move, she knew, and soon. But none of her options seemed feasible.

Something dripped down the back of her neck. Irritably, Jezebel swiped at what she assumed was sweat falling from her upswept hair. Then, fingers arrested at her nape in surprise and disgust, she realized that she hadn't been dripped on after all. She'd been *drooled* on.

Turning her head sharply, her astonished gaze was met by a pair of twinkling, long-lashed, limpid brown eyes. The newly dubbed Lucinda stood staring down at her, one end of a broken picket rope dangling from her constantly chewing mouth. Jezebel could swear she saw the gleam of mischief in her eyes.

God bless contrary females! Jezebel had just found the accomplice she needed to make good her escape. Even better; Lucinda, who, as luck would have it, had carried Jezebel's secret stash of provisions on her back, had apparently had the good manners not to shed any of her packs when she'd broken free of the men who held her. Water, food, clothing, and the one other small, oddly shaped bundle Jezebel never traveled without were all securely strapped to her mountain-shaped hump. It wasn't much to work with if Jezebel was going to be traveling cross-country, mostly through the unforgiving desert, but it was a start. A start was all she needed!

And so, without maps, without much money, and carrying only the bare essentials needed to sustain her, Jezebel Montclair set off south, headed for the destination she'd had in mind all along. Though disturbed by the events just past and concerned over her shortage of supplies, she felt lighthearted and hopeful, for she was also without the one thing she'd most wanted to shed—her guardian.

# *Chapter Eleven*

~

*E*h-hem."

The light wavered, throwing grotesque shadows upon the more-than-life-sized figurines carved into the sandstone wall of the temple's inner sanctum. Startled by the noise, Jezebel nearly chipped the wing off the hieroglyphic vulture she was uncovering with tiny strokes of a chisel and a brush made from specially treated boar bristles. Engrossed in her work, she didn't bother to turn around when she scolded the boy who held the lantern for her. She knew that deep in the most sacred recesses of the temple of Rameses, a massive shrine hewn into the very face of the cliffs at Abu Simbel, finding an assistant not afraid to test the wrath of the pharaohs was extremely difficult. The boy she'd hired—native to a nearby village—was the only one she'd been able to find who was willing to enter the temple's catacombs, and that only after a hefty bribe.

"Mahmud, in the name of all Allah's sweet blessings, *please* don't distract me when I'm working!" she chastened in harsh Arabic. "I might have lost a vital piece of text because of your carelessness." Her irritation came through clearly in her tone as well as her words.

"A thousand apologies for the interruption," returned a sarcastic voice. It wasn't Mahmud's.

For one thing, Mahmud didn't speak English. For another, the intruder's rejoinder, though clearly not in direct response to her unfamiliar words, was replete with enough irritation to more than match her own. Her young assistant would never dare speak to her so disrespectfully. No, Jezebel knew only one man who would take that tone with her.

A shock of fear—and something else she couldn't identify—had the slim archaeologist instantly leaping out of her crouch by the wall inscription she'd been examining. The pencils, sketchbooks, and various odd tools of her trade that she'd deemed essential when she'd packed Lucinda's bags for her escape flew in all directions. Instantly she reached toward the back of her sash for her knife or her pistol. And then she remembered she'd taken both of them out of it several hours ago when they'd begun to dig uncomfortably into her kidneys as she squatted to view the tiny, unusual carvings near the bottom of the wall. A quick, darting glance was enough to show her that both weapons lay upon the altar, too far away to reach before she was caught.

Dread clotting the blood in her veins, Jezebel straightened to face the figure standing in the doorway of the holy of holies. Blinded by the glare of the lamp he held, Jezebel couldn't see the face of the tall man the light concealed, but she didn't need to. She knew very well who it was.

Her heart leapt into her throat and her stomach careened wildly about inside her body, leaving Jezebel with an unpleasantly queasy feeling. The duke of Ravenhurst, it appeared, had caught up with her.

But that was impossible! She'd been so sure she'd covered her trail! Once she was certain she'd gotten a good lead on her guardian in her initial rush to leave the Giza plateau behind, she'd chosen her path carefully, pushing on toward Abu Simbel through the desert at a breakneck pace, putting her faith in the belief that Rafe would never expect her to travel to the very location to which she'd originally planned to take him. All the while she made her way south, however, she'd remained mindful of the determined nature of the man she knew would be following. She'd done her utmost to make sure she left no tracks to follow, letting the shifting sands of the Sahara wipe out all traces of her passage behind her.

Jezebel had employed every bit of her superior knowledge of the terrain and language of this country to lose her blasted nuisance of a guardian, dressing as a man and hiding in abandoned ruins, going it alone on short rations in the desert until she thought she would perish of thirst before she came upon a band of Bedouins willing to lead her to their hidden oasis. She'd tried to stay out of sight as much as possible even in her male disguise, for the fewer people she came in contact with, the fewer could betray her to the duke.

And still, despite his obvious inexperience with the territory, he'd managed to find her, when she knew even the most experienced tracker would have been hard-pressed to do as much. Had he guessed she'd had an ulterior motive in wanting to take him to this place, and chosen to look first for her here on the strength of that hunch? Or had she left some clue behind she couldn't remember? However he had done it, Jezebel thought, the man must have expended a monumental effort in terms of money and manpower to catch up with her so quickly! Despite herself, she was impressed.

Though she'd known it was risky to visit her friend Belzoni's new find in Abu Simbel, Jezebel hadn't been able to resist the lure of this newly reopened monument, knowing, from certain things the engineer had told her about the site, that it might contain information vital to her quest. And so, after a goodly length of time had passed with no sign of pursuit, she'd (foolishly, it seemed) deemed it safe to come out of hiding in the wastelands nearby and examine the ruins of this magnificent temple.

She'd needed to copy its unique hieroglyphics into her notebooks, to study them to see if Lord Clifton had been right about what they might indicate. She'd figured it would take no more than a few days at most, and when she was done, she'd planned to move on again before Lord Ravenhurst could possibly catch wind of her presence. Apparently, however, Jezebel had misjudged the strength of that wind, for it had borne him unerringly to her side.

"Damn it all. What are you, some sort of bloodhound? Why do you insist upon following me?" she demanded. "And what have you done with Mahmud? If you've hurt him . . ." She let the threat trail off.

"Oh, I ate him," the duke responded sarcastically.

For one horrible moment Jezebel actually believed him. Then common sense took hold, and she realized that, as deeply as she'd been concentrating on the wall inscription at the time, she probably just hadn't heard it when the duke took her young assistant's lamp and silently bade him leave. It didn't matter now anyway. However he'd crept up on her, he was here now, and she would have to deal with him—with or without weapons.

"I wouldn't put it past you to do something so monstrous, you great intimidating bully!" she growled, stalling for time.

Rafe lowered the lantern now and paced deliberately toward her. "Three *weeks*, Jezebel. I've spent nearly three weeks on your trail, and all you're going to do is bandy about a lot of idle insults and nonsense? Have you nothing more to say to me at this moment?" He reached her side in one more angry stride and took her upper arm in his iron grasp.

Jezebel glared furiously. "That's not good enough for you? Then how about this? Go the bloody hell *away* and leave me in peace, do you hear me, you arrogant, overly persistent, son of a—Ow!" She cursed as he tightened his hold and began to haul her toward the front of the temple. Jezebel dug in her heels, swearing and trying to pry Rafe's fingers from around her arm. But he didn't let go. Instead he simply sighed, hefted her slight weight into the air, and let her fall none too gently over his shoulder.

Her breath whooshed out of her lungs as her solar plexus connected with the muscle and bone of the duke's brawny shoulder. Her hair came loose from its braid, blinding her and muffling her outraged shrieks. She twisted, she writhed, she cursed him roundly in a dozen languages, calling him every foul name she'd ever heard in any slum or filthy port-of-call, but the duke didn't waver. He simply carried her out into the sunshine, then flipped her back over to land on her feet once more.

Jezebel stumbled for an instant, fighting layers of robes and loose hair that refused to settle into place. She'd landed in the doorway of the temple, and now she squinted in the sudden brilliance of the outdoors after the dimness of the interior. At least half the light of the blazing afternoon sun was blocked by Rafe's broad shoulders as he loomed close to her like some wrathful angel. The full weight of his anger, blazing from his aquamarine eyes, combined with the day's heat to hit her like a slap in the face, but she didn't back down. Her own eyes, lightened to the color of lapis lazuli by her anger, shot sparks at her tormentor.

"Don't you *ever* give up? Why can't you leave well enough alone? Any sensible man would have gone back to England by now—*on his own!*" she raged.

Rafe glared down at the little spitfire, half in shadow, half in light. He was equally upset, though he was sure his reasons for being out of sorts weren't the same as Jezebel's. *God, but she's magnificent,* he thought with unwilling appreciation. Even dusty and defiant, cobwebs and dirt smudging one alabaster cheek, she was the loveliest vision of pure womanhood he'd ever seen, and somehow this only made him angrier. What right had she to twist him in knots like this? Rafe couldn't believe the turmoil she'd managed to bring into his normally well-ordered life. He wanted to take those slender shoulders in his hands and shake her silly for leading him on such a merry chase.

Rafe had more trouble acknowledging the other urge that had come over him upon first seeing his ward alive and well just a minute ago. Even in his own mind, it was hard to admit that, when he'd first caught sight of her slight form at the back of the temple, he'd wanted desperately to gather Jezebel in his arms and simply hold her, giving in to his profound relief at knowing she was still unharmed. He had spent much of the past several weeks frantic for her safety.

His concern for Jezebel Montclair had been strong enough to prove uncomfortable even before he'd met her, Rafe thought ruefully. But now that he'd gotten to know her, however briefly, the degree of his caring for her had risen to an alarming degree. He didn't like having to worry over this girl—not one damned bit. It wasn't as if he didn't already have plenty of dependents back home, from his tenant farmers to the workers who labored in his coal mines to the children who lived in the foundling homes he maintained.

But he *did* worry for her, and he *did* care about her fate. However, as he was barely able to concede this to himself, the duke had absolutely no intention of admitting as much to this strong-willed vixen. Lord knew what she might do with the information. By God, the girl was so impetuous she thought it safe to take off across the desert, alone and unaided, at the slightest provocation!

Well, perhaps the provocation had been more than slight. Rafe admitted the fault was his for driving his ward away with his amorous tactics in the pyramid, and he regretted the action as much as a man could who had derived the most intense pleasure of his life that day, just from the mere taste of her lips crushed beneath his own. A pleasure, he reminded himself as he stared down at Jezebel, that he must deny both himself and her from now on. The thought didn't improve his mood.

Rafe was hot, tired, and out of all patience with both the situation and his ward. His eyes narrowed in ire, but he spoke with absolute control, even a sort of sardonic calm.

"Well, I certainly couldn't leave without my camel," he said finally, after a pause that was perhaps too long. *Perish the thought,* his sarcastic tone added. "Lucinda and I had grown quite fond of one another before you absconded with her, don't you know." The duke had to grit these facetious words out through his teeth. The knuckles of his clenched fists whitened as he struggled to remain in control, when all he really wanted to do was take this disobedient, ungrateful minx across his lap and give her a right proper spanking! But that would be beneath his dignity.

In his entire tenure as duke of Ravenhurst, he'd never once been forced to use more than words to gain obedience from anyone under his authority. Of course, the problem here was that Jezebel refused to concede that she *was* under his authority. He'd soon show her differently, but he refused to sink to her level of ill-bred savagery, no matter how uncivilized he felt inside.

"While I'm here," he said, still in the same droll tone, "I thought I might as well collect the conniving little baggage she's been carrying on her back as well." Then, seeing her huff and prepare to toast his ears with an insult of her own, Rafe dropped the pretense and snarled, "Get your things, Jezebel. We're leaving."

Jezebel bristled at this autocratic command. Who the devil did he think he was? Maybe back in England the arrogant, wealthy Lord Ravenhurst was used to people leaping to fulfill his every whim, but that wasn't going to work for him here! She didn't care how intimidating his towering height and piercing glare made him, or how overwhelming his very presence was to her senses when he stood so close to her. She didn't care if he looked and acted like some vengeful god of legend coming to berate a lesser mortal like herself. Jezebel wasn't going to quail before his wrath! She only hoped her watery knees wouldn't betray her.

Some part of her understood that the duke's infuriating behavior stemmed from a misguided sense of chivalry, of responsibility for her. But why should this man, who had been a stranger to her only weeks ago, give a damn about her fate? She couldn't comprehend it. Glaring up at the gorgeous blond duke with a mixture of frustration, fury, and confusion, she tried and failed to make sense of it. Just as quickly, however, Jezebel shook off the concern. It didn't matter *why* he wanted to oppress her, she reminded herself. What mattered was that he would not succeed!

Thinking fast, she realized that she only really needed to get him out of the way for a moment to make her getaway—just long enough to run up the cliff path that wound along the canyon wall housing the temple with its four colossal statues overshadowing the recessed portico. If she could make it up the path and back to her much-disputed camel with enough of a lead on the duke, Jezebel might gain enough time to effect an escape. She would have to flee across the open desert and some of the most barren, desolate wastelands in God's creation, yet she thought she had a good shot at outriding him once she was astride her feisty former racing camel.

But first she must get past him, for he barred the only egress with his body. Huge piles of windblown sand and rubble, still left from the excavation efforts of her friend

Belzoni and his men, made the path narrow and difficult to navigate. The temple itself was set into the sheer face of the rock wall, its sides impossible to climb. The only way out was up the trail, for below, dozens of meters down, the Nile rushed and frothed dangerously at this point in its course. No convenient air shaft or hidden passages existed anywhere in the temple to help her this time. Indeed, the temple had become a trap with only one way out.

Once again, Rafe stood between Jezebel and freedom, and he seemed to sense it, for he folded his arms and raised one sandy brow as if to ask if she intended to come along quietly.

"What's it going to be, Jezebel?" he asked. "Do you walk out of here under your own power, or must I carry you out like a child?"

*Didn't we just leave this ridiculous situation?* she thought with rising hysteria. The intervening weeks seemed to vanish from her mind, and the explorer's niece was thrown back into the same tense standoff with her guardian she'd fled before. This was really beginning to get tiresome! But right now she couldn't think of any clever way to extricate herself, and she knew the duke was not going to wait much longer for her surrender before he did something to secure it himself.

And then Jezebel remembered the tiny, sharply pointed chisel she still held in her hand. It wasn't much as weapons went, but since she'd so foolishly left her usual arsenal like a sacrifice on the altar of the temple behind her, it would have to suffice. Her mind latched on to the idea with both relief and reluctance. She didn't really want to hurt him. *But*, she asked herself, *what choice do I have?* He would never desist of his own accord. Jezebel braced herself to strike.

"Go to hell!" she cried, lunging at Rafe. Her small implement plunged toward his shoulder—not a lethal wound, she hoped, but enough to spin him around and stop him from chasing after her for a while.

Not lethal indeed, for, in a blindingly swift move, Rafe managed to deflect the blade with one hand, earning only a minor gouge for his trouble. Hissing with anger more than pain, he knocked the chisel from her grasp and clamped down on her wrist with fingers of steel. Though Jezebel fought him, he kept hold of her without seeming to make any effort at all, dodging her kicks and the sharp nails of her free hand as she struck out at him. Then one of her booted feet managed to connect solidly with his shin, and Rafe cursed.

"That's *it*, Jezebel!" he bellowed. "I've had about enough of your willfulness!" Grabbing her under one arm, he hefted his infuriated ward like a sack of meal and started up the cliff to the spot where he'd left his camel picketed next to hers.

Jezebel had a nauseatingly kaleidoscopic view of the campsite she'd left, Lucinda kneeling patiently, if disconsolately, beneath the meager shelter of a rock outcropping, Jezebel's minimal gear stored neatly by her knees. A second camel rested nearby in the sand, but Rafe seemed to have brought nothing else with him when he came to collect her—no extra supplies, no porters, no guides. They were alone atop the barren plateau, no one in sight for miles. No one to hear her scream, she thought morbidly. Where would he take her now? Jezebel wondered as she wriggled and pushed against the unyielding clamp of his arm. And what was he going to do to her when they got there?

She was soon to find out.

*T*o hell with his dignity, Rafe swore, and to hell with his ban against corporal punishment! This little harpy needed a lesson in obedience, and it seemed he must be the one to give it to her. His hissing, clawing burden secured in a viselike grip under one arm, the duke stomped up the path to the top of the cliff, looking for just the proper spot to set her down. He had some discipline to deal out! He found what he was looking for almost immediately.

The kaleidoscope whirled once more, and then Jezebel found herself set down, but in a most peculiar fashion. Her guardian seemed not to have noticed that he had plunked her down, face to the earth, upon a seat that was already taken—by his own lap! Her legs dangled embarrassingly off to one side, and her torso from the other. Beneath her belly and hips, she could feel the bunched muscles of his muscular thighs through the layers of their clothes. He must do a great deal of riding to achieve such impressive muscle tone, she thought, apropos of nothing.

"Ah, Your Grace? What exactly are you—" she ventured cautiously, lifting her head and craning her neck back at an awkward angle to see the duke's face.

"Be quiet, Jezebel," he snapped. "This is obviously well overdue for you, and none of your chicanery will help you evade it any longer!" He pushed her head down firmly and placed one forearm across the small of her back.

*What* was overdue? And what was she supposedly evading? Though completely lost as to what the duke was referring to, she knew these portentous words didn't bode well.

Then, with a shock that ripped through her body like white lightning, Jezebel found out exactly what he was talking about.

The first blow was completely unexpected when it landed full force against her buttocks. The second caught her still stunned, unbelieving.

By the tenth, Jezebel had turned to stone.

*H*ad he used too much force? Rafe wondered anxiously. He'd expected screams, yells, curses—certainly a vicious fight. He'd gotten none of them. Instead, his ward had gone still upon his lap, stiff and silent like a statue as he meted out his punishment. And in the face of that lack of response, his wrath had faded until, sanity having returned, he was horrified by the way he'd let her actions make him lose control. His hand wavered on the tenth spank, stopped about an inch above the flesh he'd been abusing. The firm, tender, rounded mounds of flesh . . .

Even covered decently in layers of cotton robes and a pair of men's trousers, he could see how perfect, how enticing her bottom was. Beneath his hand he'd felt the warm resilience of that flesh. But the rest of Jezebel had gone cold. For an instant he gave in to temptation and rested his hand upon her backside lightly, but the message his tingling palm sent to his brain was too much for Rafe's overheated senses to handle, so he slid it up her back until he could reach beneath his ward's arms to pull her upright. Again, she gave no resistance as he repositioned her to sit like a child upon on his lap.

"Jezebel," he began, searching her eyes and reading nothing in her blank, stony stare. "Jezebel, I'm sorry I had to do that, but you've left me no choice. Do you understand?"

She said nothing. She did not even bother to turn her gaze away from his.

Rafe tried again. "At least tell me you're all right."

No reply.

Rafe began to worry. Where had his usual hotheaded spitfire of a ward gone? The woman on his lap could have been a puppet, she displayed so little animation. He took her chin in one large hand, turning her face gently so he could read her expression better. He might as well have saved the effort, for she wore absolutely none upon her normally vivacious features. Her cheeks were chalk-white and her eyes stood out like enormous dark pools in winter, frozen and unfathomable.

What had he done? Rafe had never heard of a spanking inducing such a state of stupor in a person, but then he'd never delivered or been the recipient of one before, so he really didn't know for sure. He must assume it was merely more stubbornness on her part. How could he get through to her?

"Jezebel," he said urgently. "Listen to me. I regret my actions at the pyramid. Hell, I regret this whole farcical arrangement your uncle has made. But since we're both well and truly stuck in it now, there are certain realities you are simply going to have to face. The first and foremost of those is that I am in charge of your welfare, and I must make such decisions as I see fit to protect you. You are not always going to like those decisions, but they will always be made for your benefit, whether you can see that immediately or not." He searched her shuttered features once again for any response.

Jezebel stared straight ahead blindly, an unnerving act for Rafe since her face was pointed directly toward his own. Rafe got the sense that he had about as much significance to her at this moment as a fly she wouldn't even deign to swat. Still, he hoped that whatever malady had overcome the girl in the last few minutes, her ears had continued to work. There were things he must say to her if they were to have the slightest chance of making it through the tenure of his guardianship, and it was vital that he lay them out before her now, before she tried to flee him again.

Rafe continued. "The second reality you must come to terms with is that, unless you amend your ways, and amend them to my satisfaction, your life here in Egypt will most assuredly be over very shortly. Now, I am willing to be generous with you . . . far more generous that I need to be, my dear." Rafe shook his head and sighed, completely unaware of how condescending he sounded.

"I'm even prepared to let our original agreement stand, if you like—though I must tell you that after this outrageous stunt you've pulled, I have my doubts you will ever be able to prove your responsibility to my satisfaction." Rafe paused, as if trying to determine exactly how to phrase his next words.

"I believe it may be to the benefit of us both if we simply consider our previous wager to have been nullified—no winners or losers—on account of the hasty actions of which we have *each* been guilty during the first days of our acquaintance. My boorish behavior and your childish flight have equally violated the terms of the bet, as I see it, bringing us both back to where we were at the outset of our, ah . . . association," he pronounced. He cringed inwardly, feeling that the words emerging from his lips were far more pompous-sounding than he'd meant them to be. He'd meant to come off as the very model of a magnanimous, kindhearted guardian, but somehow he had the feeling he wasn't creating exactly that effect in his single, hate-frozen listener. Still, Rafe was determined to finish what he had to say, even if his speech didn't seem to be working out quite the way he'd originally planned it. He went on.

"However, since it seems we were both at fault, I now propose that we reinstate the terms as we had agreed to them originally. In other words, should you find it within your powers to act like a proper lady, as well as display your capability to manage your affairs here on your own, I may still prove willing to reevaluate my decision at the end of our journey. For though I intend that we should head back to Cairo together now—and, in all likelihood, take ship for England as soon as we arrive—I see no reason not to continue making stops occasionally along the way on the chance that you will be able to change my mind. And I don't mind admitting I still have a great curiosity to see the ruins of Egypt's past glories. I shall require a skilled guide to show me the sights you and I had originally planned to visit, but missed because of the . . . ah . . . abrupt manner of your departure from Giza. You can still be that guide, if you so choose."

Rafe stopped there to see if she would take him up on his offer to continue with their wager—an offer he was really only making as a sop to the girl's pride, anyway. He knew there was no way he could let an impetuous, heedless female like Jezebel Montclair take care of herself out here in the barely civilized climes of Egypt. No matter that she seemed to have managed just fine for the past few weeks with nearly no supplies and little money. No matter that she'd kept him guessing every second, that he'd nearly despaired of ever finding her before sheer chance had led him to stumble upon her trail. Well . . . chance, and an easily bribed old Bedouin woman who had sensed something suspicious about the young "boy" who'd joined their group briefly a week earlier.

Only Rafe's liberal palm-greasing and the promise of his good intentions given before Allah and all the Prophets (through the aid of one of Rafe's translators) had pried the information about his ward's last known direction out of the crone. Even so, as little trail as she'd left for him to follow, it hadn't been easy tracking her down. Now that he had her back, he was not letting Miss Montclair out of his sight for another minute!

But would the promise of freedom, dangled before her like the proverbial carrot, be enough to win her cooperation? Rafe couldn't tell anything from Jezebel's blank stare. Damn, but the chit didn't give in easily, did she? He would have to assume her silence meant cooperation.

Best he finished laying on the artillery all at once. "Lastly, Jezebel, you must also accept that should we be returning to England together, as is most likely, I intend to do as I know your uncle would have wanted. I intend to see to it that you find a suitable husband, as expeditiously as I may. I'm sure it will be the best solution for both of us," Rafe finished. *Here endeth the lesson,* he thought. *For all the good it's done.* Jezebel looked as if she hadn't heard any of it.

Perhaps, he worried again, his form of punishment had been too harsh. He hadn't meant to break her spirit, hadn't thought it possible to tame this wild beauty with so little effort. Well, there was nothing he could do now but go on, and hope whatever wounds he'd caused, physical or mental, would heal quickly. Rafe looked around the rocky clifftop as though searching for inspiration.

"For now, I suggest we leave this wretchedly hot, godforsaken place immediately and rejoin the men of my search party downriver." Rafe was unnerved by her lifeless silence and could not seem to stop talking. "After I found your trail," he rambled, explaining in case she was wondering (which he had to admit she didn't seem to be), "I left them with orders to bring the dahabeah up to meet us here. However, they were forced to put in about half a mile back since the current is so rough in this canyon, and so they are awaiting our return there. If you are ready, we can adjourn to the camp now."

Jezebel remained stubbornly uncommunicative for another long moment, forcing him to wait uncomfortably. If it weren't for the rise and fall of her chest and the warmth of her legs pressed against his own, he might have thought she was a doll—a perfect, porcelain beauty with no heart and no soul inside her.

Then Jezebel broke the silence at last.

"Are you finished?" she asked hollowly. Her eyes still refused to focus on him.

"Yes, Jezebel, I am. Though it was necessary, I truly hope this hasn't been too upsetting—" he began, but Jezebel was already climbing off his lap, moving as stiffly as if she'd suffered a hundred spanks instead of ten.

"Fine. Let's go," she clipped off shortly. It was all she said as she gathered her gear and began to load it on Lucinda's back.

It was all Jezebel would say for a very long time.

# Chapter Twelve

~~

*J*ezebel had *never* been so angry. In her entire life, such rage as she was feeling toward her guardian had never suffused her body or burned through her mind the way it did now. As she stood with her back to Rafe, cheeks flushed a deep red and abused posterior throbbing unmercifully, trying with all her might not to scream or throw something extremely heavy at him, she was surprised she hadn't burst into incandescent flames from the white heat of it. Had there been any justice in the world, her fury would have burned the duke to a crisp as he sat.

But Jezebel did not intend to let her anger show. She wouldn't give the blackguard the satisfaction of knowing he'd gotten to her! Let him beat her, humiliate her, drag her around like some Neolithic cave dweller. She wouldn't bend, and she wouldn't break, no matter what he tried.

But oh, how *dare* he take her across his knee? How dare he treat her like a naughty child he was reprimanding for some minor infraction, rather than a grown woman who had every right to escape him? No one had ever treated Jezebel with such disrespect. No one had ever thrown away her dignity with such total disregard or made her feel so helpless and pitiful. Did the duke truly take her efforts to elude him so lightly? And was that all he saw when he looked at her—a child to be disciplined?

His kisses hadn't seemed so paternal that day in the pyramid, Jezebel thought bitterly as she secured the straps of Lucinda's packs with jerky motions. But then she remembered how he'd pushed her away then too. His behavior at that time had been almost as galling as the patronizing speech he'd given her just now.

Even more than the humiliation of the spanking—an offense for which she swore she would never forgive Lord Ravenhurst—Jezebel found herself resenting the arrogant way he'd presumed to dictate to her afterward. He thought he was so generous, giving her a second chance to win their wager. Ha! She knew he intended to honor that bet about as far as she did—as far as it was convenient, and no further. He said she must behave like a lady, yet still display competence in dealing with this harsh land. What he didn't seem to realize was that sometimes—indeed, often—the two behaviors were mutually exclusive. Sometimes in order to survive in Egypt, one had to be less than perfectly delicate. To *succeed* one had to get positively uncivilized.

But if Lord Ravenhurst wanted a proper young lady . . . very well, then, she thought. He'd get one! Every minute of every day until she escaped his foul presence.

The boorish duke had no way of knowing it, but for now it actually suited her purposes to go along with his dictates. She would act like a lady and make no complaints or further attempts to escape him—but though he would be unaware of it, the truth was that in obeying his wishes, she would actually be following an agenda of her own.

If she was lucky, Jezebel reflected, the duke would not guess until it was too late that the route she was charting for them back to Cairo just *happened* to coincide with the path she now intended to take on her own. And why should he suspect anything? Ravenhurst was merely being his dictatorial self by commanding her to be his personal guide. He had absolutely no intention of helping her in her quest, but in the end, he would find he had been instrumental in accomplishing her goals, while his own plan to enslave her would remain unfulfilled. And if she had her way, the slim archaeologist thought spitefully, their journey together would resemble nothing so much as Virgil leading Dante through all the horrors of the inferno. Would that she might leave him to roast in hell at the end of it!

Despite the unpleasantness his obnoxious presence at her side was sure to cause, Jezebel couldn't help reflecting that, now that he'd found her, it was a real stroke of luck that the duke still wanted to follow their original course, to have her lead him through the sites they'd previously discussed viewing along the return journey from Abu Simbel. She was more than happy to do so—just as long as one of the sights they visited was the Valley of the Kings.

Jezebel had hoped all along that if she played the tame tour guide for His Bloody Grace, she would wind up heading exactly where she herself needed to go—after all, it had not been purely by chance that she'd planned their original stops! She'd had clues even then to feed her conviction that she was on the right track. But now Jezebel was even more sure of her footing than ever, for as she'd hoped, the wall inscription she'd been able to study so briefly here in the temple of Rameses had indicated that her next destination should indeed be a secret location hidden within the desolate, awe-inspiring Valley of the Kings.

It only made sense to travel with Lord Ravenhurst, to swallow her pride and wait to escape him until after she'd accomplished what she'd set out to do. Therefore, galling as it was, she would let the duke think he had her beaten for now. When the time was right, he'd know differently— far too late to do anything about it!

Jezebel mounted her camel without a backward glance at her nemesis, riding obediently enough in the direction he indicated. She even pointedly ignored it when he took Lucinda's reins in one large hand and began leading her along the trail like a child atop her first pony. She would say nothing now. Not one damned word. There would be satisfaction in plenty soon enough, she consoled herself, just witnessing the look in his eyes when he realized how she'd duped him into doing her bidding all along.

*H*e'd won the battle, hadn't he? So why did Rafe feel like he'd just lost a far more important war?

For the past week or so since he'd caught up with her in Abu Simbel, he'd had nothing to complain about with his ward's behavior. Indeed, except in the matter of her dress (she continued to wear the Eastern garb she'd adopted, having no other attire with her), Miss Montclair now appeared to be the very model of good manners and propriety. Remote, polite, she kept the distance between them more than proper as they traveled back north along the great river.

Gone was the open, laughing Jezebel whose company he'd so enjoyed that first day, gone as if she'd never existed. Gone too was the defiant spitfire who'd had the gall to hold a gun on him for the heinous crime of standing in her path. The woman who had replaced her was another person entirely—and about as forthcoming as the Sphinx.

Oh, she was an excellent guide, Rafe had to admit. Jezebel had dutifully planned their return journey to Cairo to the last detail, had taken over the care of their comfort and supplies with impressive efficiency, and had conscientiously made sure they'd miss none of the sights she'd originally promised he'd see.

In the days since their explosive embrace inside the pyramid of Cheops and her subsequent flight, Rafe had seen some truly breathtaking sights, if none to compare with that of his ward with her lips swollen from his kisses, eager to receive more.

As they sailed down the Nile in their single-masted boat, cruising at a comfortable pace through the warm, lazy days and pausing each evening to watch the fiery sunset paint the river in reflective shades of gold and vermilion, Jezebel diligently pointed out objects of interest along their route, making sure Rafe could appreciate every last detail of the ancient world into which he'd stepped. On his hurried journey south to find his ward, Rafe hadn't had the leisure to enjoy the landscape or stop and tour of any of the ruins he'd passed. But now, having found her, he was determined to gain as much enjoyment as possible from the time he'd had to dedicate to dealing with Jezebel Montclair. And there was certainly no lack of impressive scenery to take in.

When he saw his first hippopotamus—a creature, according to his ward, that the Arabs called a river cow—he wondered how Noah could ever have fit two of them on his fabled ark. A hunt was taking place as they watched, dozens of men and boys dressed in loincloths and little else standing waist-deep in the waters of the Nile, circling a herd of the beasts with their long spears at the ready.

Hippopotami were much larger than they appeared at first. Rafe learned as much when the one Jezebel had pointed out, at first visible only as a pair of round onyx eyes, great flaring nostrils, and wiggling ears above the surface of the water, was driven by an intrepid hunter from the muddy shallows and up the riverbank. The enormous brownish purple animal, stubby legs churning faster than Rafe would have believed, bellowed deafeningly as it turned to face its attackers. Blunt white tusks showed threateningly against the blackness of its gaping maw.

This hunt could be very dangerous, and was carried out no more than once a year in a ritualized culling of the herd that had been practiced for centuries, his ward explained that day as they stood together by the rail of the dahabeah. The meat would be butchered and would probably feed the villagers for months to come. Jezebel had offered nothing more at the time, and Rafe, unable to break through her mute Sphinx-like behavior, could only wonder what thoughts ran through her mind as they solemnly witnessed the hunt. They'd squinted into the sun to follow the hunters' movements, quietly watching the dangerous ballet between man and beast. More people were injured or killed in the river every year by these "cows," she'd told him at last, breaking her silence to speak in the offhand, disinterested manner he was beginning to hate, than by the crocodiles most Westerners so feared. Then, finished with her explanation, she'd left him by the railing and gone to her cabin.

Rafe had had the dubious pleasure of seeing a number of those cold-blooded reptiles along the way as well. Sliding with spine-chilling menace into the water from the clay banks in pursuit of their unfortunate prey, the scaly, greenish brown creatures looked like something out of a nightmare. When he said as much one day to his closemouthed ward, however, Jezebel explained that they actually ate relatively infrequently, spending most of their time basking in the sun to heat their cold blood and to conserve energy. The ancient Egyptians, she'd told him grudgingly, had even worshiped a god who took the form of a crocodile, though with their language still mostly a mystery to modern scholars, little was known about the deity anymore.

In her role as guide, Jezebel had showed Rafe the remains of the once-fabulous temples sacred to this god,
along with a host of others too numerous to count. In the
ancient capital of Memphis, they had stood staring up dozens of feet at the tops of the thick pillars that had once held
up the now-crumbled ceilings of these ancient houses of
worship. Rafe had listened intently while Jezebel explained
that the shape of these pillars was a deliberate imitation of
the reed-bundle columns that the pharaohs were thought to
have used to build their own now-vanished palaces.

At the vast temple complex at Karnak, just outside the
city of Thebes, they'd walked together through an avenue
of identical statues all of rams so numerous and finely
carved it was hard to believe the masons had been able to
construct them exactly alike. And in dozens of other sites
along their path, Jezebel had revealed her impressive store
of knowledge about everything involved in the life of the
Egyptian people past and present, from their primitive yet
effective farming methods to the disastrous consequences
of their long occupation by the Turks.

In the past week or so, he had to admit that she'd shown
him more about the history and culture of this land than
most would see in a lifetime.

But she had shown him nothing of herself.

Even with all of these wonders to occupy him, the main
impression Rafe had walked away with was of Jezebel's
complete withdrawal from him. She spoke woodenly when
she shared information, and her shuttered face seemed im-
mune to expression. At first he'd tried to shake her from
her unnatural stiffness by being genial, friendly, and warm,
all of which he felt. He'd even tried being avuncular, which
he definitely did not feel. Rafe had used every ounce of
what he'd been told was his considerable charisma, but it
was all to no avail, for he found that the charm for which
he'd been famed back in London society had no effect
whatsoever on his ward. She had refused to laugh or even
crack the slightest smile.

Whenever he'd made a joke, or even tried to engage the
girl in any conversation unrelated to their current trip, she'd

merely grimaced tightly and continued with her monologue, completely ignoring his overtures. While they walked the ruins, Jezebel took care to stand as far from Rafe as she could without actually having to raise her voice to address him, and whenever possible, she'd made sure one of their bearers followed closely behind them. Even when they were forced together by the small confines of the dahabeah, she made a point of keeping her distance.

As time went by, Rafe had become more and more frustrated with this act of hers—an act that, in any other woman, he would have taken for mere modesty. Indeed, Jezebel was behaving exactly as she should. She spoke when spoken to, she never defied him when he made a request, and she was always properly deferential to his rank and stature, even when her own unusual position as head of their little excursion forced her to take the dominant role.

It didn't bother Rafe in the least that Jezebel was leading their expedition. After all, she knew the country far better than he. As long as he was around to ensure nothing went wrong, Rafe saw no reason not to enjoy learning from his ward's undeniable expertise. No, the only thing that bothered him was this damned ridiculous passivity she'd taken on—passivity that suited her about as much as it would have suited *him*.

Though she had done a fine job of displaying her competence as an Egyptologist, Jezebel had showed about as much personality as one of the stylized wall reliefs she so obviously admired. In fact, the only time he'd seen animation light up Jezebel's lovely features was when she was describing some moldy old mummy or the symbols inscribed upon a statue whose creators had been dead for thousands of years. Rafe had begun to feel an odd jealousy at the sight of the remnants that could catch her enthusiasm and bring the smile back to her lips when he could not.

Rafe knew he was being terribly perverse. First he chided her for not acting like a lady, and then he hated it when she did. So he did nothing about the situation, though his every instinct told him to shake the girl until she stopped behaving like such a lifeless mannequin. He told himself he had no right to be upset at her for obeying his wishes. Yes, Jezebel was taking her newfound decorum a bit too far—but much as he wanted to push her, corner her, demand that she treat him with the disrespect he suspected was really more her style, he hesitated.

How well did he really know this woman? And what right did he have to disrupt her life in such a fashion? No right at all. When it came right down to it, he supposed Jezebel might have the right idea in treating him with such cold indifference. They'd both be better off keeping their dealings with one another as limited as possible. Just one day of unguarded intimacy between them had wrought a near disaster.

Rafe knew it had been his actions that afternoon in the pyramid that had ruined the tenuous connection they'd just been beginning to forge, and he wished he'd been able to exercise more control—though how he could have managed such a feat under those circumstances, the duke still wasn't sure. Nothing that had happened subsequently—her flight, their fight outside the temple, the spanking—would have been necessary if he hadn't lost control that afternoon. Perhaps if he *had* behaved as a gentleman that first day, he thought with a pang of remorse, he might have spent this time pleasantly getting to know the warm, spirited Jezebel he'd glimpsed in the beginning.

By the time they were nearing the Valley of the Kings— the last stop they would make before returning to Cairo— Rafe had begun to wonder if he'd only imagined her.

*T*heir small party was camped for the night on the west bank of the river, in a quiet spot between two picturesque villages composed of wattle and daub huts. They'd put in on a lush, fertile strip of farmland, bordered, as always, by the encroaching desert. Places like these reminded Rafe of just how dependent the Egyptians were on the Nile for everything that made life livable. They ate of its fishes, they drank of its waters, they irrigated their fields from its bounty, and refreshed their very earth when the river loosed its annual flood of nutrient-rich silt and soil upon the land.

The river was the Egyptians' primary mode of transportation, their connection to the outside world, and the reason so many conquerors had coveted sovereignty of their nation for centuries. Yet, mere acres from where they camped among the rushes and sweet-smelling grasses of the water's edge, the hilly riverbanks turned into sand dunes and the Arabian desert spread out in a vast, shifting plain that had proven deadly to many an unwary traveler.

They'd decided to camp here as a break from the constant motion of the dahabeah, and because tonight there was a rare, cool breeze to refresh them. It slid between the reeds on the river's edge, sighing, and woke the crickets and bullfrogs to begin their nightly song. As he lay wakeful after the camp had settled down for the night, Rafe reflected that even the smells of river and grass here were different than they were at home, though he couldn't see why that should be. Grass was grass and water was water wherever one went, weren't they?

Jezebel could probably explain the phenomenon, he thought as he soaked in the intoxicating scents and sights of Egypt. Everything here, including his exotic ward, seemed like a fascinating new mystery to him, one he might investigate forever and never comprehend. But at least the study would never be boring, he thought.

Rafe was lulled to sleep finally by these thoughts, bivouacked beneath a moonless sky so full of stars it was fair to bursting with white pinpricks of light. Hours later, however, he suddenly found himself waking again, although it was past midnight and they had done a good deal of hiking in the hot sun the day before. He listened for a while to the sounds of the small party's porters snoring around him, wondering what had aroused him. No one had stirred, as far as he could tell, not even Jezebel, whom he could not actually see from where he lay.

To preserve her modesty, Rafe had set up a tent for his ward to sleep in when they were not spending the night aboard their pleasure boat with its small but comfortable separate cabins. When they camped ashore, it had become his habit to lay his own bedding across the opening to hinder anyone thinking to get in—or out, he admitted ruefully. He wouldn't put it past his ward to assay another escape attempt, despite her recent good behavior, and so, along with guarding her virtue (a novel experience for the rakish duke, to say the least) he had made himself her watchdog.

Rafe was sure there was no way Jezebel could have left the camp tonight without his notice, especially as he'd taken the precaution of tying bells around her tent's door flaps. But those bells were silent, no chime warning him of any impending flight. He remained still upon his bedroll, wondering what else might have awakened him, if it had not been someone from the camp.

After lying quietly and listening for a moment, Rafe felt sure what he had heard was some strange noise in the distance—a faint, echoing cadence just on the edge of hearing that had drifted in on the cool night wind. It sounded like music, he thought, but that was ridiculous, wasn't it? He could see that the people of the nearby villages among the hills were all asleep, the last of their oil lamps doused hours ago, not even a stray dog barking. There was no traffic just now on the calm river, their own boat the only one tied up on the banks nearby. And it seemed highly unlikely that anyone would be wandering about in the desert wastes, playing some sort of melody to themselves in the dark.

But there it was. Faint but unmistakable, growing louder bit by bit, it was undeniably music he heard. The soft strains of a violin, played with masterful skill, rode the breeze and trickled into his delighted ears. Could someone really be playing out here? It seemed impossible, yet as Rafe strained to make out the sighing sound, his skin prickled with gooseflesh.

He *knew* that melody.

Rafe was on his feet and following it to find the source before he'd even consciously decided to investigate.

# Chapter Thirteen

～

*J*ezebel stood with her back against a stone outcropping atop the hill where the desert met the border of the richer farmlands, devouring everything living with its scouring wind-borne sand. The rough-edged rock still retained some warmth, though the day's heat had faded, bringing a welcome chill to the air. From where she was leaning against the wall of rapidly cooling granite, a magnificent vista opened out for Jezebel to view.

She stood on the border of two worlds. Before and below her, past a number of rolling green hills and marshlands, stretched the wide, dark river. Placid and smooth, it gleamed like a sable satin ribbon, occasional ripples showing whitely in the starlight. Behind her, the vastness of the baked, barren desert spread out endlessly. And overhead, bridging the two, the vaulted arc of the ink-black sky was so liberally strewn with stars its radiance almost hurt to look at.

But Jezebel saw none of it.

Her eyes were closed and she swayed just a little in time with the music that poured from her violin, note after note dragged forth without volition from the well-loved antique instrument.

There had never been a time when she'd been without her violin. Keeping it safe in the worn, oddly shaped traveling case she'd constructed for it long ago, Jezebel had carefully transported it with her everyplace she and her uncle had roamed; across oceans and over mountains, through deserts, rain forests, and everything in between. It was her most prized possession, the one object she would never willingly leave behind, and the greatest source of comfort she had.

Jezebel never knew what she would play before she set her bow to the strings. Sometimes she'd launch into one of the great Bach sonatas or solo violin partitas she'd learned in her early childhood. Other times she composed as she played, bringing whatever was in her heart to the music instinctively.

Tonight was such a night, for Jezebel was troubled, and she knew of no other way to soothe herself. The music, she prayed, would help to clear her mind and unburden her soul of the weight it carried. Her fingers flexed, her bow moving caressingly over the instrument, and the words and thoughts she couldn't speak spread themselves throughout the darkness as melody.

She told herself that it was only the accumulated worry and anger of the past several weeks that had left her so unsettled that she could not sleep, and had at last caused her to slit the back wall of her tent open tonight and flee stealthily, instrument case in hand, seeking this place of solace. Spending these last weeks with Lord Ravenhurst had placed a strain on her in ways she'd never calculated, dredging up painful memories and fears she hadn't ever wanted to think about again.

But Jezebel knew she must endure her discomfort for a little while longer. Despite the roiling tension she felt simply being in the duke's company day after day, she must continue with the charade of compliance she'd adopted at least until they arrived at the Valley of the Kings in another two days. Very soon after that, their odd, uncomfortable relationship would end, she told herself. There would be no more pretense, no more lies. No more Rafe Sunderland always underfoot, troubling her with his questions and his commands and his sheer magnetic *presence*. Yet though it should have overjoyed the archaeologist's niece, the knowledge brought no pleasure to Jezebel's heart.

It had indeed been excruciating never saying what she thought to her tall, handsome companion, keeping herself so completely in check she thought she would scream at times from holding back. But she had done well. She'd kept her thoughts and her feelings—not to mention her secrets— to herself this whole time, displaying nothing more revealing than calm competence before the duke even when he'd done his damnedest to crack her composure.

It hadn't been easy. Rafe had treated her as though the unpleasantness at Abu Simbel had never happened, as if the two truly were at peace and enjoying a cruise down the Nile for the sheer, leisurely pleasure of it. The man had displayed more charm than a snake-oil seller, Jezebel could swear—and she should know, having encountered many varieties of subtle charmers and charlatans on her travels. She'd found herself wanting to succumb to the duke's allure more than once, forgetting for long moments how much she hated him, how he'd humiliated and scorned her. With his wry wit, ready laugh, and acute intelligence, he was a hard man to resist. But Jezebel felt sure he was trying to cozen her with this sudden affability, to fool her into letting down her guard and making a mistake.

To what end, she still wasn't sure. Where Lord Ravenhurst was concerned, none of the usual logic applied. The duke was a hard one to figure out, she mused, posing the question of her violin, letting it hover, unanswerable, as a cascade of poignant notes in the still night air—and an even harder man to hate when he set his mind to winning someone over.

His behavior of late had been above reproach, she had to grant him that. The devious rogue had given her no reason for complaint, though she'd looked for it in every gesture, every word. Charming, debonair, a good listener and a model tourist, Rafe Sunderland had seemed happy to simply follow her lead as they traveled down the Nile, taking in all she had to say with curiosity and enthusiasm—much more than she'd expected from a pampered blue blood. He had seemed to understand the importance of her work here, and even to approve of it to a certain degree. Almost, he had made her long to tell him her real purpose in Egypt, the reason she was fighting so hard to remain here alone when life had become so difficult for her of late. She had wanted to share her plans with him, to let him see what drove her and what mattered to her.

In fact, it unnerved Jezebel to think just how often in the last week or so she'd found herself yearning to accept her new guardian's protection, the safe haven he offered so casually. She'd caught herself wondering what would happen if, after confiding her plans to the duke, she asked for his forbearance in pursuing her uncle's avenue of study until she'd proven what she'd set out to prove. Perhaps then a trip to London would not seem so impossible, Jezebel had thought at the time. And even at this moment, alone atop the hill with only the music to confide in, her mind turned the possibility over once more. Perhaps in that case, she dared to consider, taking him up on his offer to care for her would not be so bad. . . .

*No!* she rebuked herself sharply, the discordant notes of the violin echoing her suddenly increased tension. *That can never be!* Much as she wanted to, Jezebel still didn't dare trust the man any further than tomorrow, and perhaps not even that far. She knew that despite his veneer of thoughtfulness and admiration, the duke had absolutely no intention of taking her work seriously—or of giving her the freedom to pursue it.

His seeming kindness was only that, she reminded herself sharply—an illusion. Jezebel could never let herself forget that Lord Ravenhurst was society's darling, a master of the kind of perfunctory social intercourse she herself had spent the better part of her life trying to avoid. Coming from a man like that, the charm Rafe displayed could only be a facade meant to keep their relationship afloat on its current superficial level—and to keep her at the proper distance.

It made Jezebel sick to think that the signs of friendship he had shown her were really just the sort of courtly dissimulation a man in his position must often be forced to display, but how else could she interpret the signals he had sent her? One moment he was kissing her as if she were the most desirable woman in the world. The next he treated her as if no intimacy had ever occurred between them, as if he'd forgotten their brief embrace entirely—and perhaps he had. Her face flamed with embarrassment even now, thinking of it once more. A corresponding wail came forth from the violin, echoing her distress.

She still couldn't believe she'd invited his kiss so brazenly. She must have been insane, deranged from the heat, perhaps, even before he had scattered her wits by taking up that invitation. But though her brains had been scrambled by the erotic contact of their mouths that day in the Great Pyramid, Rafe's had seemed unaffected, both then and now. Probably, she realized as she considered it now, her shameless and ill-considered advance had seemed hopelessly naive to the sophisticated duke, and he'd simply been too polite to express his disgust. In any case, it was clear their kiss had meant so little to him that he'd been able to shrug it off without another thought.

But Jezebel could not. The memory of that brief caress was etched indelibly upon her mind. Even in her mortification, even as she was determined to wriggle out from under his crushing thumb, there was a small part of her that still yearned to taste Rafe's firm, masterful lips just one more time. . . .

And that was really what had driven her out here tonight, Jezebel admitted to herself at last. It wasn't anxiety over her future plans, and it wasn't frustration over the role she was being forced into playing. No, the true cause of her misery was the undeniable fact that, even after everything Rafe had done to humiliate her, to break her will and dominate her, Jezebel still couldn't shake the powerful longing she felt whenever she was with him.

Jezebel let the resonant sounds come forth from her violin, asking it to purge her, note by note, of the feelings that overwhelmed her. She allowed the music to express her frustration and upset, and in return it helped her think more clearly, helped soothe her turbulent emotions. As always, the violin responded to her touch, working its calming magic little by little.

It became clear in her mind that although she didn't understand the feelings she was having for the duke, she was deeply afraid of them, for they were of a kind she had never had before. Though she'd grown up in an almost exclusively male environment, still worked closely with men all the time, she'd never experienced anything like the sensations she felt now. And this was one experience Jezebel could do without.

Until Rafe Sunderland had arrived in her life, Jezebel had been in complete control, mistress of her own destiny and emotions. Now, however, she wasn't sure of either. She'd felt completely out of control from the moment he'd confronted her in the hotel—had it really been just weeks since then? Her whole life had changed dramatically in that time. Why, oh, *why,* she wondered yet again, had her uncle ever brought this man into her life?

The duke made her feel things that she couldn't afford to fcel, offered her gifts that would have been all too easy to accept at the price of her very soul and sanity. And yet the man had no idea what sort of dangerous pot he stirred when he offered to take care of her. But no, that wasn't quite true, she amended. In point of fact, he simply didn't *care* what pot he stirred. He didn't care about *her.* And as long as that was true, she could never trust him, never tell him about the mission she'd set for herself, never ask for his help or surrender herself into his care.

For to Lord Ravenhurst, it meant nothing to take her in and guard her from those who might seek to do her harm. It meant nothing to him to feed her, provide for her expenses, to see that she was properly outfitted and escorted and wanted for nothing. But it meant a great deal to Jezebel.

Her existence had never been easy, living as she had with an uncle who more often than not forgot to take thought for even their very food and shelter; a man who, she'd sometimes thought, had felt more for his archaeological finds than he did for anything living. Though he had loved his niece, Lord Clifton had sometimes had a very poor way of providing for her welfare. And though she had always claimed to relish her independence and to enjoy taking care of both of them, secretly she'd often wished her uncle would share just a little bit more of the burden. The duke, on the other hand, was more than willing to share it—indeed, if his words were to be believed, he insisted on taking it over completely!

Standing on the hilltop with only stars to light the darkness of her isolation, Jezebel let herself imagine what it would be like to rest safe in Rafe Sunderland's care. Safe in his arms . . . She knew she could never let it happen in real life, but there were times when she would like nothing more. There were times when she wanted to melt into his embrace, feel again the wonder of his kiss. When he was near, her feelings became so overpowering she sometimes wasn't sure she could stop herself from throwing herself at him again.

*Dear Lord,* Jezebel thought, suddenly stricken, *I have become like my mother after all.*

Long, anguished notes sang forth from her violin in a dizzying arc as she put voice to the fear that had haunted her all of her young life.

Fragile, emotionally unstable Natalya Montclair had been Jezebel's only example of the relations between men and women, and for her, love had been a form of mental illness. She'd clung to her husband, Jezebel's father, and declared her passionate need for him countless times. As a little girl, Jezebel had watched her mother throw herself upon her father with kisses and clawing arms every time he had returned to her side, and weep for months when he left again. If that was what passion could do to a woman, Jezebel had decided she wanted no part of it. She could never let herself need another person in that way.

But now, for the first time ever, Raphael Sunderland had her wondering if what she felt was similar to the overpowering emotions her mother had once endured. No other man had ever given her cause to fear for the solidarity of her heart and mind as he did now, and Jezebel was deeply worried. She couldn't share this gnawing fear with anyone, but it had been with her as long as she could remember.

Even as a small child, she'd accepted the truth. She'd always known, somewhere in her secret heart, that in temperament she was far more like her mother than her father or her uncle, for she'd recognized in herself all the signs of her mother's violent, volatile spirit. When Natalya had died so tragically all those years ago, young as she was, Jezebel had made a vow to herself never to allow her feelings to overcome her as they had done to her troubled parent. By sheer force of will if necessary, Jezebel was determined to avoid the curse of her mother's madness.

She'd practiced stillness, calm, and focus until she was

sure that, at least on the surface, she resembled the unemotional members of her father's side of the family. In the
normal run of things, no one would ever read turmoil or
upset on Jezebel's features, or hear her raise her voice. Oh,
she laughed, she enjoyed herself as much as the next person, but Jezebel never truly let go—at least not where anyone would ever see it. Since she'd been a small child, she
had never let anyone break her composure. But Rafe
seemed to do it now with alarming regularity. And that was
precisely why it was so vital that she leave him.

Jezebel hated the man with a passion. And she wanted
him even more, though she knew that to give in to her
desires was to give in to the very madness that had eventually taken her mother's life. She couldn't take the risk of
getting close to the duke, no matter how much she wanted
to. She could never let him see how much he affected her.
But she could dream about what it would have been like if
things had been different. . . .

Only now, because no one would hear, did Jezebel feel
secure enough to voice the instrumental song that exposed
her inexpressible desires. Perhaps by giving free rein to her
fantasy with music, she hoped, she could purge herself of
her obsession with the man. Perhaps once she had finished,
she would return to her normal, sane self, troubled no
longer by these unwanted emotions. Dear Lord, she prayed
it would be so.

As she played those four little strings that spoke so eloquently, the night echoed with a surging melody that told
of fantasies and girlish wishes, of longing for a different
past and future both.

The music swirled out over the sandy earth, was carried
across the waters of the Nile beyond. The notes swelled,
filled the arid land, and soared up to challenge the dark
vastness of the heavens above. It was Jezebel's way of ex-
orcising the demons inside her, of forever putting behind
her the longing for everything she knew she could never
have. The duke of Ravenhurst was one of those things.

The violin wept heartfelt tears. But Jezebel's eyes remained dry.

* * *

*W*ith only starlight and the entrancing music bewitching his ears to guide him, Rafe found his way to the top of the hill with its rocky crown. When he reached the summit, however, he stopped dead, dumbfounded by the sight that greeted him.

His ward stood swaying in a robe of gossamer white cotton, her hair a glorious mane of black silk blowing loose about her shoulders and her back. It hung as far as her waist whenever the breeze let it go, and whipped around her face with a life of its own when it was caught. Her eyes were closed in seeming rapture, and she appeared totally unaware of her surroundings—like a sleepwalker. He couldn't tell what she carried in her arms, though he noticed she held them out before her in a most peculiar manner.

At first it did not even occur to Rafe to associate the unearthly music flowing through the darkness with his ward. Indeed, he thought for one insane moment that she was cradling a baby. But then it all came together in his mind, and he realized that though she might rock it with as much love and reverence as an infant, what Jezebel was holding was a violin. She was *playing* the violin.

Somehow, Rafe was not surprised.

The melody she was performing was one he'd heard many times before tonight, though he knew these notes had never been played in this exact pattern by any human being before. To Rafe, Jezebel's melody was the essence of longing for all that could be, for all that wasn't, for all that might never come to pass.

He recognized it from his dreams.

It had been a long time now since he'd had the dream that began and ended with this same seductive song, but Rafe would never forget the music that had haunted him from his earliest boyhood—or the woman who played it. Never before had her face come clear, but he knew now with an undeniable certainty that Jezebel was the one, the illusory woman who had captivated his fantasies so completely all his life.

Unable to keep memory from overwhelming him, he recalled how the recurring dream always started.

*Rafe found himself alone, in the dark, standing in the midst of some great sandy plain. He could see very little, but a sound was filling up his ears, a music so beautiful and beguiling he instantly felt compelled to follow its promise and to confront its unknown composer. The sound was faint, however, and growing fainter, so he chased after it, though his legs felt leaden and they dragged in the sand with each agonizing step. And finally, after an interminable struggle, he came upon the mysterious musician whose melody had so enchained his soul.*

*All he could see through the vast distance between them was an indistinct, willowy female figure. She was dressed all in white, he saw, and carried a violin in her hands— the instrument casting such a spell upon him that he was helpless to do anything but open his ears to its enchantment. He stopped to watch her, mesmerized, feet sinking deep into the sand without his notice, his only concern the distant specter who held him fast in her power.*

*She swayed like a dancer as she played, a mistress of starlight and sorcery. Her face was hidden behind a veil of wind-driven hair, but somehow he knew that if he could but glimpse her features, he would find her fair beyond comparison. Rafe felt the compulsion to go to her growing ever stronger within him, and he tried to call out to the woman to wait for him, to let him catch up, but he found himself utterly powerless to stop her as she began to drift farther from his sight.*

*Sand began to trip up his feet as he chased her, the wind to take his cries, and, worst of all, the unforgettable music began to fade from his ears. A terrible certainty came over Rafe as he sank into the treacherous desert's grip that if she escaped him now, he would never find her again. Yet no matter how he struggled, he could do nothing to prevent the weight of the sand from slowing him down. He could only sink deeper down into its sifting, ravenous grasp.*

*He looked up one last time, only to find it was already too late, and he had lost her. The violin's last promise trailed behind, the final faint notes a mocking farewell that only brought his failure home more painfully. Devastated, Rafe gave himself up to despair, letting the desert devour him slowly.*

He'd always awoken from the dream with a feeling of being crushed by a terrible burden. Yet despite the sadness that accompanied it, he had still welcomed its arrival each time it came, for the vision allowed him, even for a brief moment, to see *her* once more—the unknown woman whose rhapsody commanded his heart.

And now, standing here awake and lucid in the chill desert night, hearing the music he'd once thought existed only in his imagination, seeing the selfsame figure with her long blowing hair and white garments, there was only one conclusion he could draw.

Jezebel was the woman of his dreams.

*Ridiculous,* Rafe thought faintly. After all these years of searching, sometimes without even knowing it, the Honorable Miss Jezebel Montclair—his *ward*—simply couldn't be the one.

Could she?

# Chapter Fourteen

⁓

$\mathscr{I}$'d no idea you played," a voice spoke softly into the silence that fell after the last echoing note had died.

Jezebel whipped around with a startled cry—coming dangerously close to tumbling down the steep edge of the hill as she did. Rafe was at her side in seconds, cupping her shoulder gently in his hand and leading her back toward safer ground. He seemed to sense her confusion, the lingering trancelike state that always came upon her after these impromptu concerts.

"What are you doing here?" she asked inanely. Jezebel couldn't seem to catch her breath. The sight of her guardian, when she'd just been playing such an intimate melody involving him, threw her completely off balance. For a moment she entertained the fantasy that somehow, with her performance, she had conjured the duke out of thin air. But she'd been trying to *bury* her thoughts of him, not bring forth the far more intense and disturbing reality! Rafe Sunderland, clad only in boots, form-fitting buff trousers, and a thin white cotton shirt, his manly figure lovingly detailed for her eyes by the light of a thousand stars, was somewhat more than Jezebel wanted to deal with in her current emotional state.

"I followed the sound of your violin," he replied quietly. "It drew me here."

In a way, then, Jezebel supposed, her fantasy really was true. She *had* brought him here, though it hadn't taken any magical powers on her part. She'd simply woken the man up with her overloud playing. But why had he not made his presence known immediately when he arrived? Maybe, she thought with a mental wince, he had been so horrified by her performance that he hadn't known what to say. It was not an uncommon reaction, Jezebel had found, when she played her original compositions.

She'd never meant anyone to hear what she played tonight, least of all her guardian, who was already looking for wrongdoing on her part. Surely he would take her to task for her wildness, her unladylike ways. After all the effort she'd put into convincing him she had lost her spirit, the one thing he'd know now was that she was anything but spiritless!

Thank God there was no way for him to interpret the true meaning behind her melody, to guess that it had been her feelings for him that had sparked it. But even without understanding the content, the style would make him realize she was not, and never could be, a proper lady—no proper lady would be filled with such wild extremes of emotion. After what he'd witnessed tonight, the duke could not help but be aware of things about her that she'd intended to keep hidden forever, both from him and from the rest of the world.

But what would he do with the information? she wondered, feeling a rising sense of panic. "How—how long have you been listening?" Jezebel demanded, flustered. And how much had he read into what he'd heard? she wondered. "Just how long were you skulking there in the shadows, spying on me?"

"Only long enough to see you put forth the most incredible performance I've ever been privileged to attend," Rafe said softly. He chose not to respond to the anger or defensiveness in her tone. Instead, his own reply verged on reverence. "I've heard nothing of its like before."

Well, that wasn't *quite* true, Rafe had to admit to himself, but no matter how shaken and amazed he was at hearing, in real life, the music that had echoed throughout his dreams for so many years, he definitely was not prepared to reveal as much to Jezebel—not now, and possibly not ever. He still had trouble believing it himself, and he wasn't at all ready to contemplate the possibilities presented by the unlikely coincidence. His ward was dangerous enough to his equanimity without her knowing that she had captured a place in his fantasies as well as in his waking life.

Still, seeing the vulnerability stamped upon his ward's lovely features, having heard the poignant sound of longing so plainly described in her music, Rafe desperately wanted to comfort Jezebel. She was clearly in pain, and he ached with the need to ease it. Yet he found himself afraid to do so—afraid of the strength of the feelings building inside him for this one slight girl, this unexpected and completely unique young lady who had fallen into his care.

He hesitated to aid his ward, and he knew damn well it was because his feelings for her were not purely protective. If he held her once more in his arms, his embrace would not stop at a mere offering of solace. And though he wished for the sweet conclusion of their unfulfilled passion more than anything, he knew he must be strong enough for both of them, must not give in to the desire that raged inside, seeing his fantasy woman come to life.

Jezebel knew nothing of his dreams, could have no idea how deeply her melody had resonated in his soul. No, all she knew was that he had witnessed an intensely personal moment, and he could tell she was afraid of his reaction to it. With her sapphire eyes clouded and the hunted expression she wore on her face, Jezebel looked like a wary animal, expecting to be beaten for some transgression. Nothing could be further from his mind than taking her to task, however, and Rafe wanted to reassure her of that much, at least. "I hope it will not be long before you delight my ears with a second performance," he said with awkward gallantry. It was nothing like what he had meant to say. "Come," he urged, taking her cool, trembling hand within the warm reassurance of his own. "Let us sit awhile and talk together."

Oh, this was even worse than she'd feared! Lord Ravenhurst was making fun of her! Or worse, being patronizing. Jezebel knew he could not have liked the raw sounds her bow had produced tonight. This wild free-form sonata was not meant to be enjoyed. Compared with most contemporary pieces, it had no real structure or cohesive movements, no limits imposed by traditional Western musical conventions. No, it was a release, pure and simple, too ragged and full of mad emotion to be appreciated by anyone with normal sensibilities. Only someone with as much passion in his heart as she, Jezebel thought, could ever take pleasure in this music. A blue-blooded scion of society like Rafe Sunderland never could. Yet he claimed that he *did*.

Jezebel gazed wonderingly at the duke, allowing him to lead her over toward a patch of green rushes that grew lushly in the shade of a different portion of the same rock outcropping she'd been leaning against when he'd first come upon her. Gently, he urged her to sit down, and Jezebel did not have the wit to deny him. After weeks spent avoiding his intimate company, now he was far too near, too real, and too enticing to refuse.

She could feel the warmth of Rafe's well-muscled thigh brush against her own as he sat down with his back against the rock, close to her in the darkness. She could smell the clean, slightly salty fragrance of his skin as it mingled with the sweeter scent of the crushed greenery. Her pulse started to race. A quick, stolen glance at his face, however, gave her no indication if he was feeling a similar desire. In fact, she was finding it very difficult to read the duke's mood at all tonight. His normally open, honest features were pensive, inwardly focused. He seemed almost . . . subdued. But that was ridiculous, she told herself.

Why would Lord Ravenhurst be feeling pensive when he had nothing at all to worry about except enjoying the next leg of his cruise down the river? As far as he was concerned, she reminded herself, he was still holding all the cards. He knew nothing of her plans to deceive him. Most likely, Jezebel assured herself, the duke was just gathering his thoughts, trying to find the least offensive way of telling her he'd found her conduct wanting.

But he said nothing for a long moment, staring down across the width of the placid, night-dark waters in thought while Jezebel fidgeted. At last, tired of waiting for the axe to fall, she spoke up. "You don't have to feed me false compliments, Your Grace," she said bitterly. "I'm grown up enough to know better than to believe them, and such unctuousness doesn't suit you at all."

A smile of genuine amusement spread slowly across his sensual mouth. "Unctuousness? My dear, no one's ever accused me of being a flatterer in my entire life. Just the opposite. I am said to be a very harsh critic, and I've never been shy about making my opinions known. But Jezebel, I found nothing to criticize in what I heard tonight."

She wanted to believe him. Somehow this man's opinion mattered to her very much—so much more than the rest. Let society as a whole scorn her, it didn't matter to Jezebel. But Rafe was different. If he accepted her music rather than condemning her for it, it meant he might also accept the turbulent nature of her soul. No one but her uncle had ever done that, and even Jonathan Montclair had not been privy to these occasional solo "concerts."

Wasn't it *possible,* a small, rebellious part of her brain asked, that he might really have liked her music? "Do you truly mean that?" she questioned, fearing to hear him rescind his praise, or worse, to read insincerity in his gaze when he confirmed it. But there was no deception in Rafe's sea-blue eyes when he replied.

"Of course I mean it. My God, Jezebel, in a lifetime of watching the finest maestros performing in the grandest opera houses and symphony halls of Europe, I've heard nothing to compare with what you just did up here, alone with no one but the jackals for witness. You infuse more passion into a single note than most of those dried-up old men who pass for artists in Europe could put into an entire symphony. How could you have kept such a talent hidden for so long?" He shook his head in wonderment. "Have you never played before company? I can't believe that no one bothered to mention your talent in this area—your archaeological colleagues back in Cairo were certainly voluble enough about your other skills."

Voluble in condemning them, she'd bet. Lord Ravenhurst had probably heard any number of nasty disparagements about herself and her "dotty old uncle" before they'd even set forth on this journey. And yet he'd remained seemingly open to her opinions at every turn. Again, Jezebel forced herself to remember that this was only how things *seemed,* not how they were. She must remain wary. She must remember the past, distasteful as it was, lest forgetting it leave her open to more pain.

Jezebel Montclair had indeed once played for company. Over the years, she recalled reluctantly, she'd scandalized any number of proper British ladies and their husbands with her performances—proving, as if she'd needed more proof, that what she felt inside her wasn't normal or acceptable to society at large. It was part of the reason she always sought out solitary places now before she released the rhapsodies that filled her mind and soul.

It had been a bitter disappointment to Jezebel when it had become clear that she could never make music her profession. No one would listen to a woman violinist. No one would take her seriously or listen to her compositions. It was not because she played poorly, Jezebel knew—far from it. No, the truth was she was simply *too* damned good. Women in her social strata were encouraged to learn music, of course. Being able to pick out a tune on the pianoforte was thought to be a requisite accomplishment for most ladies of good breeding. But one was not supposed to be *good* at it. One was not supposed to shine.

No one had ever heard of a famous lady violinist, especially not one belonging to the nobility. The few times that Jezebel had agreed to play before company, years and years ago, had been unmitigated disasters. Whatever country or principality she and her uncle were living in at the time, her audiences, usually composed mainly of transplanted European gentlefolk and British diplomats eager for a musical reminder of their faraway homes (played perhaps no more than adequately), had always been far from appreciating her raw, impassioned genius and dazzling solos. Instead they had sat silently at the conclusion of her performances, clearly embarrassed by the unseemly display of emotion Jezebel infused into her music.

From a man—an Italian maestro, perhaps, who was expected to act the part of virtuoso—the performance would have elicited cheers and repeated calls for encores, but in a young girl of Miss Montclair's age and station, it was absolutely unacceptable.

This was why women were not encouraged to take up the violin, the ladies would whisper disapprovingly, clucking their tongues and shifting uncomfortably in their chairs.

These disgraceful displays just proved what they'd always suspected at heart—old Lord Clifton had clearly been remiss in his niece's education. Such a shame he'd let her grow up so wild, they would say to each other behind the cover of a fan or a gloved hand, never curbing her far-too brazen ways as he ought. Their husbands, of course, would have to agree in condemning the girl's overly passionate public displays, if they knew what was good for them!

With her budding good looks and the fortune she stood to inherit, the young Jezebel Montclair might have been quite a catch had her uncle not allowed her to become such an odd little bluestocking—but then, the ladies would remind each other with sage nods and sidelong glances, eccentricity was known to run in Miss Montclair's family. A shame, indeed.

Jezebel hadn't needed to actually overhear the gossip of these so-called paragons of good taste and manners or witness the pitying looks they'd sent her way to understand they hadn't appreciated her performances. The hideous silence that would reign while she stood upon whatever stage or dais had been erected for her little musicale was enough to tell her everything she needed to know. She'd shut her violin case firmly after a few of these disasters, loftily informing her uncle that she would not deign to play for fools like these any longer. She'd hidden her tears of hurt and shame from him, however, knowing they would only upset the kindly old archaeologist who'd been the one to encourage her to perform in public in the first place.

Jonathan Montclair had reluctantly been forced to agree with his niece that the world was perhaps not ready for a woman of her scope, but he had begged her not to give up playing entirely. He'd been so kind, so supportive, Jezebel recalled with a knot of sorrow in her throat. Many nights reclining before a campfire, bivouacked out beneath the stars, he had asked her to play a melody to lull him to sleep, and she had happily obliged him.

Jezebel's uncle had always encouraged her musical ambitions. It had been she, finally, who had relegated her music to the sidelines of her life, finding it easier to focus on other pursuits that did not seem so heartbreakingly futile.

Well before they'd settled here in Egypt, she had put that dream aside and tried to forget it. Perhaps that was when she'd begun devoting her life solely to her uncle's work, Jezebel thought. Indeed, the only times she had played in recent years (aside from these lonely nocturnal concerts) had been at her uncle's request. No one else had heard her play in ages—which, she told herself, was exactly as she liked it.

Lost in these reveries, it took Jezebel a moment to realize that Rafe was watching her curiously, the inquisitive light in his aqua eyes telling her he was still waiting for her answer. She had been silent too long.

"My so-called colleagues never mentioned my music because I've told no one here about it," she finally replied. "There are many things those men don't know about me," she said shortly. Jezebel was still not sure what to make of his reaction and was uncomfortable with the unaccustomed praise. "Even more *you* do not know."

She realized even as she said this that the same was true in reverse. She didn't know enough about her new guardian to judge whether or not he was upset, disgusted, or if he'd honestly liked what he heard. But though she couldn't explain why it should matter to her, she wanted badly to believe he had. . . .

"You're right, Jezebel," he said, looking down at her with a strangely searching gaze. "I really don't know anything about you. But I should very much like to learn." His lips as he formed these provocative words looked velvety soft and yet deliciously masculine in the pale light of the stars. His warm breath fanned her blushing cheeks as he leaned ever closer. Too close. Jezebel was suddenly afraid she might kiss him again if he didn't move back.

"Why?" she asked sharply, her absent defenses finally returning to save her before she let down her guard too far. She mustn't allow Rafe to see any more of her inexplicable weakness for him! Jezebel could afford to give him nothing he might later exploit, for she could already feel her mother's madness rising in her far too strongly to take that risk. She knew she would not be able to bear any further rejection from this man. "Why would you want to know

anything about me, Your Grace? I thought your only object
was to be rid of me as swiftly as possible."

Rafe leaned back under the lash of these words, though
his eyes studied her even more keenly than before. His little
ward spoke truly. Why was he sitting here alone in the dark
of this starry night beside the very embodiment of temptation if what he really wanted was to remove her from his
life? *Because,* his own mind answered him, *you* don't *want
to get rid of her. You want very much to* keep *her.* Yet how
could he ensure that she stayed in his life when she seemed
so determined to leave him?

Just as in his dream, this mysterious woman sought to
escape him, dancing always just out of his reach and leading him a maddening game. But in the real world, Rafe
reminded himself, he wasn't paralyzed, trapped, and unable
to recapture her. Here, however much she might vaunt her
cherished independence and her clever evasions, he knew
he had the ultimate control over Jezebel's actions. The only
question was, how would he use his authority? If he did as
his lustful body told him, and not as his conscience dictated, the results could be disastrous for them both.

Rafe knew he must be careful in what he said next, but
he could not resist telling his ward at least a part of the
truth.

"It might once have been," he admitted. "But I am not
quite sure *what* the object is now."

Jezebel leaned back silently next to her guardian with
her spine pressed against the stone slab, absorbing that admission as she stared out blindly into the darkness. Rafe
too remained quiet, letting the frank comment linger in the
air.

"I don't think it is so surprising that I want to know you
better, Jezebel," he said after a while. "You are my ward,
however strangely that event came to pass, and you are also
a very unique woman. You possess seemingly any number
of hidden talents to spring upon me just when I've begun
to think I've seen them all." He smiled again and Jezebel
found herself blushing. "I would like to understand the
forces that drive you, that make you think you want such
a life as the one you've chosen here. Perhaps if I under-

stood, I might be able to aid you in some way."

She sucked in her breath sharply, looking away before he could see the sudden panic in her eyes. It was impossible to give him what he wanted, Jezebel thought. Even more so than her own private ambitions, hopes, and dreams, she was not prepared to share Lord Clifton's secrets with Rafe, now or at any conceivable time in the future. He wouldn't understand the need she felt to vindicate her uncle's beliefs, to prove the old earl's detractors wrong. He would never let her do her duty to the man who had raised her, but there was no one else to see justice done if she did not. Those men who had mocked the earl, called him a crazy old fool left out in the sun too long—his own colleagues and supposed friends—had driven her uncle to his death. They'd goaded him with their taunts and scorn to work beyond the limits of his fragile health, until in the end he'd become obsessed with the need to prove his beliefs had merit.

There was no doubt whatsoever in Jezebel's mind that these men were to blame for the sudden respiratory illness that had felled Lord Clifton as he worked feverishly to uncover the final clues that would lead him to the ultimate proof of his claim. After his death, the archaeologist's niece had vowed to do anything she could to make sure his loss was not in vain—and that included denying the truth to her guardian, even when she wanted very much to lay it all before him and ask his assistance. Jezebel couldn't afford to stake her uncle's legacy on this man's uncertain clemency. He might well decide she was as batty as her uncle and ship her off to England all the sooner if he knew what she sought to accomplish.

"I don't *think* I want this life; I *know* I do," she said with a hint of returning anger, deflecting his question. "It is only men of your ilk who think it inappropriate when a woman desires to pursue a life of study such as mine."

His *ilk*? Just what sort of class of men was she lumping him in with? Rafe didn't even like to think of it. "It is not your studying or your love of antiquities to which I object, Jezebel. On the contrary, I have always believed women should strive to develop their minds. It is only the dangerous manner in which you seek to gain your knowledge that concerns me. You cannot simply stride through the world alone and unprotected, unconcerned with the reality that there are men out there who would do things to you which are unspeakable for a young lady to even hear of, let alone endure."

"Do you think I'm so unaware of the dangers around me?" Jezebel scoffed. "I assure you, that's hardly the case. I haven't been sheltered in blissful ignorance my whole life the way you men like to keep most women. I've seen and done many things which would surprise you, I'm sure. And I am not without weapons to protect myself. I believe you saw one of them not so very long ago, Your Grace," she reminded him pointedly, still rather proud of how neatly she'd outfoxed him the day she'd held the gun on him in the pyramid.

"And I believe you discovered just how easily those defenses of yours can be breached," he replied even more pointedly, referring to their altercation in Abu Simbel.

"You only caught me then because I did not truly wish to injure you," Jezebel retorted hotly, then flushed when she realized how revealing that statement was. "In any event, Lord Ravenhurst," she hurried on, hoping to deflect his attention from the slip, "I hardly think it fair to base your whole decision regarding my future on that one afternoon—or on what you've heard tonight." Let him think she still believed his lies about abiding by the terms of their wager. She hoped he would continue to think she still meant to play by his rules.

"As I told you before, I don't intend to," he answered. "I am still weighing my decision. But if you think this lifeless marionette act you've been treating me to all week helps your case, you're mistaken. I believe I will need to know much more about you before I can decide how best to arrange matters between us."

*Well, isn't that a noble gesture,* Jezebel thought sarcastically. *Still weighing his decision, indeed.* She considered telling the duke to stuff his "decision" right up his unmentionables, but she held her tongue with an effort. Staring down at the nearly forgotten violin she still cradled in her hands, she reminded herself that further emotional outbursts were exactly what she should *not* allow herself at this moment. Right now she needed to play the cooperative, demure female. She should make a show of obeying him.

Jezebel didn't want to tell the duke anything more about herself tonight. He'd seen far too much already, in her opinion. But if it would help remove this disturbing man from her life ... and that *was* what she wanted, wasn't it?....: "What do you want to know?" she asked grudgingly.

Rafe ignored his ward's less-than-enthusiastic response. He could not help his sudden need to know her better, to gather every last piece of the puzzle that was Jezebel and try to put her together in his mind. Yet he did not want to frighten her away with the intensity of his interest—or, in truth, intrigue her too greatly. If she parted those rosebud lips of hers once more in an invitation like the one she'd offered back in Giza, there was no way he would be able to decline. For that reason, Rafe kept his tone carefully light when he replied. "Well, there are any number of fascinating things about you, I imagine, but why don't you start by telling me who taught you to play the violin so brilliantly? You couldn't have attained the mastery I heard tonight all by yourself. Surely; inborn talent aside, you were not born with a full-blown knowledge of the instrument?"

"No," Jezebel admitted. "My mother taught me the basics when I was a little girl. The rest I picked up on my travels, but I could not have begun without her tutelage."

In fact, she thought now, the best part of her itinerant lifestyle had always been the many wonderful new forms of music she was lucky enough to come across during their journeys. In each country she and her uncle had visited, Jezebel had always homed in on the musicians among the people they met. Afghani nomads, Hindu snake charmers, and African tribesman had all been her tutors at one time or another. The result was that, in addition to the traditional Western music she practiced on her violin, Jezebel had learned to incorporate many more exotic sounds into her repertoire.

She'd practiced every piece of sheet music she'd brought with her from England until she could play them all blindfolded and the parchment pages were almost transparent from handling. But that had not been enough for the lonely, gifted little girl, and she'd quickly begun to pick up the native songs and melodies of the places they visited. Although she had a deep, abiding love for the beautiful symphonies and sonatas of her own culture and had collected as much Western music as she could lay her hands on, Jezebel had also found herself utterly fascinated by the Eastern rhythms she learned on her travels, the atonal notes and nonmathematical structure of their music.

In addition to her violin, over the years Jezebel learned to compose and play original pieces on a myriad of other instruments ranging from six-foot-long sitars to tiny, hand-wrapped reed flutes. Indeed, there was no sort of music she could not love or find peace within. This was the true gift her mother had given her. Much as she hated to remember Natalya sometimes, it had been she who had first opened Jezebel's mind to the sublime world of sound and harmony.

"Your mother?" Rafe prompted.

"Yes," Jezebel sighed, just the thought of her mother instinctively making her wedge her back farther into the solidity of the stone wall against which they sat. Memories once again overwhelmed her.

The one bright spot in Jezebel's relationship with her mother had been the violin lessons they'd shared. Unpredictable as Natalya Montclair could be, when she taught her daughter how to hold the varnished spruce and maple instrument in her little hands, correcting her bow position or showing her how to make the notes soar forth cleanly from the catgut strings, she was all patience and encouragement. It was as though the music she coaxed from the violin drew Natalya out from the world of mental anguish she inhabited and into a place where emotions were safe.

Though most gentlewomen did little more than pluck dispiritedly at the strings of a harp or plunk out a tune on the pianoforte, such was not the case with Jezebel's mother, who adored music and was an accomplished performer on several instruments. Having seen early indications that her daughter shared her own keen ear for music, from the time Jezebel was four years old Natalya had given her the basic instruction she needed to perfect her own natural talent.

Though most of her memories of her mother were bitter-sweet at best, Jezebel admitted to herself that she owed her love of music, along with the heirloom violin itself, entirely to her.

As a child, Jezebel had used music as a bridge to span the distance between them, to form a common bond. And when her mother suffered one of her "spells" and could not care for her, she took solace in the music she created, wrapping it around her loneliness and her fears like a lullaby to ease her sorrows. Yet it was unthinkable for her to speak of these things, even to Rafe, whom Jezebel instinctively knew would be a sympathetic listener. She could only tell him the facts.

"My mother loved music, and she began teaching me everything she knew, from proper fingering to bow position and stance, from a very young age. I was barely bigger than my own violin when I first started to practice. But my mother died when I was eight years old, and I had to teach myself what I could from then on. This violin is the only thing I have left of her." Jezebel stroked the varnished wood of the instrument in her hands.

"You must have loved her very much," Rafe sympathized.

Jezebel just looked at him blankly. He couldn't know anything about the tragic events surrounding Natalya's death. He couldn't know anything about how chaotic and fearful she had made Jezebel's life.

"Sometimes," she said at last. It was all she could say with any honesty.

Rafe saw that Jezebel was not telling the whole story, but though he wanted to ask what she'd meant by giving such an ambiguous answer, he hesitated to dig further into that painful part of his ward's past just now. She'd had enough emotional upheaval for today, if her music was any indication of the state of her feelings. "Yet she did give you a fine ear for music, and that is a great gift. If you ever performed in London, you would surely bring the house down," he predicted.

Jezebel's laugh was more like the croak of a raven. "You must be joking."

Rafe could see the disbelief fairly radiating from her, and he thought he understood it. "Well, I doubt the *ton* would appreciate a melody such as you played tonight," he agreed, "but your technique and musical interpretation are both extraordinary. If you played them a piece by Beethoven, say, a gavotte or one of the other popular dance tunes, I'm sure you would be an instant success."

"And I am sure I would not. Believe me, you have no idea what you are talking about." Again Jezebel remembered the horrified reactions she'd garnered from her past performances, trying not to flinch at the memories.

"In any event," she concluded, unwilling to discuss her shortcomings as a performer any further, "I do not choose to perform for company. I don't like the feeling of people watching me when I play," she said, shooting a pointed glance his way. Jezebel's lips twisted in sour humor. "Besides," she admitted at last, "when I do perform, it seems my audience shares my aversion. I find they tend to run with great alacrity in the direction directly opposite from my own, very soon after I set bow to strings."

"But now I have heard you play," he reminded. "And I am still here."

"You must be tone deaf," she joked weakly.

"No, but am not the judgmental monster you seem to think either, Jezebel." Rafe looked down at her, just inches away in the dark. "I want to help you in whatever way I can."

It was as though Rafe had overheard her thoughts and not just her melody. The temptation was mighty just to lean on him, put her head against that broad shoulder for a while, and simply sigh. If she had any sense, Jezebel told herself, she would bolt right back to her cozy little tent this instant, tuck her head under the blanket, and tomorrow behave with no greater warmth toward her guardian than she had all along.

But things had changed tonight between herself and the duke in some fundamental way from which there could be no going back. Jezebel could sense this change, though she could not guess what it foreboded. All she knew was that there was something between them now, a connection formed of starlight and music and rare honesty. She felt weak and shaky, mesmerized by Rafe's words and wanting very much to melt into his comforting strength.

Flutters of unwelcome pleasure made their way down Jezebel's spine. The blood sang in her veins, rushing to her extremities until she was tingling all over. The indecent longings she'd thought she'd purged earlier came back with a vengeance, and there seemed nothing she could do to stop the feelings.

The duke wasn't interested in her, Jezebel reminded herself forcibly, however much her own body might clamor for his touch. He'd shown as much quite clearly when he'd shoved her away after her clumsy, girlish embrace in Cheops's tomb. Yet, if that was the case, why was he sitting so close to her now, staring at her with such slumberous warmth in his eyes? He did not seem repulsed by her at the moment. Indeed, he was gazing at her with every evidence of rapt attention.

And then she shivered—whether from her thoughts or because of the chill night wind, she didn't know—and Rafe wrapped one rock-hard arm about her shoulders, pulling her into the shelter of his body and chafing her cold arms gently with his palms to keep her warm. Jezebel grew weak all over, overwhelmed and surrounded by his large frame and his masculine scent. Fiddling with the bow of her violin nervously, she looked down at the instrument in her lap. She felt strangely submissive wrapped in the circle of his manly arms, and the only thing she could think to say at that moment was uncharacteristically apologetic.

"You must consider me quite a burden, Your Grace. After all, I've dragged you halfway around the world when it's clear a man in your position must have pressing matters calling for his attention at home. I'm truly sorry for all the trouble you've gone to on my behalf." This statement, she found to her own surprise, was true. Though she might intend to deceive him and leave him at her earliest convenience, a part of Jezebel really did appreciate the great lengths this man had gone to in fulfilling what must have been an onerous duty. How many other men would have done as much?

Rafe thought of the women who waited back in London for him, of the horse races and card games and gala balls and routs. He didn't miss a single one of them. "Don't be sorry, Jezebel. I am not. Right now"—and he marveled at how true the statement was—"there is no place I would rather be on this earth than right here by your side. And I'm very glad we've had this opportunity to talk tonight. I've wanted to speak candidly with you ever since we began our journey back down the river, but there has never seemed to be a good time." Indeed, she hadn't given him the chance. She'd rebuffed every effort he'd made to thaw the ice around her heart. But now, he sensed, that ice had melted, though he wasn't sure of the cause of her newfound vulnerability toward him. He took the opportunity gratefully.

"I wanted to tender my apologies once more for what happened, for destroying your trust in me so early on with my unconscionable behavior. I would ask you now to give me another chance to prove we can be friends. This strange 'situation' of ours doesn't have to leave us forever at loggerheads if we choose to get along." Rafe paused, smiling wryly. "Besides, I'm not sure I can stand feeling like 'His Bloody Grace, Annoying Tourist Extraordinaire' much longer."

Despite the confusion of her warring feelings, Jezebel felt herself smile. "You weren't that bad, my lord. I've seen far worse tourists than you." She gnawed her lip, deciding to be honest with him. Her sense of fairness required as much, painful as it was. "And though it's very chivalrous of you, you do not have to apologize for what happened between us in the pyramid—the intimacy, I mean." Blushing painfully, Jezebel stumbled over the phrase but continued on. "I know it was my fault. You were only being kind to respond at all, and you had every right to stop what you did not want to happen."

Rafe could only stare down in disbelief at the woman tucked into the curve of his arm. Was *that* what she'd thought? Had Jezebel truly spent the past weeks believing it was lack of desire that had caused him to push her away? Dear Lord! He started to laugh.

Jezebel stiffened immediately, a dagger of pain lancing through her breast. "I'm glad you find my apology so amusing, Your Grace," she choked, struggling to throw off the weight of his arm and rise to her feet. She spun to face him once she gained her footing, her lovely features tight with fury and hurt, her night-dark hair swirling about her like a living shield. She wielded her precious violin like a club, shaking it at him to emphasize her words. "But be sure I'll give you no more opportunity in the future for levity!"

Rafe leapt up as well and grabbed her before she could run, sweeping her into an embrace that locked her struggling form tight against his rangy frame. He easily took the violin and bow from her nerveless fingers, laying them carefully upon a shelflike protrusion in the rock embankment, out of harm's way. One of his large hands came up to frame her face, to hold it in place while he studied her features with intent tenderness.

"Jezebel, sweet Jezebel," he murmured. "How could you think such a thing? How could you *ever* think I didn't want you? My God, I've practically had to tie myself to that wretched camel for weeks to keep from taking you in my arms." He knew he should not be saying this, knew that, even if it hurt, it was better if she believed he had no interest in her as a woman. But seeing the anguish and self-doubt in her face, he could not bear to let her go without knowing the truth.

Jezebel's eyes welled with sudden tears and she tried to look away from him, but he held her face fast in his gentle grasp. "You're lying," she whispered, her gaze downcast. "I know you are." She knew how he must view her. She was the eccentric, mannish niece of a crackpot explorer. No one had *ever* wanted her.

"What do I have to do to prove it to you?" he asked, dipping his head to catch Jezebel's dejected gaze until her anguished blue eyes, their sooty lashes clumped with crystalline tears, finally accepted his insistence and met his own. He simply looked at her for a long moment. Then his eyes narrowed with tender triumph.

"Never mind. I know."

## Chapter Fifteen

~

*R*afe's lips came down upon Jezebel's in a kiss that spoke eloquently of his admiration, his acceptance, and his deep desire for her.

"Jezebel," he whispered over and over again as he worshiped her with slow kisses, lingering kisses, lush openmouthed kisses. "I want you. I want you. Never doubt that I want you."

His tongue swept inside and her knees buckled, a soft, throaty moan escaping her lips. Rafe then transferred his attentions to the curve of her slender neck, tracing a path with ardent lips, tongue, and teeth to a spot just beneath her ear that made her collapse bonelessly against him. If it hadn't been for his arms about her waist, his hand cradling the back of her head, she might have slid to the ground completely. His tongue laid a river of molten lava down the tendons of her neck, his sweet caress making her shiver and gasp and arch up for more. And then, just when she thought she couldn't stand this delicious torture one moment longer, his lips returned to capture hers again.

She'd thought the storm of her passion was over for tonight, but now another tide swept Jezebel up, this one far stronger than the last. She clung to Rafe's waist and shoulders, pressed her body up to his, and greedily drank of the nectar of his mouth. Dear God, he tasted so good, so right! Rafe's kiss was like life itself, sweet and exciting and vibrant, mysterious and thrilling and dangerous all at once. Every vital feeling she'd ever had was in the touch of his lips, the loving pressure of his mouth shaping hers. She wanted it to go on forever. She wanted to climb right inside his very skin. Rafe was warm and fragrant with the scent of man, strong and virile and completely different from herself. Jezebel could not help sending her questing palms out to touch his skin through the thin fabric of his shirt, learning the contours of his masculine form.

And everywhere she touched seemed to bring intense pleasure to the duke. He groaned as her fingers traced the sinews of his arms and shoulders, slid across the slablike muscles of his chest, curved around the trim circumference of his waist to stroke his sculpted back. Her fingers dipped beneath Rafe's loose shirt to feel the heat of his flesh, singeing her nerve endings as she did with lightning bolts of ecstasy.

Dear Lord, but she was marvelous, Rafe thought hungrily. He angled Jezebel's face to deepen their kiss with one hand tenderly cupping the back of her head, his other hand tightening its grasp about her tiny waist as he drew her ever closer. He wanted to devour every bit of her, to draw her very essence into his own body with his kiss. Without conscious thought, Rafe began backing Jezebel up against the rocks, holding her against the barrier so that he had her at his mercy. Jezebel gasped when he pressed the turgid evidence of his desire against the taut flesh of her belly, but did not flinch away. Instead, she wedged herself more firmly into his embrace, kissing him with wild adoration until his head spun dizzily.

Rafe's good intentions evaporated. He'd meant only to reassure her, but now . . . though he tried to stop himself, knowing what he did was wrong, his callused hands still sought out the fastenings at the neck of her gauzy cotton gown, freeing the loops from around the small, pearly buttons that went down the front of the garment all the way to her waist. Pushing aside the fabric impatiently, his palm swept across the smooth flesh of her torso to cup one ripe, pink-nippled globe. His mouth swallowed her cry of pleasure even as his fingers plucked the hardened nub of her sweetly rounded breast. Telling himself he would stop after he had filled his eyes just once with the full perfection of her body, Rafe pushed Jezebel's robe farther back toward her shoulders to bare her more completely to his gaze. Her breasts were every bit as enticing as he'd imagined—firm, upturned, and of a size to fit his hands perfectly.

Rafe found he could no more stop at this juncture than he could have hewn the Sphinx out of living rock with his pocketknife. "You are so beautiful," he groaned in a harsh whisper against her nape. "So incredibly, unbelievably beautiful." Even his dreams had not exceeded this reality. Rafe bent at the waist, and as he pressed her back against the wall, one arm protecting her from the roughness of the stone, his mouth sought the solace of those nipples. He laved them one after the other with his seeking tongue, and Jezebel cried out, writhing against him helplessly.

She couldn't get enough of these amazing new sensations, couldn't help wanting more of the duke's practiced touch upon her newly sensitized skin. Even the strange feel of his golden beard stubble abrading her tender flesh where no man had yet touched her could not bring Jezebel back to her senses. Indeed, each sweeping stroke of his knowing tongue sent her further from any thought of sense or reason as she gave herself up entirely to passion. For the first time in her life she truly understood carnal desire, and as she'd feared, once aware of it, she instantly became its slave.

Though part of her realized it was utter madness to be twining herself around this man, half-naked in the rushes beneath a black, star-strewn Egyptian sky, Jezebel was helpless to deny the fierce need she felt, the joy that sang in her veins. *He wanted her!* She didn't question it now. Rafe worshiped her with his body and Jezebel greedily took all that he offered, giving of herself everything that she had in turn. Once caught in the grip of these violent, powerful feelings, she was unable to retrieve so much as a trace of sanity. She would have to ride out this storm until it reached its natural conclusion—though what that would be, Jezebel could only vaguely guess. Whatever it was, she craved it desperately.

Even as he kissed and suckled the sensitive tips of her breasts, she wanted more, felt the caress send excruciating pulses of desire much lower down in her body, where not even she had dared to seek her own pleasure before. Yet now she needed him there, in that place that burned and clenched itself in knots of aching tension and anticipation. But how could she express her desire?

Jezebel slid her slender hands through Rafe's hair and down the column of his neck to clasp his nape, firmly turning that beautiful head with its burnished curls upward so that he was forced to let her distended nipple go and look up at her face. Suddenly confident, though she couldn't have said where she had gained this feeling of surety when she was on such unfamiliar ground, she pushed him back a little, taking a small step forward away from the stone embankment and nudging him with her hip to give her space.

Perhaps it had to do with knowing that *this* time, there could be no doubt Rafe wanted her. Every inch of his body screamed his desire, his overwhelming ardor for her. Jezebel could feel it in his trembling flesh, the tightness with which he held her, the insistent pressure of his swollen shaft against her belly. Rafe's lust for her was like a heady wine, a draught or magic potion making Jezebel drunk with her own sensual power. She felt like a siren bewitched by her own sorcery. She felt completely unlike herself, wrapped in pleasure and knowing instinctively how to fan it further in both of them. It was, she thought, marveling at herself with the last lucid remnants of her consciousness, as if she'd always been meant for this sort of seduction.

Jezebel smiled a tiny smile, almost as if to say, *In for a penny, in for a pound,* and slowly shrugged her shoulders, freeing her soft cotton gown to fall with a whisper into the grass. She stood before the duke entirely naked.

"Oh, sweet Jesus," Rafe breathed, sinking to his knees before her as though she were a goddess and he her most devoted acolyte. He pressed his forehead to the satiny flesh of her belly, rubbing his face against her soft white skin and breathing hard, trying to slow the raging lust that suffused every bit of his body. He wanted to throw her to the ground instantly and plunge inside her so deeply that they would become one, locked together forever. He wanted to ravage her perfect, untouched body until her screams of ecstasy echoed across the river and woke the villagers for miles around. He wanted to lose himself within this impetuous, exotic beauty and never, ever recover. But he could not. Would not.

Dimly, he felt her hands tugging at his shirt, freeing it from his trousers, and pushing it back to fall behind him, leaving him bare to the waist. The heat coming off his body was so intense that Rafe did not even feel the coolness of the nighttime breeze off the Nile. He could sense nothing but the woman before him, his whole being focused on her ethereal loveliness, trying desperately to remember that she was an innocent, and he her sworn protector. But was he not also her provider? his sly brain asked, using a convenient sort of twisted logic. And was she not right now in need of something only *he* could provide?

He knew what she wanted. The ache inside her, if it was even half as bad as the one he was experiencing so fiercely in his own body, needed some form of satisfaction. It *demanded* satisfaction, and Rafe wanted more than anything to give it to her, even at the price of his own pleasure. But despite the raging fire within him, when he touched Jezebel he was gentle, reverent. His hands slowly swept their way up the outsides of her shapely legs to caress her hips, then slid around her waist, stroking with his thumbs as he lavished her belly and the undersides of her breasts with hot, wet kisses.

Jezebel moaned, a long, whimpering sound that expressed her burgeoning desire as the handsome duke knelt before her on the grass like a knight pledging fealty to his queen. She wanted to touch him everywhere, but could not seem to concentrate well enough to stay in any one place for long. Her fingers fluttered from his rock-hard, broad-spanning shoulder blades to his neck, his face, and around to tangle in his hair. She didn't know if she wanted to push his head lower to assuage the ache she felt, or drag it away from her belly out of some vestige of maidenly shyness.

Everything she felt was so foreign to her that while she encouraged and accepted each new sensation, she did not know exactly how to react to it. She was tossed, thrashing and writhing, from one level of passion to the next, like a drowning sailor without anything solid to cling to. Finally, Jezebel settled on grasping the overhanging lip of stone above her, too new at the game of love to do more than simply hang on while her more skillful lover showed her just how good it could be.

She gasped when his fingers curved around behind her hips, sliding across her buttocks to stroke her briefly there and then dip lower, grasping her inner thighs with hot, lean-tendoned hands and widening the stance of her legs. She felt a cool breeze caress her most intimate flesh, and sobbed helplessly in delight before he even touched her there.

That touch was not long in coming. Rafe, sensing Jezebel's willingness and need, turned his body so that her side pressed against his chest, and one slim leg rested between his own spread thighs. All the while he continued covering her torso with nipping kisses, tender kisses, long strokes of his tongue that swirled deep into her navel or across her ticklish sides. He wanted to bury his face deeply between her legs and taste her sweet honey, but instead, he first sent his hand gently stroking up the inside of one silky alabaster limb until he reached the juncture of her thighs.

Rafe glanced up, saw Jezebel arched back and clutching the wall behind her for support, her face a mask of want and her pale skin glowing in the starlight. It was time. He sent his fingers questing between the downy curls that hid her damp petals, reveling in her cry of pleasure as he stroked the incredible wetness and heat of her femininity, finding and circling her tiny, erect pleasure bud with his thumb while he carefully urged one finger inside her body. Her reaction was everything he could have asked for.

Jezebel screamed hoarsely, bucking against his hand and sobbing. Rafe pushed another finger into her tight, slick passage, eliciting another cry as he slid them both slowly in and out of her once, twice, a third time. Her whole body was trembling, and with his other arm wrapped tight about her waist, Rafe was taking most of Jezebel's weight. The rest was supported by the rocky wall, her head tossing and her hair catching, unnoticed, on rough patches of stone. Rafe had never seen a more beautiful sight, and, unable to help himself, he gave in a little more to the temptation raging through his veins. His kisses drew a line ever lower down on her belly until his breath fanned her soft black curls, and then his tongue took over for his thumb. Jezebel went wild.

From the instant she'd felt those talented fingers thrust themselves inside her body, touching her innocent flesh in ways that were far from innocent, Jezebel had known there was no going back. But now she knew nothing at all. A feeling unlike anything she'd ever experienced before was growing upon her, fast and furious, unstoppable as a tidal wave and nearly as frightening. It felt like pain, except that she wanted more, could not get enough of this sweet agony. She cried out again and again, pressing herself shamelessly against his fingers and mouth until the dark tide suffused her, sending her spinning and screaming into oblivion.

When she came, Jezebel's knees gave way entirely, and Rafe caught her limp form as she fell, laying her tenderly on the grass and stretching himself out alongside her. Propped on one elbow, still bursting with his own need and his unaccustomed restraint, he kissed her softly back into wakefulness, lavishing her lips with her own fragrant moisture and stroking her hair with one trembling hand. Jezebel's eyes fluttered open, lambent with spent desire.

"What happened?" she whispered, dazed.

"I think you fainted," Rafe replied with a smile, leaning down to kiss her again. The touch of his mouth held no urgency, only lush generosity.

The archaeologist's niece took a moment to absorb that astonishing idea along with her lover's delightful kiss. She had never swooned before in her life, had not even thought herself capable of it. But then, she'd never felt the full measure of Rafe's intimate touch before tonight either. Nothing was as it had been; the old truths could no longer be counted upon. "I mean before that."

"Before that, I gave you pleasure."

"And took none of your own?" Jezebel asked quizzically, not understanding why he would deny himself. Her mind was still hazy, and she could not think very well, especially with those bright aquamarine eyes gazing down into hers with banked passion and a curious kindness she couldn't interpret.

"Oh, I assure you, sweet Jezebel, I took a great deal of

pleasure in what we just did, wrong as it was." Rafe nuzzled her ear, seemingly content to do no more than coax her through the aftershocks of her pleasure, though his swollen member, pressed hard against her hip through the cloth of his trousers, told another story entirely.

Jezebel ignored the moral judgment in his statement for the moment, still fixed on the physical act and savoring the slow tingling waves of rapture that continued to shake her body.

"But why did you not . . ." Somehow, even after what they'd just shared, even though they lay entwined together in the tall grass, herself completely naked and the duke in nothing more than boots and breeches, she still felt shy talking about their lovemaking, or lack of it. Why would he deny himself, when he was so clearly aroused? She didn't understand his restraint at all.

"Why didn't I make love to you, do you mean?" he finished for her.

Jezebel nodded against his shoulder, suddenly feeling unsure of herself again. She didn't like it that while she had flown to the dizzying heights of heaven, Rafe seemed to have remained quite firmly here on earth. Her fears began to resurface. Had he not wanted her as much as she'd thought, after all? How could he so easily walk away from all that she offered? She needed to find out—almost as much as she needed to know the full scope of passion he'd denied her when he denied her his body.

"I wanted you to—still want you to," she confessed in a small voice as she turned onto her side to face him. She stroked the line of his jaw with her fingers, then skipped her hand down to his chest, pausing to play briefly with the light, fluffy curls that covered the upper part before continuing downward to draw a line of cool fire until she reached the waistband of his pantaloons. Stretching to kiss him, Jezebel simultaneously took her courage in her hands even as she took *him* in hand.

"Christ, woman!" Rafe yelped, yanking her palm away from his aching shaft. "Do you think I'm a saint?" He pressed her back down onto the grass, putting space between their bodies, though space was the last thing he wanted at the moment. "I stopped when I did because, wrong as it was to carry things that far, it is nothing compared to the damage that would be done to your reputation and your honor if I did what I'd *really* wanted to do." Rafe was leaning over her now, practically growling with frustration.

"If I'd done what I *really* wanted, I'd have made love to you right here in the grass until the sun came up, and probably some poor sod who'd only meant to water his ox or yak or whatever-the-devil kind of farm creature it is they have around here would come upon us tumbling about in the dirt like a couple of randy goatherds!"

Jezebel started to giggle, his ferocious expression failing utterly to chasten her. She couldn't help relishing his admission of the extent of his desire for her, nor could she prevent the warmth that spread through her even as the cool breeze fanned her naked flesh. She grinned up at Rafe, imagining the look on the face of the poor farmer coming upon them in the dawn's pink light—or on the ox's, for that matter.

"It is not a matter for levity, do you hear? Someone had to take responsibility for calling a halt to our madness before it went too far. If I hadn't stopped when I did, your reputation would have been completely shattered, your chances for making a decent marriage utterly ruined."

Both of them grew quiet at the mention of the word *marriage,* the laughter dying from Jezebel's eyes, and the pent-up desire from Rafe's.

For Rafe, the idea of some other man enjoying what Jezebel had given him so sweetly just moments ago made him sick at heart. He wanted to keep her for his own, take Jezebel to some secluded bower away from the prying eyes of society and make passionate love to her until neither of them remembered the meaning of the words *guardian* or *ward* anymore. But he could not forget that it was his duty to keep her virtue intact, her reputation pure and unsullied, until the day he would hand this precious gift off to some other man—a man who, he was sure, could never begin to appreciate the extent of Jezebel Montclair's many charms, mental and physical, the way he already did.

For Jezebel, Rafe's mention of her possible marriage was like a slap in the face. Though she'd had no illusions about the duke's finer feelings for her, it still came as a shock, after the intimacy they'd shared, to hear him talk of wedding her off as if it were a foregone conclusion that she would agree to this plan, even desire such a thing herself. Nothing, it seemed, had changed between herself and the arrogant Lord Ravenhurst. He still presumed to dictate her life, preach to her about morals, even when the bastard couldn't keep his own hands off her!

Jezebel forced herself to choke out another laugh, though ire and hurt were rising within her almost as quickly as passion ebbed. She tried for a light tone, failed miserably. "I should think I am capable of deciding for myself whether or not I will 'sully' my reputation, don't you?" In truth, she thought with a pang of despair, she had *not* been able to choose. Had he not so high-handedly taken the decision from her, Jezebel doubted she would have had the wit to halt their lovemaking before its ultimate consummation. She wasn't even sure she would have wanted to . . . then. Now, however, the thought of what she had almost done sent cold dread shivering down her spine.

The consequences of such a foolhardy, brainless act were legion, not least of which was the possibility that, once she had tasted the full measure of passion with Rafe Sunderland, she might never be free of his influence. It would be that much harder to leave him as she'd planned, that much harder to lie to him, and that much harder to continue on alone. She should be thanking the man for having the good sense to stop them both before they did something disastrous, instead of feeling hurt by his rejection. But Jezebel didn't feel the slightest bit grateful, only cut so deeply that she knew this was a wound that would never truly heal. Still, she could not afford to let the duke see her pain. Only her anger was safe to show. "After all," she argued, righteous indignation saturating her voice, "it is *my* reputation, *my* honor, to do with as I choose."

"No, Jezebel, it is not!" Rafe practically shouted in return. "It is, in fact, *my* benighted duty to ensure you remain innocent and do no damage to your hopes for the future. It is *my* duty to guide you, choose for you, see to your safety. It is I who must protect you at all costs, even if it be from yourself." *Or* my*self,* he thought, ashamed.

Several dozen hot retorts crowded into Jezebel's throat simultaneously at this incredibly obnoxious pronouncement, the words thankfully choking each other off before she could utter any of them and thereby inflame the volatile situation even more.

"You are insane," was what she settled for at last, a statement delivered flatly as she yanked her robe back over her head and rose unsteadily to her feet. She looked down at the duke, sprawled in all his magnificent glory upon the rushes, his hot gaze glaring up at her. "Completely and utterly insane."

She grabbed her violin off the rock shelf above them in one hand, jerkily ran the other through her snarled hair. "Protect me from *myself*? I cannot begin to understand, nor do I even wish to comprehend such a bizarre and ludicrous statement, Your Grace."

With that, Jezebel turned on one heel, stalking stiff-backed from the scene of her aborted seduction and heading deliberately for her tent.

Rafe could see her shaking her head as she went.

"That, my dear," His Grace said to the empty air, one hand covering his eyes wearily, "is exactly why you need a guardian."

# Chapter Sixteen

*Jezebel* had never been so happy to see anyone in her life.

"Belzoni!" she cried, leaping from the dahabeah so hastily the large, wide-keeled boat wobbled and rocked as if it might capsize. In another second she was in his arms, pounding the gigantic engineer on the back with such hearty slaps that even he was a bit staggered. From the way she greeted him, any outside observer would have to assume the two had been parted for years, rather than the scant month that had passed since their last meeting in Cairo.

Nonplussed, the normally effusive Italian patted her awkwardly on the back. "So nice to see you too, *cara mia*. Did you have a pleasant tour?" Belzoni's gaze wandered curiously behind her and took in the tall, scowling duke just now disembarking a deal more cautiously than his ward.

"Fine, fine," Jezebel assured breezily, brushing off the topic as if the past weeks of her trip with Lord Ravenhurst had been a routine occurrence, rather than the greatest series of emotional upheavals she would ever hope to suffer. "But where is my dear protégé Gunther? He hasn't been giving you too much trouble, has he?"

"I have not burdened Herr Belzoni overmuch, I hope," Gunther said sulkily, coming down the hill to greet the group at the landing site. The fabled Valley of the Kings—actually a series of rocky hills and valleys pitted with man-made caves and crevices that stretched for nearly a square mile—began just beyond their sight beneath the western cliffs opposing the city of Thebes across the river.

Belzoni rolled his eyes, but politely did not dispute Gunther's statement.

"Of course you have not," Jezebel said warmly. Her dazzling smile erased any sting her earlier comment might have caused. "Well, I'm sure we all have a great deal of catching up to do, my friends—you must tell me all about your excellent finds, and His Grace and I will of course fill you in on our own little adventures." The ones she could recount in polite company anyway, Jezebel thought darkly, which weren't many. Shaking off the thought, she linked arms with both men and turned to steer them away from the little jury-rigged pier, ignoring the duke entirely.

"Yes, indeed. We shall have a great deal to talk about tonight." She sent a glance replete with significance in Belzoni's direction, and he nodded his understanding discreetly, obviously recalling where she had just been and what she had hoped to find there. "But for now, why don't you show us about the camp, and then we can get our things settled in." The trio started up over the hills to the dig site, seemingly oblivious to the fact that the duke was not following.

Rafe stood abandoned on the rickety little dock while the party's bearers edged their way around him warily, carrying his own and Jezebel's gear off the boat. He watched as the porters who'd gone ahead with the camels and lighter supplies (as they had on each previous leg of the journey) reunited with their fellows from the dahabeah, spitting endless streams of betel juice from their stained lips and exchanging river gossip jovially. He himself was not feeling particularly jovial. No, he thought pensively. Jovial was assuredly *not* the word he would use to describe his mood.

It seemed he was the only one his little ward was not happy to see.

$\mathscr{I}$t was possible, Rafe had been told upon arrival by the obsequious, frequently bowing Turk who seemed to be the encampment's version of a majordomo, to have almost any modern convenience the duke desired delivered for His Grace's comfort within an hour of the asking. Indeed, he'd soon discovered, the little settlement was quite a bizarre study in upperclass British taste. Bone china and Irish linen were de rigueur for the obligatory high tea, served precisely at four in the shade of an enormous, eagle-faced statue that had certainly never been meant to preside over the poppy-cakes and cucumber sandwiches that were included.

If one wanted to bathe, as Rafe learned the hard way that afternoon, a dozen eager servants would practically dunk you into a copper hip bath (produced from Lord only knew where) and knock each other over competing to scrub your back. If you wanted a brandy, the finest oak-aged distillation, served in a leaded crystal balloon snifter, appeared before your nose so fast the fumes would burn your nostrils. And all this took place in the eerie shadow of the desolate valley's walls, slotted here and there with deep rectangular shafts where once had rested kings so mighty the world had quaked beneath the stomping heels of their golden sandals.

Coming after the much more spartan comforts of his sojourn with Jezebel, which, until now, he'd deemed surprisingly comfortable considering the uncivilized terrain, this sudden overwhelming luxury felt rather surreal to Rafe. The men of this expedition certainly lived well!

Still, despite the comfortable surroundings, after a communal dinner replete with polite chitchat and awkward silences, the group had quickly disbanded, each going their separate ways. Jezebel, in particular, had expressed a desire to retire early, claiming exhaustion from their journey. Rafe was fairly sure her exhaustion stemmed from the extraordinary lengths she'd gone to in the last two days to avoid him—even more so than she'd done before their illicit encounter by the riverbank.

Doing a little avoidance of his own, he'd made sure that the tent Jezebel had been assigned was pitched well away from his own, yet still within his line of sight. Though he didn't have the fortitude to test himself with too much of her proximity after what had nearly happened two nights ago, he didn't trust his ward not to flee him again should the opportunity arise. Though she'd shown surprisingly little inclination to escape of late, seeming to have accepted the decree he'd laid down regarding her future at Abu Simbel, he still wouldn't put it past her—especially after their latest debacle.

He had been an utter cad, Rafe thought remorsefully, staring out into the evening's blankness. Night had fallen, the lucent blue dusk fading slowly to black while he sat by the tent he'd been given, thinking miserably about how he'd failed in his duties over the past month or so. He had truly let his ward down, for she had a right to expect far better from him, he knew. His oh-so-noble "restraint" two nights ago was no better than a joke—and a poor one at that.

*Restraint,* he scoffed, cursing himself. *Ha!* When it came to Jezebel, he had none. Though he might not have taken her virginity that night up in the hills, he had most certainly taken her innocence, and the guilt was eating him alive. No proper young lady should experience such carnal knowledge with a man not her husband, even though, in her naïveté, she might think she wanted it. And no self-respecting gentleman would dream of providing it. He was an absolute bounder.

How had this uncharacteristic behavior come about? he wondered. How had this little chit, a girl still barely out of the schoolroom, managed to twist him into such knots and caused him to act with such astonishingly bad grace? He'd always been known for his rather cosmopolitan preferences, leaving the young misses to line the walls of society's ballrooms while he and his more worldly partners performed their own pas de deux in private. Never once had he been tempted to dally among the innocent, would not even have dreamed such an inexperienced young woman could begin to pique his fickle interest or satisfy his somewhat jaded tastes.

Yet Jezebel had captured his imagination far more than the most sophisticated of Rafe's past lovers without making even the slightest effort. Indeed, even when she did her best to anger or disgust him, as she frequently did, the Honorable Miss Montclair enchanted and charmed him in ways he could not comprehend—ways he did not want to explore. He had but to look at her, and he wanted her.

He wanted to hear her low, throaty voice mumbling a taciturn greeting at him while she hunched irritably over her morning coffee. He wanted to see the enthusiasm shining in her eyes when she described some archaeological theory so esoteric even the well-read duke had trouble following her train of thought. In truth, he wanted all of her—constantly, consistently, completely maddeningly.

To date, he had not found any trait in Jezebel that did not make him want to toss up her skirts (or pull down those scandalous pants of hers, he thought with a hint of reluctant humor) and ravish her endlessly. And to date, he had controlled his impulses no better than a randy sixteen-year-old catching the eye of a comely milkmaid.

But things would be different when they reached England, Rafe told himself. They had to be.

Resolved, the duke rose from his seat upon the chunk of crumbled statuary, probably no less than a thousand years old, that anchored the front flaps of his tent against the desert wind. In Egypt, as he'd witnessed many times already, people quickly lost their reverence for the antiquities they were so keen to dig up—if it wasn't made of gold, it was often tossed carelessly in a heap while the discoverer went on to bigger finds. At another time Rafe might have found a certain ironic humor in that, but right now he had bigger concerns.

Taking a deep breath, he set off toward Jezebel's tent. He would apologize to his ward again, reassure her that he would treat her with all honor from now on, and ask if she would not desist from the stubborn, cold silence she'd displayed toward him since the incident. They would leave this place and return to Cairo for the journey home very soon, and Rafe did not want to leave things as they were much longer. He hoped his genuine remorse would thaw Jezebel's heart enough to allow them to rub along somehow.

But when Rafe reached Jezebel's tent, his apologies died in his throat, turning to bitter gall when he realized that not one, but two people occupied the canvas walls.

He felt marginal relief when he recognized the voice of

the second person was Belzoni's, and not the handsome
German's or that of some other young man from the camp
he'd yet to meet. But relief turned to outrage when he heard
what they were actually saying. Their words, carrying quite
clearly through the canvas walls, showed the duke just what
a dupe Jezebel had made of him.

"My friend," Jezebel was saying urgently, "I need you
now as I've never needed you before."

*Y*ou know I will help you however I can, *cara*. What is
it you need?"

"I will explain that momentarily," Jezebel promised,
pacing the confines of the tent agitatedly. "But before I do,
there's something you should know." She stopped and took
a deep breath, hating to entrust her secret even to Belzoni.
The man's lust for treasure, she knew, was legendary. Still,
he already knew more about her quest than anyone else,
even Gunther. Now, with no other choice, she realized she
must tell him the rest. If he would stifle his innate greed
for anyone, she knew it would be for her sake.

"I've found the proof my uncle was looking for."

The Italian sucked in his breath. "The tomb?" he asked
incredulously.

"Not yet." Before Belzoni could say anything more, she
cut him off. "Don't look so disappointed, old friend. What
I've found is something almost as good. You know what I
went to Abu Simbel in search of?"

Belzoni nodded.

"Well, I found it. The same inscription, the same scribe's
hand. Giovanni, *the same cartouches carved upon the
wall!*"

"Not the ones . . ."

"Yes. When the bey ordered you to leave Abu Simbel
so abruptly after opening the temple, you must not have
had time to study all of the writings on the walls. But I did.
And in the inner sanctum, I found something incredible. I
saw the exact same series of symbols there as those you
told my uncle you had uncovered in the tomb of Seti I,

right here in this valley. The cartouches of Rameses II, his father Seti, even Thutmose III, whom you call Young Memnon, and whose great bust you shipped with such difficulty across the seas to the waiting crowds in England—they were all there, together."

The engineer ignored the flattery. "But how does that prove anything? Your uncle thought to find the hidden mummies of all these mighty pharaohs lumped together like so many sticks of firewood among their treasures in one great hidden tomb." He shook his head, obviously believing along with his fellow archaeologists that this theory was ridiculous. "Such a monumental find will never be achieved in this day and age, *cara*—not even by a great excavator like me. You must face the facts, little one, as I urged your uncle to do before he wore himself out on such a fruitless quest. Too many robbers have come and gone before us. All the tombs have already been opened."

"But that's just it!" she broke in excitedly. "The priest who wrote the inscriptions must have been the very one who moved the bodies. He had to know it was only a matter of time before his royal charges were ripped from their burial chambers and defiled, and so he and his fellows secretly removed the mummies from those tombs whose locations were no longer secret, and placed them where thieves would not be able to find them. Why else would all these pharaohs' tombs be empty, and all their names appear together?"

"*Cara*, I can think of a dozen reasons—" Belzoni began, but she cut him off.

"But I'll wager you cannot explain this!" With a flourish, she produced a scrap of paper from her sash, much crumpled and charcoal-smeared. "This was carved directly below the cartouches in Abu Simbel, almost worn away by time. I was forced to redraw it from memory when Lord Ravenhurst"—Jezebel sneered the name—"abducted me from the temple and all of my papers were scattered. But I'm confident of its accuracy."

"This looks like—"

"It *is*. Belzoni, this is a veritable map of the secret tomb's location! See, it's not like the other hieroglyphic text on that wall—not like any I've ever seen or studied in all my time here. You yourself found it when you opened Rameses' temple for the first time in three thousand years. You just didn't see it, you were in such a hurry to leave before the bey made you give up all your treasures." A look of chagrin crossed Belzoni's weathered face, but Jezebel didn't give him a chance to defend himself.

"Lord Clifton suspected there would be an inscription in the temple of Rameses matching the one in Seti's tomb, but he never got the chance to look before his death—as you well know. But not even he could have guessed the scribe would leave what amounts to an actual diagram of the location! I admit, I had my own doubts my uncle would ever find the secret tomb—until I saw this. Right away, I knew what you have just deduced for yourself: the picture looks exactly like a view I've seen a hundred times before—right here in the Valley of the Kings. If only we could decipher the hieroglyphs around it, instead of just identifying the names in the cartouches, I'm convinced I would right now be reading precise directions to the hidden tomb."

Still not willing to completely trust him, Jezebel tucked the paper back into her sash before Belzoni could get a really good look at it. "But I don't need to read directions to find the tomb. I know the landmarks. And I'm betting the entrance isn't completely sealed off—the priests would never have put this inscription on the walls of the temple sacred to Rameses if they did not intend future generations of their brethren to care for his tomb and guard its secret. I'm telling you, it's exactly as my uncle predicted!"

The explorer's niece took a deep breath, excited to have finally shared the incredible discovery with someone who would appreciate it. "And that brings me to the reason I have told you all this, the reason I ask your aid."

Still looking dubious, Belzoni nodded. "As I have said, I will give you any assistance I can. You have only to name it. For your uncle's sake, whom I loved as a comrade in arms, and for you, who seek to do him honor." His broad, mustachioed face was solemn.

"What I need is simple. I need you to get rid of the duke."

*   *   *

*C*rouched outside in the shadow of the tent, Rafe nearly choked at hearing this. She couldn't mean . . . could she?

He felt like the biggest fool in creation. All this time he'd blithely gone about believing he had Jezebel under his control, when the whole while it had been *she* who was leading *him* around by the nose, and he had never suspected a thing. Their whole trip, he now realized, had been orchestrated, not with his edification and pleasure in mind, but solely to satisfy his ward's own clandestine agenda.

From the very start she had known exactly what she was doing, and she had never had the slightest intention of sharing the information. In fact, when she'd realized she couldn't get rid of him as easily as she'd obviously planned to do—and Rafe now wondered if that whole dramatic escape in the Great Pyramid had been engineered ahead of time—she had simply used him and the protection of his presence to get her safely back here to the Valley of the Kings. The stops along the way, designed to keep him from suspecting anything, he guessed, must have been torturous for Lord Clifton's crafty niece, when all she wanted was to get back here as quickly as possible to search for the remainder of the proof that would vindicate her uncle beyond the grave.

It all made sense now, he thought bitterly. The strange sense of urgency he'd felt in her, the silences, and the deep wariness. She had been guarding a secret all along, and she feared he would try to stop her if he knew the truth. She was right about that, Rafe thought. He wasn't sure he believed Lord Clifton's theory as Jezebel had explained it, no matter what proof she claimed to have. And he didn't care how noble her goal was, he told himself, didn't care how cunningly she had planned or how well she had managed to achieve her ends up to this point. He would not allow her to continue searching indefinitely for some mythical tomb while he cooled his heels waiting for her in the middle of some godforsaken desert, neglecting his own affairs! Rafe had played the fool for her long enough.

But that wasn't even Jezebel's plan, was it? he reminded himself with angry amazement. She'd never intended to tell him about her little mission, and she'd certainly never thought to get his permission to fulfill it. No. She had a different scheme in mind.

He could scarcely believe it. Rafe labored under no misconceptions regarding Jezebel's tender feelings for him—she'd showed him again and again that she wished to be shed of him more than anything else. Still, it hurt more than he liked to admit to be confronted with the proof that the incredible passion they'd shared meant nothing to her. After collapsing so sweetly in his arms, spent with the ecstasy he'd given her, he couldn't believe she was cold enough, hard enough, to calmly plan his demise like this. She was a Jezebel in truth if she could do such a thing, the duke thought with a surge of pain. But did she actually think to enlist the engineer's aid in this plot?

Thankfully, the conspirators' next words dispelled that awful fear. Apparently, Belzoni had had the same mistaken impression.

"Get rid of him?" the engineer croaked, appalled. "*Cara,* I don't know what rumors you may have heard about my unsavory past, but I assure you, I have never dabbled in that sort of criminal activity!"

"No, no, you buffoon. I didn't mean kill him! I may despise the man for his arrogant, inflexible ways, but I certainly don't wish him dead!"

Jezebel hoped she managed to sound convincing when she told Belzoni she despised the duke, though she was far from sure that was the right word to describe her feelings for him. The emotions she felt toward Rafe were a great deal more complicated than simple disgust or anger, she knew, but she could hardly tell her old friend as much. Instead she went on as if nothing were wrong.

"Even if I did, I certainly wouldn't ask you to do it," Jezebel said, infusing a hint of laughter into her voice to bolster the effect of nonchalance. "There are cheaper assassins to be bought on almost every street in Cairo. No, all I require from you, my friend, is to distract His Grace tomorrow while I search for the tomb."

"You think to find it in one day?" Belzoni asked skeptically.

"It seems unlikely," she admitted, "despite the precise location on the pictogram. But regardless, I will still only really need you to keep him away for that length of time. If I do not find it in one day, I intend to escape from him once again, but this time, I will make sure he shan't find me. This time I shall be free of him for good."

"How will you do it? The man appears quite determined to me. It seems doubtful that he should give up so easily."

"That's the beauty of my plan, my friend. He will have to give up when he learns that I am dead."

"What?"

A grin spread across Jezebel's face, the emotion honest this time. "I shall fake my own death, of course. With your help. Whether I find the tomb tomorrow or not, I won't be coming back here while Lord Ravenhurst remains in Egypt." Her plan really was brilliant, she thought, and if it caused the duke some pangs of concern at first, well, she was sure he'd not mourn overlong. Indeed, he would probably be grateful to be relieved of his duty to her, once he had the chance to realize the ramifications of her demise. Obviously, duty meant more to him than she did—his refusal to make love to her two days ago had been ample proof of that. Soon enough, she knew, he would be back to his rakehell ways, living it up with his cronies back in England, having forgotten all about his onetime ward.

Jezebel could not explain the sudden pain that blossomed in her heart at that thought, and she dismissed it angrily. She had no time for missish regrets now.

"But what of your inheritance?" Belzoni asked. "If he thinks you dead, you won't be able to receive it. The money will go to someone else."

"That's true." She shrugged. "It seems it is a price I must pay, both for my uncle's sake and for the sake of my independence. But perhaps," she teased, trying to dispel the concern on her friend's face, "someday I shall rise from the dead, like an Egyptian queen of old, and claim my fortune."

The former strongman could see how serious Jezebel

was, despite her jokes. And he knew just how stubborn she could be—very much like that uncle of hers, he thought. "Is there nothing I can do to dissuade you?"

"Nothing."

"Then I must help you, I suppose," he sighed.

"I knew I could count on you, old friend," she said warmly, much relieved. "You'll send me word in hiding once the duke has gone?"

"Of course. But you must tell me your plan for convincing him you have perished. I still don't see how it can be done."

"It will require all of your former acting skills, of course. And perhaps some of Gunther's unique brand of sullen charm as well. . . ."

But Rafe chose not to stay around to hear the details of their dirty little plot. He had heard more than enough to sicken him already.

# *Chapter Seventeen*

～

*T*he duke had been suspiciously compliant when Jezebel suggested he go off alone with the men this morning to view their recent excavations, or so it seemed to her now. He'd left her behind supposedly suffering from a vague "female complaint" with only a polite wish that her health improve quickly. She wouldn't have thought Lord Ravenhurst the type to fall for that sort of flimsy excuse, but then, it was all to the good that he had, wasn't it? She couldn't believe she was wasting time worrying about what her guardian did or did not believe at a moment like this. She should not give him another thought, she reprimanded herself sternly. Not one more damned minute of her time.

For now Jezebel stood on the verge of history. Well, she amended before hyperbole could carry her away, that was only strictly true if history could be said to resemble a rather unprepossessing little hole hidden in the scrub brush about halfway up the side of a cliff. The narrow opening she'd found was located in an area of the King's Valley neglected by most respectable Egyptologists because it was believed to have contained only the burial sites of minor nobles and priests. No one much bothered with this region, the supposedly richer pickings to be found elsewhere being far more alluring to treasure hunters, and so it had been left relatively untouched. Nothing moved here today, except for a high, keening wind that howled fitfully around the weathered edges of the hills. In the strange orange light that had permeated the area since Jezebel had arrived at dawn this morning, the whole place looked haunted.

A legend had spread that this desolate section of cliffs and caves was guarded by an *afrit*, a demon said by the ancient Egyptians to protect the spirits of the dead from all who sought to do them harm. Jezebel, however, was not afraid of demons. She'd never met one in all the tombs she'd explored, and she didn't expect to now. If she was lucky, she *would* encounter a goodly number of dead people today, but she very much doubted if she would find a single vengeful spirit among them. Unwinding the heavy coils of rope she'd brought with her and looking for a place to anchor the end, she could barely contain her excitement.

This was it! She knew it was. She was standing exactly in the spot the pictogram depicted, everything from the slant of light over the cliffs to the curve of the valley floor matching perfectly. And here, just where it should be, was the tiny slot in the sloping cliffside. Below might lurk the greatest discovery in modern Egyptian history.

*Well,* Jezebel thought, *what am I waiting for?* She tried to ignore the tingle of unease inside her, telling herself it was only the isolation of the place and the odd quality of the light today that had unnerved her, and not any fear over the descent she was about to make. True, she usually would not attempt to enter a new burial chamber alone, knowing that it might be full of snakes or hidden pitfalls, but this time she had no choice. Any trouble she got into, she would just have to get out of on her own. But that was fine, she reassured herself. Really, everything was going to work out perfectly. She had Lucinda with her, the gear she'd need for their trek later strapped atop the faithful beast, and, as always, she kept her wits handy. She could handle anything this new adventure threw at her.

*No more delays now, lily-liver,* she chided herself. *Better get going before someone sees you standing around dithering.* Making fast one end of her rope to a large boulder nearby, she quickly lit her lantern and prepared to rappel down into the narrow opening.

*G*old.

The first thing to greet Jezebel's stunned vision when she reached the bottom of the shaft was the unmistakably rich yellow gleam of gold. Piled about everywhere, great heaps of funerary offerings mingled with heavy gilded headdresses, precious jewelry, and electrum-plated statues of every god ever worshiped in the pantheon of the ancient Egyptians. The light from Jezebel's small horn lantern glinted off more riches than a dozen Belzonis could hope to carry. But what interested her was not the immense treasure strewn so carelessly about the narrow chamber deep within the rock. It was the mummies.

*If only I had more light!* she wished futilely. Jezebel let the rope go, ignoring the small shower of stones that rained down about her head. Before her, piled one atop the other against the walls of the tight corridor, were more mummies than she'd ever seen together in one place at one time. *There must be at least thirty bodies here!* she thought jubilantly. But whose bodies were they? That was the important thing. Taking a charcoal pencil and paper from the pack she carried, the determined archaeologist set to work.

*I*t wasn't until the lamp started to gutter and the light to fade that Jezebel snapped out of the trancelike state of utter concentration that had held her in its grip. Good Lord, what was the time? she wondered. There was no way to tell down here, and what little light came from above seemed to have mostly faded, so she thought perhaps evening had already fallen. So long! Jezebel stretched out from the crouch she'd been in, hissing when her knees protested painfully.

So far she'd done no more than catalog the location of most of the mummies, identifying them by some of the many protective amulets they'd been wrapped with and marking their places down on the diagram of the tomb she'd made. The walls of this place were blank, rough-hewn, showing that it had been unfinished, perhaps originally meant for some other less august personage than the ones who'd come to occupy it now. And they were, indeed, among the most famous in history.

Lord Clifton had been more right than even he could have hoped. Studying the golden scarabs and turquoise fetishes, the beads and inscriptions and golden masks of the pharaohs lying here, Jezebel had been able to piece together the identities of many of the mummies that rested along the walls of the corridor. To her great amazement, she'd found that before her lay the immortal remains of the great Rameses himself, of whom the Bible spoke in Exodus, hastily laid out in a plain acacia-wood coffin alongside his father Seti I. Here too were Queen Ahmes, the mother of the controversial female pharaoh Hatshepsut, and, most incredibly, the body of Hatshepsut's brother Thutmose III, broken in three pieces. This man/god had once been the greatest pharaoh and the greatest general in Egypt's history, and Jezebel had stared at the dried-out remains in silent awe for a long moment before moving on.

The mummies rested one atop the other like so many bowling pins knocked down in a child's game. It was awe-inspiring. It was gratifying. It was going to make Lord Clifton the most famous Egyptologist of all time! With tears in her eyes, Jezebel realized that she had truly fulfilled her duty to the man who'd been all things to her for so long: father, mother, confidant, and teacher.

Well, not quite. First she must get out of this place alive, if she wanted to share her discovery with the world. And that was looking a little bit more difficult than she'd originally anticipated, what with the alarmingly large chunks of masonry that were beginning to fall from the opening overhead. Her rope, the only lifeline she had to the outside world, swayed and trembled as fist-sized stones sailed past it, and she could hear a strange howling coming down the tunnel. The wind must be picking up outside. Time to get out of here.

Jezebel grabbed up her satchel, filling it hastily with the pieces she would need to prove that she had found what she sought. Rings, amulets, anything inscribed with the name of a pharaoh went into her bag, while she was forced to leave behind her a fortune in gold and priceless artifacts. She slung the heavy burden across her shoulder and started for the rope. She would have to leave the lantern behind as well, since she couldn't climb with both it and the heavy satchel, and the oil inside had almost run out anyway.

Halfway up the tunnel she knew she had a serious problem. There was a diffuse sort of light filtering down from above along with the noisy wind, but choking dust and bits of stone filled the air, the heavy rope sawing into the crumbled rock and sending more debris down to blind her with each upward lurch. Climbing down to the tomb hadn't been this difficult, she thought anxiously, but then up was always harder than down. Her arms ached from the strain and an ominous rumble filled the air. Jezebel swung one foot up to shoulder level and braced it against the rock to push herself upward.

It was a mistake. The rumble turned to a roar, and, even as the explorer's niece made a desperate bid for the light above, the entire passageway shuddered and collapsed. All was dust and noise and bruising stone for a moment while she hid her head between her arms and hung on for dear life, not daring to move. At last the cave-in seemed to slow, then stop, and, still clinging to her rope with arms that felt like over-attenuated wires of pure pain, she at last dared to look up.

*Hmm,* she thought facetiously. *Not as bad as it could have been.* Ignoring for the moment that she was buried from the shoulders down to her hips in rubble and could not move her torso an inch, while her legs, hanging free beneath, dangled about twenty feet from the bottom of a very unforgiving stone crypt, Jezebel thought she was doing fairly well. It could have been worse, she decided, than being corked inside a tomb with nobody around to help, no one who would look for her in this vast, sprawling complex of the dead—one of whom, it seemed, she was shortly to become. *At least,* Jezebel thought as she struggled to wriggle free and got no more than a scraped shoulder and another rock on her head for her trouble, *there's a bit of daylight left. At least I can see.*

And then a shower of dust obscured everything, blanketing her eyes and making her cough and choke.

"I say, Miss Montclair," came a sarcastic voice. "You seem to be in a bit of a bind. Would you like a hand there?"

Jezebel reflected that that last rock must have hit her a tad harder than she'd reckoned at first. She was either hallucinating or dead already. But the dusty, elegant hand that reached down for her was not imaginary, and it was not the hand of God, either.

"Ravenhurst," she gasped, dismay warring with an absurd elation. "What the devil are you doing here?"

"Shall we discuss that later, my dear, seeing as how you are about to tumble headlong to your death?"

Jezebel nodded enthusiastically up at the blond head that resolved itself above her as the dust cleared. Lord, but he was a sight for sore eyes—which hers, filled repeatedly with dust in the last few minutes, definitely were! Even disheveled and looking about as angry as any human being she'd ever seen, he made her heart leap. "Good idea," she agreed faintly.

Rafe surveyed the situation, keeping his demeanor calm and controlled, even as, inside his brain, a loud voice shouted, *This is* not *good!* His ward was in a very precarious position, wedged between several sizable rocks, her arms pinned in the rubble so that he could not grasp her wrists to lift her to safety. The position she was in reminded him of nothing so much as a babe stuck in the birth canal. However, he doubted he could count on anyone from inside giving her a push. He must think of something else, and quickly, for if her arms gave way, he didn't think the rocks would support her. She would fall back into that dark, deep hole, tons of stone crashing down atop her.

Then he saw it.

"Jezebel, I want you to remain very still."

"I can hardly do much else," she retorted, just to show she had some spirit left.

He ignored the attempt at humor, reaching behind him out of her sight for a moment. When he brought his arm forward again, Jezebel blanched.

"Please, Your Grace! I know I have been a terrible ward, but I don't deserve *that*—please!" She went white with horror at the sight of the large, gleaming knife in his hand.

"Don't be an idiot, girl. I'm not going to kill you, I'm going to get you free. Hold still." Rafe leaned down, his legs dangling outside the entrance to the tomb, the rest of his body angled precariously inside the steep shaft only a foot or so above where Jezebel was trapped. With one hand he took hold of the wide canvas strap of her satchel, his callused fingers brushing her cheek briefly as they moved toward her shoulder. Jezebel held her breath. With the other, he slipped the blade of the knife beneath the strap. Too late, she realized his intention, realized what it would mean.

"No!" she cried.

"I told you, I won't hurt you. Let me just . . . there." The strap parted beneath the sharp blade, and the bag began to slip downward of its own weight.

"Oh, no. No, no, no, no," Jezebel moaned in despair. A moment later, the grip of the stone around her lessened by the absence of the heavy bag, she was free. Even as Rafe pulled her to safety, all she could concentrate on was the distant, heavy crash as the only proof of her uncle's beliefs smashed to the floor of the burial chamber, immediately followed by a storm of heavy boulders that sealed off the entrance. It was all she could do to lie among the dry brush and let the desolation wash over her.

"Are you insane, girl? Do you want to lose your life over a bunch of musty old relics?" Rafe had scrambled to his feet and now stood towering over her, shaking with rage and the concern he would not show.

She sat up, tossing her head angrily. He did not even want to know what she'd found, she thought in amazement. No, all the damnable duke cared about was chastising her for her so-called disobedience. Would he never understand her? "Those relics *are* my life! Haven't you realized that by now?" Hating to be loomed over, Jezebel rose to her full height to face him. It didn't help. Rafe was still a full head taller, and glaring down at her with those flame-blue eyes, he made a menacing sight. "How did you know I was even here?" she demanded. "You weren't supposed to know anything about this. Did you force Belzoni to tell you?"

As if he could force such a colossus to do anything against his will. "Damn it, Jezebel, I knew what you were trying to do because I overheard you last night. Were you trying to make me *think* you were dead with this little stunt, or were you really trying to make a go of it this time?" He was yelling by now, control completely gone. "You are the most reckless, stubborn, foolish, mule-headed woman—"

He would have continued on in this fashion indefinitely, had not Jezebel chosen that moment to place one dainty, dirt-and-cobweb-stained hand across his mouth in mid-rant.

"We don't have time for this right now," she said quietly. Her frightened gaze was fixed at a point on the horizon just over his shoulder.

Not noticing her sudden alarm, Rafe pulled her hand free, looking mad enough to take a bite out of it. "Don't you dare try to hush me, Jezebel! I have finally had as much as I can take! I've got some things to say to you, and you are going to listen to them this time, by God, or you'll be begging for the flat of my hand by the time I'm finished!"

But Jezebel was already stepping past him, headed down the slope toward their camels. With a sinking heart, she saw that both Rafe's beast and Lucinda were kneeling, confirming her fears. In itself it wasn't unusual for them to rest that way, nor a sign of trouble, but when they faced themselves away from an approaching saffron-colored cloud that filled the entire horizon, the long lashes of their triple-lidded eyes squeezed tightly closed, that was a definite, unmistakable signal of danger to come.

"Fine," she tossed over her shoulder as Rafe scrambled after her. "But can we talk about it after the sandstorm?"

# Chapter Eighteen

⌒

"Sandstorm?" Rafe echoed. His voice came out hollow, and his darkly bronzed face went gray with realization.

"Yes," Jezebel confirmed shortly. "There's rather a nasty one headed in our direction as we speak. I estimate it should hit anywhere between five and ten minutes from now." She kept her tone conversational, but her flying fingers, unstrapping their gear from the hunkering camels and tossing necessary items to the ground willy-nilly, told another story altogether. She was terrified.

There had never been a storm of this kind in the Valley of the Kings, not in living memory, and not in any of the legends she'd ever heard. Normally they only hit in the open desert, much farther west of the Nile. Otherwise she would have recognized the signs much earlier—the sullen quality of the light, the oddly pregnant wind blowing in fits and starts—and prepared accordingly, at least as much as anyone could in the face of a killer sirocco. But now it was too late for elaborate preparations. They would have to take their chances in the open, with just the supplies they'd brought with them.

Jezebel had with her only the sturdy canvas tent that she had packed for her planned flight, along with a few woolen blankets and miscellaneous garments. She must assume Rafe would have little more of use. But no tent, staked to the ground in the usual fashion, could hope to withstand the howling winds or the mercilessly abrasive airborne grit that would descend like a horde of angry locusts to devour them alive. They would have to wrap the layers of cloth about them like a shroud and pray it would not become one in truth. What the storm would do to them, trapped in these desolate cliffs where the sand could erase an entire ridge or valley in seconds, Jezebel truly didn't know, but she guessed she was about to find out. She made herself move faster.

Wordlessly, Rafe stepped in to help.

*A*s a matter of fact, the roaring, screaming wall of sand hit them just over six minutes later. By then, the two were wrapped in a cocoon of canvas and wool, the heavy cloth shelter nestled between their two camels and anchored underneath the sturdy humped bodies. Jezebel could only pray for the beasts, knowing that they were better equipped by nature to ride out the simoom than the two humans they protected.

She wondered, somewhat inanely, if Rafe was still angry with her. It was hard to tell. The large, muscular man lying atop her, his long legs surrounding hers, his heavy torso pressing her body into the ground below, his arms like a cradle on either side of her head, didn't move or say a word, but even had he chosen to speak, she wouldn't have been able to hear him over the incredible din. She guessed he had decided to continue his dressing-down of her at some later date—if, in fact, they survived to make such an occasion possible.

They lay still in the grip of the storm, breathing the same air, occupying the same space, wrapped in darkness and noise and each other. And slowly, Jezebel became aware of a third presence hanging heavy in the space between them. Desire.

She couldn't avoid it. There was no place to go, nowhere to escape the sudden surge of unwelcome heat that had nothing to do with the searing wind outside. They were wedged together between the breakwaters composed of their two camels, in a space barely big enough for one but shared by two, Rafe taking the upper position to shield her should the frighteningly fragile barrier of the cloth be rent and the scouring sand take over. But for now the shelter held, rippling and flapping and enclosing the two in a world all of their own.

This moment had been a long time coming, and whether hers was a lunacy created by the shrieking of the wind, or some deeper madness within, Jezebel suddenly knew that she wanted the inevitable to happen. It might be wrong, it might be disastrous for her sanity and self-respect, but she wanted it—more than anything she'd ever wanted before. And she knew they might never have another chance to explore the full measure of the attraction that bound them. They could well be dead by morning.

Above her, she sensed that Rafe was feeling the same pull—his whole body had gone rigid, as if he still sought to fight the temptation she knew in her heart she'd already yielded to. Just to make sure he could not resist any better than she, Jezebel curved one hand about the back of his neck and brought his mouth close to hers, almost daring him to deny her. Their breathing, hot and rapid, mingled in the bare inch of space between them.

She thought she heard her name being sighed in the wind, but could not be sure, and in another instant ceased to wonder about it, for other concerns had taken precedence. Rafe's lips had taken hers in a kiss so meltingly alive and rich with sentiment that all his earlier skillful caresses seemed to fade in comparison. This was something different, something more.

This was a surrender and a conquering both, an acknowledgment of what was to happen and a deep yearning for its culmination. It was lush and seeking and giving all at once, and Jezebel's desire, newly roused, roared to life more powerfully than the storm outside. She gasped with the intensity of it, clinging to the man she hated and needed and wanted so deeply, the man who had saved her life and so often sought to control it.

"Rafe," she whispered achingly, though she knew he couldn't hear. And then she kissed him back.

He sank beneath a world of heady desire when she returned the tender caress of his mouth, every last shred of decency and reserve lost in the need to have Jezebel, to take her at last as he'd wished from the moment he'd first seen her—and even before, in his dreams. Though he knew it was wrong, the fear he'd felt for her safety and the anger

at her deception now were transmuted into the deeper, truer
emotion that rested in his heart. He could not name it, but
he could express it with each kiss he laid upon the sweet,
rosebud lips of the woman who'd ensnared him so deeply
in her wiles.

He kissed her with long, slow caresses of his lips and
tongue, his arms sliding around her slender back and swan-
like neck to hold her ever closer to him. He felt, rather than
heard, her sigh of pleasure as his mouth shaped hers, and
he wedged his body more firmly against the pliant curves
below him. He could feel each inch of her curvaceous figure beneath the layers of their clothes, knew that these bar-
riers must be removed, and slowly set to work easing the
fabric from their bodies.

Sooner than she could have imagined, they were both
naked and the shock of Rafe's warm, hair-roughened skin
pressing against her own made Jezebel cry out with longing. She surged up against him, urgency overcoming her.
She needed to feel him everywhere at once. She needed his
hands upon her body, his lips tasting her breasts and her
belly as they had before. And she needed what he had not
given her before. But Rafe was taking his time.

It was as if he'd never made love before tonight, Rafe
thought. Nothing he'd ever experienced with any other
woman could compare to the rapture he felt simply kissing
Jezebel. Even as his body raged and pleaded with him to
hasten his pace, he yet found a strange contentment confining his attentions to her velvety lips, kissing her over and
over until she was sobbing with need. But at last even that
ecstasy was not enough, and Rafe began a slow, tender
exploration of her body that left her weak and writhing
helplessly beneath him. His lips never left hers as he
stroked her luscious breasts, fondled the nipples, and teased
the undersides. They never left her mouth when he sent his
sensitive fingers questing lower, across her belly and down,
combing through the soft curls guarding her femininity.

He caught her moan of delight in his mouth as he tenderly prepared her for his loving, spreading her thighs with
the gentle urging of his knees, his fingers dipping in between them to spread her own honeyed moisture across her

nether lips with lingering strokes that had her weeping her pleasure in his ear, lurching upward for more of the delicious torture. Her own hands were sliding frantically back and forth across the smooth, hard-muscled flesh of his back and hips. She urged him closer with her own kisses, showing him her readiness with the complete surrender of her mouth and the unrivaled passion of her soul.

The storm raged outside, the noise and heat drowning out the rest of the world, drowning out sanity until there was only feeling, raw and elemental, rising to unbearable heights between them.

Just when Jezebel thought she could not stand the torment of longing one moment more, felt sure she would die if he did not fulfill her instantly, she felt Rafe's weight settling carefully between her spread legs, the blunt tip of his phallus pressing against the entrance to her body. For an instant, she tensed as he stretched her with his swollen length; then, as he deepened their unending kiss, she relaxed and let him inside her body as if he'd always been meant to rest there.

There was no pain, only a sensational fire such as she had never known before. Every cell and nerve in her body screamed a welcome to her lover, flowering for him as he sank his heavy shaft inside her to the hilt.

This was beyond lovemaking. This was pleasure so intense that pain paled before it. Rafe cried out helplessly, overwhelmed with tender rapture as he felt Jezebel surround him with her incredible wet heat. Again and again he surged into her, finding the rhythm of her untried body and matching it to give her maximum pleasure, for each ripple of ecstasy she experienced sent him spinning atop a similar wave.

They strained lovingly against each other, sweat-slicked flesh sliding against flesh until the moment when the storm outside and the storm inside became one. In one blinding instant, climax overcame them, and, crying their pleasure against each other's lips, Rafe and Jezebel ascended the heights of passion together.

This time, Rafe was fairly certain they both fainted.

# *Chapter Nineteen*

*She* didn't want to leave him. It shocked Jezebel to realize just how much she truly did not want to let Rafe go.

She lay in the curve of his arm and listened as the sounds of the slowly dying wind mixed with the soft sighing of her lover's sleeping breath. Next to her ear, it was a gentle respiration, reminding her painfully of the exquisite tenderness he had shown—tenderness that had been almost entirely absent from her life up to now. No one had ever recognized her deep, aching need to be treated with such gentleness before. No one had ever cared enough to notice. But ironically, it was his very caring, his protectiveness, that had devastated Jezebel so completely. Her gut clenched around a knot of sorrow.

There was nothing here for her now, that much she had realized even in the moments before the storm had struck last night. With only the best of intentions, Rafe had managed to destroy Jezebel's last hope of fulfilling her oath to Lord Clifton when he cut the cord of her satchel, sending the proof she needed crashing back to its resting place inside the unfinished tomb.

He had saved her life, but with the very same act he had taken away the purpose that had guided it. Still, Jezebel knew she was lucky to be alive, and she could not honestly say she regretted the quick action the duke had taken to release her from the collapsing tunnel.

Nor did she regret any of what had happened afterward. Being caught in the grip of a sirocco with Rafe Sunderland had been the most intensely moving experience of her life. But now the storm was over, and she must salvage what she could, gather both the scraps of her life and her sanity as best she could. It would probably be easier to rebuild her life than her shattered emotions, Jezebel thought sadly.

Miraculously, the sand seemed to have been scoured from their shelter, rather than piled in drifts upon it. She could see the first inkling of dawn's pinkish light leaking even through the weave of the heavy cloth, and the air was fresher now than it had been, rather than growing more stale and stifling as she'd feared would happen if they'd been buried. Even the camels seemed to have been spared, for she could feel their breathing on either side of her as she reached out to touch the living walls that had been their saving grace. Everything within their little refuge seemed to be untouched.

The same would not be said of the rest of the valley, Jezebel knew. When she slipped out from beneath their tiny canvas refuge, she knew she would find before her a world that was utterly changed. There would be no trace now of the pharaohs' tomb she'd sought so diligently. Every crack and crevice within miles would have been eradicated or reshaped. If the cave-in had not been enough to conceal the entrance to the chamber, last night's freak sandstorm had surely obscured it beyond all recognition. It might take years, and the work of hundreds of diggers, to find it again in the altered landscape. Years and resources she did not have. Her life here, as Rafe had said what seemed a thousand years ago, was over.

Briefly, she considered doing as the duke willed and accompanying him to London as his ward. *Would it really be so bad?* she dared to ask herself. *Would it be such a mistake to accept his guardianship?*

Rafe's muscled forearm, dusted with a light furring of golden hair, tightened about her waist at that moment, pulling her closer against his chest, and Jezebel's heart turned over.

*Yes*, the answer came. It would be the most terrible mistake she could ever make. Even now, feeling him nuzzling her neck as he slept, hearing the soft sigh of pleasure that eased from his sculpted lips, she knew she had already succumbed to the same madness that had destroyed her mother so many years ago. Her need for this man consumed her in ways she'd never dreamed of, made her weak and help-

less and frightened—sensations she had never once experienced in an entire life spent adventuring!

Perhaps it would be different if she knew his feelings
for her were similar, if she knew Rafe needed her with the
same obsessive desire she felt each time he was near. But
Jezebel did not know that. She had seen no indications that
the duke shared her lunacy. What she had seen was only
the lust of a man faced with an eager, willing woman who
had fairly begged him, time and again, to give in to temptation and take what was so freely offered.

Ravenhurst had probably had a hundred encounters as
earthshaking as the one they'd shared last night. Such carnal ecstasy was probably quite commonplace to him, Jezebel told herself, forcing herself to acknowledge the bitter
truth. The only thing keeping him with her was the over-
developed, misguided sense of duty that seemed to rule
Rafe's life—without it, she knew he would have left her
already. It was only she who was possessed by such madness, only she who could not see their passion for the mo-
mentary pleasure it had been. Only she who wanted more.

She didn't want Rafe to return to England without her.
Therefore she would make sure he did. It was as simple as
that.

But first she would take one last memory to carry with
her in the lonely days to come.

Even as daylight began to penetrate the sullen clouds of
dust still slowly settling over the Valley of the Kings, Jezebel turned in Rafe's arms and woke him with the sweet
fire of her feverish kisses. She caressed him as if to memorize every line of his lean frame, to imprint the planes of
his body on her palms. She rose above him, sliding her
slender body atop his larger one as if she would blanket
him with her silken flesh, driving him on with hot words
and hotter touches.

His response, slow at first but infinitely willing, mounted
as their bodies mingled in the first light of morning, their
caresses ever bolder and more intimate until at last he could
deny them both no longer. Rafe urged her down upon his
straining shaft, gasping with his eagerness and her frenzied
need. She took him inside her as if they had forever to

squeeze into a day, her urgent cries and the frantic writhing of her body telling eloquently of the desperate longing she could never admit. And when she peaked, Jezebel almost believed the loss of her soul to this man, a gift she hoped he'd never know he possessed, was a price she'd pay again.

*H*e'd known she was going. Even as he felt himself falling into an exhausted sleep after that second incredible round of lovemaking, Rafe had known he would wake alone. He'd learned at least that much of Jezebel Montclair in the past weeks, if not enough to make her stay. Being proven right didn't make the ache in his heart any less painful, however. And it didn't lessen his determination to get her back, willing or no.

Knowing she would probably run when he came after her yesterday, he had planned ahead for Jezebel's defection. Rafe had no fear now that he'd fail to recapture her, for he had taken the one thing he knew she would always come back for, the one thing she could not do without.

While she'd been inside the tomb yesterday, rifling the bodies of kings, he himself had not been wholly idle. He had arrived just in time to watch Jezebel lower herself into the passage—no coincidence, since he'd been following her from the moment she left the camp, having shrugged off the anxious Belzoni and his German cohort as soon as the group of men had ridden out of view of the camp. After assuring himself his ward had not been injured in her harrowing descent into the burial chamber, he'd calmly gone through her baggage, finding and transferring the item he sought from her set of packs to his. Then he had set himself down in a patch of shade beside the crevice where she'd disappeared, determined to wait her out.

He could not explain why he had given Jezebel that last chance to find what she'd been looking for, when he'd every right to storm down there and yank her out by her glossy black hair, dragging her back to camp—and to England for that matter—whether she liked it or not. If he *had* gone in to fetch her, or stopped her from entering the tomb in the first place, perhaps she would not so nearly have perished during the harrowing cave-in. He had exposed her to danger by allowing her to pursue her ambitions, against all sense and duty. But with Jezebel, none of his former logic seemed to apply. And so he had inexplicably waited for her to emerge on her own, letting her take the time she needed to finish her business in the tomb.

Now he would wait again, for he had at least accomplished one act of intelligence during that day full of lunacy.

Rafe arose from the remnants of their former refuge, shaking sand like a wet dog and blinking in the glaring sunlight. As expected, only one camel's bellow greeted him, and only one pack of supplies was at his feet. But it was the *right* pack. As he stared out into the reshaped landscape before him, with grim satisfaction the duke patted the heavy canvas bag that held his belongings. It was the heavier by the weight of one heirloom violin.

He would see Jezebel again.

# *Chapter Twenty*

∽

 𝒯he note read simply:

> *Come and fetch your property aboard the clipper ship*
> *Gertrude by nine o'clock in the evening on the twenty-*
> *ninth, or I shall toss it overboard.—R. S.*

When Belzoni relayed it to her, saying little but offering silent apologies with his eyes for failing to distract the duke, Jezebel only smiled painfully and patted her anxious friend on the back, telling him everything would be all right. Saying a quick good-bye and asking the man to look after Gunther for her should she not return, Jezebel herself was far less sure.

Only one thing was certain. She would see the duke again.

𝒯hey were to meet in Rafe's spacious cabin aboard the clipper ship, or so the steward who'd directed her here had assured her. But when Jezebel arrived promptly at nine, it was to an empty cabin. It seemed her nemesis had not deigned to make an appearance as yet. Anxiously, she searched the room, tried every chest and cabinet in the place, but all were securely locked and she could not locate any keys. Somewhere in here, Jezebel was sure, the duke had hidden her violin, and her frustration grew as she pried uselessly at the heavy furnishings.

At last she gave up the effort, settling for taking up a sentinel post by the door and watching the last purple streaks fade from the clouds, framed by the duke's north-facing window. It shouldn't surprise her that he would have secured himself a berth on the so-called "posh" side of the ship, she thought irrelevantly, her nervousness making her thoughts scatter randomly. Of course he would know the meaning of the newly coined acronym "portside out, star-board home," having learned from the East India Company men who traveled this route regularly how the unbearable heat of the southern sun would bake one side of the ship heading east, the reverse on its return to England. And of course he would make sure his accommodations were nothing but the best. He was the duke of Ravenhurst, after all.

Christ, what was she doing thinking such inane thoughts at a time like this? Jezebel chastised herself. She knew she would need all of her wits to survive the coming encounter, yet she was already wound tighter than a Swiss clock, feeling crazier than the cuckoo inside.

It was full on nine-thirty before Rafe sauntered into the room, and when he did, he did not even pause to greet her! The duke simply made his way across the darkened cabin, carrying a single candle to light the space, the flickering flame throwing more shadows than light across the tense tableau until he set it in its holder upon a small table in the corner next to a wing-backed chair. At last, moving as if he had all the time in the world, Rafe sat himself down and turned his face to her. One brow rose expectantly as if to question her presence in his cabin.

Unnerved by his strange attitude, Jezebel spoke harshly. "I'm here," she snapped. "Where is it?"

"Where is what, my dear?" he asked, pausing to light a fragrant cigar and puff it into glowing life. "I'm afraid I don't know what you're talking about." Rafe sprawled out in the padded grip of the enormous leather chair, his expression evincing a scarcely polite level of interest. If she hadn't known better, she would have thought the duke was barely awake, his heavy-lidded eyes and slouched posture suggesting he'd much rather be napping than talking to an insignificant little nuisance like her. But Jezebel did know better, and if her anger hadn't matched his own, she would have run from the enormity of the banked fury she sensed in him.

The smoke drifted across the space between them and stung Jezebel's nostrils. Fleetingly, she wished for a cigar of her own, thinking perhaps if she had one, she might appear as relaxed and in command as the duke. She was anything but, however, and she knew it showed. The sight of him, tall, loose-limbed, and handsome as sin, was making her knees weak and tampering with the bracing anger she'd mustered to defend herself against this meeting.

The last time they had met, they'd made such sweet love that the memory of it still brought tears to her eyes. It seemed as if only moments instead of days had passed since the intimacy that had so devastated her soul. But she must not show Rafe how much he affected her, she told herself sharply; not when the only emotion on *his* shuttered face seemed to be pure, absolute contempt for her.

"You know damn well what I'm talking about," she said after a pause that was telling. "My violin. I want it. It's mine and you've no right to keep it from me." Not for anything else would she have returned after the craven way she'd left Rafe in the aftermath of the storm. She could barely stand the pain of seeing the disgust written on his longed-for visage, when she'd resolved only days before to shut him from her memory for good. But her mother's violin was the one possession Jezebel could not bear to leave behind.

In her life she'd been forced to abandon many things as her travels with her uncle demanded. Friends, homes, pets, and practically every possession she'd ever prized at one time or another had all been sacrificed for space or practicality or simply because her uncle was in a hurry to get to his next destination and could not be bothered with extensive packing. She hadn't complained, doing whatever was necessary to keep her life with Lord Clifton on an even keel. But through it all, Jezebel had managed to hold on to her violin, keeping it safe beside her while everything else was scattered to the four winds. She could not leave it now, even when it meant facing the agony of seeing Rafe again. Even when he was behaving like such a cruel, taunting stranger to her now.

"Oh, that." He waved negligently as if the matter were

of no importance to him. "Of course you may have it back—just as soon as we reach England." He smirked.

She'd known this meeting was a setup, that he would try to return her to the homeland she'd abandoned when still only a child. What else could he want? What else had he wanted all along? But she'd had no choice about appearing tonight, so it really didn't make a difference that Rafe sought to trap her. Jezebel sighed and removed the pistol from her sash. This was becoming a very familiar refrain.

"I would rather have it *now,* if you please, Your Grace," she demurred. Her tone was utterly implacable. "I won't ask again."

A very similar pistol appeared in Rafe's hand, seemingly from thin air. "I believe I've already given you my answer," he replied levelly, holding his gun pointed directly at her chest. "The matter is not up for debate."

The move surprised a laugh out of Jezebel. "You wouldn't shoot me," she scoffed.

"And neither would you shoot me, Jezebel. If you were going to, you'd have done it by now."

"You don't know that—"

"And you don't know that I'm not just sick and tired enough of your constant disobedience and wayward ways to put a bullet through you and end both our miseries right here and now. Think about it, my dear. Who would ever know if I simply tossed your sweet body over the side of this ship tonight? Why, you'd barely make a splash, I'll wager. And then I'd be free to return to England, having only to claim I never found you—or better, found you were already dead upon my arrival. I could even claim your little fortune for my own, should I so desire," he finished, a thread of cruelty lacing his conversational tone.

Jezebel's mind was so busy entertaining these lurid images that she didn't notice that the rhythm of the rocking floorboards beneath her feet had shifted to a deep, rolling swell sometime in the past few minutes. She was too mesmerized by the mocking blue flames of his eyes to notice anything else. Then she shook her head, clearing it of her morbid fantasies. "You'd never do that. You're far

too . . ."—she choked off the word as if it sickened her—
"*responsible*. You're not capable of such a dastardly act."

"Well, thank you *so* much for that tremendous vote of
confidence," Rafe said dryly. He tapped out his cigar in the
ashtray conveniently placed beside him, then rose from his
chair, ignoring her widening eyes and the wavering pistol
that tracked his every movement. "And you're right. I am
not such a bastard as all that." He strolled over to one of
the large, locked cabinets set into the wall, placing his pistol
casually down next to the ashtray on the side table as he
went. Sighing dramatically and shaking his head like a man
who has given up trying to be a tyrant when everyone
knows he is really just a soft-hearted fool, he fished for a
moment in his trousers pocket, coming up with a key and
unlocking the cabinet.

"I'm not even hard-hearted enough to keep your little
treasure from you any longer, to tell you the truth." Rafe
removed Jezebel's violin, still carefully packed in its worn
case, and proffered it to her, neck first. "Here, take the
thing. I certainly have no use for it."

Jezebel made a grab for the case, still holding her gun
protectively in front of her. The precious instrument in her
hands, she hesitated warily, uncertain why he was letting
her have it so easily, but not about to miss her opportunity.
Now that she had what she'd come for, it was time to make
her escape. She wanted to say something—to curse him,
rail at him, or possibly just say good-bye—but no words
would come forth from her tight throat when she tried. Instead, under Rafe's inscrutable gaze, she merely turned
mutely for the door and fled.

She got about three steps before his casual question
stopped her.

"Just as a matter of curiosity, how do you plan to swim
for shore with that case strapped to your back?" he asked
idly.

Her heart sank straight to her toes.

He didn't have to say it. Like a cat toying with a mouse
it has caught firmly between its paws, he'd played with her,
and she had fallen for the bait. All the while he'd kept her
talking, the *Gertrude* had been putting out to sea! Now that

she was paying attention, she realized that the ship was already in motion, its sailors shouting to and fro as they sent the clipper off on its long voyage to England. She was trapped.

"But . . . the steward assured me the ship was not scheduled to depart until tomorrow's tide . . ." she protested feebly.

"Yes, I really shall have to commend the man on a fine job of acting. Not his usual forte, or so he assured me, but I find it's amazing what talents people will suddenly develop when you make it clear you own the controlling interest in their shipping operation." Rafe smiled mockingly at her.

She had lost.

The situation was beyond hope—there would be no miraculous escape for Jezebel this time. No one on board would help her, she realized. Not when the duke probably owned the entire shipping line this clipper belonged to, and not when all he had to do to brush aside any protests she might make to the passengers or crew aboard her was to shrug and say his new ward was being recalcitrant about returning to her homeland. Indeed, should she attempt to explain the truth of her situation—omitting the intimacy they'd shared, of course, for she'd no intention of ever revealing *that* to anyone—Jezebel knew it would do her no good. In the eyes of the world, Lord Ravenhurst had every right to do as he was doing. Every right to abduct her and drag her off to a foreign land.

Jezebel acknowledged her defeat with a dull sense of amazement. It seemed that, after years of avoiding it, she was finally going back to England, and she was doing it in the company of the very *last* person she would have chosen to smooth her return. She saw the pistol shaking in her hand, and, knowing it was useless now that the ship was under way, she absently tucked it back inside her belt. There had never really been a question of her shooting Rafe. But even emptied of the weapon, her hands continued to tremble. She was afraid, she realized. Deeply afraid, and not just of her confusing feelings for the guardian who had tricked her into this abominable position.

For the first time, Jezebel admitted to herself that there was more to her reluctance to return to England, the homeland that seemed so much more alien to her than any of a dozen more exotic destinations, than she'd previously admitted. Jezebel, who had already seen and done so much more in her short life than most women ever would, who was known and respected even by her detractors for her bravery and adventurous heart, felt a terrible, gnawing anxiety in her gut at the mention of merry old England.

What would they make of her there, a girl who hated to wear skirts and felt more at ease climbing mountains barehanded than decorating altar cloths with tiny needlepoint stitches? How would London society take to a woman who felt greater joy dancing with Gypsies by the light of a crackling bonfire than pacing the steps of a gavotte beneath a crystal chandelier? They wouldn't take to her at all, she knew. Just as they hadn't taken to her mother, once Natalya's wilder side had shown itself.

They had shunned the Russian émigré who'd married into their world, left her alone in the country with a husband who neglected her and a daughter who could not help stave off the pain. And that isolation had killed Natalya as much as her growing madness had done. It was loneliness, in the end, that had driven her over the edge of endurance. In a deep, secret part of herself that she could barely acknowledge even in her mind, Jezebel had always feared that this would be her fate as well if she returned to face her birthright.

At least in Egypt, her eccentricity had been indulged, for the European expatriate community was filled with those who had chosen to live outside the normal scope for one reason or another, but Jezebel did not delude herself that such would be the case in London. Society was much stricter there, she knew, more formal and rigid in what it would allow. The elite clique of snobs, social climbers, and overprivileged aristocratic parasites who had closed ranks against Natalya Montclair for her immoderate ways might well attempt to destroy her daughter as well. Though she told herself it was cowardly to fear the very group that had spawned her, Jezebel simply could not bear the thought of being exposed to their casual cruelty and having no means of escape. But it seemed she was going to *have* to bear it. Rafe had left her no choice.

"Damn you," she swore. It seemed hopelessly inadequate.

"Damn me all you like, Jezebel," Rafe countered, and for the first time his anger leaked through the facade of insouciance he'd masked it with. "But it won't do you any good. You are coming back to England with me."

He paused. Then, as if he'd just thought of it, he added, "Oh, and here's another little fact for you to swallow while we're at it. When we get there, you'd better prepare for a wedding." He stopped again to let the importance of his next words sink in.

"You and I, Jezebel, are getting married."

Had the world gone mad?

A red haze of fury came down over Jezebel's eyes as she stared in disbelief at her guardian. Did he truly think to taunt her thusly? It was beyond bearing! First he told her she must learn to swim with the sharks that inhabited his perilous, glittering world, and then he threw *this* at her? As jokes went, this one was beyond cruel. She knew the rakish Lord Ravenhurst had no interest in spending the rest of his life with her, would as soon hand over his duchy as his freedom. Hadn't he admitted his plans to pawn her off on someone else as quickly as possible right from the very start? So why would he now turn around and tell her he wished to wed her himself? It made no sense at all!

Rafe had no love for her—indeed, his hatred at this moment was quite palpable. This bizarre pronouncement of his must be a jest meant to hurt her somehow. Unless . . . unless, Jezebel thought incredulously, he really *did* mean it, and he demanded they wed simply because his damnable sense of duty required it of him. It was just possible, she realized. The man had more stiff-necked honor than a Round Table full of Galahads. Yet, whether he was serious in his proposal or not, the insult was just as vicious.

To be taunted was bad enough. To be wed out of pity was even worse.

Wounded to the core, Jezebel struck back with as much

cruelty as her aching heart could muster. "I'd sooner wed a goatherd than bed down with you again!" she hissed.

Rafe's face grew stiff, and sparks seemed to shoot from his light eyes when he snapped, "Marry me, or marry another, Jezebel, but whichever you choose, you *will* be wed. What happened between us demands no less."

His words made the truth clear to Jezebel. It *was* pity that prompted this reluctant proposal—pity or guilt, or both. He obviously felt a deep regret for what they had done in the Valley of the Kings. The act that had been so poignant and beautiful for her had been no more for Rafe than a tumble the duke already rued. The pain that rose inside Jezebel was intolerable.

"Then I choose to marry another!" she cried recklessly.

For a moment she feared that he would strike her, so great was the fury that suffused his handsome features. She refused to flinch, staring with blazing defiance at the man who'd dared to make her such an ultimatum—the man who had dared to pity her.

Rafe took a deep breath. "So be it," was all he said. Then he turned his back on her.

Not another word was spoken between the two during the whole of the six-week voyage.

LONDON HARBOR, LATE MAY 1818

It wasn't often one received a plea for help from the duke of Ravenhurst.

The missive had arrived at Lady Allison Mayhew's abode earlier this morning, and now, rousted out of bed well before her usual hour but far too curious to mind, she sat in her carriage on the docks of London Harbor, waiting for the ship carrying her cousin and his little ward to clear customs and allow the passengers to disembark.

Allison tapped the single sheet of thick, creamy vellum thoughtfully against her perfectly rounded chin. The note had been singularly terse and uninformative, merely reminding her of the promise she had made several months earlier to assist His Grace in chaperoning his young ward when she arrived, and telling her that, delays notwithstanding, he would still appreciate her assistance. Would she mind very much appearing today on the docks to greet them?

The Season was in full swing by now, and Allison had had to cancel a number of engagements to be here, but she did it willingly, eager for the chance to repay her cousin just some of the longstanding debt she owed him. But more than that, she was simply *dying* to see what sort of young miss had led her powerful cousin on such a merry chase halfway across civilization! Why, it had been the talk of the town when Lord Ravenhurst had gone to Egypt in search of the mysterious chit back in December.

She thought she might like a girl who· could move the duke to such extraordinary lengths. Yes, she might like her quite a lot indeed.

*W*hen Jezebel stepped down the gangway, her fingers just barely resting upon the sleeve of her guardian's jacket of stylish blue superfine, she was dressed and coifed and festooned with enough layers of frilly muslin and rib-crushing corsetry to choke a horse. She'd been aided in this effort to no small extent by the duke's valet, who had recovered from his malady just in time to make the return journey and who, apparently on the duke's orders, had packed up her belongings from her uncle's bungalow in anticipation of her arrival on the *Gertrude*.

Unfortunately, the man seemed to have brought aboard only her most stylish feminine attire, leaving behind the far more comfortable masculine garb she would have preferred to wear. So now, stepping foot in London for the first time since her eighth year, whether she wished to be or not, Jezebel Montclair was the very embodiment of proper virgin British womanhood.

She was also thoroughly sick to her stomach, though it had nothing to do with her confining apparel.

Just *who* was that vision of blond perfection waving so gaily at Rafe from the pier? she wondered. And why did he have to smile back at the gorgeous, ripe-figured woman with such genuine pleasure? Everything else faded—the chaos of the busy docks, the strange sounds and smells and sights, even the unfamiliar misting chill of the late spring drizzle that fell upon Jezebel's cheeks. All she could see was the woman who had to be Rafe's mistress.

In her late twenties or early thirties, dressed in a soft peach and white frock that perfectly complemented the pink and cream coloring of her stunning, angelic face and the spun-gold curls of her upswept hair, the woman waiting for them below on the docks effortlessly captured the essence of the fashionable ideal every other woman in England strove for hours with hot tongs, paint, and powder to achieve.

Jezebel thought she might throw up.

$\mathcal{A}$s the two stepped off the gangway and crossed the dock to greet her, it was immediately clear to Lady Allison that not all was well between her handsome cousin and the exquisite creature on his arm. She must assume this was Rafe's new ward, though Lord knew she'd not been expecting the girl to be such a stunner! Yet though the young woman was strikingly beautiful, the fair coloring of her porcelain cheeks setting off glossy raven hair that was simply styled beneath a white feathered bonnet, her petite frame in its demure muslin ensemble curvaceous enough to turn the head of nearly every man on the wharves, Miss Montclair did not carry herself with the confidence such loveliness should have given her. Instead, she resembled nothing so much as a rabbit caught in a trap, Allison thought, studying her shrewdly. And she noted that the girl's escort seemed to have taken on the role of trapper, hovering over her as if she might bolt at any moment. Lady Mayhew had never seen two more miserable people. Instantly she stepped in to help.

"My dear!" she enthused. "How glad I am to finally make your acquaintance." Absently, she bussed Rafe's cheek and turned to smile warmly at Jezebel. "You poor girl, you must be simply exhausted from your long journey."

"Actually, I'm not really very—" Jezebel began, bemused by the dazzling smile and genuine warmth in the other woman's face. Who had ever heard of a mistress being kind to another woman leaning on her protector's arm? She wanted to question this lady, to ferret out her position in the duke's life—not that she cared if Rafe had a mistress! she told herself hastily. It was simply best to know everything about one's enemy, a position Rafe had most definitely come to fill since he'd effectively kidnapped her six weeks ago. But before she could even get as far as to deny her exhaustion, let alone ask any pertinent questions, Allison cut her off.

"Come, I'm sure this ill-mannered beast has been tormenting you long enough, Miss Montclair. I am here to see to it that he does so no more." Lady Allison grinned cheekily at Rafe, who gave her a pained smile in return but made no comment. "I've taken the liberty of having your coach brought up here along with mine, dear boy," she said to the duke, who didn't seem to mind the woman referring to him in this appallingly disrespectful fashion, "and I think it best I take Miss Montclair up with me whilst you go on alone. I'm sure she and I have a great deal of getting acquainted to do, and you'll only be a hindrance while we gossip."

Both the duke and his new ward seemed unable to catch up, bowled over by her quick stream of chatter, which was just as she had intended. Satisfied, Allison continued blithely, "I shall have the things I'll need for the rest of the Season transferred to your townhouse by evening, Rafe, if you'll be good enough to have your staff prepare the Green Suite for me—you know it is my favorite. I'm sure Miss Montclair here will wish the Blue. 'Twill match her lovely eyes so well." She barely paused for breath. "Well! That's all settled, then. Run along, cuz," she said, patting Rafe's cheek with one dainty lace-mittened hand. "We'll join you soon enough!"

And she linked arms with Jezebel, dragging the younger woman off in her frothy wake, much like a leaf caught in a tsunami.

They were in the carriage, the wheels already beginning

to turn, before Jezebel regained her voice enough to sputter, "Who—who *are* you?"

Lady Allison let out a tinkling laugh. "You mean His Grace didn't tell you?" At Jezebel's negative head shake, she *tsk*ed her tongue reprovingly. "Rotten boy. Never did have any manners. Never mind! I am Lady Allison Mayhew, actually Baroness Mayhew, if you want to be absurdly formal, which I assure you I never am, and I hope you are not either."

Seeing that, if anything, her explanation was only confusing the girl more, Allison sighed, reminding herself to slow down. "More importantly, I am Rafe's cousin, and your chaperone."

Jezebel merely looked at her blankly. "Good Lord, he really *hasn't* told you anything, has he?" Allison's pretty forest-green eyes narrowed. "He didn't mention he'd asked me to assist your launch into society? As I understood it, my main task this Season is to help you find a husband. I can't believe he didn't tell you that much, at least. Whatever has been going on between you two to make Rafe forget himself so?"

To her horror, Jezebel felt her eyes begin to well with unexpected tears. "Oh, he told me that much, all right," she choked.

Before she could blink her tears away or say anything to deflect this effusive, kindly woman she was still not entirely convinced was not, somehow, Lord Ravenhurst's mistress, Lady Allison's eyes filled with sudden understanding. Understanding, but no condemnation.

"Oh, my poor dear," she breathed. "He didn't . . ." she shut her eyes in commiseration. "That bastard made you fall in love with him, didn't he?" she asked. Before Jezebel could think to deny it, to protest that this was anything but the truth, Allison had shifted neatly to Jezebel's side of the carriage and taken her in her arms. Her lilac-water perfume enveloped Jezebel in a cloud of sweet reassurance.

Though the younger woman withstood the embrace stiffly, Allison held her until she yielded just a little. When she spoke, all levity had fled her tone, and her keen intelligence shone through fully for the first time. "As deeply as I hold my cousin in affection, Miss Montclair," she told the dark-haired young temptress who was struggling so mightily not to cry in her arms, "such behavior on his part is wholly unacceptable. If there was ever any doubt, my dear, you may now count upon my loyalties resting firmly in your camp. We women have to stick together in times like these, after all. When it comes to affairs of the heart, we must consider ourselves at war!"

# Chapter Twenty-one

~

$\mathscr{I}$t was a very odd sort of war, if war it could be called, that was waged between Jezebel and her guardian for the next full week. She never saw him once.

Jezebel didn't know what Rafe did with his time—she could barely account for her own, for her new chaperone had swept her up in a whirl of activity so hectic she hardly had a moment to think. Shopping, sightseeing, shopping again (one could never have enough shoes, according to Lady Allison), paying calls, and, to Jezebel's great dismay, more shopping ("Really, we must get you properly outfitted right away! It's shocking how inadequate your wardrobe is") occupied her to the exclusion of all else—as, she suspected, her unlikely duenna had intended.

Later, she never could say exactly how Lady Allison had managed to persuade her to stay. All she knew was that almost as soon as the carriage had pulled up beside the imposing gray stone facade of Lord Ravenhurst's Grosvenor Square townhouse (the duke's own impressively crested black-lacquer coach being nowhere in evidence yet), she had been lured inside a charming little yellow salon and encouraged to rest herself upon a seductively comfortable striped satin settee, her parasol and pelisse having been handed off to the butler who waited impassively by the door.

Over a delicious little sherry much finer than any Jezebel had ever tasted before, Lady Allison had begun to converse with her, seeming content to exchange idle chitchat while their rooms were being aired. Jezebel had been planning to get right up again and run before any chambers could be made ready for either one of them. Yet somehow the baroness, like a cunning but kindly spider, had spun such a

web of irrefutable logic around her in just those first few
minutes that she'd managed to convince Jezebel London
was really *exactly* the place she truly wanted to be.

Perhaps it was the travel exhaustion that Jezebel had
tried to deny earlier, or perhaps all the strain of the past
few months she'd spent battling the devilish duke had finally caught up to her, but it had all made so much sense
at the time. . . .

*C*urving one slender arm about the back of a sofa and
settling back comfortably, Allison looked her over carefully, then nodded, seemingly content with what she saw
in her new charge. "My dear, you just leave everything to
me," she said soothingly. "We'll have you settled in before
you know it, and then we shall have all the time in the
world to decide what to do about . . ."—she paused delicately—"that other matter."

"Lady Allison," Jezebel began firmly, intending to refute
this formidable woman before she could get carried away,
"you've been naught but kind to me in our very short acquaintance, but I must tell you I've absolutely no intention
of 'settling in' here. Nor do I intend to do anything about
any 'other matters'—though I'm sure I don't know what
you're referring to on that score," she bluffed. "His Grace
has made a grave mistake in bringing me here, I'm sorry
to inform you, and I plan to correct it by taking my leave
just as soon as I may. Today, in fact," Jezebel finished,
polite defiance radiating from her stiff posture.

"And where will you go?" Allison asked shrewdly. Jezebel's suddenly arrested gaze was enough for her to pounce
on. "You don't have the faintest idea what you would do
once you left this house, do you, Miss Montclair?"

Out of nowhere, Jezebel felt tears spring to her eyes—
for the second time in one day! Since she'd reached England she'd turned into a veritable watering pot, she
thought disgustedly. Her mouth opened and closed silently
as she tried to form words to deny what Lady Mayhew was
saying. But she had no answer for that simple question.

Her heart full of a bracing anger that helped mask the pain underneath, during the voyage Jezebel had not thought much beyond reaching England and, once there, defying her guardian in any way she could. Her few vague imaginings of the future had all ended with her walking off into the distance, proud and alone, having repudiated the need for any protector. . . . As for what lay in that distance, what she strode toward, she really hadn't had a clue. But she was hardly going to admit as much to Rafe's cousin, kind as she might appear to be.

"Pray, do not trouble yourself about my welfare," she said at last. "It is truly not a matter for your concern, my lady. Where I choose to go or what I choose to do is no one's business but my own. Perhaps in a few years, when I have reached my majority and may claim my inheritance legally, we shall meet again. Until then . . ."

Jezebel rose from her chair and curtsied stiffly to Lady Allison, sorry to be leaving her, for already she felt the woman might have been a friend to her. But Jezebel had left many people behind in her life, and she knew it was necessary that she remove herself from Raphael Sunderland's household immediately, before the autocratic duke had a chance to stop her. Straightening her dress and trying to make it look as if she had every idea where she would go after she left the salon, she said tightly, "I'll just go and fetch my things from the carriage." She turned then to leave the room, but Allison stopped her.

"Surely there's no need for such haste?" the older woman asked innocently. "I was so enjoying getting to know you, my dear, and I would count it a shame not to learn more about you before you go on your way. And perhaps," she offered gently, "we may discuss your future plans a little further. I should hate to worry after you when you have left, Miss Montclair."

Jezebel was worried quite enough for both of them. It was one thing to make a show of bravado and head for the door. It was another to point her feet in a constructive direction once she'd left! She truly didn't know where to go. The painful truth was that the only life she'd really known had ended on the day her uncle had died. Ever since then, she'd been living on borrowed time, and now she was faced with creating a new existence for herself. Egypt no longer held the same promise for her it once had, that much she'd been forced to acknowledge already. And even should she choose to return, it would cost a great deal of money to book a passage there. Her private funds were disturbingly meager and might not suffice.

It was galling that she couldn't lay a hand on the fortune her uncle had left her without Ravenhurst's assistance—his permission, she corrected herself. *No matter!* Jezebel told herself bracingly. *I've lived through worse situations before, and I shall come through this as well.* She opened her mouth to say as much, but Lady Allison spoke first.

"If I may make a suggestion, dear Jezebel—I may call you Jezebel, mayn't I?—I believe I may be able to help you with this very difficult decision. Please, come sit and talk with me awhile." Invitingly, she patted the gold-striped fabric of the sofa she sat upon, and Jezebel found herself getting up from her own seat and drifting without volition toward the other woman.

Lady Mayhew frequently had that effect on people, had Jezebel only known it. The seduction had begun.

"It has been quite some time since you were last in London, has it not?" Lady Allison queried, seemingly idly.

Suspicious, but seeing no harm in answering, Jezebel nodded. "Not since I was a child, my lady, and then only briefly with my father, on our way to join my uncle abroad. I've never even seen the Tower," she confessed frankly, feeling like the most provincial of bumpkins.

"Oh, but my dear! You really must allow me to take you sightseeing before you leave us!" As Jezebel was about to protest, she hurried on. "You've made it plain that you are anxious to leave Lord Ravenhurst's company behind, and I understand your desire for freedom perfectly—*I* was married once, you know—but think about the marvelous opportunity you would be missing by leaving prematurely. Why, London is surely the greatest city of the world. Everyone who is anyone lives here . . . if you have not spent any time exploring all the city has to offer, then, well traveled as I am told you are, Miss Montclair, I fear your education remains sorely lacking."

Jezebel paused to consider the other woman's words, thinking with a surprisingly strong surge of longing of the many diversions this sprawling city had to offer. The museums, the bookstores, the many diverse cultural societies, and the music . . . oh, the music she might hear! Thinking on Allison's words, she realized that London's unique intellectual offerings really did appeal to her quite strongly.

But there was one little problem. Jezebel would not be free to leave when she was done sightseeing. Lord Ravenhurst had other plans for her.

"I do not believe the duke is very interested in the matter of my further education, Lady Mayhew," she ventured cautiously, wondering whether the woman was offering her assistance, or only stating her opinion. "He seems to think there is but one matter with which I should concern myself. You see, he has been most adamant that I marry in short order—an edict that is absolutely unacceptable to me."

"Please, call me Allison," Lady Mayhew soothed, waving her hand to dismiss Jezebel's concerns. "I shouldn't worry so about His Grace if I were you, my dear. I'm sure he can be persuaded to temper his demands should you choose to remain with us a little longer—just long enough to decide your next course of action, naturally. Though I grant that because of the rather, ah . . . difficult circumstances of your acquaintance, he may not have displayed it in your presence as yet, I assure you I myself have always found the duke to be of a most reasonable nature. I'm quite confident that with my assistance we may successfully plead your case before him."

"His Grace has never been inclined to temper his demands in all the time *I* have known him, nor have I seen any shred of evidence to back up this 'reasonable nature' you claim on his behalf," Jezebel argued obstinately, truly wanting to believe the baroness, to grasp the lifeline she sensed the other woman was offering. She knew she was being swayed by temptation too easily. Had she any other options, she would not even be listening to these falsely reassuring words. Still, despite her lack of alternatives, she

told herself she must remain firm against Lady Mayhew's
blandishments. "No," she sighed. "I am afraid it is quite
impossible, Lady . . . ah, Allison."

Allison just shook her head reprovingly. "Nothing is impossible when you have enough wealth or enough intelligence on your side, my dear. You'll learn that eventually."
Patting Jezebel on the shoulder kindly, she made her a
promise. "I will speak to His Grace and convince him that
he must allow you the time you need to become adjusted
to your new circumstances before you make a permanent
decision about wedding with any man. I shall remind him
of his duty to see you have a little 'town polish' before you
settle down, and I'm sure that once you assure him you
will take the choice of a suitor seriously, he will not force
you to decide on one before you are ready."

"I shall *never* be ready," Jezebel vowed ferociously,
"and I've no intention of assuring him I will be!" Unlike
most women, she'd never had a great longing to marry, but
now, after what had happened between herself and Rafe in
Egypt, she had become doubly convinced the state of mat-
rimony was not for her. Never again would she open herself
to the kind of closeness—or the pain—that she'd experienced with Rafe. But Allison knew nothing of their history,
and so the older woman could not hope to understand Jezebel's certainty.

Allison simply seemed amused to hear Jezebel's fierce
avowal. "Well, His Grace does not have to know that you
don't intend to go through with it. Just as long as you throw
a sop to his conscience by appearing to take the courtship
rituals of the *ton* seriously, he will be content. All you need
do at the end of the Season, Jezebel, is simply fail to pick
one of your suitors for your husband. If you still wish to
leave at that point, you will have had plenty of time to
decide upon your next course of action by then—and, I
give you my word, I will personally do all I can to help
you on your way if you ask it of me. There can be no
disadvantage to you in what I am suggesting! Come, my
dear, you know I am right. What do you say?"

*You don't know Rafe at all if you can claim that,* Jezebel
wanted to say. *He will never let me go.* But how could she

explain all of what had gone between herself and the duke to Lady Allison? It was impossible.

Oh, how she hated Raphael Sunderland! Despised him and his authoritarian ways, spat upon his dictatorial demands. It was intolerable to think that she should do anything to salve his conscience, when what she most wanted was to slap his arrogant face. But she could not think of a better option just now . . . unless she wanted to wander the streets of London, alone and practically penniless. Still, that might just be preferable to acceding to his will, she thought.

She said as much to Lady Mayhew. "I'd rather starve in the streets than bide under Ravenhurst's roof, making a charade of parading about endlessly in search of a husband. God! All that simpering and posing just to catch the eye of some sniveling, overbred fop who'd rather be rogering the chambermaid! It is unbearable, my lady, a foolish waste of time and not at all what I had in mind for my future."

She expected the woman to be put off, but Lady Allison only burst out laughing at Jezebel's crudity, saying delightedly, "A woman after my own heart! I only wish I'd been as outspoken—and as smart—when I was your age, my dear. Such misery I could have avoided. And I assure you that I personally have no wish to put you through the horror of the marriage mart, no matter that Rafe has asked me to be your chaperone. I would never want to keep you anywhere against your wishes. However, I do still think it would be wise of you to stay. There are so many advantages, and so few detractions, if you play your cards right.

"What I was thinking," she continued, "was that if you remained for just the Season—and a bare two months are left of it, after all—you would have the chance to enjoy the pleasures of the city, be introduced to all of the best people, and, not least of all, have a rollicking good time enjoying all the lovely parties sure to be held this year, as I intend to do. Why, we could have such fun together, Jezebel!" Allison grinned at her like the newfound friend she was fast becoming. "And I've no doubt you'd set our stodgy society on its collective ear within a week of your introduction. You would be a breath of fresh air to them. You'd have those dour dowagers and persnickety peers eating out of your hand in no time—not to mention impressing the stuffing out of your guardian—with just a little help from me, of course."

"But I don't want them—*or* him—eating out of my hand," Jezebel protested. "I just want everyone to leave me alone!"

Allison paused then in her efforts to persuade Jezebel, obviously sensing she had not yet hit upon just the right tack to take. But after a long moment of silent contemplation, her eyes narrowed triumphantly.

It should have been a warning to Jezebel, but the words that Lady Mayhew spoke then were so tempting, so exciting to her imagination, that she didn't stop to ask herself why Rafe's cousin, a woman she'd only just met, would be so eager to help her.

"Oh, well, then," Allison said offhandedly, "if that is how you feel, then of course you must go. But I must say I'm surprised that after all Lord Ravenhurst has put you through, you don't have even the slightest urge to take advantage of this perfect opportunity to get a little of your own back from him—to best the man at his own game, as it were." She stopped for a moment, a slight smile on her rose-pink lips, sensing she now had Jezebel's complete attention.

"What do you mean?" Jezebel asked warily. "I'm not sure I quite follow you."

"He expects you to be a burden to him, does he not? He expects to have to lead you through your paces before the *ton*, to escort you and protect you and watch over you at every moment—all the while attempting to find you the perfect husband. But what if you showed him you do not need his help? What if you showed him, instead, just how very little you need him at all? I mean, *think* about it, Miss Montclair . . . a woman of your beauty and wit, set loose in society? There's no limit to the mischief you might cause. And no limit to the irritation to which you might subject the man with the task of playing guardian to you." Allison's musical laughter rang out in hearty amusement. "He would spend all of his time running along behind your skirts, just trying to keep up!"

Jezebel's eyes started to gleam with an unholy fire as Allison spoke these words, and a truly wicked smile spread itself slowly across her delicate features.

The Honorable Miss Montclair began to envision the possibilities.

Forgetting for the moment how much the thought of entering society had always frightened her, forgetting how she despised the whole false, indolent lifestyle of the *ton,* she took a moment to think about how very, very good it would feel to show Rafe she was no country cousin, no ignorant provincial overawed by her first taste of real sophistication. There was more to her than that! Rather than cowering away and hiding in the face of adversity, Jezebel would instead delve deep inside the well of her will and exert all of her own seldom-used but still powerful charm to conquer it. And she would conquer society along with it!

She would dance and laugh and flirt outrageously with every man she met, she decided defiantly. And to have her arrogant guardian witness how other men reacted to her flirtations . . . well, he might care nothing for her himself, but Jezebel was willing to bet Rafe would not like the sight of her being surrounded by a bevy of eager suitors. No, indeed, she laughed inwardly, beginning to feel a giddy surge of mischief. He would never dare to pity her again.

*Damn it all,* she thought, still under the spell of Allison's enticing imagery, *it would be a fine thing indeed to watch him chasing endlessly after me!* With the other woman's aid, she might just be able to pull off a social coup that would have Rafe yanking those golden curls of his out by the roots!

She'd always had a certain talent for playing the social chameleon, as much as she deplored the role. She'd just never had a good enough reason to use it before. But making Rafe miserable, showing him he would never be able to rule her; well, that was a bloody good reason.

At long last Jezebel felt her courage returning, warming her with the heat of righteous indignation. She realized in that moment that she had been licking the wounds Rafe had dealt her for far too long already. She had been behaving with uncharacteristic meekness ever since he'd inveigled her into returning here to England—in truth, ever since they'd made love. She had been acting as if he really did have the right to command her, as if he had won the battle between them just because she'd once surrendered to his intimate touch.

The baroness's words to her in the coach just moments ago came back to Jezebel: "When it comes to affairs of the heart, we must consider ourselves at war." And the other woman was quite right, Jezebel thought. She was indeed engaged in the fight of her life against Lord Ravenhurst. But now was not the time to surrender. Now was the time to fire back!

Jezebel mulled the proposition over a moment longer, but she already knew what she would say to Lady Mayhew. She wasn't giving in, she told herself. She was merely doing as Allison suggested—getting a little of her own back from the duke. Rafe had pushed her around for long enough!

"You can guarantee His Grace will not force me to wed?"

"Will you stay if I can?"

Jezebel remained silent for a long moment. Then she smiled brilliantly. "Yes," she said. "Yes, I believe I will."

Allison simply sat back on the sofa in satisfaction, smiling a broad smile of her own.

*A*nd now here Jezebel stood a week later, on the morning of her court presentation, feeling like the most expensive bird's nest in history.

Posing before her cheval glass and eyeing her reflection critically, she thought she looked plenty ready to go as she was, but apparently she was the only one who thought so, for at least three maids hovered around her, continuing to make minute adjustments to her costume and coiffure. Every once in a while one of these twittering birds would swoop down to alight upon her, adding a bauble of pearl or crystal or a silken ribbon to Jezebel's already busy outfit or to her elaborately styled hair.

Lady Allison too fluttered about the spacious blue-appointed dressing chamber, picking up kidskin gloves and choosing and discarding dozens of fans, her own simple, tasteful pastel green morning gown in stark contrast to Jezebel's overbearing finery.

Jezebel stifled the urge to take a swipe at one of them, feeling like a cat caught in a dovecote. The whole household was in a flutter over her presentation, servants running to and fro with freshly starched crinolines, curling tongs, and mending kits to make last-minute tucks and alterations to the already (in Jezebel's opinion) overly tucked and ornamented oyster satin gown. Today she would make her curtsy before the queen, decked in feathers and an absurdly long train that she must not (she'd been warned dramatically) even *dream* of tripping over. Everyone was nervous except Jezebel herself (including, she hoped, the absent Rafe, who, if there was any justice in the world, would right now be sweating it out over the impression his ward was going to make).

She couldn't see what all the fuss was about, but as often as she tried to explain to Lady Allison that she'd been presented before many foreign potentates, pashas, and kings, the other woman persisted in hovering nervously over her charge, twitching at the low neckline of the gown and making sure the coils of Jezebel's dark hair sat just right against her neck. After all, she said in defense of her fussing, Jezebel couldn't make her social debut without first making her bow—and there would be plenty of sticklers lurking in the court drawing rooms today, women with daughters not half so attractive as Jezebel, who would be eyeing her jealously, praying for just one slipup.

Jezebel didn't intend to slip up, though it would not much upset her own peace of mind if she did. Really, what was one more fat, overdressed monarch (even if it was one's own) to her? But since it meant so much to Allison, she turned from the mirror to reassure her.

"Two steps forward when my name is announced, left leg crossed before the right, and curtsy." Her eyes twinkled as she recited. "Do not speak until the queen addresses me, and then answer as briefly as possible. Say nothing outra-

geous, and back out of the audience chamber decorously—
without tangling myself hopelessly in this dratted train—
when I'm dismissed." She grinned cheekily at her new
friend.

"Insolent girl." Allison smiled back, thinking she'd
never met a young woman with as much poise as Jezebel
Montclair. "Well," she concluded, looking over her charge
one last time and being unable to find fault with Jezebel's
couture. "Shall we go down and greet His Grace? The poor
man's probably been waiting for us an age."

Jezebel barely smothered the childish urge to mutter,
*Good.* Though she was not nervous about meeting the
reigning queen of the entire British Empire, she was extremely tense indeed about her upcoming confrontation
with her guardian. In just moments she would see Rafe for
the first time since their return from Egypt, for though she
was sure her guardian would love to continue avoiding her
indefinitely, as her sponsor he had no choice but to make
an appearance at this ridiculous ceremony. If he wanted
Jezebel to move in society, they would both have to endure
today's antiquated rituals.

It made Jezebel feel a tiny bit better knowing that Rafe
would probably be suffering every bit as much as she.
Though she knew he'd do his duty and escort her to this
formal presentation, *and* take her to the ball she was scheduled to attend tonight as well, she couldn't imagine Lord
Ravenhurst, a man so full of impatient energy he made
other people fidget just by standing next to them, enjoying
these stiff, ritualized events. No doubt there were other activities he enjoyed more, she thought darkly. Activities best
not mentioned within reach of a lady's ears.

What had he been doing while she'd been preparing herself like a Christmas goose for her debut? While she'd been
enduring an endless round of fittings, suffering innumerable
pinpricks, and standing agonizingly still for hours while the
modiste Lady Allison had engaged and her flock of assis-
tants took reams of measurements she hadn't even dreamed
could be necessary, he had probably been visiting all his
old mistresses, having a roaring good time reacquainting

himself with his favorite whorehouses and pleasure palaces, Jezebel thought sourly.

Certainly, though he'd been eager enough to spend every waking moment with her in Egypt to make sure she didn't slip his grasp, the duke had changed his tune now that he was back on his home ground. Jezebel hadn't seen hide nor hair of the fiend since the day she'd moved in to her luxurious new apartments—her gilded cage, she thought sardonically. Now that he thought he had bested her, it seemed that Rafe was already taking her for granted. Why, since their arrival, the man hadn't so much as inquired about her health or stopped to check if she was settling in comfortably! Just as she'd suspected, as soon as he was confident that she was well and truly under his thumb, Rafe obviously felt no need to see her at all. He assumed he'd beaten her, that he no longer had to worry about any rebellion from her quarter. Well, she vowed, he'd soon regret his presumption!

Ready for battle, Jezebel scooped up her train with a defiant flourish and sallied forth from the dressing room, Lady Allison following a short distance behind. She was engaged in a war for her very freedom, and she was bound and determined to win!

## Chapter Twenty-two

$\mathcal{F}$or the past week, Rafe had barely had time to breathe, let alone engage in any of the debauchery his ward imagined on his behalf. He hadn't had the chance to see even his closest friends, for he'd been engaged in an exhausting round of account reviews, estate tours, and never-ending business meetings, not to mention dealing with the enormous amounts of general catch-up work (including handling the towering piles of correspondence his harried secretary had gratefully handed over) that his ducal responsibilities required after such a long absence. There'd been even more work than Rafe had originally assumed he'd return to find when he'd left in search of his ward, because of all the extra time he'd ended up spending chasing Jezebel up and down the Nile. He'd barely had time to race from one looming crisis to the next, averting disaster in one place only to find another springing up somewhere else.

After a mere sennight, Rafe was still far from finished putting all of his affairs back in order. But his duty to his ward could not be put off any longer, as his wayward thoughts, constantly drifting to dwell upon the raven-haired minx, reminded him with infuriating frequency. Just because he had not seen her, that did not mean he had forgotten Lord Clifton's niece since returning to London. Far from it. He thought of her practically every waking moment.

He'd received regular reports from Lady Allison regarding Jezebel's doings, and much to his surprise, the baroness had repeatedly reassured him that the girl seemed happy enough to be here, content with her role in society. Content to put herself on the marriage mart in the coming days and weeks. The thought made Rafe want to go back to account tallying! Yet though he longed to immerse himself in work and not look up until the maddening, headstrong Jezebel was well past thirty and firmly on the shelf, he knew he would have to find her a husband much sooner than that. For, as much as he might like to bury the whole issue of Jezebel's future, to ignore his responsibility to her in favor of his own selfish desires, he knew that he would be doing her a grave disservice if he did so. After the disgraceful way he had dishonored her, it was of paramount importance that she marry, and quickly too.

The longer the tempting minx went without a man to tame her wild ways, the more likely it was that she would become involved in a scandal that would sully her good name permanently—and Rafe was painfully aware that *he* was the most likely candidate to cause that black mark on her character. His control when it came to his ward was practically nonexistent. It had been simple luck that their indiscretion had come at a time and in a place where the genteel world was perforce excluded from ever catching wind of it, but the next time their passions overcame them, they might not be so fortunate.

It wasn't hard for Rafe to see that if Jezebel remained in his household, under his roof, sooner or later he would give in to temptation again. He would take her in his arms and make love to her with all the frustrated passion in his soul—it was inevitable. And with her fiery, intemperate nature and innate sensuality, he doubted Jezebel would deny him for long, even if at this moment she swore she hated him. Sooner or later, he knew they would wind up in one another's arms—and beds. But though Rafe longed with all of his heart for that event to take place, he knew that if she would not wed him, it would be as disgraceful for them to conduct a liaison as if he had made the girl his mistress. And she would *not* wed him—she'd made that clear in no uncertain terms. "I'd sooner wed a goatherd," she'd said. The words still bit like the lash of a whip.

Before the night of his unforgettable encounter with Jezebel, Rafe had thought he might never marry, and the thought had never troubled him—indeed, it had been a comforting one to a man who had for years been witness

to the many well-publicized misalliances and infidelities
with which the British upper class was rife. But that night
in the desert had changed everything. Their lovemaking had
made him rethink his long-held belief that he would remain
a bachelor forever. He'd tried to convince himself that he
was offering for her out of duty, solely because it was the
right thing to do. But Rafe knew that was not the whole
truth, for instead of the grudging willingness to do the right
thing that he'd expected to feel upon making the decision
to wed Jezebel, he had instead experienced a curious lightness of spirit.

Inside his heart, a joy had blossomed that was both fleeting and profound—fleeting, because he knew Jezebel did
not share this strange desire he suddenly felt to spend his
life with her; and profound, because he had never felt such
a strong connection to a woman before she had come into
his life, and he knew he never would again. The thought
of having a lifetime to spend chasing Jezebel and all the
wondrous mysteries she represented to him had infused
Rafe's spirit with excitement.

Until she had refused him.

He still had trouble believing it. Since his sixteenth year,
when he'd inherited the Ravenhurst duchy and the enormous wealth and prestige that went along with it, women
had been throwing themselves at Rafe with a degree of
verve and creativity that would have been comical had it
not become so deuced inconvenient. He'd never been foolish enough to delude himself it was solely his charm or his
looks that had won him such concentrated female attention,
and over the years of waking to find women in his bed,
women in his carriage—hell, women fairly falling out of
his linen drawer!—he'd grown less and less inclined to
accept the majority of the invitations he received. He'd as-
siduously avoided the marriage traps in which these trained,
conniving females sought to catch him, and had found himself growing increasingly cynical over the years, believing
there was no such thing as an unmarried woman who did
not covet either his name, his title, or his wealth.

But not Jezebel. Jezebel was different, and had been so
from the start. She didn't want anything from him at all.

Standing at the foot of the grand staircase, waiting for her to come down to make her bow before the queen, Rafe realized that this was really the crux of the matter. Painful as it was to acknowledge, the only thing Jezebel wanted from the duke was for him to leave her alone.

Even had he wanted to, he could not have fulfilled her wishes, but Rafe saw now that he did *not* want to. If the Lord Himself came down from heaven in a shower of sparks and told him it was perfectly safe to let Miss Montclair go off on her own, he still wouldn't want to do it. It wasn't just the incredible, once-in-a-lifetime lovemaking they'd shared, though that was part of it. It was the way she smiled, the way she challenged him—hell, even the way she lied to him and tried to run from him. He didn't blame her for wanting to be free. He himself had longed for just such freedom from the expectations of the world many times. But unlike Jezebel, he was a realist. There were certain rules that had to be followed, damn it, and certain realities that couldn't be wished away.

Why could she not see that for herself? Rafe thought with angry sorrow. Why couldn't she see that he didn't place these restrictions on her because he enjoyed it, but because they were necessary? He only wanted to do what was right for Jezebel, to fulfill the trust her uncle had laid upon him, and to see that no harm came to her, from himself or any other man. If she would only admit what was in her heart, instead of letting her temper get the best of her, she would see that his offer of marriage was the perfect solution for both of them. Damn it all, why couldn't Jezebel stop defying him for one blasted minute and see that everything he did was because he cared for her?

The duke answered his own question. Because Jezebel was the most incredibly obstinate, contrary, pigheaded, short-sighted . . .

. . . beautiful woman he'd ever met in his life.

He'd seen her in all sorts of situations. Dusty and defiant in her flowing Arab garb; deceptively cool and conniving in the muslin morning gown she'd worn to sweet-talk him that first day at the hotel in Cairo; even gloriously naked one evening in the hills between the desert and the banks

of the Nile, bathed in the light of the cold white stars. But
he'd never seen her like this.

Poised at the head of the curving marble staircase in her
extravagantly beaded, lace-ruffled, and embroidery-
bedecked court gown with its matching foot-high headdress
of dyed ostrich feathers, she should have looked ridiculous.
But to Rafe, Jezebel looked simply breathtaking. The week
they'd been apart here in London and the unbelievably long
six weeks during which she'd ignored him aboard the *Gertrude* seemed to have had no effect whatsoever on his overheated libido. Even knowing she hated him for what he'd
done to her, knowing that she returned none of his admiration or desire, Rafe wanted her more now than ever before.

He scowled furiously.

*J*ezebel couldn't help it. She laughed. It started with a
tiny, half-suppressed snicker, but soon the smothered
sounds that escaped her lips had built up into full-blown
belly laughs. Riding home from Russell Square in the coach
with her guardian and her chaperone, after what was supposed to have been the most serious, momentous occasion
of her life, she began to giggle uncontrollably.

A feather from her headdress took the opportunity to fall
from its nest and hang crookedly before her mirth-filled
eyes. She only chuckled harder, hands clasped desperately
about her tightly corseted waist as a series of silent, hitching little exhalations began to shake her slight frame. Jezebel looked as if she were suffering a fit. She slapped her
knee helplessly, the blow making no sound through the
dozens of layers of her garments, and cackled like a fiend.

Allison and Rafe stared at her as if she'd gone mad.

"Ah, ha, ha, ha . . . did you see it?" she gasped. "That
little puffball in the puce satin with all the blond lace?"
Jezebel was nearly choking with glee. "Good heavens! She
was so overwrought with excitement, I thought she was
going to faint! I feared she would roll headlong down the
aisle and bowl the throne right over before she could even

make her bow. And then when she finally *was* presented, did you hear that little squeak that came out of her mouth?"

She paused to double over again, as much as the stiff, old-fashioned stomacher of her court gown would allow. Little hiccuping bubbles of hilarity escaped Jezebel as she struggled for breath. Allison had begun to smile as well, as much because of the infectious nature of her charge's hearty laughter as from the admittedly amusing antics that had taken place in the royal drawing rooms.

*"Your Majesty,"* Jezebel mocked in a high, lisping voice, *"It ith an honor!"* Tears of mirth formed at the corners of her jewel-bright eyes. "And the look on old Queen Charlotte's face! I thought someone had handed her a toad, she looked so sour."

"She has always looked like that—at least since her husband George's regrettable madness took hold," Allison said, a chuckle of her own sneaking out. "But I think this time her sourness was made worse by the terrible fart let go by the little chit in the appalling yellow sarcenet—the one who came before the girl in puce—just as she bent to make her curtsy."

Jezebel roared with renewed laughter. "She *didn't*! Oh, Lord, I wish I'd have been close enough to hear it . . . though how I could have kept a straight face for my own presentation after that, I'm sure I don't know."

"Believe me, my dear," Allison said dryly, "you would *not* have wanted to be close enough to hear that particular sound, because had you been within earshot, you would also have been within sniffing distance, as I and the other lady sponsors were. Simply appalling! His Grace was just lucky to have been on the other side of the room with the gentlemen." Allison withdrew her fan and began to wave it vigorously before her nostrils as if the mere recollection were enough to send her swooning. Merriment gleamed in her moss-green eyes as the two exchanged mischievous grins.

At that moment, the duke finally chose to break his long silence.

"If you two have finished discussing the unfortunate scatological indiscretions of the young ladies present at

court this afternoon," Rafe broke in repressively, "I believe
we have several matters of more import to go over before
Miss Montclair's debut at Lord and Lady Netherland's gala
tonight."

Instantly all levity fled the coach.

Jezebel's teeth snapped together with a click, and she
shot her guardian a venomous glare. Before she could toast
his ears with a scathing retort, however, she caught Lady
Allison's warning look out of the corner of her eye, and
held her tongue with a visible effort. Allison's speaking
glance reminded her, as it was intended to, of her vow to
keep her temper in check. If she wanted to beat the duke
at his own game, the look said, she would have to do better
than to rise to each baiting taunt the man threw out. The
war between them had barely begun, but in these opening
skirmishes, Rafe already seemed to be winning, showing
none of the distress or discomfort she herself felt.

He had said virtually nothing to her since their return to
London, not even this afternoon when they'd gathered in
the townhouse's grand foyer before attending the absurd
ritual of the presentation. He'd looked so handsome in his
high-collared jacket of deep blue wool and simply tied
white cravat, his buff pantaloons and gleaming Hessians
conforming so much like a second skin to his indecently
well-turned legs that Jezebel's knees had gone weak. The
only thing marring his virile masculine beauty was the deep
frown that had darkened his rugged countenance.

He'd had no words of gallant praise or even of condemnation for his ward, merely offering both ladies his arms to
escort them to the vehicle that awaited outside. His seeming
indifference had been a blow to Jezebel's confidence almost
as strong as the rush of desire she'd felt at the sight of him.
Lady Allison must be right to counsel coolness, she thought
bitterly. If she did not deign to return Rafe's barbed words
now, no matter how much she was burning to tell him what
a contemptible swine he was being, she would probably
succeed far better than if she bristled with offense. Her new
plan called for restraint and cunning, not hot-tempered
words that would show the duke just how easily he still
affected her emotions.

Allison, however, not burdened with Jezebel's reasons for remaining closemouthed, was able to be more voluble in response to Rafe's surly comment. She rolled her eyes, saying, "Honestly, Ravenhurst, you can be such a killjoy when you set your mind to it. Don't you want to compliment Jezebel on the excellent job she did today at court? *I* think Her Majesty was very favorably impressed with our little charge's aplomb, even if the gracelessness of the other girls making their debuts made her task rather easy in contrast."

Rafe did not appear inclined to praise his ward. In fact, he looked a good deal more likely to smother her with one of the carriage pillows. "I hardly think it appropriate to encourage this sort of disdainful behavior in the girl, Allison," he said sternly, not looking in Jezebel's direction. "Such disrespect for convention is highly inappropriate in a young lady her age, and it seems to me that our dear Miss Montclair is already quite unconventional enough. She must learn to hold the traditions of our society in greater esteem if she is to be successful in her Season."

"Rafe!" Allison boggled at him in astonishment. "What in heaven's name has come over you?" It wasn't at all like her cousin to act in such a pompous and self-righteous manner, as Allison well knew. In the normal run of things, the duke was the first to crack a joke at the expense of the *ton*, given even the slightest opportunity. He'd never taken the insular social world they inhabited seriously, perhaps knowing he was above such superficialities. "What has brought on this foul temper?"

"I am not in a temper of any sort, Allison," he growled. "I am simply stating a fact. If Miss Montclair wishes to be accepted and to find an appropriate husband, she cannot be encouraged to poke fun at the very people among whom she must mingle. A little less levity and a little more serious-mindedness is required—on both your parts."

In fact, despite his denial, Rafe's temper was extremely foul, but it was not because of any embarrassment Jezebel had caused him. No, he thought, her grace and poise this afternoon would have been a credit to any protector. Miss Montclair had swept into that fussily decorated, overheated chamber as if *she* were the queen and the woman on the dais a mere nobody with whom she was graciously condescending to converse. And, amazingly enough, the aged, ill-favored, and normally ill-tempered Queen Charlotte had seemed quite content to accept this attitude, instantly falling under the spell of Jezebel's natural charisma and currying her favor with compliments and invitations to visit the royal family at Balmoral once the Season was over.

Against his will, Rafe had found himself feeling extremely proud of her self-assurance, wanting to cheer when she sashayed up to the queen as her name was announced without the slightest trace of nervousness or hesitation, executing a flawless curtsy and charming the older woman with her bewitching smile and easy conversation. He'd been so proud he'd wanted to snatch her up in his arms and give her a triumphant squeeze. He'd wanted to land a big kiss right on those smiling pink lips. Those lush, sensuous lips . . . those lips he'd kissed a thousand times in the heat and chaos of a storm-swept Egyptian night. . . .

God, how he'd wanted her in that moment. He could have torn all the clothes from her sleek body right there in the queen's own audience chamber and made love to her in front of half of the biggest sticklers in their small social world.

Of course he was pleased with her. The problem was that he was far *too* pleased. It was a cruel dilemma. A dilemma, he reminded himself, that Jezebel herself had created. It was she who had bewitched him, and then refused him. She did not want him—would rather marry a stranger! he reminded himself yet again—and the knowledge was burning him up inside. While he suffered the torments of desire, his ward now seemed cooler and more distant than the most remote ice maiden, content to forget all that had gone between them. But he himself was snared in her web so deeply by this time that he had not even the vaguest idea how he would ever extricate himself.

So instead of praising Jezebel, Rafe was intentionally baiting her. It was a matter of self-defense. Her charm was killing him!

"Oh, come, now, Rafe." Allison was saying. "I hardly

think you have anything to worry about with our dear Jezebel. Why, she is an absolute treasure." Lady Mayhew beamed at her charge.

"That *treasure* is the same woman who has twice brandished a pistol at my person, and on a third occasion made a rather good try of skewering me with an awl. I do not think it at all safe to take her good behavior as a given. What if she decides to attack someone over the buffet? Believe me, it wouldn't be unheard of for her." Rafe shot a glare at Jezebel before continuing to address his cousin. "I have spent far more time dealing with my cunning little ward than you have, cousin, but she has not managed to pull the wool so easily over *my* eyes as she seems to have already done with yours. I tell you, with Jezebel Montclair, one can never be sure what she will do next. Just wait until she comes after *you* with a pickaxe, and see if I speak the truth. If you are wise, you will take my advice and help me formulate a plan for dealing with tonight's party in advance, in case of, shall we say . . . unpredictable behavior on her part."

Allison looked ready to leap to her defense and dispute Rafe's insulting words, but Jezebel interjected before the older woman had a chance, at last breaking the long silence that had gone on between herself and her guardian. What she said was practically inaudible, however, spoken while she looked down at her lap with an expression that might have been shame. Jezebel's voice was so low that both Allison and the duke had trouble hearing it.

"What was that?" Rafe demanded sharply.

"I said: 'A chisel,' Your Grace," she repeated with seeming patience. "It was a chisel that I used—not an awl or a pickaxe." Her words were sweetly offered.

When she looked up, however, her sapphire eyes were blazing with a rage that was no longer banked. She'd resolved not to lose her control, not to let the duke get under her skin, but this was just too much to take lying down. "And I would that it had gone straight for your black heart! If you are so concerned about being disgraced by my behavior at tonight's ball, perhaps you will recall that it is only on your orders that I go at all—not by my own choosing. I daresay you will just have to take your bloody chances with my 'behavior,' and pray I don't decide to forget my manners in the midst of a quadrille!"

"Is that a threat, Jezebel?" Rafe asked softly.

"It is a statement of fact, my lord. Nothing more, nothing less."

"Well, then let me share a little fact of my own with you, my dear little ward. If I see you pulling any stunts tonight simply to annoy me or to ruin your chances of success with the *ton,* I shall not be inclined to take it at all well. I won't hesitate to discipline you as I see fit."

"What, the way you did before?" she sneered. She leaned forward, taunting Rafe from across the seat. "Is the flat of your hand the only weapon you know how to use? You cowardly blackguard! You just *try* that again and see what it gets you . . . you . . . !"

Allison laid a cool hand on Jezebel's knee, the single, calming gesture stopping her heated young friend from saying more and possibly escalating her argument with the duke into real violence.

"I'm sure our dear charge is merely a trifle overcome by the excitement of the day. What Miss Montclair *means* to say is that she is very much looking forward to tonight's affair, and hopes her conduct will be a credit to you and the Ravenhurst name." She shot Jezebel another speaking glance, silently warning her not to inflame the situation any further. "In fact, it is her fondest hope that she will make a success of herself both tonight and at future events, earning society's full approbation and esteem. Is that not right, Jezebel?" Her voice held a stern warning—and a reminder.

Jezebel visibly swallowed the retort she was aching to make. It was a long moment before she could speak again.

"Indeed, Lady Mayhew. I *live* to please society." The strangled, sarcastic words came painfully from her throat. Oh, how it stuck in her craw to knuckle under to the duke even this much! But it was all in a good cause. If she wished to win in the end, Jezebel reminded herself, she must continue to follow Lady Allison's plan no matter how much it cost her to rein in her turbulent emotions. Her success so far in that arena had not been good, she admitted.

Still, even this unplanned outburst might be put to good effect. Her mercurial mood shifts would keep the duke off balance, that much was sure. She'd laid the foundations of worry in his mind already, she could see. Let Rafe wonder which Jezebel would appear at the ball tonight—this morning's engaging sophisticate, or the savage he so obviously expected. Let *him* sweat it out. *She* knew exactly how she would proceed. This, she vowed, was the last time she'd let him under her skin!

Rafe was not at all mollified by this disingenuous acquiescence on the part of his ward. It wasn't much of a promise to behave—if it had been a promise at all. His angry gaze studied the delicate features of Jezebel's flushed profile suspiciously, but she refused to meet his eyes now, staring in the direction of the coach's half-shuttered window and showing neither defiance nor remorse for her words. But just as he opened his mouth to challenge her sudden, grudging surrender, the carriage finally rumbled to a halt before the door of his townhouse, and the duke thought better of it. Perhaps now was not the best time to continue this argument.

It was three very relieved gentlefolk who piled out of the conveyance almost before the footman could let down the carriage steps. With undignified haste, each of them in turn fairly flew up the front stairs and bolted for their separate regions of the house.

They had a ball to prepare for.

# Chapter Twenty-three

～

$\mathscr{R}$afe had thought Jezebel couldn't possibly appear more enticing to him than she had at this afternoon's presentation. He'd been wrong. The way she looked tonight, on the verge of entering her first ball, made her earlier beauty pale in comparison.

If he hadn't known better, he would have sworn she did it just to torment him.

As his ward shrugged off her lightweight gray silk cloak in the vestibule of Lord and Lady Netherland's opulent Mayfair residence, he caught his first glimpse of the outfit she and Lady Allison had chosen for her initial foray into society. The duke swallowed heavily and turned away before the sudden, embarrassing condition of his arousal became apparent to the world. Had he been worried about her potentially bad behavior? Now he began to take thought for his own.

*Think of dead kittens,* he told himself grimly. *Think of the way the Thames smells in summer. Think of anything but the curve of her silky white shoulders or the swell of her breasts in that sinfully delicious gown!*

Wearing a stunning evening dress of silver tissue with an overlayer of drifting, filmy gauze strewn with iridescent Austrian crystals in a whimsical leafy pattern, Jezebel presented a shimmering vision of radiance as she waited to hand off her wrap to a servant a few paces from him in the dimness of the candlelit entrance hall. The high waist of the gown, resting just beneath her gently rounded bosom, was cinched with a wide sash of silver ribbon adorned with more glittering crystals, perfectly accentuating the natural slenderness of her willowy figure. Her glossy black hair was caught up atop her head in a swirling braided bun wound through with matching silver ribbons, but left free to fall in back in a wealth of untamed curls. The simple coiffure gave her a fresh, girlish look that was nevertheless wildly erotic. Each brush of her hair across those milky shoulders was like a lick of fire to Rafe's already inflamed senses.

She looked, he thought, like a graceful wood nymph or a siren risen from the sea to lure men to their doom—certainly, she'd lured *him* into folly often enough!

Rafe could hardly look away. The neckline of the gown was not improperly low for a young lady of her age or social standing, as he was forced to acknowledge, but the crisscrossing, off-the-shoulder bodice was cunningly designed nonetheless to draw the eye to the sweet shadow of her cleavage. And his eye was drawn indeed . . .

*Dead kittens!* he barked to himself again.

Thankfully, the duke heard his name being called at that moment, and turned with relief to greet the man who'd hailed him from beyond the ballroom door. "Damien!" he said with a grin of welcome as the other man rudely elbowed his way to Rafe's side through the crush of people waiting to enter the main ballroom. "It's bloody great to see your ugly face again, old man."

"You wouldn't know it from the time it's taken you to get 'round to seeing me, you scoundrel," his friend replied, trying to look offended but failing as a cheerful smile broke through his feigned displeasure. "I hear you've been back a week and entertained no one but your blasted solicitors." He clapped Rafe on the back with hearty exuberance.

Rafe smiled, squeezing his friend's shoulder in return. "You know how it is. Duty first."

"As always. Demme if you ain't the most boringly responsible fellow I know," Damien teased, his voice an exaggerated dandy's drawl. "I can't seem to shake you of that nasty habit, hard as I've tried over the years. In fact, if anything, the condition seems to be worsening with your old age. You really ought to have a physician look into it."

Rafe merely rolled his eyes, used to his friend's ribbing. "I'll be sure to do that—the same day you give up your predilection for practical jokes." He excused himself mo-

mentarily, taking the opportunity to hand his topcoat to one
of the footmen standing by the cloakroom on the other side
of the vast foyer for just that purpose.

Damien, meanwhile, turned to greet Allison, who had
come up silently as he and the duke were talking, Jezebel
trailing a few steps behind. "Lady Mayhew, you're looking
lovely as ever this evening," he said, bowing gallantly over
her hand.

Allison, who was still smoothing the folds of her sky-
blue satin skirts, dimpled prettily at the marquis. "Always
a pleasure to see you, dear Marksley." Without offense, she
noticed that his attention, ever fickle, had already wandered
to light upon the girl who stood in her shadow.

"And just *who* is this ravishing creature by your side?"
Damien asked. He favored Jezebel with one of his signature
smiles, a crooked grin that had been known to send young
ladies groping for their smelling salts at a dozen paces. His
gray eyes were bright with interest as he took her hand and
held it lingeringly in his own, masculine appreciation written clearly upon his open, handsome features. "I thought
you and Ravenhurst were sponsoring Clifton's homely little
niece for her come-out tonight," he muttered to Allison out
of the side of his mouth.

"Oh, they are," said the young goddess whose hand he
still held, speaking before her blond companion could reply. Her voice was low, throaty, and edged with honeyed
venom. "*I* am Clifton's 'homely little niece.' "

Lady Allison put her hand around the back of Jezebel's
waist, gently drawing her forward just a bit more. "Jezebel,
it is my dubious honor to present His Lordship Damien
Marksley, the marquis of Rutledge, and one very embarrassed gentleman at the moment. Marksley, this young lady
is the Honorable Miss Jezebel Marie Montclair, niece to the
late earl of Clifton."

Damien's eyes widened comically. In them were both
distress at his blunder and a sudden, deep flare of interest
that went beyond embarrassment. His glance wavered between the seductive, raven-haired young beauty now facing
him, a mocking challenge filling her cobalt-blue eyes, and
the tall duke whom he could see watching her from across

the room. There was such heat in the duke's gaze when he looked at her, Damien now noticed, that he could have incinerated half the Netherlands' guests with a single sweeping glance. It was not at all like the expression of cavalier disinterest Ravenhurst commonly sported at affairs like these. *Very interesting, indeed,* thought Lord Marksley. *The duke's long sojourn in Egypt begins to make sense. . . .* He turned his attention back to Rafe's ward.

"Pray accept my humblest apologies, Miss Montclair. I'm afraid I've really put my foot in it this time, haven't I? I wouldn't blame you if you favored me with the cut direct, but I beg you will prove yourself as generous as you are beautiful, and forgive my oafishness though you have every right to despise it—and me. I spoke in ignorance, and regret my error deeply. Lord Clifton was a lucky man indeed to have a niece such as you."

He looked so woebegone and remorseful that Jezebel had to laugh. "I've been called worse things than homely in my life, Your Lordship. I believe my self-esteem will survive, especially after so graceful an apology."

Just then Lord Ravenhurst returned to his ward's side, coming to stand protectively behind her, as though with his very body he could blockade her against the interest she was beginning to garner from all sides of the room. But the whispers and sidelong glances had already begun, as both eligible gentlemen and the ladies who hoped to snare them sized up this exquisite creature arriving in their midst, mid-Season and under the protection of one of the richest men in England. Not all of the glances were friendly, but some were a trifle *too* friendly—including, in Rafe's opinion, the marquis's.

"Marksley. I see you've met my ward."

"Indeed, and managed to insult her already, it seems."

Rafe quirked one brow. "Oh? Should I be getting ready to polish the floors with your hide in her defense?" The edge in his voice was just a little too sharp for humor.

"Nonsense," Jezebel said firmly, choosing to deliberately misunderstand her guardian. "No one is going to be polishing any floors tonight. I'm quite sure that is the sort of thing for which the Netherlands employ this astonishingly large

fleet of servants." She gestured to indicate the several powdered and liveried footmen who could be seen weaving
their way through the guests in the foyer and the ballroom
beyond. "And contrary to what he's told Your Grace, I find
Lord Marksley perfectly charming."

She smiled up at the tall, dark-haired gentleman. "Perhaps, if I am lucky, His Lordship will save me a dance later
on?" There was a definite note of flirtation in her tone, and
Jezebel noticed with satisfaction that the duke was beginning to scowl as he watched their interplay. It seemed he
didn't like her attempts to charm his contemporaries—an
interesting development, Jezebel thought, considering his
stated intent to marry her off to one of them.

"It would be my honor, Miss Montclair," said the marquis, bowing deeply.

"We'll see if her dance card has any spaces left open at
the end of the evening," Rafe said gruffly. "For now, it
seems to me that we have lingered quite long enough in
this drafty hallway. It is time for my ward to make her
debut."

He offered Jezebel his arm, which she took with notice-
able reluctance, and steered them toward the doorway,
where a steward waited to announce the guests to the hosts
and assembled peers in the rooms beyond.

Damien and Allison remained behind just a moment
longer. The marquis studied his friend's exit, observing the
way the duke and his ward seemed to circle one another
like wary cats. Then he returned his gaze to Allison's face.

"You and I, dear lady, simply *must* have a little chat
later on this evening."


*R*emember what I said to you earlier," Rafe admonished
Jezebel as their names were announced and they stepped
through the door. Anger at his own unconquerable lust
made his tone unnecessarily harsh. "None of your tricks or
wild behavior, I'm warning you. . . ."

But Jezebel only gave him a serene smile in return. She
crooked her finger, beckoning him near as if she had a

secret to tell. He stopped to hear what she would say, but his ward barely paused, merely standing on tiptoe for an instant to whisper something in his ear, then disengaging her arm gracefully as she continued on her way. The two little words she spoke so pleasantly as she glided into the ballroom hung behind her in the air like Montgolfier balloons.

Rafe was so astonished to hear the shocking profanity that had issued from Jezebel's innocent, rosy lips that it took him a moment to go after her. By then it was too late.

$\mathcal{S}$he is a resounding success," observed the marquis.

Rafe's inarticulate grunt might have been agreement, or simply a growl acknowledging he'd heard his friend's opinion. He tossed back a hefty slug of brandy, draining his glass, and leaned back against the section of oak-paneled wall that he and Damien were holding up. Having nothing better to do, they hovered aimlessly around the door leading to one of Lord Netherland's several card rooms, where they'd been banished by a smiling Lady Allison.

That gracious lady had gently shooed them on their way not long ago, claiming that with two such towering, powerful gentlemen standing over her like sentinels, Jezebel's prospective suitors would be much too intimidated to approach her. But neither man had felt much like playing cards tonight, not when the real action was taking place on the main dance floor. The duke, at this moment, was beginning to think it might be no bad thing if he decided to casually stroll back over to check on the ladies—all in the course of his duty, naturally. Perhaps those panting swains who clustered so closely around his tempting ward could *use* a little intimidating. He knew he wouldn't mind doing the job.

Both Rafe and Lord Marksley were watching Jezebel's progress with keen interest, though for different reasons. She had already attracted quite a crowd of eager admirers, only an hour or so into this first ball, and had danced several times with young men who, after partnering this graceful, laughing miss in a quadrille or a gavotte, could not seem to do enough for her. The young beaus invariably returned Miss Montclair to her chaperone with dazed smiles upon their faces, hopelessly bewitched by the pleasure of her company. They fought over the right to bring her punch, to fetch her a shawl, to claim even a moment of her attention. Lady Allison stood by her side all the while, beaming. She made introductions as needed and stood ready to assist should her charge falter.

But Jezebel didn't look like she was going to falter anytime soon. No, Rafe thought morosely, she looked as if she had been born to move in high society, as at ease and in command in this setting as she had been atop a camel in the Sahara, or floating down the Nile in their dahabeah like the fabled Cleopatra of old cruising on her pleasure barge. She looked happy, gay, at home. His frown deepened.

"But then, with a face and figure like hers, and the wits to match them—which she's clearly got in spades—Clifton's niece could hardly be other than an instant triumph in these stagnant waters," Marksley was saying blithely. "You haven't been around to notice, but there's been precious little fresh blood among the *ton* this year. It's hardly been a bumper crop of marriageable females, I tell you. I venture to say your ward will be the pick of the bunch, with all she has in her favor. Lovely manners she's got too—and of course there's that very attractive dowry her uncle left the girl. Very winning creature, all in all. Ought to do well."

Rafe's already stormy expression grew positively thunderous. He didn't *want* her to do well. He didn't want her to be enjoying herself as she so obviously was, lapping up the male attention that was coming at her from all directions, laughing and dancing and having a lark. He wanted her to be having as miserable a time as he was.

*J*ezebel was having a miserable time. If she had to smile at one more inane compliment, or let one more oaf trod upon her slippers in the course of a reel, she thought she might wreak serious havoc upon the gentry assembled here tonight. Though she'd brought it on herself, exerting every bit of charm in her body, flexing every latent muscle of social grace she'd never bothered to use before, she was hating each moment she must spend among these foppish, vacuous, useless specimens of the landed upper class.

Their cloying odor of misspent privilege overwhelmed her even more than their heavy use of colognes and perfumed pomades, and she wondered if any of the young ladies and gentlemen present tonight had ever so much as done a single day's work. She doubted it. Jezebel couldn't believe that this was the group from which she was expected to choose her prospective husband! Even had she had any intention of actually picking a suitor to wed this Season, which she most certainly did not, there were no truly worthy candidates for her to choose among, as far as Jezebel could see.

Why, not a one of them had an ounce of the fire or wit Rafe Sunderland had. Not a one of them had so much as an iota of his intelligence or his undeniable, virile attractiveness. . . . Oh, dear God, what was she thinking? Comparing her potential suitors to her guardian was *not*, Jezebel told herself, a wise move. Still, her willful mind could not help extending the comparison of its own accord, once the subject was opened.

How could any one of these men ever give her the kind of intimate ecstasy Rafe had provided her so easily, so thoroughly, and so generously? Jezebel asked herself. How could any one of them challenge her, tease her, infuriate or amuse her as he had from the very start? How could any of them make her pulse race or her heart beat in her chest as if she'd been running for her life? They couldn't, the answer came. None of them was a match for the duke, and never would be.

If she hadn't known better, she'd have thought he'd brought her here tonight with the express purpose of proving that fact to her. The cream of society's wealthiest, most exquisitely well-mannered and well-bred sons littered the Netherlands' ballroom floor like so many grouse flushed out for her hunting, yet Jezebel could see none of them for the scowling, angry man she knew watched her from one corner of the ballroom, just waiting for her to make a mistake.

The only thing keeping Jezebel from losing her temper at this foolish charade and storming out of the ball was the expression she'd caught on her guardian's face every time she'd turned around to gauge his reaction tonight. He looked both stunned—poleaxed, she thought spitefully—and irritated beyond belief. His was not a face that brooded easily, being by nature much more suited to wide, sunny smiles and mischief, but the duke was definitely doing a fair imitation of a brooder tonight, she saw. Obviously, Rafe had expected her to act like a perfect cow, blundering about the ballroom as though she'd been raised in a barn, mannerless and graceless and hopelessly out of her league. Therefore, she would remain among these stuffy, pretentious bores and show him she was anything but—if it killed her!

Miss Montclair increased the potency of her smile even more, fairly blinding the young squire who was its current recipient. She could stand a little misery as long as she knew Rafe shared it.

But it seemed she was not destined to suffer all the night away.

"Little Jezzie? Can it really be you?"

Jezebel spun about at the sound of her old nickname, an incredulous smile spreading across her gamine features as she realized who addressed her. She dropped the thread of her conversation with the sweating, stuttering young squire as if it had burned her, instead holding out both hands in glad welcome to the distinguished, attractive man in his late thirties who had just come upon the group. Instantly the younger men surrounding Jezebel, sensing they were outclassed, fell back to give the two room to converse. Allison, however, made no protest at this usurpation of her charge's attention. She merely kept her eyes open and her lips shut around a tiny smile that judged nothing.

"Lord Belmore!" cried Jezebel, taking his big hands in her own gloved ones with warm enthusiasm. "No one told me you'd returned to England. I'd heard rumors your party was still off adventuring down south of the second cataract near Nubia, making a pilgrimage to the temples there. What a welcome surprise it is to see you here instead!"

"And I certainly never expected to see *you* here in London, my dear girl," said the earl of Belmore, his brown eyes crinkling with pleasure. "And so grown up as well! How long has it been—two or three years now? Let me look at you." He held her arms wide and studied her lithe frame with an interest that might have been just slightly more prurient than it was benevolent. "I must compliment Lord Clifton on a fine job of raising you," he said approvingly. "Is he here tonight?"

Jezebel's smile faded. "No, my lord. I regret to inform you that my uncle died several months ago, whilst we were still in Egypt. It was a respiratory illness that felled him."

"Oh, my dear Jezzie. How dreadful for you." The earl touched his hand to her back briefly in sympathy. "Did it happen before he could find that great tomb he wrote so often about in his letters? I'd so hoped he would discover it, if only to shove the find up the noses of those pompous know-nothings who took such delight in cutting his theories down."

Jezebel felt her eyes tear up at Belmore's sympathetic words. "Yes, unfortunately he passed on too soon," she choked out. "He was never able to locate the tomb's exact position, though he came very close shortly before his death." She chose not to tell the earl about her own subsequent discovery and disheartening loss in the Valley of the Kings. She could not bring herself to talk about that yet, and even had she wanted to, Jezebel knew that now was neither the time nor the place.

She looked around her at the glittering swirl of color and light and richness that was the crowd surrounding her. *Good God,* she thought with an aching heart, *whatever am I doing here?* She did not belong in London among these swells, and she never would. "My uncle had an extremely determined mind, my lord, but his body simply could no longer keep up with its demands." She could feel the tears threatening to brim over her dark lashes, and she swallowed hard, trying to hide the emotions that were so dangerously close to the surface tonight.

But Lord Belmore must have seen something in her face, for he said, "Come, my dear, let us go somewhere where you can tell me all about it."

Jezebel glanced briefly at Allison in question. Getting out of here, even momentarily, sounded heavenly, but . . . "I am here with my new guardian, my lord. I must inform him—"

"Nonsense, my girl," Allison broke in. "Go on with your friend now," she said, having looked the attractive earl up and down and apparently approved of him. "There are several quiet salons and drawing rooms in this great mausoleum of a house, and I'm sure one of them will be free if you wish to talk with His Lordship privately. I will see to it that His Grace is informed of your whereabouts."

*R*afe didn't need informing. He'd been watching Jezebel like a hawk, and when the handsome, darkly tanned earl—a man who had had, at one time, quite a notorious reputation among the polite world as an adventurer both in and out of the bedroom—had made a beeline for his ward, his expression had grown absolutely fulminating. It had only grown worse when he saw the obvious pleasure spreading across Jezebel's face as the man greeted her, the closeness between them that told the duke the two were old acquaintances.

Now it seemed that they were leaving the ballroom with every intention of renewing that acquaintance. But *he* had every intention of preventing it.

Rafe started off in the direction in which his ward and the earl of Belmore had vanished. Nothing and no one would stop him.

*D*amien didn't even try. After his friend stalked off in midsentence, leaving the marquis alone in the middle of a discussion of the merits of a particularly fine gelding he was thinking of purchasing at Tattersall's the following week, he simply shrugged and headed in a new direction of his own.

A glass of champagne in each hand, Lord Marksley approached Lady Mayhew, who was assuring the last of her charge's suitors that Miss Montclair would return soon—and that if they did not see her again tonight, surely they would encounter the young miss at one of the many balls, fetes, and soirees that were to be held in the coming weeks before the Season ended.

"My dear," he said after the last disappointed young man had left, "just what exactly do you think you're doing?"

"Why, whatever do you mean, Marksley?" Allison asked, dimpling up at him innocently.

"Well, I hate to be the man to remind you of propriety, since I'm the first to admit it really smacks of hypocrisy coming from me, but I do distinctly recall hearing, at least once or twice, that it is the express duty of a chaperone to ensure her charge does not go off alone with strange gentlemen—not to encourage her to do so!"

Allison laughed merrily. "I'll grant you that is usually the case, and so I will forgive you for doubting my devotion to my task. But in this case, I have a much higher duty than that of mother-hen to fulfill, my lord."

"Oh? Would you care to tell this rather perplexed gentleman just what the devil you are talking about before he bursts of curiosity?"

"I should think it was obvious, even to a thick sort of fellow like yourself."

Damien's sour glance was enough to make her sigh and stop teasing.

"Oh, very well, I shall explain the matter, though by now you should be able to see it for yourself." Allison opened her mouth to speak, but the marquis beat her to it.

"Are you referring, by any chance, to the fact that our own dear Rafe, a man you and I both know has never so much as raised an *eyebrow* over a woman in his life, is now deeply, hopelessly, and disgustingly in love with his ravishing little ward?"

"And that she is every bit as much in love with him.

Yes. You're not as witless as you look, Marksley."

"Would you prefer this champagne on your head, or in your hand, my lady?" Damien queried in all seriousness.

"My mouth, actually, though I think I can arrange to put it there under my own power, thank you," Allison said as she took the delicate crystal stem in hand and sipped.

"Well, since you've deemed me sufficiently intelligent to observe the obvious fact that those two wretches are miserably enamored of each other, and probably have been from the moment they met in that uncivilized backwater where the girl's been hiding all these years, perhaps you'd now like to explain how you think it helps either one of them for you to give Miss Montclair your blessing to go off with another man? A fellow I'm told the ladies find extremely handsome, I might add. And on top of that, to do it in front of the very man who's so in love with her. . . ."

Damien shut his mouth with an audible click, but his eyes filled with mirthful appreciation for Lady Mayhew's conniving. "Oh," he said. "Never mind. I catch your drift now. By damn, you are one devious woman, Allison!" Damien clinked glasses with the dainty blonde.

"Thank you, my dear." She accepted the compliment absently. "I must admit I thought it rather brilliant myself. If I've done my job right, I doubt we'll see either Rafe or Jezebel again tonight."

"Sure you're not simply shirking your duties in order to go off with a certain M.P. I see not-so-discreetly trying to get your attention over by the potted palm?" Damien teased, his clear gray eyes twinkling.

"Well"—Allison smiled archly—"there *is* that. Now, would you care to shut up and listen to the rest of my plan? The sooner we do our good deed and get these two stubborn idiots to realize they're perfect for each other, the sooner *we* two can go back to enjoying the debauchery that is so much more in our nature."

"I'll drink to that, my lady." And Damien did just that.

# Chapter Twenty-four

~

$\mathcal{S}$tep away from her," Rafe said quietly into the stillness of the darkened drawing room. "Right now."

The couple engaged in the passionate embrace upon the sofa leapt apart guiltily, confusion coming over their faces as they realized the furious gentleman looming over them with such suppressed violence was not a member of either of their sets of equally disapproving parents.

"Lord Ravenhurst!" the brown-haired youth stuttered, wiping his lips as he tried to hide the brunette he'd been kissing behind his skinny body. "I apologize, Your Grace. I . . . that is . . . we didn't realize anyone . . ."

But Rafe had already abandoned the chamber, the same expletive Jezebel had earlier whispered in his ear now issuing much louder from his own sculpted lips—minus the personal pronoun, of course. Behind him, the two he had interrupted *in flagrante delicto* gasped, but seemed to get over the shock quickly, for they had found their way back into one another's embrace before he'd even cleared the hallway.

The duke finally found the correct pair outside in the darkened, shadowy gardens.

This time he did not bother with words. When he saw Jezebel standing in the embrace of the earl of Belmore, her head resting trustingly on his shoulder and the man's strong arms held tight about her back, something snapped inside Rafe. It was his ward this time, all right. And there was no mistaking the intimacy of the clinch she shared with the ruggedly attractive Lord Belmore. Rafe saw red.

An inarticulate snarl of rage issuing from his throat, he lunged for the earl, yanking Jezebel from his arms and swinging the man around in one lightning-quick move. In the next, his fist was streaking toward Belmore's stunned face. The punch landed with a sickening thud, and Belmore went down, grunting heavily.

Rafe stood over him, waiting for the other man to rise so that he could hit him again. "Get up, you swine," he invited menacingly. "Get up so I can beat you properly. I swear I'm going to thrash you to within an inch of your life for touching that girl."

Jezebel didn't scream. She didn't swoon. Before the tears of grief for her uncle that she had shared with Lord Belmore had even dried in her eyes, she had picked up a rock from a nearby flower bed and lobbed it at her guardian's head.

It was unfortunate, to her way of thinking, that the stone didn't knock him out then and there, but it certainly did get his attention when it *thwap*ped squarely against the short curls at the back of his skull. Rafe swiveled in her direction, his face a mask of rage. "You dare . . ." he breathed. "After what you've done, you dare . . . ?"

"Damn right I dare, you bastard!" she hissed, keeping her voice down so as not to invite unnecessary attention to this ridiculous tableau Rafe was forcing them to play out in the manicured gardens of Lord and Lady Netherland's London abode. Just beyond a row of blooming white oleander, all the brilliant lights and brittle gaiety of the ball in progress were visible through a series of French doors lining one side of the house. Many of those doors were open to capture the cool spring breeze, and the last thing Jezebel wanted was to have a bunch of curious busy bodies gaping over what was surely the most humiliating experience of her life. "What the bloody hell do you think you're doing, knocking down my friend like that?" she demanded in a harsh whisper.

"Your *friend*," Rafe sneered. "I saw just how 'friendly' you two were getting! If I hadn't arrived when I did, you'd have been getting 'friendly' beneath the shrubs in another minute."

By this time Lord Belmore had struggled to his feet, ignored by the two who seethed so hotly at each other, eyes blazing in shades of blue and hands clenched so tight the knuckles on both of them were dead white. "Excuse me," he began, wiping blood from his lip with a monogrammed handkerchief. "I believe there's been some sort of misunderstanding here—"

Rafe rounded on the slightly older man, sizing him up even as he levied his threat in a tone of deadly seriousness. "Lord Belmore, is it?" At the other man's curt nod, he continued. "Let me give you a few rules to abide by, one man to another. First, you will keep your filthy hands off my ward in future. You are never to see her again, or make any attempt to contact her, do you understand? And second, if you refuse, I shall make your life a living hell. Count on that much."

Lord Belmore did not look much impressed by the duke's enumerated threats, but he could obviously see that the situation was quite volatile. He tried to defuse it with placating words. "Your Grace. Let me assure you—"

"Spare me your assurances. I know what I saw, man, and I tell you it will not happen again. Do not tempt me to make sure of the matter with pistols at dawn."

Jezebel gasped. A duel was a serious threat indeed! Even should both survive the fight, the winner would be sent into exile in disgrace, the loser possibly facing a long recuperation in bed as well as the censure of society once he was well again—if he were not maimed for life. And she had to acknowledge that with the way her guardian was looking right now, she did not believe both men would survive. Rafe would destroy the earl, tough as the other man was. Behind Rafe's back, she shook her head frantically, begging Lord Belmore with her eyes not to accept the challenge.

"However," Rafe went on softly, "if you were to leave immediately and swear on your honor never to speak of this night to anyone, I should consider the matter concluded to my satisfaction—provided, of course, that you leave Miss Montclair strictly alone in future. Which is it to be?"

Belmore sighed, looking one last time at Jezebel's distraught face. "Much as I'd relish whipping some respect into your insolent hide, you young pup," he said conversationally, "I shall bow to the lady's wishes, and take my

leave of you both at this time." He bowed in their direction.
"Jezzie, it was a great delight to see you again, especially
looking so well, and I will hope that our conversation does
not wind up causing you more trouble than it did pleasure."
He grinned despite his split lip, clearly not able to resist a
last parting shot at the duke. "Until we meet again, dear
child."

Bowing once more, Lord Belmore retreated back toward
the ballroom, still dabbing drops of blood from his lip. Rafe
and Jezebel were left alone.

"Damn you!" Both spat the words simultaneously. Neither saw any humor in the coincidence, however, and in
seconds, Rafe was upon Jezebel, grabbing her arm in a grip
of steel and dragging her around the far side of the house.
He circumvented the party by means of a small garden gate
and an alley that led to the street beyond, where a line of
black carriages waited with their drivers to pick up the
guests.

Jezebel fought him all the way. "Where do you think
you're taking me?" she protested. "You can't just abduct
me in the middle of a party, you great bully! This isn't
some petty pasha's dominion in Arabia; this is London, for
heaven's sake! You can't do this!"

"Watch me," Rafe said grimly.

And abduct her he did. Jezebel found herself tumbling
in a heap of skirts and petticoats across the plush leather
seats of the duke's closed barouche, fighting her way up
for air just in time to see the Netherlands' townhouse recede
in the distance. Rafe was already sprawled on the seat opposite hers, glowering at her. His arms were folded and his
long legs were stretched out across the carpeted floor, feet
brushing her skirts. In his rumpled formal attire, he looked
dashing, debonair, and devastatingly dangerous. Her heart
turned over in her chest. Lord, why did he have to keep
doing this to her? Jezebel thought furiously. Every time she
should have wanted to smack him, she wanted to kiss him
instead! Yet she knew she must ignore the feeling at all
costs.

"I'll be missed soon," she warned. "How will it look for

my precious reputation if I simply disappear in the middle of my very first ball?"

"Lady Allison will make your excuses, Jezebel. Have no fear; she will take care of that much. You, my dear, have far more important concerns to worry about right now."

"Oh, and what would those be, Your Grace?" Jezebel sneered. "Perhaps the fact that I seem to be possessed of a guardian who's completely and utterly, one hundred percent bloody *insane*?" Her voice had risen so much that the last word was a veritable shriek.

"Is it insane to require that my ward remain chaste whilst she is under my protection?" Rafe yelled back. He had lost all control over his temper. The sight of Jezebel in that man's arms had made him want to do murder, but the best he could do now was wound with his words. "Is it insane to ask that she not engage in lewd and illicit embraces in the gardens on the night of her come-out ball with one of the most notorious rakes in all of England? Is it insane to require *that much* decorum?"

"Lewd and illicit?" Jezebel gasped breathlessly. Outrage warred with disbelief. "I know the man's *wife*, for God's sake! Lady Ellen was one of the few women who ever showed me any kindness back in Egypt. How dare you suggest—"

But Rafe wasn't ready to listen to any explanations. The hurt and betrayal he'd felt when he saw her embracing the robust earl had blinded him to all sense. "It's all the worse, then, that you could do what you did. How could you take another woman's husband in your arms when you call yourself her friend?" Shaking in the clutches of his jealousy, what he said next was like a dagger to Jezebel's heart. "You truly live up to your whorish namesake, if you can do as much."

Jezebel cried out sharply at these words, whether wounded or angry or in a state beyond both feelings she did not know. She flew across the carriage seat at her tormentor, attacking him with both hands, slapping him furiously across the face and head several times and cursing him wildly before he finally caught her wrists and made her stop. She was straddling his lap, her skirts and undergarments having ridden up to her thighs unnoticed in the struggle.

There was a small silence in the coach as it continued to rumble across the cobbles. Both could hear the tipsy driver singing to himself and his horses as they stared at each other, panting. Rafe's face was bright red with the several imprints of her palms. Jezebel's was completely white, even her naturally red-tinted lips and pink cheeks devoid of color. He let go of her wrists.

She uttered a tiny sound. It could have been a gasp for the breath she had been holding. It could have been the last of her cries of rage. But Rafe knew it was a sob.

"*You're* the only man I've ever whored for, you hypocrite," she whispered. "Or wanted to." Her eyes closed in desolation, and the tears she'd never let him see before carved streams down the delicate planes of her face. All the animation had been leeched from her features, and her body, in his grasp, felt like stone. Her lips quivered, but her teeth were clenched tight as though she were engaged in some great inner struggle.

It was the rictus of pure agony, Rafe knew, and he had caused it in her.

"God," Rafe whispered. "Oh, God, Jezebel, I'm so sorry. I didn't mean to say such a horrid thing—I swear I didn't. Please don't cry. Please, sweetheart, I would never truly believe such things of you. I was crazed when I said that— insane, just as you claimed. I know you are honorable, and good, and loyal above all things. I have never thought you wanton—and none of what has gone between us changes that in my eyes. Please, please stop crying."

Jezebel's tears continued to flow unchecked, even as he slid one powerful hand into the tangled curls of her raven hair and brought her close. She opened her jewel-bright eyes and stared into his as Rafe's sweet, brandy-laced breath caressed her face. "I hate you," she whispered.

An instant later her tear-wet lips covered his.

*But I* love *you,* he thought, the surprise of her kiss stealing all of his defenses and stripping his feelings down to the barest, deepest truths. And this was the truest thing he knew.

He hadn't looked for it; in fact, he had tried to avoid it with all of his might, but this was one battle he'd lost before it was even begun. He had loved this woman, Rafe saw with sudden clarity, from the very first moment he'd seen her in that hotel in Cairo, smoking a hookah and defying him with every fiber of her being. And he had ached for her in his dreams for far longer still. The emptiness he'd felt in his life before he'd met Jezebel had vanished the moment she'd come into it, he realized now, replaced with more joy and excitement—and yes, more frustrated anger—than he'd ever expected to experience. She was a precious gift, one he'd taken for granted long enough. Somehow, some way, he must make amends for his cruel words.

Rafe had only meant to press her head against his shoulder for comfort—much as Belmore must have done earlier, he realized with a surge of remorse—but Jezebel had turned the tables on him again, as she had so often in the past. Now, instead of comfort, he sensed she needed wild abandon; frantic, furious loving that he could not deny her. Rafe wrapped both hands in the soft waves of her hair and held on while she ravaged him with all the stormy passion that was in her heart. If this was what Jezebel needed of him, then he would gladly give it. More than gladly.

Dear God, how he loved this sweet, savage woman. Loved her as he'd never loved another woman, needed her as he needed breath in his body. And he had almost lost her with his blindness and jealousy. "Jezebel, Jezebel, Jezebel," he groaned into her mouth endlessly, his lips shaped by hers and their tongues dueling with frenzied need. "Forgive me." But his words and his kisses weren't enough to assuage her pain.

Before he knew what she was about, Jezebel had found the opening of his tight buckskin trousers, had undone the flap with fingers made clumsy by her trembling eagerness, and released his aching shaft from its confinement. "What . . . ?" he began, then ended the question in a sharp gasp of ecstasy as she shifted impatiently upon his lap, sinking down relentlessly until she was impaled upon the full measure of his hard, throbbing length.

Rafe smothered his cry, knowing they could be heard

outside the coach. But Jezebel seemed not to care. Her fingers were tangled painfully in his hair, and she alternately pressed forward to kiss him and leaned back upon his lap to feel the fullness of his possession, riding him with a natural expertise that came of complete unrestraint. She rose up sharply, plunged down upon him with her slick heat, rocked and circled with her hips until he thought he would die from the urgency of the sensations she caused.

Again and again he whispered her name, but she would not look at him now. She would kiss him, stinging his mouth with rapturous, deep caresses. She would take his shaft within her body and lavish it with all the liquid fire that was in her. But she would not look at him.

Rafe became aware that she was murmuring something, over and over again, like a litany of prayer. But when he pulled her mouth close to his ear, his heart squeezed in pain, even as his loins clenched with the incredible pleasure she forced upon him. "I hate you," she was whispering. "I hate you, I hate you, I hate you."

At last, as she was nearing her climax, and her murmurs became cries that grew louder and louder, he was forced to slide one hand up the satiny column of her neck and put his palm across her lips to muffle them. And just as her incredibly powerful inner muscles began to spasm around him, both became aware of a noise that came from outside the conveyance.

"Yer Grace?" came the slightly slurred voice. "Yer Grace, we've arrived. I'll jest be fetchin' the coach steps now, so I will."

It was too late for Jezebel. The first waves of her climax had already overcome her, and Rafe saw the anguished embarrassment of realization cross her face even as the tide of rapture submerged her. He kept eye contact with her, willing her to see his encouragement, his protection, and, yes, his love for her. Mutely, he offered his hand for her to bite down on, and she took it, mercilessly grinding her sharp white teeth into his flesh to stop the cries that overwhelmed her. Rafe simply held her tightly with his other arm, gritted his own teeth against both the pain of her bite and the far more unbearable need to let his own pleasure overtake him simultaneously.

Within seconds it was over. Jezebel collapsed, and Rafe went to work.

*P*oor girl seems to have fainted from all the excitement of her first ball," he said to the dumbfounded coachman, who opened the door to find his sweating and rumpled employer with the young miss slumped bonelessly across his lap. The driver's wondering eyes followed them dubiously as the duke bounded past him up the steps of his townhouse carrying his disheveled burden, her skirts and long unbound tresses flying every which way. He brushed similarly past the concerned butler at the door, climbing the two flights of inner stairs two at a time to the third floor, where the bedrooms were located. In the corridors he scattered chambermaids and footmen like leaves in his wake.

"Attend her!" Rafe barked to Jezebel's startled personal maid as he shoved the door to her suite open with his foot, speaking far more sharply than was his wont. The sweet, round-faced girl's eyes went from sleep-closed to saucer-wide when she saw her new mistress, swooning in the master's arms, being so precipitously borne into the chamber. She leapt to her feet, knocking the hard-backed chair she'd been napping in across the dressing room floor in her haste. "The young miss has need of your assistance," the duke said more gently, obviously seeing he'd frightened her.

"Oh, what's 'appened to poor Miss Jezebel, Your Grace?" quavered the girl, whose name, if he remembered right, was Sophie. Rafe thought quickly.

"Too much champagne and too much excitement her first night out, I imagine," he said, striving for a tone of boredom. "It's naught to be frightened about. Simply attend to her toilette quickly, and then leave her to rest undisturbed for the night—you may bunk upstairs with one of the parlor maids, for I'm sure Miss Montclair will have no further need of you until the morrow. She looks fair to be sleeping it off well past noon."

"Oh, yes, Your Grace, right away!" Sophie anxiously followed the duke as he strode into the bedroom, heading directly for the wide feather bed with its blue satin counterpane. The duke deposited his dazed burden carefully upon the cover, then turned to leave.

"You're a good girl, Sophie. Now, no gossip about the young miss, you understand? She'll be quite embarrassed enough in the morning without a lot of talk going 'round about her unfortunate excesses, I imagine."

"Oh, yes, Your Grace—I mean, no, Your Grace!" Sophie bobbed a curtsy, then nervously added another, as if the first were not enough to convey her sincerity. "I'll not speak a word!" Awed, she watched him stride from the room, not noticing the stiffness of his gait or the way he held one hand close to his chest as if it pained him. All she saw was every girl's knight in shining armor come to life.

*O*h, miss, ain't he just dashing?" the ladies' maid gushed, helping Jezebel out of her shoes and stockings as her mistress lay limply on the bed.

*Dashing.* That was not the word Jezebel would have chosen, she thought dully. *Maddening* was more like it, for he had indeed made of her a madwoman. She wished she *had* overindulged in alcohol tonight, if only to bury the memory of what she had just done, or excuse her actions. Lewd, he'd called her, and lewd she had been. Outrageously, unbelievably brazen. She had just practically raped the man in his own carriage, never mind that he'd seemed to enjoy it. *How* could she have done such a thing? There was only one possible explanation, Jezebel knew. Her mother's madness had finally descended upon her, for at last she had dared to love.

She closed her eyes in despair, ignoring the chatter of the maid and the actions of her clever fingers as the girl divested her of her crumpled gown and underthings. She let Sophie sit her up and brush out her long tresses, let her slip a wispy nightrail over her head and tuck her under the covers. She even managed to whisper good night to the maid when she departed, leaving a single candle lit by the bedside. Jezebel couldn't have called the girl back now even if she'd wanted to. She had no will left, for she had succumbed to Rafe Sunderland: body, mind, and soul.

She truly hadn't been able to help herself in the coach, had needed the feeling of his masculine possession even as she vowed to hate him with every last breath. One moment she'd been furious with him, the next swamped with desire. It made no *sense,* she thought, anguished. No one could love and hate at the same time—unless they were subject to the curse that made love a kind of insanity, as Natalya Montclair had been. As Jezebel had always feared to become herself.

She'd feared that if she ever fell in love it would be the end of her hard-won composure and self-discipline. She'd feared her emotions would rage out of control and she would become the sort of frighteningly unstable woman her mother had been toward the end, subject to wild rages and unbearable suffering. If ever a man took over her heart, she'd feared to lose her mind.

And now all of her fears had come true, in the form of a blond Adonis who gave her more pleasure and more heartache than she could possibly bear.

Jezebel lay in the darkened chamber, her body still pulsing with the strength of her climax and her mind still reeling with the knowledge that she was doomed. There could be no hope for her now, nothing but a slow spiral into deepening madness, misery, and death. She'd seen it happen to her mother when her father could not return Natalya's love, and now it would happen to her. History would repeat itself, for Rafe, like Martin Montclair, did not love the woman whose affections he'd captured.

Oh, he desired her, that much she could see now. She might still be relatively innocent, but she knew no man could fake the sort of response he'd displayed. Yet desire and love were two separate feelings, and when it came to feelings, the one the duke displayed most often in her presence was simple irritation. She was a bother to him, a temptation to his body and a distraction to his mind. She was

someone Rafe would rather do without. But he was someone she *could not* do without.

He would return to her tonight, however, whatever the
future might hold. That much was certain. She'd seen it in
his eyes, felt the impatient tremors of lust in his body as
he'd taken her upstairs in his strong arms. He would not
deny himself again—why should he, when the damage was
already done? Honorable as Rafe had always tried to be,
she had tempted him too far to refuse the gift of her body
this night. She'd been every bit the Jezebel he'd called her,
had ravished him with her body and then left him wanting—no matter that it had not been by choice that they had
stopped. He would come for what she had denied him. But
how would she face him when he came?

Was there really any point in trying to resist the enchantment of his touch anymore? she wondered hopelessly.
Why should she, when he'd already taken possession of her
soul? *No,* Jezebel decided. *If this is to be my fate, then I
will savor the moment while I can. Come tomorrow, regret
may come to destroy me, sorrow teach me how to suffer,
but tonight I will be his.*

Slowly, she got to her feet, her hands going to the neck
of her gown. In moments she had the ribbons undone, and
it slid quietly to her feet. Naked and resolved to revel in
her madness, Jezebel climbed back upon the bed, laying
herself upon the cool satin of the coverlet as a sacrifice to
the god of passion.

She did not have long to wait before he came to
claim it.

*R*afe barreled out of his ward's chamber, striding down
the corridor toward his own master suite, shaking his head
in feigned disgust for the benefit of any servants lingering
in the hallway. She'd gotten herself foxed, his faintly
amused expression seemed to say, and she could damn well
deal with the consequences of the sore head she'd have
tomorrow on her own.

The instant he reached the privacy of his bedroom, how-

ever, Rafe's expression changed. He leaned heavily against
the door, his breath coming in shuddering gulps. Shaking,
he looked at his left hand, seeing the angry purple marks
of Jezebel's teeth making half-moons on both sides of the
heel of his hand. He would suffer a thousand bites like this
one just to taste the fire of her kiss again. He would suffer
far worse for her unforgettable brand of savage, untamed
loving. But for her sake, he knew he should not go to her
tonight. Hadn't he hurt her enough, tormented her fragile
heart sufficiently for one night?

Apparently not.

Despite his moral struggle, Rafe found himself standing
on the threshold of Jezebel's boudoir within short order,
quietly sliding shut the panel of the secret passageway con-
necting their suites. Thank God these old houses always
seemed to have been built by incorrigible lechers, he
thought with a hint of humor, for at the sight of the woman
on the bed before him, he was definitely experiencing some
powerfully lascivious thoughts. God, but she was beautiful.

Jezebel saw him then, alerted to his entrance perhaps by
an errant draft of air coming from the passage, perhaps by
the soft, admiring exhalation he could not keep from
crossing his lips as he made out her figure in the dimness.
She turned on her side to face him, her luminous sapphire
eyes reflecting no surprise, no anger, only welcome and a
sensual surrender that was breathtaking to witness.

Her pale body glowingly outlined against the ice-blue
satin bedspread, her long, ink-black tresses spread in waves
upon the pillows, her rosy-crested breasts visibly pebbled
even in the flickering light of the lone candle by her bed,
and the sweet shadowy V of downy curls just visible at the
juncture of her slender thighs, Jezebel was every man's
fantasy—and his own heart's desire. He had waited long
enough.

Two seconds later he was on top of her.

"I thought you would never return," she said as Rafe
settled himself between her legs, impatiently stripping off
his shirt and waistcoat—he'd already discarded his evening
jacket on his way to her bedchamber. His naked torso, gold-
furred and beautifully muscled, was soon bare against the

paler flesh of her own. His massive frame dwarfed her delicate one, and yet the picture they made together, Rafe like a majestic lion and Jezebel the sultry sylph who'd tamed him, was both mystical and deeply sensuous.

"I couldn't stay away," he replied softly, looking deeply into her eyes. "I tried, darling. God knows how I tried." Rafe's sense of failure was plain in his voice, and the apologies he did not know how to speak were written in his gaze.

Jezebel swallowed. "I didn't want you to stay away," she whispered achingly, her hand framing his slightly stubble-roughened cheek. Forgiveness was in her eyes, all anger forgotten for now, the battles between them subject to a tender truce for this one night. And then there were no more words between them. Rafe could not wait a minute more before claiming her, and Jezebel knew it. He had waited too long, both tonight and in the months since their last explosive coming together, and nothing could stop him from taking her now. His aching heaviness, shielded once more behind the constricting cloth barrier of his tight pantaloons, pressed hard against the juncture of her thighs, his unappeased hunger having grown to enormous proportions. But Jezebel didn't fear Rafe's heat. No, she welcomed it with everything in her being, for it matched her own desperate need.

His mouth took possession of hers with an ardor that was unknown to either one of them in previous kisses, a need that the love they could not express only made deeper and more poignant. His tongue swept across her lips, parting them before plunging inside to conquer the strawberry-and-champagne-flavored territory of her mouth. But he had no need to conquer what was already his. Jezebel gave him everything with a sublime sort of surrender: her kisses sweet, the touch of her strong musician's hands upon his body worshipful, the exquisite instrument of her body sharing her passions with him while the perilous love in her heart played a melody of its own.

Faint with sensual hunger, she barely felt him shed his boots and trousers, only sensed his brief absence while he took them off. But then he was back in her arms, naked, his hands stroking her cheeks with sweet, adoring tenderness even as his knees urged her legs to part. And then he was inside her body, fusing them so deeply that Jezebel cried out, while Rafe went still and rested his sweat-damp forehead against her own.

"I don't think I can wait," he said hoarsely. "I'm sorry, love."

In answer Jezebel only kissed him deeply, her tongue encouraging him to take all that he wanted of her as it dipped and darted inside his mouth. With a rough cry, he did as she bade, his hips plunging compulsively between her thighs, harder and faster and harder still until, with a roar of completion, Rafe collapsed atop her body, his seed pumping hotly into the welcoming depths of her womb. Yet even as the incredible intensity of his climax had him helplessly shuddering in her embrace, he was careful to make sure his elbows, resting on the pillows on either side of Jezebel's head, took most of his not-inconsiderable weight. Completely undone, Rafe buried his head in the curve of her neck, panting harshly and still gasping periodically as tremors of pleasure shook his body.

Jezebel was content to hold him, even though her own desire, fanned by his rough, desperate loving, had not been fully appeased. Her inner muscles clenched around his still-swollen shaft, loving the feel of him there, wanting him inside her forever. But he would not be hers forever, she knew. He would not want her for much longer.

*At least he is here now,* she thought with a hint of sadness. Her hands came up to stroke the beloved head that nestled next to hers, her fingers sifting through damp curls and massaging the muscles of his neck. Tears came to her eyes once more, but she did not want to shed them now. No. Now she simply wanted to savor the feeling of having her lover in her arms, his body warm and fragrant with the scent of satiated male, his heart beating strongly next to hers.

But Rafe was not content to simply lie with Jezebel, leaving her unsatisfied.

It started with slow kisses that lavished the side of her neck with tender fire: erotic, explicit kisses that had her

shivering and trembling and whimpering in his ear. Before
she knew it, he had lifted his head to hers and transferred
the kisses to her lips, laving and suckling each of her lips
individually with such openly carnal caresses that they
made her womb contract sharply. His shaft, still buried
deep inside her, seemed to leap in response, and Jezebel
gazed up in wonder. "So soon?" she asked breathlessly. "I
thought it was impossible. . . ."

Rafe laughed shakily, hitching himself up on his elbows,
his manhood pushing even deeper into her with the movement, so that both paused to savor the ecstasy. "Sweetheart," he said with a whimsical smile, "with you, nothing
is impossible."

And until dawn, he proved just that.

He taught her things about her own body that she would
never have guessed were possible, wrung smothered
screams of rapture from her kiss-swollen lips until her voice
was hoarse and she was sobbing from the intensity of her
pleasure. For hours he made love to her, showing her tech-
niques and positions she'd never dreamed of. And Jezebel
absorbed every lesson eagerly, learning so quickly that she
managed to show even the sophisticated duke a few new
things of her own. But mostly, it was Rafe who led the
intrepid explorer into uncharted territory this night.

At one point, while Rafe had Jezebel positioned close to
the foot of her high bed, stretched on her back while he
stood gloriously nude between her legs, slowly thrusting in
and out of her tight passage, he took her small hand in his
own and drew her fingers into his mouth. He smiled at her
expression when he bathed her fingertips with his tongue,
sucking them with wicked suggestiveness. She looked up
at him slumberously, trusting that she would like whatever
he did to her body. But what he did next shocked even her.

Rafe took her fingers, wet from the loving of his mouth,
and slid them slowly down her own body until he'd reached
the place where they were joined. Her eyes widened and
she held her breath as he guided her moist fingers to explore
her own flesh, to feel the thickness of his shaft where it
entered her, to feel his heavy sac, and then, most incredibly,
to touch the exquisitely sensitive nub just above the spot

where their bodies were joined. A stab of pleasure went through her so strongly that she stilled, looking up at him with wondering questions in her eyes.

"Show me," he commanded. "Show me how to pleasure you, Jezebel."

Too shy even to watch what she did, Jezebel tentatively stroked this new source of rapture, slowly learning her own body's needs while Rafe watched with narrowed eyes, keeping his own passion in check with iron control. He continued to thrust gently in and out of her body, not increasing his pace until she begged him to do it, her slender form writhing and bucking beneath him. And then he took over for her, his skillful fingers stroking her clitoris with sure, intuitive motions even as he pumped harder and harder into her body.

Her climax this time went on for what seemed like hours, with Rafe's coming only moments later in a hot flood of seed that bathed her with the proof of his possession. It was so much more than she'd ever thought her body capable of feeling that Jezebel actually laughed, incredulity and euphoria making her giddy. Rafe grinned back, tenderly stroking her flushed cheek with one callused thumb.

And that was only the beginning.

Neither would relinquish this one stolen chance for love, not now, not though it cost them the world. Though they tried to take it slowly, to savor every moment, the dark hours before dawn fairly flew for Rafe and Jezebel in a haze of mad, reckless pleasure.

# Chapter Twenty-five

$\smile$

$\mathcal{B}$ut dawn did come, hard as the lovers strove to hold it off, and with dawn came sanity—or at least what remained of it. The wreckage of pillows, discarded clothing, and unwanted bedcovers strewn about the bed and the floor all around it made it look as though a hurricane had passed through in the night. And in a way it had, thought Rafe. Both he and Jezebel had been completely devastated by the intense force of their loving.

He must leave her soon, he knew. Despite the command he'd given the little maid Sophie to leave her mistress undisturbed, it was not safe for the duke to remain in Jezebel's chamber much longer. All it would take was one overly conscientious chambermaid getting it into her head to stoke the hearth or replace some linens, and the whole world would know within hours that the duke of Ravenhurst had been found stark naked in his ward's bed.

Rumor would spread like wildfire throughout the servants' network and on to their employers, so that by breakfast time, all of society would be avidly discussing their indiscretion over biscuits and hot chocolate. The talk would not be kind, he knew. It never was. And despite the fact that he could think of no better fate than to be found in such a state every morning for the rest of his life, Rafe didn't think a servant's shriek of moral outrage was the best way to inaugurate the future he hoped to spend with Jezebel.

Provided he *had* a future with Jezebel. That was still undecided, he knew, for he could not be sure the unpredictable Miss Montclair would accept his suit, despite the welcoming way she had accepted his body. She had a rather unnerving habit of doing and saying whatever was least expected, as he'd had cause to learn time and again over the last several months. Who knew in what mood she would arise today? *Well,* he thought, taking a deep breath, *there's only one way to find out, isn't there?*

Rafe turned onto his side, gazing down at Jezebel. He knew she wasn't asleep, though her eyes remained closed, lashes like dark fans against her fair unblemished cheeks. She lay on her back, head turned away from him, one arm thrown out across the bed as if reaching for something. Something he could not give her? he wondered. There had been a sorrowful quality in her surrender last night, almost a sense of despair. Did she regret their intimacy already, or did she feel as he did, wanting only for it to continue, sorry only that they had fought for so long? He hadn't been able to tell anything from her behavior during the endless hours of the night except that she desired his body. But what went on in that guarded heart of hers? Rafe still knew little more of that than he had the day he'd met her, though it was his fondest hope to spend the rest of his life unraveling the mystery.

"Jezebel," he whispered softly, leaning down to kiss her. She opened her eyes slowly, her expression unreadable this morning, as though she had been having serious thoughts of her own. Her lips were warm and welcoming, however, greeting him and the day with soft solemnity.

"Hmm?" She leaned up on her elbow so that they were face-to-face, skin to skin. Her hair fell like dark rain about her shoulders. Her beautiful breasts, their nipples hardened and rosy from his caresses, rested inches from his chest. Still smoldering with the night's desire, she looked as if she might bridge the distance with another kiss at any moment.

Rafe had difficulty concentrating suddenly. "I have something I must ask you, sweetheart," he said. "Something very important. I—"

*Oh, not yet,* she thought. *Don't let this night be over yet. I'm not ready for it to end, not ready for morning's consequences.* Jezebel didn't think she would ever be ready. "Don't!" she said urgently, putting her hand across his mouth. "I know what you want to say, but please, don't ask it of me. Don't spoil this night for both of us," she begged, moisture growing in her eyes. But it was too late.

"Spoil it!" he said incredulously. "I want to marry you and you think that will spoil our lovemaking? What kind of sense does that make?" Rafe's tender mood was fast fading, replaced with bewildered hurt. He'd had a feeling Jezebel might persist in her refusal, but having it confirmed didn't make it any easier to take.

"No sense at all," she replied sadly. *Madness is inherently nonsensical,* she thought. "But I cannot marry you nonetheless."

"Well, why the hell not?" he demanded. "Can you honestly say you have no feelings for me? Can you tell me you'd rather marry some stranger who, for all you know, might very well abandon you on your wedding night to go visit his mistress? It's not unheard of among our set, as I'm sure you know." Rafe blew out his breath in frustration, seeing from the stubbornly closed expression on her face that he was not having any effect on Jezebel. But whether he could make her change her mind or not, he needed to understand her reasoning.

"Explain to me how you can prefer such a fate to sharing your life with me, with whom you have already shared so much," he implored, one hand stroking across her silky shoulder. "I am prepared to protect you, care for you, honor you above all other women for the rest of our lives. Can you not, in return, learn to love me just a little, Jezebel?"

Learn to love him? Pain shot through Jezebel's already bruised heart, and she squeezed her eyes shut. There was no "learning" involved. Her heart had always known him, worshiped him, needed him. Of course she could love him. Yet could he do the same?

Throughout the long night during which he had lavished her so thoroughly with his tender lovemaking, he had refused her all words of love. He'd said nothing of his feelings, though his body had spoken eloquently of its lust. And now he still could not speak the words, even as he asked her to marry him. Rafe did not love her any more today than he had yesterday, she thought wretchedly. He had simply given in to his body's needs, and, out of honor, wanted to make things right.

Now he asked her to admit her love for him. But it was impossible to open her heart in such a reckless way, when all his own heart felt was that damnable sense of duty that pervaded everything he did. His proposal was simply another example of his guilty conscience, she knew, and Jezebel could not marry a man who felt only pity for her—not when what she felt for him was so much more.

Marriage to Rafe would kill her, she thought wretchedly, and worse, make *his* life a living hell. He would learn to hate her before long, to despise the bonds of need she placed upon him. As she grew weaker, less able to control the madness that would grow within her, he would turn from her in disgust. And she would wither beneath his scorn, his indifference. It was not a future Jezebel wanted to contemplate for either of them.

For her own sake, she might accept his proposal, cravenly clinging to him despite the insanity his touch brought about, but for his, she must decline it. There was no other way to set him free, for she knew Rafe would never forsake his responsibility to her, no matter how much he might eventually yearn to do so. Jezebel couldn't let him make such a sacrifice.

"No," she said at last, heart breaking in her chest. She looked down, letting her hair fall in front of her eyes, for she could not look him in the face while she gave him such a terrible lie. "I could never love a man like you." But the real truth, the truth she could not speak, was that she *must* never love a man like him.

Rafe felt the words enter his body like a saber thrust. He stared down in wonderment at the woman he adored, feeling as if his life's blood were draining away. "A man like me," he repeated slowly, digesting the words. He thought he understood her meaning, suddenly. In fact, a lot of things were abruptly becoming clear.

He wasn't adventurous enough for her.

He wasn't exciting enough, or daring enough, or carefree enough to capture her wild Gypsy heart. She wanted a man like Belmore, who might sweep her off on some exotic

escapade at the drop of a hat. Or, he thought, perhaps someone like Damien, with whom she'd laughed so merrily the
night before; someone light-hearted and gay and irrespon-
sible. Someone who would not try to hold her down or tell
her what to do, as she had so often accused him of doing.

Anger rose again in the duke. Damn it! After all he had
done for her sake, all the time he had spent trying to protect
her and see to her happiness, she still wanted no part of
him! But no, that wasn't quite true, was it? There was one
part of him his ward seemed to enjoy well enough, he
thought furiously. Curse her! She took what she wanted,
and let the rest go all to hell—her reputation, her safety,
her future. His heart. None of it seemed to matter to Jezebel.

"You won't have a man like me," he mused, something
in his tone dark and ugly. "Well, Jezebel. What if I told
you you damn well *will* have a man like me, like it or not?
What if I said I won't give you up to another man, that
I'm tired of your games and I intend to make you my wife
before the day is through?"

Jezebel lay back, shrinking from the fury in his eyes.
"You cannot do that," she said flatly.

"You think not? All I have to do, sweet Jezebel, is wait
until your maid walks in that door to find us, or better yet,
drag you outside naked and announce to the world just
exactly what it is we've been doing for the past several
hours. You'll be ruined unless you agree to marry me. Society will spurn you; no lady or gentleman of good name
will have anything to do with you. You'll be cut dead, do
you understand?"

"*Let* them cut me," Jezebel said contemptuously, pur-
posefully infusing scorn into her voice. She dragged the
sheet up to cover her breasts as she rose to her knees on
the bed, facing Rafe's anger squarely. It was imperative that
she finish this horrid confrontation before her resolve gave
out and she dissolved into a puddle of miserable tears, letting him see how very much it was hurting her to argue
with him after the beauty of the lovemaking they'd shared.
Already the pain inside her felt as if it were crushing the
very breath from her lungs, but she struggled on.

"Do you think I give a damn what society does or says about me? If you believe that, you've learned nothing about me at all, Rafe. Not one damned thing. You can drag me to that altar by the hair if you please, but I will never say the words that would bind me to you." Her voice broke then, and she dragged in a ragged breath. "I'd rather have my shame branded on my chest for the rest of my life for all the world to see than make such a disastrous mistake." Jezebel spun around, a curtain of hair masking the sorrow upon her face, and got up from the bed. When she turned to face him again, however, her expression was composed.

"Please, spare us both this humiliation, Rafe. Leave now, and let us pretend this night never happened." There. She'd given him his way out. She waited breathlessly for his reaction, not knowing if he would explode with anger, or take her dismissal with the relieved indifference of a man ending a casual affair that has gone stale. She wasn't sure which she feared more.

"You would still marry another?" Rafe asked tonelessly. "Knowing your only choice is between me and a man you've never met, you would do this?" He too came to his feet, scooping up his discarded trousers and yanking them on with controlled fury.

Her chin rose. It seemed the duke was not pleased with the release she'd offered him, after all. "If you leave me no other option, then yes."

"Damn it! What other option is there?" he yelled suddenly. "If I sent you away to one of my estates for the remainder of your minority, I would have to keep you a virtual prisoner out there in the country, knowing you as I do—you'd flee the moment my back was turned. And I do not wish to stoop to such medieval tactics any more than you wish me to. That is not worthy of either of us." He took a long, angry breath.

"But do you truly think I could bear to have you under my roof for the next five years and never touch you, Jezebel? You and I both know we cannot remain within ten leagues of one another without ending up in bed together. I would not be able to restrain myself from making you, in effect, my mistress—and I doubt you can claim to have

much more fortitude, my sweet ward." Rafe's tone made a
mockery of the endearment.

"Knowing that I will almost certainly shame us both if
you are not safely put beyond my reach, or bound to me
in the eyes of the law, how can I, with any honor, allow
you to remain unwed and in disgrace any longer? This is
not what your uncle expected of me when he made me your
guardian. It is not proper. Hell, it simply is not *right*!"

His damnable honor again, Jezebel thought sadly. For
Rafe, this was all a matter of doing what was right, not
what his heart commanded. She had been right to refuse
him, for the only things binding him to her besides their
unreasonable physical attraction were the terms of Lord
Clifton's will. "Then let me go, Rafe. Just let me go," she
pleaded, though she knew it was no use.

He ran his hand across his face defeatedly. "That I cannot do."

"Then there is nothing left to say, is there?" she said. It
wasn't a question. "We will go on as we did before, Your
Grace, and damn your stubborn soul to hell." She gestured
toward the secret door with a shaking hand, waiting, praying for him to go.

It wasn't until the panel had slid closed with soft finality
that Jezebel collapsed to the floor, letting the pain overcome
her in a hot flood of tears.

*T*he floor was where Lady Allison found her, sleeping
heavily, close to noontime.

The baroness looked around the wrecked chamber wordlessly, surveying both the rumpled, churned-up sea of bedding and the red-rimmed eyelids of the girl huddled
miserably on the carpet with an equally unreadable gaze.
What had happened here during the night would have been
obvious to a much meaner intellect than Allison's. Yet she
had no words of condemnation for Jezebel, though the
younger woman, waking to find her immaculately dressed
chaperone standing over her, feared to receive at the very
least a harsh lecture for the disgraceful behavior there was

no way she could deny. But instead, after helping Jezebel rise to her feet, she merely ordered her a bath and set about preparing her for the day ahead.

"There will be any number of young bucks calling at the house to sniff around your skirts today if I did my job properly last night," Allison said as she wound Jezebel's freshly washed and dried hair into an elegant chignon at the back of her head, having dismissed Sophie in order to attend her charge herself. "I can't tell you how many infinitely suitable young men at the Netherlands' ball asked my blessing to call upon you. You'll want to look your best for them, no doubt."

Jezebel opened her mouth to protest she didn't want to look *any* way for them, that all she wanted was to crawl back into her bed and hide from the world, but Allison didn't give her the chance.

"After all," she went on seemingly idly, "His Grace will be perfectly green with jealousy when he sees you at the center of such a crowd of fine young men. Won't it be amusing to watch him squirm, knowing there is nothing he can say, since you are only doing as you are bid?"

Allison seemed to be offering these words as comfort to her young friend, but not even the thought of making Rafe jealous could cheer Jezebel, for she knew perfectly well that he would not envy any men who came to woo her today. No, she thought miserably, rather than begrudging them their suits, he was more likely to thank them profusely for taking her off his hands after the way she had angered him this morning.

Blast Rafe and his stubborn self-righteousness for making her go through this charade! It was cruel to order her to choose another man when it was him she loved, Jezebel thought. No, it was more than cruel. It was pure torture. Yet strangely enough, she found she no longer had any desire to take vengeance on the duke for the pain he was causing her. Perhaps even as recently as last evening Lady Allison's idea of tormenting Rafe had pleased her, but all thoughts of revenge had fled her mind the moment she'd realized she loved him.

If she hurt him, she hurt herself as well, for as angry as

she was at the man who had taken her innocence and stolen her heart, Jezebel had discovered last night that his well-being meant more to her than did her own. She didn't want to make Rafe as miserable as she was, the way Lady Allison was suggesting. Still, she knew it would not be hard to accomplish that task if she chose, with or without jealousy on his part. All she had to do was agree to marry Rafe, and he would suffer every bit as much as she.

Jezebel knew full well that if he even suspected how much her heart was aching to be with him, he would press her again to be his wife—out of guilt if nothing else. And as strong as she was, she didn't know if she could refuse Rafe a third time. Therefore, for his sake she must pretend to be content with the situation, content to give her heart and hand to a man like the ones at last night's ball. She must greet her suitors with as much false enthusiasm as she could muster, and go through the motions of encouraging them to woo her.

Whether or not she would marry one of them, however, was another matter.

Though she felt more lost and confused than she'd ever felt in her life, Jezebel was not yet entirely ready to sacrifice what was left of her future in order to obey her guardian's decree. He ordered that she become wife to one of the effete fops who seemed to be all the *ton* had to offer. Well, she might already be suffering from a madness that was doomed to grow and perhaps one day destroy her, but she wasn't *that* far gone yet! Since she could not change his mind, she knew she must instead find a way to escape Rafe and the strict code of honor that dictated his life. It would be better for both of them in the end.

What she might do, Jezebel was not yet sure, but she still had time to decide that, just as Lady Mayhew had suggested when she'd persuaded her charge to stay awhile in London—had it really been just last week? She would think of something before it was too late, but until she did, she would just have to play along with the uncomfortable role she'd been assigned.

What was a little discomfort anyway? Jezebel thought. Compared to the ache in her heart, the minor annoyance of surviving a short time in society was nothing to her. What she did, where she went—none of it really mattered to her anymore. As long as she managed to break away from Rafe before she did them both irreparable harm, any pain she might endure along the way was incidental. And after she had left the duke and his world behind, she would have a lifetime to spend attempting to forget the memory of everything that had happened to her here—a lifetime of failing to forget.

So she said nothing in response to Lady Allison's words, merely allowing herself to be dressed and readied for the day like a lifeless doll.

Behind her, unnoticed by Jezebel, her chaperone frowned with deep concern.

Miss Montclair was in deeper than she'd feared.

*R*afe returned that afternoon from a ferocious, bruising bout at Gentleman Jackson's boxing salon to find his house so crammed with fresh-cut flowers that he almost could not wade his way inside through the bouquets stacked up in the entranceway. The smell of the chocolate confections in their gaily wrapped parcels strewn upon the sideboards mingled with the scent of the blooms to form a heavy cloud of cloying sweetness permeating the halls.

What was going on here? When he'd left his ward this morning, striding furiously out the door in search of an outlet for his overpowering emotions, the house had been quiet, empty. Even the servants had still been sleeping, and Lady Allison, if she had even spent the night in the townhouse, had been nowhere in evidence. Now, however, the place was filled with the sound of many merry, boisterous voices—almost all of them male. But it was only the single, sultry female voice he heard that had the power to start his pulse pounding.

Jezebel's contralto laughter floated above the tenor and baritone masculine hum, a distinct musical counterpoint that had her guardian frowning mightily and marching for the salon from whence the noise came.

When he realized the significance of what he saw there, it did not please him one bit.

As Rafe entered the room, he was greeted by a sea of dandies, Corinthians, and young pinks of the *ton*. All rose at the sight of the duke, bowing low so that their colorful morning coats bellied out over tight buckskins and mirror-polished boots, reminding him of so many birds displaying their plumage. "Good afternoon, Your Grace," murmured a dozen voices simultaneously.

These men were here courting Jezebel.

This fact was instantly obvious to Rafe, and so was the rather sickening realization that, as her guardian, it was supposed to be *his* task to weigh and encourage their suits. At the thought, Rafe instantly felt about nine hundred years old. Methuselah must have had a similar experience when his daughters and granddaughters brought home suitors for him to approve. Except Methuselah had not been in love with his progeny as Rafe was with his ward.

He'd known this day would come, had been dreading it for months, in fact, but he hadn't expected the job to begin so soon after Jezebel's debut. Nor so soon after the heart-break of this morning. Yet he must face the torment despite his feelings, for his ward had given him no choice. He could not be responsible for ruining her future, which would most certainly happen if he did as he wished and tossed the lot of these gallants headfirst down the front steps. Rafe must do his duty, though duty had never before seemed such a crushing burden.

"Sit down, sit down, for heaven's sake," he ordered the anxious swains. "This isn't a military parade." Belying this statement, he began prowling about the salon, hands clasped behind his back, studying the faces of the gentle-men whose attention Jezebel had attracted and recognizing a number of the same young bucks who had been her part-ners in the dancing last night. All had come back for an-other taste of her charms, it seemed. He could understand why.

Rafe's eyes sought out Jezebel in the midst of this crowd and found her seated among a circle of her most ardent admirers, smiling winsomely at the young men. She was dressed in a modest confection of flower-sprigged white poplin, which covered her from neck to slippers and should have made her look both girlish and innocent, but which, to Rafe, made his ward appear almost unbearably sensuous after the night he'd spent exploring every inch of the skin so teasingly covered now. He could have stared at her forever, remembering both the pain and the rapture of their evening together. Could it really have been only hours ago? Rafe ached at the sight of her as though they had been apart for years.

When she caught sight of him, however, Jezebel's expression tightened in seeming distaste, and she looked away quickly, turning to listen to one of the men seated nearby as if he were the most fascinating orator of all time. Allison, he noticed, sat beside her on the sofa, looking over the proceedings benignly until she glanced up to see her cousin. When she turned her gaze in his direction, Rafe could have sworn a look of displeasure crossed the blond woman's angelic features before she covered it with a smile of welcome.

"Greetings, dear boy. Isn't it the most wonderful day? Miss Montclair and I have been entertaining these fine gentlemen with the help of your good friend Marksley, but we have all been awaiting your return so that you might grant permission for your ward to partake of an outing with the suitor of her choosing. All have been deeply anxious to claim the honor of her company, I can assure you!" Allison laughed good-naturedly.

For the first time Rafe noticed Damien among the crowd, strolling over from across the room where he had been engaged in conversation with a couple of nervous-looking fellows.

"How does it feel to be the guardian of the most successful young lady to debut in London this Season?" Marksley asked as he came up to the group. His expression was suspiciously innocent. "There is no woman in England to compare with her, I vow—excepting our dear Lady Allison, of course."

Allison took the compliment as her due, but Rafe noticed that Jezebel barely seemed to hear it. Her expression was faraway, haunted, and her lids were heavy—from lack of sleep, he guessed, an affliction they shared.

How did it feel to be Jezebel's guardian? It felt like hell, the duke thought. "I'm overwhelmed," he said with a patently false smile. "But how is our dear charge taking to all this new attention?" He directed his question pointedly at Jezebel, and she reluctantly met his gaze.

"Very well indeed, Your Grace," she said neutrally. He could read nothing in her eyes, no recognition of what had gone between them, though he very much wanted to see it. Then she turned to take in the roomful of beaus with her next words, speaking much more warmly. "It is an honor to make the acquaintance of so many fine gentleman, and I am flattered that they should extend their efforts to make such an ignorant provincial girl feel welcome in town."

Instantly her words were decried from all across the salon. "Nonsense! It is our honor to be allowed into the presence of such fairness," said one gallant, bowing deeply. Another spoke up, saying, "We are privileged even to be admitted within the circle of radiance cast by your exquisite beauty." Yet another swore, in all seriousness, "If yours be ignorance, then let me spend the rest of my life in that sublime state of witlessness, dear lady."

*No need to wish for that,* Rafe thought uncharitably. He thought he caught his ward rolling her eyes, but when he looked closer, he saw she was smiling upon the fool graciously. "You are too kind," she said, sweeping them all with her gaze and placing one hand to her chest as if swearing to her sincerity. "You are all much too kind. How can I repay you for the sweetness of your words?"

"Let me take you out walking," said one.

"No, come riding with me!"

"I would be honored to accompany Miss Montclair for ices," said a third man, and then the rest of the proposals merged together in a hubbub of competing offers. Jezebel looked a bit overwhelmed, and Rafe was less than pleased as the noise level grew and the rivalry between the swains became less civilized.

"My curricle is much finer than yours, you popinjay,"

said one to another. "Miss Montclair will not wish to rattle about in that rusty old trap you sport."

Two other young men, remarkable only for the loud colors of their waistcoats, started bickering over who had the right to ask the lady out to Lloyd's coffeehouse. "I saw her first, damn your eyes," said one, a baronet.

"Maybe so, but I outrank you, now, don't I?" gloated the other, who happened to be a viscount.

Finally, Lady Allison was forced to step in. "Gentlemen, gentlemen, please," she said loudly, gesturing for quiet. "Your enthusiasm is extremely gratifying, but Miss Montclair cannot possibly choose whom she will accompany this afternoon if you all continue squabbling like a lot of schoolboys. Pray, a little more decorum, if you please." ·

Shamed silence ruled for a moment while the young men hung their heads. Marksley took it as his cue to step in.

"Well, *I* was wondering if Miss Montclair might not like to visit the museum this afternoon, seeing as I understand she has quite an interest in antiquities, and I have a standing invitation from the trustees to bring guests."

Jezebel's head came up and she smiled brilliantly, her blue eyes showing genuine interest as she gazed at the handsome marquis. "Why, that sounds delightful, my lord," she said. "I should love to accompany you to view the exhibits."

"Well", Allison smiled, "that's settled, then."

"No, I am afraid it is *not* settled. Not remotely," the duke retorted smartly. "Would you care to step outside the salon with me, Marksley?" he asked. Rafe's tone made it clear that this was not a request. It was a threat.

"Certainly, old boy," replied the marquis, seeming not at all concerned. He grinned tauntingly at the disappointed beaus still crowding around Jezebel, as if to say, *Just wait till it's your turn, lads!*

*J*ust what the bloody hell are you up to, Damien?" Rafe growled once they'd reached the empty hallway.

"Up to?" Damien asked innocently. He leaned one

shoulder nonchalantly against the silk-papered wall,
crossing his legs at the ankle as he responded to Rafe.
"Why, I've no idea what you mean. I'm simply spending
a delightful spring afternoon escorting a beautiful lady to
the entertainment of her choice. Lucky fellow, ain't I? It's
sure to be a fascinating outing, what with Miss Montclair's
unusual background and all. I can't wait for her to share
her unique perspective on the exhibits."

"That's rubbish, and you know it. You haven't even the
slightest interest in antiquities. In fact, I distinctly recall
your knuckles being rapped more than once for falling
asleep in history classes back at Eton. So why are you really
so interested in taking my ward out this afternoon?"

Damien looked offended. "Can't a man ever escape the
infamies of his past?" he complained, sighing theatrically.
"Seriously, Rafe, forgive me if I have this wrong, but did
you not specifically ask my help in getting your little Miss
Montclair married off all those months ago?"

"Yes, I suppose I did," Rafe conceded reluctantly, still
frowning. "But I don't see how separating her from her
suitors is supposed to assist in that effort."

"Well, old boy, it may shock you to hear this, but the
way I see it, I'm not actually separating Jezebel entirely
from her beaus," the marquis fibbed. Lady Allison had better be right about the efficacy of making Rafe jealous, he
thought, or he was going to be out one best friend very
shortly! But he had faith in the baroness's Machiavellian
talent for deception, and he'd already agreed to play this
part last night. He would not back out now.

"You see," he continued blithely, "ever since I met your
charming ward last night, I've been seriously thinking
about throwing my own hat in the ring for the girl. I tell
you, she's enough of a temptation to make even a confirmed bachelor like myself reconsider getting leg-
shackled."

There was a small, ugly silence while Rafe sized up his
erstwhile friend.

"I think you had better just reconsider that decision a
second time, my friend," he said softly. "Jezebel is off limits to you."

"Oh, really?" Damien replied, eyebrows rising incredulously, as if this were the most astonishing thing the duke had ever said. "Is it my lack of fortune you object to, if I may ask, or is it that you find fault with my character?" He knew it was neither of these things, considering his wealth nearly rivaled Rafe's own and his character had not stopped the two men from sharing each other's companionship for the past twenty years. A hint of mirth glinted in his eyes as he baited his unfortunate friend. Allison was a veritable genius, he thought. Rafe was jealous already.

The duke scowled. "Damn it, Marksley, I don't have to have a reason. I say you may not marry her, and that is the end of this debate, do you understand?"

"Oh, I understand, all right, old friend," Damien said with a grin. "The only thing I *don't* get is why you don't give up this ridiculous pretense of searching for a husband for the chit and marry her yourself."

There was another pregnant pause.

"She wouldn't have me," Rafe said at last, stonily. His face turned a deep red as he made this admission, and he glared at the marquis as if challenging him to laugh.

"She wouldn't *what* . . . ?" Damien gaped, his mind boggled by the notion of any young lady refusing the much-sought-after Lord Ravenhurst. Why, women had been pursuing Rafe ever since he'd been old enough to run from the visions of wedded bliss in their eyes! To think that not only had the duke been swayed from his long-held opinions about marriage enough to actually propose to Jezebel, but that she had had the nerve—or the foolishness—to refuse him, was almost more than Damien could believe. He'd seen that Rafe harbored feelings for his ward, and that there was more to their relationship than either wanted made public, but he had not dreamed things had already progressed so far. "The girl actually turned you down?"

"Twice," Rafe said tightly.

*"Twice!"*

"You heard me, Marksley. Now shut that foolish mouth of yours before you start catching flies. This discussion is closed. You may take Miss Montclair to the museum today and provide escort for her to other affairs as we originally discussed—as long as Lady Allison accompanies you, of course—but you are to dismiss all notions of developing any sort of intimate relationship with my ward. If you seriously wish to find yourself a wife, then you must look elsewhere, do you understand? If you cannot accept this decree, then you are no longer welcome in my home."

"It will be as you wish, Your Grace," the marquis said deferentially, giving the other man a low, formal bow. With troubled eyes, he watched Rafe stalk, stiff-backed, down the hall toward his study.

The duke was in deeper than he'd realized.

# Chapter Twenty-six

By the time Jezebel had returned from her expedition to the rapidly expanding British Museum, she had already changed her mind about her level of tolerance for a lengthy stay among the *beau monde*. Had she believed it would no longer matter to her if she stayed? Nothing could be further from the truth. No. Now she realized it was quite imperative that she remove herself from London quickly—before she became completely and utterly unbalanced!

It was not Lord Marksley's company that had caused this feeling in Jezebel. Indeed, he'd been the perfect companion—charming, attentive, and, of course, handsome enough to turn any girl's head. He'd squired her about, Lady Allison in tow, through the many exhibits scattered about the dusty, dimly lit rooms of the burgeoning museum, asking insightful questions about some of the Egyptian relics they passed and displaying a good deal of curiosity about her days exploring the world with Lord Clifton. Marksley had been as entertaining and thoughtful as a young lady could ask.

But he was not Raphael Sunderland, and that was all Miss Montclair could truly say she noticed about him that day.

Nothing the marquis said or did on that afternoon could lighten the leaden feeling in Jezebel's heart, and though she tried to hide it from both her companions beneath a sunny smile and animated chatter, she knew neither one of them was fooled. The duke of Ravenhurst had torn a hole in her heart, and no amount of sightseeing, no matter how amusing the company, could hope to heal the wound. The pain of knowing Rafe would never love her as she so desperately loved him made Jezebel feel like an injured animal, bleed-

ing inside and unlikely to survive. She could think of nothing but the golden beauty of his face, the flame-blue light
of his eyes gazing tenderly down into her own as they had
last night—before she had denied his proposal.

All through the day, memories of their loving and the
treasured moments over the past several months that had
led up to it had come back to torment her. Jezebel could
see nothing that was put before her by her two concerned
companions, overwhelmed as she was by the bittersweet
remembrances that crowded into her mind's eye. The only
thing she could think of was how Rafe, with his special
brand of magic, had stolen his way into her well-guarded
heart bit by bit, until at last he had conquered it. Not even
this rare chance to view the wonders of the world's foremost assemblage of historical artifacts could distract her
thoughts.

When, in an area of the museum's collection set aside
for recent acquisitions, she studied a drawing of the Great
Pyramids made by one of Napoleon's many commissioned
artists, she could not help but remember how they'd first
kissed there, in the heated darkness of a pharaoh's tomb.
While she gazed at the proud sculpted musculature of a
magnificent Greek god in the museum's Hellenic wing, she
thought solely of how favorably the duke compared to the
statue in his naked state. Even the sight of the sunlight
breaking out of the late spring clouds as they stepped outside the large, still-under-construction building at the end
of their tour reminded Jezebel of nothing but the brightness
of her lover's smile as he'd lain beside her in bed, caressing
her gently during the night. Remembering, knowing she
would never see that intimate smile again, nor taste the
incomparable sweetness of his lips upon her own, was unbearable agony.

All day, even as she'd strained to behave pleasantly to
the very kind-seeming Lord Marksley and to Lady Mayhew, to whom she felt she owed a great debt of gratitude
for the way the other woman had unquestioningly taken her
under her wing, Jezebel had felt as though the mere effort
of appearing normal might make her lose her mind. At any
moment, she thought surely she would scream, or tear her

hair, or fly completely out of control and do something even more destructive, either to herself or to another. Harsh sobs battled their way up the tight passage of her throat and choked her breathing. But instead of crying, she'd continued to cling to the fraying remnants of her restraint, trying not to offend the only two people who had shown her true kindness since coming to London by making a public spectacle of herself.

Through sheer force of will, she'd managed to do nothing to disgrace anyone today, but how much longer could she endure?

She had to get away soon, Jezebel thought desperately as she headed for the privacy of her rooms to change for the evening's planned entertainments, having said a brusque farewell to her escorts at the door. Otherwise surely she would run mad with a cleaver!

*It* wasn't until several weeks later, however, that Jezebel figured out how it could be done. Though inwardly she was a wreck, outwardly she remained calm, composed, and obedient during this time—not that Rafe was often there to appreciate this unusually good behavior on her part. And whenever he *did* happen to be around to witness her activities, the duke did little more than glower angrily at Jezebel before stalking off to closet himself in his study or going out to attend to business matters in town. They spoke little, and only stiltedly, when they did happen to meet.

It was all Jezebel could do to paste a serene, untroubled expression on her face during these encounters for Rafe's benefit, for each time she caught sight of him, she felt as if she'd swallowed her heart whole. She could not help but be aware that Lord Ravenhurst, on the other hand, wore a uniformly stony expression whenever they were faced with one another, closed and cold and absolutely unforgiving. She had no reason to hope they might reconcile, for nothing about the situation had changed since their terrible, gut-wrenching argument. And even if she'd wanted to say something to her guardian to ameliorate his anger, she was no longer sure how to bridge the seemingly insurmountable distance that had grown between them.

Rarely did Rafe make an appearance at any of the evening affairs Jezebel spent so much of her time enduring, and never once did he actually escort her to one of the many balls, cotillions, and soirees at which she dutifully danced and flirted along with every other unmarried girl of the gentry. The duke seemed content to delegate most of his escort duties to his cousin and to his friend Lord Marksley, spending less and less time at the Grosvenor Square residence as the days went by, and also stopping in with less frequency to lend the support of his presence at the many affairs the ladies attended.

Never once, of course, did he repeat the single, shattering clandestine visit he'd made to her chambers on the night of her debut, though Jezebel spent many nights sleeplessly tossing, fruitlessly yearning for him to slide open the secret panel that connected their rooms.

She was still under Rafe's patronage, but sometimes she wondered if he had managed to overlook that fact entirely. He might as well have forgotten her very existence for all the notice he paid her now, she thought. The duke seemed to have cut her completely out of his life and his heart, if she'd ever truly had a place there to begin with.

Jezebel kept herself from succumbing utterly to the sorrow of this only by allowing herself to be caught up in the hectic social pace Lady Allison set for them; attending all the right parties, toadying to all the right members of the *ton*, and, most of all, saying all of the right things to the new beaus she found she now had in plenty. Until she'd formed a solid plan for leaving London and all its entanglements behind, she had no other choice.

In the mornings, she accepted invitations to ride in Hyde Park, galloping hell-for-leather in Rotten Row, as well as trotting along the more sedate "Ladies' Mile" whenever Lady Allison prevailed upon her to slow her breakneck pace in the saddle. Often in the afternoons the baroness allowed a select young gentleman or two to accompany them for shaved ices or tea at the Clarendon Hotel, and in the evenings, before attending an opera or a new play on Drury Lane, they frequently strolled the public gardens of Vauxhall, listening to music and watching the fireworks displays in the company of some blissful young swain. Jezebel could barely remember any of their names, to tell the truth, and if it hadn't been for her chaperone's greater social élan, she would surely have offended more than a few of them.

She survived several tedious evenings of lackluster dancing and mediocre refreshment at Almack's, after being approved to enter by the straitlaced patronesses. And every day, rain or shine, she settled herself into the duke's carriage with Lady Allison to call upon, and be called upon in return by, all the "best" people in London. Cards and invitations piled up in silver salvers in the hallway. Society, it seemed, was welcoming Lord Clifton's bluestocking niece with open arms, contrary to what she'd once feared. Indeed, they lapped her up as a cat does a bowl of cream, calling her an "original" and "a breath of fresh air," just as Lady Mayhew had predicted.

Jezebel began to wish they had spurned her instead.

*T*hat thought became the germ of an idea that blossomed into full flower one afternoon several weeks after her debut as she and Allison returned to Rafe's townhouse from yet another interminable round of social calls. The two ladies had just adjourned to the salon for tea and a rest from all the smiling and posturing of the day, and the baroness had begun to sort through the various invitations that had been delivered during their absence. No few were tossed into her reject pile after a mere glance at the return address of the sender, but the attractive blonde opened the majority with interest.

After a few minutes of quiet "hmm's," murmured "possibly's," and amused head shakes, even Jezebel, who had been staring disinterestedly into space, was startled into alertness when Lady Mayhew said, "Now, here's one that looks like fun! How do you fancy a costume party, my dear?"

*As a cobra fancies the mongoose,* Jezebel was about to say, when all of a sudden an extremely wicked thought struck her. It had been so long since she'd had the will or enthusiasm to entertain any sort of mischief that she almost didn't recognize the excited feeling that came along with

the notion that had entered her mind. But as she turned it
about in her mind, there was no doubting that this thought
was most definitely mischievous. Indeed, if she went
through with the idea that had just come to her, she might
truly wreak havoc!

Instead of the tart retort she'd intended to make, Jezebel's lips began to form a smile.

At first the expression was just a tiny lightening of the
features, a rusty beginning that was still the first natural
sign of happiness to cross her face since the night of her
turbulent come-out. But soon the smile had grown so much
that even Lady Allison appeared startled by the genuine
pleasure of it. The older woman looked at her charge
askance as Jezebel replied, "I should like it very well. Very
well indeed!"

"Should you?" Allison asked cautiously. Suspicion grew
in her mind. This was quite a vigorous show of zeal on
Miss Montclair's part for what was really a rather commonplace social engagement, not so very different from
many of the fetes and entertainments they had already par-
ticipated in during the past weeks. Yet until now, Jezebel
had not seemed able to muster a speck of genuine enthusiasm for anything—not since Allison had been forced to
practically peel the girl off the floor of her boudoir the
morning after Lord and Lady Netherland's ball. In fact,
she'd been so dejected of late that the baroness had begun
to worry for her health.

Jezebel had done her best to bear up beneath the strain,
she knew, and really, no one could fault her behavior.
Everyone was talking about this mysterious new addition
to the *ton,* wondering about the background she carefully
made so little mention of, speculating about everything
from the state of her fortune to the kind of flower bouquets
that might win her favor. Despite the fact that she was
suffering from the worst case of heartache Lady Mayhew
had ever seen, Jezebel had, perhaps unintentionally, managed to make quite a splash since her debut. And she had
done a right proper job of distressing her guardian as well,
though Miss Montclair herself no longer seemed so eager
for that. Allison had never seen Rafe so off balance.

The baroness's dashing cousin, usually so debonair and relaxed during social occasions, had become a veritable recluse of late. People were beginning to notice his odd behavior, and to comment on how little he was seen in company with his ward. At parties, when he did deign to show up, he either drank heavily and ignored the guests who attempted to engage his attention, or snapped at those who dared approach him with such a scowl of annoyance that they trembled at his displeasure. Many seemed of the opinion that they had somehow annoyed the duke for him to behave so uncommonly rudely, but Allison had taken note of the direction of his frowning stare and she thought she knew the truth. Every time she had looked over at him during the past weeks, Rafe had been watching Jezebel, and the hungry look in his eye was one she'd never thought to see her cousin wear. He was desperate for the girl.

Matters had to come to a head soon, she thought, for if they didn't, both the lovers would surely suffer a collapse. And until this moment, she'd have bet on Jezebel failing first, for she'd been utterly miserable. Now, however, the girl was fairly lit up with joy. Over some little masked affair? Allison didn't think so, but neither did she intend to spoil her charge's newfound happiness with her suspicions. The girl almost certainly had some misbehavior in mind, but whatever was causing Jezebel's sudden animation, her chaperone was all for it—naughty or not.

"Well, then," she said mildly, sipping her tea, "we shall of course accept. I believe the party is to be held a week hence at the home of Lady Devonshire."

" 'Tis perfect," said Jezebel, still with that unholy gleam in her eye. "There will be just enough time to make the necessary preparations." She paused in thought for a moment. "And first of all, I shall need to engage the services of a very good modiste."

*R*afe would be furious when he found out what had happened in his absence, Jezebel brooded anxiously as they were about to enter the duchess of Devonshire's Belgrave

Square mansion, but by then, there would be nothing he could do to undo the damage she had wrought. Really, it was his own blasted fault for not keeping a better eye on her, she thought, trying to cover her nervousness with spite. He should have known better than to believe she'd sit back meekly and do nothing to prevent his plans for her from coming to fruition.

She might be doomed to love Lord Ravenhurst more than she'd ever thought possible, but she would never be ruled by him—in this or in any other matter. She knew they would inevitably grow to hate each other if she allowed him to force her into marriage, and hatred between them was the one thing she could not bear. Better, she thought, to cut out her heart and let the wound bleed cleanly than to let it fester inside for the rest of her life, destroying both of them.

Jezebel had made up her mind. But that did not mean she was at ease with her plan.

From the moment she strolled into the party with Lady Allison and Lord Marksley, who had again graciously agreed to escort them for the evening (the duke once more having made no firm commitment to attend in response to his cousin's written request), her stomach began fluttering wildly. Wrapped tightly in a long, hooded white cashmere shawl that covered her from the top of her head to the heels of her golden sandals, Jezebel held on to the arm of Damien's particolored satin harlequin costume tightly, nervous and determined at the same time. She knew she looked little different from the crowd of nymphs, goddesses, and shepherdesses that filled the ballroom before her. That would change, however, the moment she removed her wrap—she'd made sure of that when she'd commissioned a most unusual costume for Lady Devonshire's party.

Even now, despite her nervousness, remembering the seamstresses' reaction to the design she'd requested brought a tiny smile to Jezebel's lips.

After more than an hour of hushed argument and impassioned pleas for reason, the modiste Lady Allison had recommended had gone sailing out of Jezebel's dressing room, her face white and her lips pinched, muttering things like "Shocking!" and "Most inappropriate!" as she went. She had clutched her fashion dolls and sketches under one plump arm, marching down the hallway with a militant stride and descending the stairs shaking her head angrily as though what she'd been asked to do were a cardinal sin.

But her pockets had been the heavier by a good deal of gold, and she had agreed to do as the young lady ordered. Miss Montclair would get the costume she'd requested, though the modiste claimed she was sure no decent woman would dare wear it in public.

Yet this was exactly Jezebel's plan. In another moment, she would lay aside her cashmere covering, step forward into the sight of some of society's most critical, sanctimonious hypocrites, and, she hoped, be deemed thoroughly unfit to move among them.

From then on, Jezebel knew nothing would be the same. Suddenly relief began to take the place of the fear she had been feeling. This was what she'd wanted, and when she'd done what she'd set out to do, there was little doubt but that it would irrevocably ruin her. One way or the other, she hoped the misery of her suspended life would end.

Though the future she looked forward to might not be a pleasant one—indeed, promised to be lonely and difficult in the extreme—it would at least be a release from the terrible pain of being so close to the man she loved, yet never able to touch him. She would be an outcast among her own class, and no matter what Rafe might have planned for her future, she would have made herself utterly unmarriageable. He would have no choice but to concede her lack of fitness for this life, she reasoned, and would finally be forced to see the wisdom in letting her leave his protection. As she saw it, he really had no other choice, if he was not to keep her in bondage for the next five years, and she knew the duke did not have the requisite cruelty for that. He would let her go, for in the end it was always society's rules that dictated Rafe Sunderland's actions, and society was about to turn against her.

Though she told herself she did not care for anyone's opinion here, it was going to take all her courage to flaunt her defiance in the face of the assembled guests' displea-

sure. But at least, Jezebel thought with an echo of her former spirit, no one would ever forget the impression she
made tonight!

She gave Allison, who was costumed in a Marie Antoi-
nette–inspired shepherdess outfit, a small, guilty smile. This
was one shepherd who was going to want to beat her little
lamb stoutly with her crook before the night was done.

*A* collective gasp went up from the crowd as Jezebel
handed off her shawl to a footman and stepped across the
threshold to stand at the top of the short flight of stairs that
led down into the sunken ballroom.

Jezebel had expected her chosen costume to cause a sensation at Lady Devonshire's masked ball. In that, she was
not mistaken. However, she had also anticipated she would
be thrown out on her ear within minutes of revealing it
before the hundreds of gently bred, easily shocked guests
gathered in the dowager duchess's town residence. But in
this second expectation, she could not have been more disappointed. There was one little thing she had not counted
on when she'd formulated this daring plan: their incessant,
obsessive craving for titillation. And that was most definitely what she was giving them.

From the top of her head to the soles of her feet, the
archaeologist's niece had chosen to outfit herself in a completely accurate re-creation of an ancient Egyptian queen's
regalia.

It began with the hundreds of tiny braids she'd woven
her coal-black locks into, the whole mass of them parted
down the middle of her head, little golden beads anchoring
the base of each slender plait and two turquoise and lapis,
lotus-shaped hair-clasps holding the sides of her braided
hair back above her ears. As she moved, the beads clicked
and shifted, making a sensuous music. A golden cobra
bound her brow, and her sapphire eyes were heavily lined
in kohl from the inside corners all the way to the edges of
her winged brows. Her rouged lips were invitingly pouty,
but in truth, no one was looking at Jezebel's face, for the

costume only began to test the limits of outrageousness from there.

The bodice of the gown, below a wide gold and lapis torque from Jezebel's own jewelry collection, consisted of two cloth straps and nothing more. These bands were made of a sheer, pleated gauze starting at the shoulder in an inch-wide strip that widened only slightly into an A shape as it went over the bosom, leaving a wide swath of her pale, satin-skinned chest bare down the middle and clearly defining the lush swells of her ivory breasts. Nearly the whole of these lovely, upthrust mounds were exposed invitingly by the straps, and what was hidden, just the small, pink-tinted nipples, seemed to peek through the filmy material teasingly.

Just beneath them, the wispy gauze fabric of the tubelike skirt, figured with a delicate pattern in blue and green to resemble fish scales, clung to Jezebel's torso like a second skin, revealing every lissome curve. The diaphanous gown fitted tightly across her waist and hips, and then followed the lines of her body straight down to her feet, which were enclosed in golden sandals topped with wide ankle bracelets that matched the set of bands circling her bare upper arms.

It was safe to say no one else in Lady Devonshire's ballroom had on anything like it.

Silence reigned for the longest minute of Jezebel's life as she stood in the glare of society's close scrutiny. And then, to her horrified dismay, someone in the crowd began to clap.

In moments, the lone clap had turned into thunderous applause.

# Chapter Twenty-seven

~

*I* say, what an absolutely *fascinating* costume, dear girl," said the portly figure who had begun the ovation, coming up to Jezebel with a mincing gait a moment later. Dressed as King Henry VIII, complete with velvet short pants and hose that did nothing to disguise the lumpy texture of his limbs, the man was cinched so tightly into his girdle that one could hear the stays creaking as he moved. A half-eaten capon drumstick dangled from one hand as he leered openly at Jezebel's cleavage. "I must declare I've never seen anything like it."

Jezebel was about to make a sharp retort about his own costume's lack of originality, angered at this man who seemed to have effortlessly tipped the delicate balance of society's opinion in her favor when she'd worked so hard to have it fall against her, but at that moment she noticed the large group of ladies and gentlemen that had begun to surround herself, her chaperone, Lord Marksley, and this newcomer as they clustered near the entranceway. Everyone, including her two escorts, made a great show of bowing or curtsying as the tall, middle-aged man with his weak chin and dissipated features swept his gaze across them.

Instead of the nasty comment she'd intended, Jezebel made a curtsy of her own, as best she could manage with the fitted skirt of her costume. "Your Highness is too kind," she murmured stiffly as she stared into the face of the Prince Regent. Inwardly, her heart sank down to the tips of her beringed toes.

The future king of England himself had just foiled her plan.

With his favor for her so obviously declared, Jezebel might never succeed in offending polite society as she'd intended. She could see it in the faces of the lords and ladies around her. They'd been ready to crucify her just a moment ago, but once Prince George showed his admiration for her daring, they'd changed their minds in a heartbeat. Whether she willed it or no, Miss Montclair's stamp of approval had just been sealed.

Her mind reeled with the knowledge that she was trapped, that her stock on the marriage market had just risen to an unprecedented pinnacle of desirability, and she could not think what to do to erase this terrible error. When the Prince Regent spoke once again, she barely listened.

"Nonsense, gel. You've put these other ladies and gents here to shame, I daresay. Look at 'em! Same old dull, spiritless round of tragic Shakespearean heroes, lusty satyrs, aging nymphs, and wretched Punch-and-Judy couples. It's enough to make a man weep. But *your* costume . . . well, now. You make a fine Queen Cleopatra! Mistress of the Nile, what?" He chortled. "Where did you ever get such an unusual idea for a gown?"

Jezebel didn't bother to correct the Prince's mistake, though the costume she'd chosen was more along the lines of something the ancient queen Nefertiti might have worn, not the much later-born Macedonian Cleopatra, who would almost certainly have been robed in the Grecian style of her time. What good would it do to correct the man? He did not care for the authenticity of her gown any more than did the rest of the people here. He only cared for what it revealed.

She'd intended to expose her difference tonight, her unsuitability to live in their world, but now she realized that all anyone was really seeing was her body. Skin crawling, Jezebel wanted nothing more than to run from the nightmare she'd created.

Sensing her charge's distraction, Allison stepped in with her usual aplomb. She'd realized immediately what Jezebel was trying to do, and had exhaled a sigh of thanksgiving when the Prince, all unknowing, had squelched the girl's rash plans. Now, instead of assuring her downfall, they had just scored the social coup of the Season! She should have guessed that Jezebel's excitement over this party meant she

was up to something like this—and it had been a valiant
bid for freedom, Allison had to admit.

But the baroness had other plans for young Miss Montclair, and none of those plans involved her succeeding in
breaking away from Lord Ravenhurst. Now, with her raised
profile among the *beau monde,* that goal would be harder
than ever for Jezebel to achieve. Lady Mayhew could not
have been more pleased had she planned tonight's events
herself. When she spoke, she chose her words with careful
calculation.

"Miss Montclair spent several years in the East with her
uncle, Lord Clifton, before his recent passing. The late earl
was quite an antiquarian, don't you know. His niece has
followed in his footsteps, studying the lost culture of the
Egyptians for quite some time while living in Cairo, and
before that, I believe they traveled and studied together in
many other exotic parts of the world during her formative
years."

This was more than most had learned about Miss Montclair to date, for the two had decided early on that Jezebel's
social success might well hinge upon the *ton* believing she
had had an unexceptional rearing—or at least upon their
*not* knowing the whole truth about its extremely unconventional nature—but at this point the baroness judged it would
do no harm to her charge's reputation to admit her unusual
background. As Allison saw it, since Jezebel herself, in
attempting to jeopardize her social standing, had instead
cemented her status as society's newest plaything, now the
girl would simply have to deal with the consequences—
including the interest she'd garner from having grown up
in such intriguing circumstances.

But surprisingly, their stout future monarch seemed un-
interested in pursuing a conversation on antiquities or long-
dead queens with the explorer's niece—perhaps because his
attention was focused so exclusively on Miss Montclair's
very much living flesh. The prince regent merely expressed
his condolences on the earl's passing briefly to Jezebel, and
then turned to converse with Lady Mayhew.

"Baroness," he said jovially. "Always a delight to have
you in company. So you're watching over Lord Clifton's

niece now, are you? I'd heard you were assisting Ravenhurst, though I haven't seen the fellow himself anywhere
about tonight. He really ought to do a better job of playing
watchdog, what with a stunner of a gel like this to protect!
You, my dear lady, don't seem near old enough to be shep-
herding such a lovely young creature about, your own costume notwithstanding."

Allison released one of her tinkling laughs, curtsying
again in her wide hoop skirts and tapping the Prince teasingly on the shoulder with her shepherdess's crook. "La,
Your Highness, you are the most shameless flatterer! I daresay I am more than aged enough to guide an innocent
young girl successfully through her first Season. Certainly
I've experience enough to point out all the worst rakes and
to warn my charge against succumbing to their honeyed
wiles." The baroness spoke these words pointedly, though
her smile remained dazzlingly bright, and the Prince
seemed to take note of her words.

"Harrumph. Yes, well," he said, glancing about the ballroom searchingly and catching a glimpse of his wife, Princess Caroline. "Think I see Ann Boleyn over there with a
look of vengeance in her eye," he joked, "so if you'll excuse me . . ." He took the ladies' hands in turn, kissing each
one lingeringly. Prince George's squinty eyes rested once
more on Jezebel's exposed chest. "Very original getup, indeed. Wish more women had your spirit!" And then he took
his leave.

There was an awkward silence among the fawning circle
of admirers who had come along in the Prince regent's
wake. Avid eyes looked Jezebel up and down—some with
more friendliness than others. And then they all began to
speak at once.

"Were you really brought up among the savages in the
Far East?" a scandalized yet fascinated dowager asked,
straightening her tall orange turban as if to indicate her own
worldly knowledge of the Orient. Of course, wearing this
unfortunately hued silk turban was as close as the old lady
had ever come to making a study of any Eastern culture,
as was made plain to Jezebel by the ludicrously incorrect
way she had wrapped it about her head.

"Did you ever see a crocodile eat a man alive?" another voice piped up ghoulishly.

"What was it like to live among the Turks? Do they truly keep harems of white women for their pleasure?" one man asked, a nauseatingly prurient interest in his tone. Though no one else had the bad taste to expand upon the subject, many curious eyes silently echoed this last question.

These were not, for the most part, people to whom Jezebel had been introduced as yet. Though obviously among the highest-ranked courtiers, judging by the way they had flocked about their Prince, they were complete strangers to her, and quite intimidating. Until now, knowing that any difference in a woman was looked upon with suspicion by this insular crowd of privileged, overbred nobles, she had deliberately said as little about her odd upbringing as possible, preferring not to mention anything that would make her stand out or ruin her chances among them. But tonight Jezebel had decided to pull out all the stops, let them and all the rest of society see her as she truly was—no more hiding her "outrageousness" or anything else about her nature.

Being an intensely private person, she had never wished to let strangers like these have access to her past. It was a part of her existence that could have no significance to them beyond their own lurid, wildly inaccurate imaginings, but it had been very real to her until her uncle's death and Rafe's arrival in Egypt had ended that chapter of her life all too abruptly. Having her admittedly unusual life become a topic for discussion among the idle rich was something Jezebel had always dreaded. It was only in the hope that by showing herself as she really was, she would prove to Rafe once and for all that she could never live in his world that she had dared to open herself to this excruciating examination by London's so-called "polite" society.

Now all Jezebel could think, deluged beneath their barrage of prying questions, was of how terribly her plan had gone awry. She'd given them a taste of just how improper she could be, and instead of shunning her for her wild, unconventional behavior, these excitement-starved social vampires were loving every bit of it. But they weren't truly seeing her for what she was. No, they saw her as a curiosity—something to liven up their dull existences, like a performing monkey on a leash. For once, Jezebel found herself at a loss for words, disgusted beyond measure by the fickle, jaded nature of her peers.

Luckily, her debonair escort for the evening was possessed of a more facile tongue. After a brief moment of shock—followed by another of pure masculine appreciation when he'd first seen her scanty costume revealed—Lord Marksley had contented himself with silently observing the unusual situation unfolding around Miss Montclair, but now, upon seeing Jezebel so overwhelmed, he gallantly stepped into the fray. It was clear the poor girl had no idea what she'd gotten herself into!

"Really, Lord Pimminger," said Damien laughingly to the gaunt, hawk-faced old lecher who'd spoken last. "What sort of question is that? I'm sure Miss Montclair would know nothing about any such indelicate thing as a harem, old boy. She is a lady, after all."

One pretty, dark-haired young miss dressed in a poor imitation of a Roman goddess's garb, standing next to her mama and fanning herself with an ostrich-plume fan that most assuredly did not belong with the costume, gave Jezebel a once-over that clearly questioned the marquis's pronouncement. Envy seethed in her eyes for the upstart girl who seemed to have stolen society's—and the handsome Lord Marksley's—admiration these past several weeks.

Her thoughts were the same as those of nearly every other woman in the ballroom. This latest outrage was simply too much for a lady to take lying down! Who did the chit think she was, coming to London mid-Season and stealing everybody's beaus out from under them? And now showing up at the duchess of Devonshire's house wearing what amounted to two straps and a handkerchief? A nearly transparent handkerchief, at that! The gentlemen looked ready to riot, their eyes popping and their tongues hanging out at the sight of this shameless hussy parading her wares so brazenly before them all. It was intolerable. The girl needed to be put firmly in her place, and if no one else would dare to speak up after the Prince had given his approval to the little harlot, well, *she* would gladly take on the job. She'd be doing proper ladies everywhere a favor.

"I'm sure His Lordship knows whereof he speaks," the young lady, a wealthy baronet's daughter, simpered coyly. "But sadly, I really cannot say we have seen anything to indicate as much from Miss Montclair herself. Why, everyone knows she has displayed quite an astonishing range of masculine pursuits since she arrived in our midst, from riding with the gentlemen in Rotten Row to requesting the most esoteric of dusty old tomes at the Strand. Despite her own rather suspicious silence about her past before tonight, her . . . shall we say . . . *gentlemanly* achievements have been the talk of the town for weeks." The woman paused tauntingly before delivering her final blow.

"However, I think you'll agree it's an undeniable fact that Miss Montclair has yet to demonstrate any *feminine* accomplishments at all. Really, if you ask me, it begs the question of whether anyone in those heathen backwaters where she was raised ever took the trouble to teach this poor unfortunate the proper ladylike manner of dress and deportment—certainly one cannot tell as much from the evidence before us today."

The brunette sent a vicious, gloating smile Jezebel's way. Several other women, both young ladies of marriageable age and their doting mamas, smirked and twittered behind their fans. Jezebel went red with a flush that was clearly visible as far down as her nearly naked chest. Was this the kind of spite she would have to face for the rest of her life? If she couldn't escape the life Rafe had planned for her here in London, she would forever be at the mercy of catty, vituperative females like these. It was what she had always feared—the fate that, along with her father's neglect, had destroyed her own mother so many years ago.

History, it seemed, was repeating itself. Everything she'd feared since her mother's death, every misstep she'd sworn to avoid, was coming about no matter which way she twisted to avoid it. It was like the unfolding of some ancient Greek play, with herself and her mother as the cursed family members struggling vainly to deny their fate. Was Jezebel doomed to suffer the same tragic end Natalya had? In truth, this seemed more likely to the explorer's niece with each passing hour, as though she were caught up in some hideous, ironic nightmare from which there was no awakening.

In this frame of mind, it was no surprise that the sudden attack from this cruel stranger should wound Jezebel with perhaps disproportionate strength. Though she knew she should pay it no mind, the woman's barb nevertheless sank in deep, as did the hostility in her gaze. It was true that Jezebel had few of the so-called "feminine accomplishments" to her credit, and that lack, it seemed, included the ability to win a war of insults against so determined a foe. This assault, combined with the upset in her plans the Prince had caused, left Jezebel momentarily thrown and unable to defend herself. She felt the accumulated weight of the women's stares and knew she must make some response. But before she could stutter out a reply, yet another masculine rescuer stepped in to do it for her.

"Oh, I don't think you need worry on that score—Lady Beauford, isn't it? Your kind concern is of course appreciated, but I think it's highly doubtful that anyone with an eye in her head would ever mistake my dear ward for anything but the extraordinarily lovely young lady she is," a deep, warm baritone spoke over Jezebel's shoulder. She could feel her near-naked skin tighten from her neck to her knees at the sound of that voice, even before she looked back to confirm what she already knew.

Rafe stood behind her left shoulder, tall and ungodly handsome costumed in the flowing robes of a Bedouin desert nomad. He wasn't quite touching her, yet she imagined she felt the steadying warmth of his big hand pressed reassuringly against her back. Her pulse pounded wildly in her veins, for he looked as he had that first day of their expedition in Cairo—the day he had first kissed her. Had he chosen this costume to remind her of that unforgettable beginning to their fateful journey? Jezebel's knees went weak as she watched the exchange between her guardian and the suddenly flummoxed Lady Beauford.

"Oh!" exclaimed the young lady, going red in the face and looking about her for the supporters who seemed to

have suddenly faded into the background of the ballroom.
None of them would meet her eyes, and her own mother
could be seen trying discreetly to pinch the girl into silence,
but she went on heedlessly, seeming not to care how the
tide had turned against her once the powerful duke had
shown up to defend his ward. "Your Grace."

She nodded deferentially as was proper to Rafe's
superior status, but she did not back down. "Of course no
one is questioning Miss Montclair's feminine *attributes*—
I dare swear *those* are quite prominently displayed tonight
for all to see." A few smothered gasps met this outrageous
statement, but the girl herself merely smirked at her own
wit. "I merely wondered if her womanly *skills* were as . . .
ahem . . . developed."

There was a tense standoff for a moment as the tall,
golden-haired duke stared down at the spiteful brunette as
if she were a particularly loathsome form of insect that had
just crawled into their midst. His expression suggested that
he was debating the merits of crushing her, but his tone
was quite pleasant when he responded to the foolishly daring baronet's daughter. Did this impudent little wretch really think she was going to get away with insulting the
woman Rafe loved? he wondered incredulously. He'd grind
her to dust beneath his bootheels before he would let that
happen! No one would ever disparage or insult Jezebel
while he was there to stop it.

"As a matter of fact, Lady Beauford," he said smoothly,
"in addition to her undeniable feminine charms, Miss Montclair is also blessed with a number of quite impressive
talents any lady would be proud to claim for her own. Indeed, though it is to her credit that my ward is not limited
to the usual few domestic skills most young ladies are
taught in the schoolroom, it is also a fact that she does not
lack for these more pedestrian abilities as well." Though
Rafe spoke these cutting words to the baronet's daughter,
his eyes kept drifting back to his ward again and again.

By damn, she looked unbelievably delectable in that sensational costume! Rafe thought, painfully aroused. Close
up, the effect was even more mesmerizing than it had been
from across Lady Devonshire's grand hall. He could not

get over that first image of her slender figure closely en-
cased in the green- and blue-figured gauze outfit, her sparkling eyes outlined exotically in kohl, her slim arms
shimmering with gold, and, especially, that hair! He wanted
to bury his hands in the dark silky ropes, wrap them about
his wrists and bind her to him for a kiss that would melt
the icy heart of this luscious Egyptian princess. The very
breath had been knocked out of him the moment Rafe
caught sight of his slim ward standing so vulnerably at the
head of the stairs, silently daring the world to despise her.
She had looked so incredibly stunning, so brave, and so
poignantly beautiful that his heart had twisted in his chest,
and all the anger he should have been feeling had slid right
out of his body.

He'd known instantly what she was up to with this stunt,
and, from his vantage point by the entryway as he entered
the ball, he'd had a clear view of the Prince's grand gesture
as well as the *ton*'s reaction to it. He should have been
furious at her defiance and relieved when the regent unwittingly ruined her plan with his lascivious admiration.
Instead, all Rafe had wanted at that moment was to push
his ogling future sovereign aside and claim Jezebel as his
own before all the world.

No other woman had as much fire in her heart, as much
originality and spirit as Jezebel Montclair did. No other
woman fought him or denied him as she did either, it was
true, but he would not have had her be any other way. He
wanted to laugh at the sensation she was causing among
this overly staid coterie of snobbish gentlefolk. He wanted
to snatch her up in his arms and whirl her about for the
sheer joy of her uniquely dramatic flair.

The only thing stopping the duke from doing any of this
was the painful knowledge that Jezebel was displaying her
inventive nature tonight solely in order to escape him. It
was a crushing blow to Rafe to know that she wanted to
be rid of him so badly that she was willing to ruin herself
to do so. She must hate him very much indeed. Still, whatever her feelings for him, he vowed he would continue to
defend her to the last breath in his body.

"Miss Montclair has been blessed by her upbringing and

her uncle's expert tutelage with many admirable traits and
talents most women in society could only dream of possessing. Isn't that right, my dear?" he asked, directing his
words and the approving smile that went with them at Jezebel, though his heart was aching inside his chest at the
remote look in her eyes.

"His Grace gives me too much credit," Jezebel replied
cautiously, her voice not nearly as steady as she would have
liked it to be. She was unwilling to let Rafe see how her
heart had leapt at the sight of him, though she felt overcome
by the same ridiculous surge of pleasure she always did in
his presence—a wholly elemental response her body produced uncontrollably in reaction to his.

But never mind how she felt about him. How was *Rafe*
reacting to *her*? Jezebel wondered. That was the important
thing. Was he angry for what she'd tried to do tonight?
Even though her actions had had the opposite effect of the
one she'd intended—which should please the duke, since
he was so bent on marrying her off—it was surely obvious
to her guardian, as she assumed it also was to Lady Mayhew and Lord Marksley, that her costume choice had not
merely been a bid to capture male admiration or to cause
jealousy among the ladies here tonight.

Would he attempt to punish her for her defiance? After
all, he'd ordered her most strictly not to make any waves—
had warned her repeatedly, in fact, of the dire consequences
of such an act. Yet when she gazed warily into the endless
aquamarine depths of the duke's eyes, Jezebel could detect
no vengeful thoughts. Indeed, she thought she was sensing
a distinct warmth there. If she hadn't known better, she'd
even have sworn she saw a hint of admiration, a smile in
those attractively crinkling blue eyes. But that was impossible. Rafe despised her now, didn't he? The fact that she
could not read his hatred did not mean he was not feeling
it, she reminded herself. The duke was far too skilled at the
game of social interaction to let his emotions show in public, and he certainly would never let anyone divine them
from his words.

"You are too modest, Miss Montclair," he was saying.
"Why, I recall being treated to a most extraordinary display

of musicianship not so very long ago—a very ladylike accomplishment indeed." Rafe paused as if caught up in fond remembrances. "I cannot recall ever having heard a finer concert than I was witness to that night in Egypt when you played your violin. Lady Beauford would agree, I'm sure, if ever she were to hear the same," he concluded with a pleasant smile for that fulminating young woman.

He *did* despise her! Jezebel thought, stricken. It was certain now. Why else would Rafe say such a thing, expose her greatest weakness to the world in such a heartless fashion? This was to be her punishment, Jezebel realized with a growing sense of horror. This was how the duke meant to pay her back for her defiance. She listened dazedly while the hateful Lady Beauford replied. It was as though the girl could sense Jezebel's horror at the notion of performing in public.

"Is that so, Your Grace?" the brunette asked, seemingly delighted to hear the news. "But how providential. It so happens that my dear papa is giving a musicale tomorrow evening, and we are lacking one performer, due to a sudden illness of some sort or other." She waved a hand dismissively, as if the unfortunate musician's sickness had come about solely to vex her. "We were going to cut the evening short—a grave disappointment to Papa, who, as I'm sure you're aware, is known for the wonderful maestros and divas he has always managed to entice to our home. The *crème de la crème* of society will be in attendance as usual, and I was terribly afraid we would have to shortchange their entertainment. But perhaps that won't be necessary now, if what you say about your ward's musical accomplishments is true.

"If Miss Montclair would do us the honor of filling the vacancy," she continued, "I'm sure we'd be much indebted to her—and, of course, delighted at the chance to observe this great 'talent' of hers." The girl's smile this time was positively feral. It was clear she expected Jezebel to fold under her intimidating tactics and be forced to admit her shortcomings in front of their eager audience.

Before Jezebel could fulfill her expectations by spitting out a vigorous refusal, however, Rafe had placed his hand on her shoulder, directly upon the spot she'd pictured him touching a moment ago. The sensation was so startlingly erotic that it silenced her—indeed, under his warm, callused fingers, it was all she could do not to melt to the floor in a puddle of helpless sensation.

"Miss Montclair would be delighted to assist your family in their hour of need," Rafe returned with a wolfish grin of his own. In one short sentence, he succeeded both in making Lady Beauford appear churlish, and in having it seem as though his ward was doing her a favor by agreeing to play at the musicale. The duke was very pleased with his handiwork. "Be prepared for quite an event—and I do hope you will all be there to see it," he said, spearing the assembled peers each in turn with his challenging gaze.

This statement sounded far more like an order than a mere expression of desire, and they took it as such, nodding and murmuring acceptance of the decree. Lord Ravenhurst, despite his affable words, did not look in any mood to be crossed.

"Now, I should like to dance a waltz with my ward, if there are no objections?"

If there were any, no one dared to mention them as he swept Jezebel neatly out of the influence of the baronet's daughter, who stood with her mouth agape, her plan to humiliate her rival foiled. Damien and Allison looked ready to cheer at this turn of events, and Jezebel herself was so overwhelmed that she allowed Rafe to lead her out onto the dance floor, where the orchestra was beginning to play the first strains of a well-known waltz.

She drifted into his arms so naturally it was as if they'd never been apart, but though their bodies understood one another instinctively, her mind could not penetrate the thoughts that lay in his.

"What exactly do you hope to accomplish by forcing me to do this?" she asked tightly, trying not to respond to the feel of his muscular arms around her, not to gaze at him lest she drown once again in the bottomless blue oceans of his eyes. His scent, a virile male musk, subtly tantalized her senses and surrounded her in heady sensation, while his vital energy, his uniquely sensual magnetism—less tangible

but no less real to Jezebel—sent waves of nervous anticipation coursing through her veins. It felt so good to be
within the circle of his embrace once more! But she had to
remember that Rafe was no longer the tender lover she'd
come to hold so dear, but the vengeful guardian she must
now escape. "If it's to punish me that you make me play
before these people, you'll find you do yourself as great a
harm as you do me," she warned.

"*Punish* you?" Rafe said incredulously. "What the devil
are you talking about, Jezebel?" He spun her deftly to avoid
another couple on the crowded parquet floor, and her long,
braided hair swept across the arm he held pressed against
her back to guide her, the golden beads clicking together
softly as they collided with one another. It was all he could
do to stay focused on the topic at hand. "I was trying to
rescue you from the claws of that vicious little hellcat back
there. I thought I was giving you a way to fight back against
her insults." Rafe's eyes were filled with bewilderment, and
a trace of hurt as well.

"By throwing me to the rest of the lions?" she threw
back bitterly.

"I don't understand," he protested, genuinely confused.
"How can you consider my giving you a chance to make
that little twit and her cronies eat their words 'throwing you
to the lions'? What can you mean by such a statement?"

But Jezebel just stared at him sadly as they moved together through the figures of the dance. It should have been
an intimate moment, a romantic moment, with the light
from a dozen crystal chandeliers bathing them and the
sounds of Strauss's famous Viennese waltz playing from
the musicians' balcony to guide their feet, but instead Jezebel only felt her heart breaking all over again. Could he
really not know what he had done when he'd volunteered
her services for tomorrow's concert? But then, she reasoned, how *could* he possibly guess why she so feared it?
She'd told no one about the dark nightmares of her past. . . .

It had been at an event just such as the one planned for
tomorrow night that Natalya had lost Martin Montclair's
love—or so Jezebel remembered her mother telling her
many times during her earliest years. She must never play

her music for the man she loved, Natalya had warned darkly, her eyes fervid with remembered pain as she taught her little daughter how to manipulate the strings of her treasured violin. Never, for she would lose him, lose everything, just as Natalya had the night she'd embarrassed her new husband by giving an impromptu performance during a house party the couple had been invited to shortly after their honeymoon. After that humiliation, she swore, Martin had never looked at her with the same love in his eyes. After society had turned away in disgust, he had done the same.

As Rafe would do tomorrow, Jezebel knew with agonizing certainty, if he had not already learned to hate her thoroughly by now. Perhaps an outrageous costume had not been enough to ruin her. Perhaps, because of the odd way fate had fallen out tonight, the *ton* now thought she could do no wrong, but there was still one way she could earn their disapprobation.

She could play her music for them in the only way her heart knew how—and in doing so, shame her beloved unforgivably before the elite society that meant so much to him. After that disgrace, she knew Rafe would no longer chase after her if and when she ran—none of his peers would ever admit her among their number again, let alone make an offer of marriage for her hand, so what would be the point? Besides, he would be so disgusted in his own right that he would probably say no more than good riddance when he found out she was gone.

Rafe didn't know it, but he had just handed his ward the key to the very freedom he'd spent so long denying her.

*This is exactly what I wanted, isn't it?* Jezebel asked herself.

*Oh, but not this way,* her heart answered in anguish. *I never wanted it to be this way.*

But there was no other choice. As they spun and turned in perfect synchronicity, she was already moving away from Rafe in her mind, anticipating the heartache of the morrow. She stared up into his handsome face as if to memorize every feature, to take in and capture the sensually sculpted angles and planes that made up his splendid vis-

age. She wanted to reach up and caress his ch
did not even dare do so much.

Jezebel could see from his baffled, upset expre
Rafe was still waiting for her explanation, but she ⸻ ⸺one
to give him—none that he would understand, anyway. "It's
nothing," she sighed finally. "I didn't mean anything by it.
Please, forget what I said. I am merely nervous about playing before such a large audience, that's all. I'm sure the
performance tomorrow will be fine," she said, trying to reassure him even through the burgeoning tightness in her
throat. Seeing his continued suspicion, she attempted to distract him as they continued to swirl and dip in time to the
heavenly music.

"Don't you think you're holding me a tad too close for
propriety, Your Grace?" she asked breathlessly as he tightened his grip during one sweeping turn. They were almost
cheek to cheek, and her scantily clad bosom brushed from
time to time against the flowing cotton of Rafe's Bedouin
costume. "Are you not concerned you'll scandalize your
friends with such behavior?" she inquired, a trace of her
old sarcasm returning to add some normalcy to her voice.

Jezebel didn't want to think about tomorrow anymore,
and she didn't want Rafe contemplating it either, if she
could help it. She wanted him to think only about this very
moment, this last chance they would have for intimate conversation. She wanted him to remember how it had been
between them—how the connection between them had
sparkled with challenge and zest, how they had matched
each other as neither had ever been matched before. And
when he answered her, she saw her tactic had worked.

"Well," he replied, chucking softly, "between the two of
us, you are surely the master of impropriety, but tonight I
feel like taking a page from your lesson book, my fiery
Egyptian princess. Let them all go to hell if they don't like
it. Tonight, at this masque, we are none of us ourselves. A
Bedouin raider will dance with his woman in whatever
manner he chooses, and fight to the death anyone who
would deny his right." Despite his lightly spoken words,
Rafe's tone was strangely solemn, and his gaze, sweeping

tenderly across her face, told her he understood her need to say no more of the future.

*Would that every night could be like this for us,* she thought. *A night out of time and without consequence.* But that was a dangerous fantasy, an impossibility. There would never be another like it.

Jezebel, knowing it would be the last time they would ever stand so in each other's arms, surrendered to the sensuality of Rafe's statement and the reborn kindness in his eyes she had missed so dearly. She could do nothing less, for like the bandit he portrayed tonight, Lord Ravenhurst had stolen her defiance along with her heart.

They waltzed together silently after that, and Rafe clasped her even closer, sensing his beloved's distress, feeling his own sorrow near to overwhelming him. The more firmly he tried to bind her to him, he thought, the farther away this beautiful woman seemed to drift. It was just as it had been in his dream, he realized sadly. Inevitably, he drove her away with his actions, though he did not know what he did to make her flee. Would he never hold Jezebel's heart as tightly as he held her body?

He feared someday soon she would vanish, just as his dream woman had always done. This time, he was not at all sure he could survive the loss.

# *Chapter Twenty-eight*

~

$\mathscr{I}$t was much later that night, cocooned in the warm darkness of Rafe's glass-walled conservatory, that Lady Allison found Jezebel almost entirely hidden among the lushly growing foliage. She followed the soft, weeping sounds of the girl's violin to locate her among the proliferation of exotic blooms and greenery crowding the humid, loamy-smelling little hothouse.

"Jezebel? Is that you, dear? I received your note, and I came as soon as I was able." Indeed, the baroness had canceled a long-planned assignation with her current lover when she'd seen her charge's scrawled request for a meeting tonight waiting on her night table, knowing that nothing less than desperation would ever lead the proud Miss Montclair to ask for help. So now, hours after the memorable masquerade ball had ended, Allison was here to do whatever she could for the girl for whom she'd come to care so deeply. Whether Jezebel would thank her later for the kind of aid she'd give, however, was still a matter for debate. Lady Allison's methods tended to be rather . . . unique.

At this late hour, the baroness's hair was falling casually about the shoulders of her pink silk dressing gown, her artful makeup removed for the night and her feet comfortably wrapped in a pair of old, scuffed yellow bed slippers. She should have looked less glamorous with all of the careful artifice stripped from her, but somehow Lady Mayhew only appeared more luminous now, the gentle concern on her features giving her face an even more angelic cast than usual, never mind what devilish plots were brewing behind her moss-green eyes. "Tell me what is wrong," she entreated.

Jezebel set the antique violin that had seen her through

so many dark nights beside her on the stone bench where she'd gone to ground after the ball, the melancholy Gypsy tune she'd been playing having faded to silence before it was even complete. Always in the past she'd managed to find solace in her music, a sort of peace and equanimity gained by letting her feelings flow out through the strings. But tonight, for the first time, it had failed her. The music had echoed hollowly, ringing falsely in her ears. There was no solace for the kind of pain she felt this night, Jezebel knew. Perhaps there never would be again.

"Thank you for coming to me as quickly as you did, my lady," she said quietly. "I know I have been nothing but a trial to you these past weeks, and that the hour is very late, but I am afraid I must stretch the limits of your generosity yet again. There is another favor I must ask of you—perhaps the greatest favor of your life," she warned.

Allison settled herself on the bench beside her charge, stroking the girl's still-braided hair kindly and taking in the ruin of her dark eye makeup without comment. Jezebel's eyes were dry now, but it was obvious that she had recently shed more than a few tears. From the way she'd been dancing with her guardian earlier tonight, it wasn't hard for Allison to guess the source of her troubled heart. The two had behaved as though their one waltz together must last into eternity. Stubborn fools, the both of them!

It was a good thing she was here to straighten things out, and that she had Lord Marksley as her coconspirator in this effort. Her cousin and his ward were just lucky, the baroness thought with an inward smile, that they had allies so adept in the ways of love to rescue their failing romance! The two, left to their own devices, would clearly botch the whole business miserably, and Allison cared for them both too much to let that happen.

"Tell me what it is you would ask, dear heart. You know I will do it if it is within my power. I truly hate to see you so miserable, Jezebel. No woman should ever suffer so over a man." That last part she could say quite honestly.

This time Jezebel did not bother to deny the cause of her anguish. They both knew it was Rafe she cried for. "I need you to help me leave this place, as you swore you would the very first day we met." She hated to remind the other woman of her vow, knowing she was putting Lady Mayhew in a very awkward position with her powerful cousin, but she persisted, for she had no other choice. "I must ask you to keep that promise now, however much trouble it may cause between yourself and the duke, for if you do not, I truly don't know how I shall survive another day in his household."

Jezebel's voice cracked with these words, and she hid her face behind her shaking hands, letting her hair fall forward as well to mask her shame and anguish. "It is killing me to remain Rafe's ward," she finished achingly, voice coming out muffled from behind her fingers.

"Nonsense, girl," Allison retorted, with rather less sympathy than Jezebel had grown to expect from her. "I'll grant you a man can come near to destroying a woman if he chooses—no one knows that better than I!—but Rafe Sunderland has no such plans for you, my dear. I know my cousin, and he is a good man," she declared passionately. "He is dedicated to your welfare, your safety, and your happiness."

Thinking Jezebel was about to protest, she decided to head her off quickly. This stubbornness had gone on long enough! Damien had informed her of how the girl had twice refused Rafe's suit, and though she respected Jezebel's right to say no even to so august a person as Lord Ravenhurst, she thought privately that her charge's unhappiness stemmed solely from her inexplicable unwillingness to marry the man she so obviously loved—and who so obviously loved her in return. Still, Allison knew it would do no good to simply say so—the headstrong Miss Montclair would not listen if she did. Instead, she must play a more cunning game if she wanted to ensure the couple's eventual happiness.

The baroness wasn't about to tell her charge what she had in mind, of course. She could see Jezebel was far too keen on making a sacrifice of herself to willingly fall in with such a plan as the one Allison was hatching. Still, she would give the girl a thing or two to think about before letting her believe she was leaving the man she loved for-

ever. Perhaps, though she doubted it, Allison could still
spare her charge some future sorrow by divulging a past
sorrow of her own.

"Listen to me," she said firmly. "I am going to share
with you some information only a very few people have
ever been privy to about my past. If it does not convince
you of Rafe's caring nature, I don't know what will." The
baroness took a deep breath before launching into her tale.

"Shortly after my ill-starred marriage to Lord Arthur
Mayhew—the baron who gave me my title and stole from
me so much else I valued more—my new husband took it
into his head to mistreat me with as much viciousness as
was in his corrupt soul," she began levelly. "Several times,
after staying out all night drinking and endeavoring to gam-
ble away the fortune he'd inherited, Lord Mayhew returned
home in an alcohol-fueled rage, and, unfortunately, he directed every bit of that rage at me. I was only a nineteen-
year-old girl at the time, and I found myself utterly
defenseless before him. Battered and bruised, I ran to my
parents for shelter, but my family, having virtually sold me
to the baron for the settlement my marriage brought them,
refused to help.

"They told me it was a wife's duty to submit to her
husband, and fearing to anger their powerful new relative,
they closed the door on me, their youngest daughter. But
Rafe did not abandon me. No," she said softly, "instead he
very probably saved my life."

"Though we were only the most distant of relations, and
I had never previously spoken more than two words with
my many-times-removed cousin—who seemed terribly imposing, having already inherited his title, though he was
actually even younger than I—he still sensed something
was wrong the instant he looked at me. Maybe it was my
red-rimmed eyes or the lackluster way I, once a very vivacious girl, was now comporting myself about town. He
confronted me discreetly, but I feared at first to admit to
the ongoing abuse I suffered. After all, my own parents had
been unwilling to help, and my husband had warned me of
the consequences should I dare to complain to anyone
again. When Rafe finally persuaded me to confess the

truth—and I remember he was oh, so very gentle about it—
he went directly out to give the baron what he promised
would be a severe 'talking to.' " Allison paused, satisfaction writ large across her features.

"Needless to say, my loathsome husband never so much
as touched me again, and I knew from the fearful glances
the baron shot Rafe's way whenever their paths crossed in
society that this 'talking to' must have involved a great deal
more than the use of harsh language. I could not have been
more glad, or more relieved that I would no longer have to
fear my husband's wrath. Soon after, Lord Mayhew—pardon my indelicacy, but may he roast in hell—died under
the hooves of one of his own hunters, crushed by the poor
beast when he tried to force it to take a jump that was too
steep. If I hadn't known better, I would have sworn, seeing
the duke's expression on the day they buried my husband,
that Rafe had had something to do with the accident. But
I knew that the man who had so tenderly comforted me in
my darkest hours would never stoop to murder. Perhaps if
I'd thought of it, *I* might have," Allison admitted with a
shameless smile, "but *he* never would.

"Ever since he came to my rescue nearly ten years ago,"
she concluded, "we have been fast friends. Rafe Sunderland
taught me how to trust again, how to let go of my fear and
learn the joy of my freedom. He saved me from a man who
more than likely would have killed me, given enough time,
and he gave me the strength to make my way on my own
afterwards. I still trust him as I do no other, man or
woman."

Jezebel sat silently, stunned by the picture Lady Allison
had painted of her younger self. It was hard to imagine this
poised, confident woman ever suffering beneath the yoke
of a brutal abuser. But it was not hard to imagine the man
she loved coming to Allison's rescue. It was the kind of
deed Rafe would perform without question, as naturally as
breathing.

If the baroness meant to prove something to her charge
about Rafe's goodness, then she was preaching her gospel
to the already converted. Jezebel knew Rafe would always
come to her aid. She trusted him to do his duty by her. The

problem was that he would never do so out of love. But Lady Mayhew clearly did not understand that this lack was the true root of Jezebel's conflict with the duke.

"So you see," she was saying, "if he would do so much for me, why do you assume he would do any less for you? If you would only let him, Rafe would care for you all the days of your life."

"Lady Mayhew—Allison—" She swallowed. "I am honored by your confidence. Truly I am. I know it cannot have been easy for you to share such an intimate story with me. But I must tell you it was perhaps an unnecessary lesson. I have never doubted Rafe's dedication to duty. I know he would do whatever was in his power, give whatever was needed to ensure my security. But there is one thing he cannot give me, and it is the one thing I shall die for want of." Jezebel could not continue, for tears had choked her throat to silence.

"What is it, Jezebel? What can my cousin not provide for you?"

*His love,* she wanted to say. But that was too much to admit even to Lady Allison. "My freedom," she replied instead. "And after tomorrow night, I shall need it more than ever. That is why I have asked for your help, my lady. It is imperative that I leave this house immediately after the musicale tomorrow."

"Why, what is to happen at the musicale?" Allison asked, thoroughly bewildered. She'd tried to understand her charge's position, to see what made her so terribly insistent on running from the very thing she ought to be running toward. And, having survived her own unhappy marriage, she could sympathize with Jezebel's fear of marrying a man who would not allow her the freedom to be who she truly was inside. Allison, however, feeling sure that fear was mostly founded on misunderstanding between the two lovers and not on any real repressive tendencies in Rafe's nature, had hoped to clear her charge's mind of doubts on that score with her tale.

But now it seemed she had perhaps been wide of the mark when she assumed Jezebel's heartache stemmed from a lack of trust in Rafe. Of all the reasons she'd imagined the girl giving for her need to leave London quickly, she had not expected Jezebel to say this! What possible trouble could one little performance cause to make Miss Montclair so anxious to flee the country? From the little she'd heard tonight, and the rare praise the discerning duke had showered upon her earlier, Allison assumed her charge must simply be suffering from an extraordinarily strong case of stage fright.

Jezebel looked down at her hands, which had begun toying aimlessly with her bow again without her knowledge. "This is very hard for me to explain, my lady, but because you have been so forthright in trusting me with your own secrets, it is time that I return the favor, so that you may understand the absolute necessity that underlies my request for your aid."

She paused. "It begins with the death of my mother—a scandal buried beneath twelve years of silence and the uncounted leagues of distance my father very deliberately put between us and it when he came to fetch me afterwards," she said at last. "I was barely eight when it happened, living, by Lord Clifton's grace, with my mother on the family's North Country property, but I will never forget that day as long as I live." Even now, visions of the misty February morning—the boat overturned and slowly sinking into the lake, the flowers strewn on the banks and floating on the silver-gray surface of the water—still managed to steal all the warmth from Jezebel's limbs. "My mother drowned herself in the ornamental lake on the grounds of my uncle's estate."

Jezebel ignored her companion's sympathetic gasp. "She was mad, you see," she continued tonelessly, avoiding Allison's gaze. "She thought she was Ophelia at the time, pining for her Hamlet—my father—whom she believed had spurned her." Jezebel remembered her own confusion and fright as her mother had tucked flowers from their hothouse into her dark, unbound tresses and in the pockets of the little pinafore her daughter had worn, murmuring, "That's rue. That's for remembrance . . ." quoting the then-unfamiliar lines of Shakespeare as she climbed aboard the

little dinghy the groundskeeper kept by their dock for occasional pleasure jaunts on the water.

She'd even given her mother a push, she remembered
with a surge of nausea, when Natalya had ordered it, not
realizing her mother's intent until she'd seen her, far out
into the middle of the lake, standing up and letting herself
fall deliberately into the frigid waters. There had been nothing she could do to save her, though Jezebel had nearly
drowned herself trying to drag her mother's body to the
surface.

"I watched her die," she said to Allison, all emotion
drained from her tone. "And after that day I swore that I
would never let the same madness overcome me."

"Oh, my dear . . . you poor girl, to suffer such a terrible
ordeal so young!" Allison said, her eyes filled with tears.
She didn't know what this tragic tale had to do with Jezebel's reluctance to perform at tomorrow's musical gathering at the home of Lord Beauford and his witchlike
daughter, but she knew that somehow, in her charge's
mind, the two were deeply interconnected. This was no
mere case of stage fright! There must be a reason for her
panicked need for flight, yet the baroness knew she must
let Jezebel come to that portion of the story in her own
time. "But you must know you need never fear to suffer
madness yourself. Why, you are no more insane than I,
Jezebel!"

Jezebel chuckled mirthlessly. "That is where you are
wrong, I am afraid, as tomorrow's events will prove. My
mother was also not always the lunatic she eventually became. And right now, I tell you, I am headed down the
very road she traveled to reach that state all those years
ago. I need you to help me step off that path before it is
too late!"

"But I do not understand. . . ." Could Jezebel truly fear
the onset of madness? But why now, and what had it to do
with her feelings for Rafe? Did the girl truly believe the
heartache she suffered was due to insanity? Love, Allison
knew, could well make mooncalves out of the most prosaic
of women, but she didn't think infatuation was the sort of
mental disturbance her charge was talking about. No. This

was different, much stronger and far more troubling. Jezebel honestly seemed to believe her sanity was in danger if she allowed herself to love the duke. Lady Mayhew could only pray that Rafe would be able to convince Jezebel to believe otherwise, once the plan she'd decided she and Lord Marksley would set in motion came to fruition.

"You don't need to understand," Jezebel said desperately, tears starting to flow once more. "I beg you, do not force me to explain further." How *could* she explain what would happen to her heart when she saw the disgust on Rafe's face tomorrow? How could she describe her fear that the pain of it would make what little remained of her sanity dissolve? Already, she was drowning in a maelstrom of turbulent emotion. She could not do it. "Please, just do as I ask—as you promised. I cannot remain once the concert is finished."

Allison looked at her charge steadily, reading the desperation that could indeed be mistaken for madness in her wild, tear-filled sapphire eyes. "All right," she sighed. "I will help you." Though perhaps not in the manner the girl was expecting; ultimately she was sure the scheme she was hatching would prove far more rewarding than Jezebel's for all concerned. But if she was wrong, one very troubled young woman would pay the price.

She'd better send a note round for Damien first thing, Allison thought wearily. The marquis would be playing a large part in this plan—in fact, it could not succeed without him. Until then, she must reassure Jezebel, and send the exhausted, emotionally spent girl to bed to catch what sleep she could.

"I must give some thought to how what you ask may be accomplished, and that will take more creativity than I possess at this late hour." The baroness yawned daintily and gathered her dressing gown more tightly about her shapely form. After a comforting hug, she got up from the bench and announced, "It's time for bed now. We'll talk more tomorrow, my dear, when I shall outline my plans to help you."

Allison was halfway out the door when Jezebel's voice called her back. "Wait. I . . . I need to tell you something before you go, please." She paused until the baroness had turned back to her, one feathery blond brow quirked.

"You have been nothing but kind and generous to me, and I have repaid you very poorly, I am afraid," she began tentatively. "I wronged you in my thoughts, Lady Allison, when we first met . . ." Jezebel flushed under Allison's questioning gaze, but felt the need to confess and clear the air before she could accept the other woman's aid. "I . . . I thought you were Rafe's mistress when I saw you waiting for us on the docks," she finished all in a rush. Jezebel ducked her head, letting her braids hide the redness of her cheeks, ashamed of her own unfitting thoughts.

Her mouth dropped open however, and her eyes widened when she heard Lady Mayhew's dignified reply.

"No need to apologize for suspecting the truth—I've always said you were a perceptive girl." Allison paused in remembrance. Ever since he'd saved her from her husband's brutality all those years ago, she and the duke had indeed been fast friends—and for a brief time, more than friends. Rafe had taught her how to trust again, how to let go of her fear and explore the joy her own body could experience, under the right circumstances and with the right man. Their passion had long since mellowed to a comfortable camaraderie, for they both had known the gratitude and affection she'd felt for him had never been true love— and Rafe's own feelings, though warm and certainly desirous, had never had the kind of depth his emotions for Jezebel did.

"In fact, I *was* his lover at one time—years and years ago, my dear. I can tell you this: I'm glad it's you he's finally fallen in love with, and not me. The man was far too intense for my tastes!"

The louvered glass door had closed behind Allison before Jezebel could stutter out anything in response.

# Chapter Twenty-nine

~

$\mathcal{I}$f only Lady Allison's statement last night were true, Jezebel thought longingly. If only Rafe loved her as the baroness mistakenly believed, perhaps the night to come would not be such a certain disaster. If he loved her, he would not care what she did before his friends, would understand her need to express herself and approve no matter what anyone else said.

*If* he loved her. But he did not. Rafe had never been able to accept who she was. He'd always sought to make her bend, to change her ways. He had consistently tried to twist her behavior and beliefs so that she would fit the mold of his ideal. Nothing less than her full obedience to the rules that dictated his own life would satisfy this stubborn man she yet could not help but love, and Jezebel knew that, despite her feelings for him, she could never become what he wanted of her. Doing so would be worse than madness—it would mean a total loss of self.

Just such a man as Jezebel knew the duke to be had destroyed Natalya Montclair, after all, without ever meaning to do harm.

Kind, intelligent, proud, and upstanding, Jezebel's father had been a man she'd looked up to as a fine, thoughtful, thoroughly decent person. Martin Montclair had believed in taking care of his obligations, she remembered, just as Rafe did. But he, like Rafe, had also been a product of his society—for even though her late father had often left England in search of more exotic climes, he had never forsaken the strict mores and morals of the world he'd left behind.

A scholar by nature, he simply had not been able to endure his wife's excessive emotionalism. It had embarrassed him so much, in fact, that he had abandoned both his wife and his young daughter to a life of lonely exile in his efforts to escape it. Though Jezebel had never blamed her father for what had happened all those years ago, she'd always wished he could have displayed just a little more understanding for her mother's pathos, instead of the aversion and discomfort she mostly remembered seeing in his eyes during his infrequent visits home. But perhaps, for a man with a normal, well-balanced mind, there *was* no understanding the irrational urges that had driven the once-vibrant Russian émigré. Just as, for Rafe, there could be no acceptance of Jezebel's own volatile nature—a nature which was only growing more unstable the deeper her feelings for him grew.

She would not make her mother's mistake, she vowed. She might be following a course of destiny that was eerily similar to the one her tormented parent had endured, but this time she was determined that course must lead to a different ending point. She would not allow the cycle of suffering to continue unabated—at least, if she could not spare herself this pain, she could spare her lover the deep regret her father had felt after her mother had perished. And that was precisely what she intended to do tonight—even if she must publicly humiliate Rafe in order to save him.

It was a relief knowing it was too late now for her to do anything else. The plans had been made, the wheels set in motion, and the precipitating event itself was about to take place. Allison had assured her charge that, with the help of the marquis, everything was in readiness for her exodus. And even if she'd wanted to back out, there was no way to escape now—they were already on the road literally as well as figuratively, trundling through the dusky streets near Regent's park on their way to the baronet's home.

All of the principal parties were present: the baroness, who had plotted Jezebel's course of action after the concert; the marquis, who would physically effect her escape by providing means as well as escort; Jezebel herself, who would be causing the disturbance that necessitated the escape; and the duke, who, they hoped, as yet remained completely unaware of the fierce scheming going on all around him.

For their own reasons, each of them was nervous, worried about the outcome of this evening—Jezebel most of all. Yet even Rafe, who had no way of guessing the reasons behind the unusually somber behavior of his normally carefree companions, seemed affected by their gloom. He rode in his rear-facing seat silently, seemingly brooding on dark thoughts of his own.

It was a dour party indeed that occupied the shuttered interior of the duke's closed black-lacquer barouche as it rattled to a halt before Lord Beauford's already crowded front steps. But though no one inside the conveyance was looking forward to this night, it seemed as though the dozens of others outside it were not of like mind about the "entertainment" to come. From the number of coaches lining the block, which they could see when Damien pushed aside the leather window covering nearest his seat with one finger to look out, and the stylishly attired gentlefolk alighting from those vehicles one after another, it seemed that the musicale would be well attended indeed.

Jezebel felt finality settle like cold lead in her heart. No. There would be no backing out now.

So be it, she thought sadly. She'd made her decision, and it was for the best. She stared at Rafe across the softly lit confines of the vehicle, knowing her heart was probably in her eyes but unable to dissemble any longer. He struck her more powerfully with his uniquely masculine beauty each time she gazed at him, she thought, feeling a lump grow in her throat, even when he wore such a distracted, brooding expression on his face as he did this evening. He must sense something was amiss, just as he had the night before, but again he chose to say nothing. Probably, Jezebel assumed, he did not care to ask, for he would be obligated to try to fix whatever was the matter with her if he knew for certain she was troubled. Even Rafe had his limits, and she had tested them long enough.

Jezebel laid her cold, trembling hand on the worn case of the instrument that was about to cause her downfall. It wasn't the violin that was to blame, she knew. The heirloom instrument was only the sound box that would convey her shameful secrets to society, for its strings, under the direction of her wayward hands and heart, could not lie as they should.

If she could somehow have borne to accede to Rafe's demand that she marry another man and thus satisfy his overactive sense of propriety, or if, even less likely, she'd been able to convince herself she could ensure Rafe's happiness if she married him instead as she longed to do, she'd have jumped on either solution in a heartbeat, but she knew that was an impossibility. She was not the kind of woman who could stand to live a lie, but neither could she let the man she loved bear the burden of that failing. Jezebel regretted her inability to adjust and the discomfort it had caused her guardian more profoundly than anything she'd regretted in her life—even her failure to vindicate her uncle's beliefs. But there was no way she could make up for her wretched inadequacy now, unless it was by removing herself from Rafe's life so that she could never trouble him again.

She wished they were alone in the carriage, so that she might at least say good-bye properly. She was well aware that without the other two occupying the seats next to them, her plan to leave Rafe could not be accomplished, but by damn, she could truly wish the handsome marquis and the deceptively angelic baroness to perdition at this instant!

"Give us a moment," she finally begged the two who were now waiting for her to alight from the coach. Marksley and Lady Mayhew did not hesitate, catching each other's eyes and nodding. It was a breach of etiquette, but these two were no sticklers for propriety. They vacated the space with alacrity.

However, once Jezebel was alone with her beloved, she felt suddenly tongue-tied. What could she say to Rafe without giving away her intent to leave him?

*To leave him.* Oh, how that thought hurt! Jezebel fixed her eyes hungrily on the duke's countenance, remembering everything—his laughter, his passion, his zest for life. She loved even his anger. From his cropped blond curls to the elegant bones of his big feet, she loved every part of this extraordinary man—except his inability to love her in return.

In the end, there was only one thing she could say.

Leaning across the lantern-lit space of the closed carriage, her heart in her eyes, she once again dared to kiss the duke. Jezebel kissed Rafe tenderly, lingeringly, laying her apologies like an offering upon his warmly sensual lips.

"Forgive me," she whispered, her voice a mere thread of sound as she slipped out the door of the carriage.

*T*he burning impression of that poignant kiss still tingling upon his lips, Rafe stared after the woman he loved, confusion and longing warring in his heart.

He wished he knew what pained her so, what he was doing wrong and seemingly *had* been doing wrong from the very first day they'd met. Perhaps if he'd been a man more capable of fulfilling her need for adventure, he thought, or a man who took a less serious slant on his responsibilities, Jezebel would not now be so miserably upset with him. Perhaps if he were as devil-may-care as, say, his friend Damien, she would look on him with as much favor as she had upon the insouciant marquis these past few weeks. If he were such a man, Rafe thought, perhaps instead of looking at him with sorrow and regret, she would grace him again with her rare, mischievous smile, her exuberant laughter, her breathtaking, uninhibited loving. . . .

But he was who he was, and Jezebel claimed she could not love a man like him. Oh, he could sense her affection for him, her sincere regard and concern for his feelings. She did not *want* to hurt him, he knew. It was not her fault that every rejection she made to his advances drove a dagger of pain into his breast. She had no hatred for him— even her kiss just now seemed to apologize for her inability to love him.

What did she need, he wondered achingly, what did she want that he did not already provide? What, before God, would *make* her love him? He needed her to tell him, to show him, to make him understand.

That was just what Jezebel planned.

*   *   *

𝒜s the duke took his seat again after the second inter-
mission (the musicale had been lengthy, and the various
musicians, to his mind, no better than average, despite
young Lady Beauford's boasts), he found he was quite nervous, though the girl upon the stage, tuning her instrument
with intent concentration, looked cool and collected, almost
serene.

As if she faced firing squads like this one every day, he
thought. Rafe looked around the room anxiously, noting
that among the guests who had drifted back to their chairs
after the break, the spiteful Lady Beauford was already
seated beside her parents again, a self-satisfied smile twisting her rouged lips behind the fan she waved with seeming
languor. She appeared relaxed, sure of her imminent victory
as she looked over the distinguished group of peers who
had flocked to her family's drawing room tonight.

Because of Rafe's pronouncement yesterday—which he
was beginning to regret quite heartily now as foreboding
settled over him—and the challenge thrown out by the
spiteful baronet's daughter, an unusually large number of
people were in attendance this evening, and all had clearly
been waiting for this moment. The duke could read the
avidity in the faces of his peers, could guess exactly what
they were hoping for from this occasion—they wanted
some juicy new scandal to keep them from the ennui that
forever loomed as the bane of the *haut ton*. Would Jezebel
Montclair provide them with it?

As she took up her position on the small raised dais and
waited patiently for the audience to quiet, Jezebel's guardian began to have the feeling that she would. Something
about her stillness, the way she gazed out at them all with
such grim fortitude, felt portentous to him. But then she
began to play, and Rafe forgot all of his thoughts, his worries, his fears, for when the woman he loved coaxed melody
from her violin, the duke found himself instantly and hopelessly spellbound.

The music started out familiar—Rafe thought he rec-

ognized part of a refrain from J. S. Bach's Brandenburg
Concertos—but very quickly the melody turned into
something new, something more raw and immediate, prim-
itively emotive. Yet there was another aspect to the performance even more extraordinary than the changes his ward
was making to the famous piece.

Despite their audience, Jezebel was giving him a private
performance.

From the first note that trembled forth from her violin,
it was clear to Rafe that Jezebel played only for him tonight, only *to* him. It was as if she were physically *willing*
him to hear her unspoken message and to understand its
deeper meaning. He sensed the vital importance of inter-
preting that message, both for her sake and for his own, for
he suddenly knew his beloved would never grant him another moment of such fearless, heartfelt honesty. Rafe
opened his ears, his mind, and his heart. And he heard—
almost more than he could bear.

She played pure longing, sorrow, wildness whirling like
a cyclone and sweeping him up until he had no center, no
balance, nothing but the overpowering strength of her emotions to sustain him. In a strange way, Rafe recognized the
music she played was similar to the song he'd heard before,
both upon the banks of the Nile and in his recurring dreams,
but it was infinitely more powerful now, backed with the
full force of Jezebel's bared soul.

Rafe willingly let that power sweep him up, took the
ride into the maelstrom of her mind, feeling every iota of
her passion, her free-spiritedness, and the anguish created
by her need for him to accept her as she was. He felt her
fear, the anger that she kept in check, the defiant, unconquerable spirit so many wished to crush in her. The spirit
she believed *he* wanted to crush. She was, he realized,
showing him the pain he'd caused her with his stubborn
refusal to let her be free, make her own choices, be her
own woman.

For the first time he clearly recognized the fact that Jezebel saw him as a part of the society that wanted to consume her, and that she was now telling him she could never
let that happen. She was showing him how it stifled her to

have him try to stop her, to have him deny her right to be and live as she must. With each decree he made, Rafe realized suddenly that he had been stealing a piece of that very quality which made her the woman he loved.

But Jezebel would not allow him to continue repressing her spirit, even as he saw that she regretted her need to defy him. She did not blame him for being who he was, the duke now saw, but she could not change who *she* was either. This performance was Jezebel's way of throwing down a gauntlet before all the world, making a statement that, once advanced, could never be retracted. She would do only as *she* willed, for she could not live otherwise!

The music was fierce, frightening, overpowering. It cried out, echoing through the fussily decorated parlor, throbbing in the ears of its stunned audience, threatening to drive them all to madness. Indeed, many in the overcrowded chamber even pressed gloved fingers hesitantly to their ears, as if they knew not what to make of the sounds that filled them, whether to be offended or moved by the melody's sinister beauty.

Jezebel herself, their Pied Piper, stood defiantly proud upon the stage, swaying with the turns and twists of her music, leading them all, willing or no, on the journey into her anguished soul. Her dark hair had slipped from its simple knot, swinging loose, absorbing the candlelight and cloaking her slender frame in its glossy curtain, and her eyes, haunted sapphire orbs in the porcelain whiteness of her face, sparked with icy blue flames. Her beauty was breathtaking, yet it was her music that took control of the audience with complete, ferocious mastery, stunning them into awed silence.

His ward must have been expecting him to be ashamed of her performance, the duke realized, finally putting together Jezebel's odd behavior at the masquerade with the sorrow he'd sensed in her tonight. She must have thought he would try and prevent this display. But Rafe did not want to stop her from revealing her true self before his peers tonight. Instead, he wanted to shout his pride in Jezebel to the heavens!

He could not even look about him to gauge the reaction

of the others in the room, for to him there *were* no others anymore; just himself and Jezebel, locked eye to eye and heart to heart. He found himself standing, fists clenched at his side, though he was brought to his knees in spirit, full of wonder and love for her. Jezebel's flying fingers played his insides better than they played the strings, and when he saw she wept, tears silently tracking down her cheeks while she fiddled, he felt as if she were drawing her bow like a sword across his throat.

He accepted what she was telling him at last, what she was showing him, even forcing upon him. It was everything she had inside her, every demon of fear, every angel of love, every particle of the woman she was. He knew Jezebel was trying to frighten him, drive him away, but though his ears were ringing with the spiraling notes and he felt as though he could not breathe, driving him away was the last thing she was doing. Instead, he succumbed utterly to the sorcery of her music.

All of Rafe's life, he had maintained control above everything else, had known that for duty's sake he must never let himself be seduced into forgetting his responsibilities. But now, for the first time, he knew he would forswear any vow, give up any burden, even walk away without a backward glance from the massive obligation of ensuring the Ravenhurst dynasty's legacy (a legacy he had taken great pains to uphold since his father's death had left him with the title), if that was what she wanted of him. He knew he would have been a disappointment to the old duke, who had always frowned upon and discouraged what he termed Rafe's "wild side," but the younger Ravenhurst no longer cared.

For at last he understood what his dreams had been trying to tell him. While he was blindly allowing himself to remain mired in the sands of obligation and the strict code of propriety imposed by society—a senseless code he'd always accepted without even questioning why—the woman who meant the very world to him was fading rapidly from his sight. If he changed nothing about his behavior, those burdens of power and position would suffocate him with their empty weight, their meaninglessness, and Jezebel would slip through his fingers, lost to him.

If he continued to try to force Jezebel to be something she was not, he realized, to capture her and tie her down to a way of life she had never been meant for, and which, Rafe now admitted, he himself often felt was smothering the very breath from him, he would lose her as certainly as he had always lost the mysterious, exciting woman of his visions. He knew, more surely than he'd ever known anything, that if he continued to reach for her with such a heavy hand, she would elude him forever. And without this woman to bring joy to his heart, he would be condemned to a life of bitter loneliness and care that would wear him down to an empty, dried-out husk of a man, just as it had his father.

But it was not too late to change, Rafe hoped. It was not too late yet to understand her message and respect it. Strangely enough, it was his ward's very regret that gave him hope. She must have some feelings for him if she could feel such clear remorse for displeasing him, as she mistakenly believed she had. She might not be able to change her ways, but he reasoned that she must not totally despise his own if she could play such a heartfelt apology to him. Jezebel seemed to wish she could be what he needed nearly as much as he wished he could be what *she* needed, and surely, she must love him a little in that case.

Rafe resolved that he would never again force her hand, but if she would still hear him out after all he'd done to cause her grief, he would beg Jezebel to let him remain in her life, whatever else he had to give up. He would plead with her to give him another chance. However she wanted to live—in a tent in the desert, on top of the highest mountain, or in the depths of the steamiest jungle—he would join her, spend his life helping her achieve whatever goals she thought would make her happy.

He would even learn to accept her independent ways, to hold his tongue when and if she decided to do something he thought was too dangerous or foolhardy, no matter how it frightened him to watch her hare off into danger. If she wanted to lower herself into some thousand-year-old tomb in the future, he would simply have to hold his breath, even as he held the rope for her. If she wanted to cross hostile territory or deal with shiftless pirates in some foreign land, well, then he must learn to follow where she led, do as she did. He must respect Jezebel's decisions, even if it made his hair turn white to witness some of her wilder stunts. He could only offer up his support, his love, and his unwavering loyalty. Wherever she chose to roam, he would be there to guard her back, to champion her cause, should she allow him one more chance to please her. Nothing else mattered to Rafe as did Jezebel's happiness.

He would follow where this woman led, to hell and beyond damnation, if only she would let him. Whatever consequences might result for him in the world into which he'd been born, however ostracized he might become, the duke of Ravenhurst no longer gave a damn. Society could go to hell, for all he cared!

*J*ezebel stood upon the stage as though it were a battleground and her very life the prize for which she fought. Her music poured forth unrestrained, traveling straight from her heart to the ears of the one man she could never dare have. She looked at no one else but him, drowning in his shimmering, summer-sea-blue eyes, willingly sinking beneath their shifting depths as she let herself flow into the melody echoing in her head. There was no shame left inside her for anyone's shock but Rafe's, and if she could not see the aversion emerging in those gorgeous eyes, Jezebel assumed it was due to the tears that were streaming forth from her own, blurring the edges from all but her misery.

She told him everything without a word: how she longed for him, how she wished she could have been the woman he desired, how she had failed, and how she feared to let the terrible madness that ran in her family consume him as well as herself. She told him she was sorry, she told him he was better off without her. But most of all, with each scintillating, passionate note, she told him that she loved him.

The crests of melody engulfed her, and she let herself

become lost in them, crescendos building one upon the
other almost like the waves of climax, of the ultimate pleasure she'd experienced so briefly but thoroughly in Rafe's
arms. The music surged and rose with inexorable strength,
continuing to build relentlessly, overpowering Jezebel's audience nearly as badly as her feelings overwhelmed her
own heart, until finally the seething tide broke in a flurry
of wailing notes crashing down to a rocky catharsis.

Jezebel yanked the horsehair bow from the strings
abruptly, discordantly, a harsh sob ringing out into the silence she'd created. The deafening silence. Head bowed by
exhaustion and sorrow, she couldn't bear to look up, but
then, she didn't have to—she'd been through enough humiliating performances in her past to know what this horrified silence signified. She'd done what she set out to do.
She'd sealed her dismissal from this realm, made herself a
social pariah with her unprecedented, ill-bred display of
emotion. She had also disgraced the proud duke of Ravenhurst before his peers, and she knew he would never
forgive her for this deed. She could bear the others' scorn
and hatred, but not his. Never his.

Jezebel fled from the stage, skirts and streaming hair
flying behind her as she blindly ran down the aisle between
the seats and toward the door.

It was over.

# Chapter Thirty

❧

$\mathcal{F}$eeling as if his bones were made of water, the duke of Ravenhurst slowly made his way to the abandoned stage. He moved like a sleepwalker through the crowd of spectators who held their breath, watching him uncertainly, clearly sensing the extraordinary thing that had happened here tonight but not knowing how to respond. Well, *he* knew exactly what was called for. There was but one thing he could do.

Taking a deep breath, Rafe sent his gaze steadily out across the audience.

"That," he said in his quietly resonant baritone, "was the woman I love. The most extraordinary, most passionate, talented, and beautiful woman I've ever been privileged to know. I only hope you can begin to appreciate the enormous gift she has given you tonight. I know I do."

Rafe's eyes surveyed the crowd evenly, and he caught sight of Lady Mayhew among them. She was unabashedly letting the tears caused by her charge's exquisite musical revelations flow down her lightly powdered cheeks, a handkerchief pressed tightly to her reddened nose. Plainly, she had not failed to appreciate a single nuance of Jezebel's performance. But had the others? His stare as it roamed among them was challenging, daring anyone to deplore him for championing the outrageous Miss Montclair. But to his surprise, no one in the room seemed to disapprove. In fact, he saw several other ladies wiping tears from their eyes with sodden handkerchiefs, just as Lady Allison had done.

"Brava," sniffled one. "Oh, *brava!*" And before he could blink, a chorus of other voices had taken up the refrain. Soon the entire hall was trembling with the stomping of feet and echoing with the sound of cheers and appreciative whistles. Only one face remained unmoved by the joyous spirit of the moment—that of the young Lady Beauford, who looked as sour as if she had just swallowed a persimmon whole.

But Rafe barely registered the wild accolades or the resounding defeat of the baronet's spiteful offspring, for he was already in motion. Without another word he leapt down from the stage and strode forth in the wake of his ward, no longer sparing any attention for the assembled peers. He had bigger concerns to occupy him just now. He must find his beloved before it was too late!

Thus preoccupied, as he passed beyond the threshold of the room, the duke also did not take notice of the odd fact that Lord Marksley was no longer among the gentlefolk giving such raucous voice to their approval of the old archaeologist's niece.

Very shortly, however, that little detail would become enormously significant to him.

*W*hen he reached the cool darkness of the evening streets, Rafe looked around for his carriage, assuming Jezebel would have taken it and wondering if he could still catch the coachman before they left for Grosvenor Square. But the vehicle carrying his crest was still parked at the curbside along with those of the other guests, and when he scanned the cobbled streets, the duke could see only a plain black hackney turning the corner at the edge of the park, disappearing into the distance. His heart was still racing from the emotions of the past half hour, and Rafe could not wait to find Jezebel, to take her in his arms and beg her forgiveness as she had so poignantly begged his own with her music.

Where had she gone? he wondered, the first threads of unease winding through his body. Had his ward been in that hired conveyance that had just rounded the corner? And why, if Jezebel had indeed been in the hack, would she have chosen to rent a cab rather than take his own coach home to the townhouse? Just then he heard the sound of a soft footfall behind him, and he whirled, heart in his mouth.

"Sorry," Lady Allison said. "It's only me." She smiled sympathetically, hugging the shawl she'd hastily reclaimed from a footman about her shoulders as she faced him across the pavement. Her eyes were still a bit damp with emotion, but her linen handkerchief had taken care of any damage to her cosmetics.

"Allison," Rafe began anxiously, "do you know where Jezebel is right now? It's imperative that I see her without delay."

The baroness took a deep breath. *The duke is not going to like hearing this!* she thought. *Well, here I go, anyhow.* "She's gone, Rafe. She has left London."

"Left . . . ? But how . . . ? Why . . . ? Oh, God," he groaned, grasping handfuls of his hair in his fists with frustration. "I drove her to this, didn't I? Jezebel told you she was leaving? You knew before the concert?"

"I should have known," his cousin replied ruefully. "She came to me last night with a wild tale of distress, begging for my aid. The girl was in despair, Rafe." The duke looked to be well into a desolate state of his own, Allison thought privately, hating to see him so miserable but comforted by the knowledge that her scheme was proceeding perfectly so far. He would feel much worse, she knew, before he felt better. But in the end, if all went well, he would have good cause to celebrate. The ends would justify the means—and anyway, it was just a tiny lie or two. . . .

Her manipulations were all for Rafe's own good, Allison reassured herself. She had no real cause for remorse. And so she pressed on. "Last night she begged me to help her leave here, appearing most upset and claiming, if you can credit it, that she feared to fall into some sort of state of terrible lunacy if she must stay on past the evening of the musicale."

"Lunacy?" the duke exclaimed. "But that is absurd. Jezebel is no more insane than you or I! What can she have meant by such a statement?"

The baroness quickly explained what Jezebel had told her about her mother's death and her own fear of meeting a similar fate, watching Rafe's face as he absorbed the shocking tale. He looked sick as he listened to her describe the suicide of Natalya Montclair. "I tried to dissuade the girl from her folly, but I fear she was quite intractable, unwilling to listen to reason. She became agitated, vowing that if I did not help her, she would leave on her own."

This much, Allison reflected, was perfectly true. The rest, however, would not be. "Well, I refused her, of course, knowing you would not like it, and when she saw that I could not be swayed to her cause, she seemed to accept that she must stay on here with us—at least, I believed she did, but now I see that I was too easily duped. Apparently, after realizing she would get no help from my corner, she must have gone ahead and made plans of her own to depart."

Now for the first real hint of trouble, Lady Mayhew thought. She pasted a distraught look upon her angelic features. "Oh, Rafe, I fear Jezebel has made a terrible bargain to avoid this destiny she imagines must otherwise befall her."

Now for the next step, the crucial step in her plan. This would be the worst for Rafe, she knew. The sense of betrayal he would experience would be immense. But there was no help for it, and at any rate, he would find out the truth soon enough. Allison found herself worrying that this pretense she'd come up with was perhaps too extreme, but she knew there was no going back now. She had been able to devise no better plan in the short time her charge had given her to arrange matters for her escape. If she did not wish Jezebel to leave Rafe behind permanently, breaking both their hearts and giving neither the chance for happiness they could only have together, she must be ruthless in her methods.

"There is something you must know, and I fear you will not be best pleased when I share the news." She paused delicately. "It seems Jezebel did not leave London alone." From her beaded reticule, she made a show of reluctantly withdrawing a small, folded scrap of parchment and holding it out to him. The reluctance was not feigned, though the reason for it was. "Damien asked me to deliver this to you just now. By the time I had the chance to read it, it was too late to stop them."

"*Damien* asked you? What the devil's Damien got to do
with it . . . ?" Rafe stopped, stricken. "No," he breathed.
"No, it can't be true." He stared down at his friend's hand-
writing on the sheet of foolscap, unable for a long moment
to open the folded missive. When at last he did, the pertinent words seemed to burn into his retinas with agonizing
intensity. *Eloping. Gretna Green. In love.*

Damien was carrying Jezebel off to marry her tonight.

The duke's face turned ashen as she fed him this well-
intended falsehood, and Allison's stomach clenched with
pity for him. He looked as if all the lifeblood had been
drained from his veins. Once again, she questioned the wisdom of her hasty scheme, wondering if perhaps she should
admit that the elopement was only a sham intended to send
him galloping off after his ward posthaste.

When she'd planned this confrontation with her cousin,
she'd intended to assure him that Jezebel did not love Lord
Marksley, that she was running away with the man only to
spare Rafe the burden of her care, thinking that with these
explanations in mind, the duke would approach his ward
and his friend in a less violent state of mind than if he
simply assumed the worst. She'd meant to make sure that
when Rafe pursued the two, he did not believe Jezebel had
betrayed him—that instead, she did what she did purely for
love of him. Yes, Allison had meant to do a lot of further
explaining.

But it appeared that it was too late for either second
guesses or elaborate explanations, for Rafe, biting off a vicious oath, spun on his heel and was already running for
his carriage before she could even open her mouth to call
him back.

The plan was in motion, it seemed, and nothing could
stop it now.

*Ah, love,* thought Lady Mayhew ruefully. It did make
such fools of the best of men—and women too. For her
part, she had done all she could. The two lovers would
simply have to work things out between themselves from
this point on. She could only pray that from now on the
two would make less of a muddle of their relationship than

they had to date. Cleaning up after their mistakes was becoming exhausting!

The baroness raised her fan to hide the pleased expression that spread across her lovely features as she watched her cousin tear off after Miss Montclair.

*T*he rumbling of the plain, minimally appointed hackney carriage's wheels clattering over the cobbles was the only sound breaking the silence between Jezebel and the marquis. They traveled northward along the darkened streets, heading for the outskirts of the city, not speaking or even looking at each other often. Jezebel was drained from the concert, and Damien could obviously sense it, not pressing her, only being there to provide whatever she needed, as he had earlier pledged to do.

He had arranged for the coach, had made sure her necessary items were aboard it, had been waiting for her at the curb when she ran outside—all as promised. In the part of her mind that was not still swirling with the echoes of her own musical disaster, she knew she should be grateful both to him and to Lady Allison, who had also been instrumental in this escape. Yet she could not manage to feel even that much at this moment, for there was absolutely no emotion left inside her. She had left it all behind in the baronet's drawing room, along with the man she loved. Now she was leaving London as well, and would flee the country soon after, never to return.

Earlier today, as they were partaking of a light luncheon none had had much stomach for—first, of course, making sure that the duke had eaten earlier and had left the house on business—the three conspirators had plotted the course of her uncertain future together. They had, after a short discussion, decided that Jezebel would go first to the North Country near the border with Scotland, so that she could pay a long-overdue visit to her mother's grave and view her uncle's estates, where she had been born, once more before leaving England permanently.

That this had been Allison's suggestion was a fact that

Jezebel, in her state of emotional upheaval, had taken very little notice of. The other woman's reasoning—that Rafe would never expect her to travel in this direction, that she must not leave England without saying farewell to her mother's tormented spirit—had passed over her head like words spoken in a foreign tongue. She hadn't cared *where* she went, truthfully, though she had asked that a passage be booked for her to travel back to Cairo as soon as possible after the trip north.

Allison had assured her such could be done in Edinburgh, and that Lord Marksley would take care of the costs and arrangements for the trip once they arrived in Scotland. Egypt was the only place where Jezebel still maintained any ties, and so it had seemed like the logical next step—at least until she could plan a better.

But Egypt was a long ways away, she thought dully, staring with sightless eyes as the streets of London passed by for possibly the last time. It was too bad, she reflected with a sense of surrealism. She had been so bent on the quest to leave it that she had never even had the chance to enjoy this famous city. Now she would probably never see it again.

What did it really matter? she asked herself miserably. The memories here were far too bittersweet for her to ever think of returning, even if she had not just sealed her social demise tonight with her own actions. No, she would never be able to think of London without picturing her beloved, without remembering how she had disgraced and disgusted him.

Better that she never come back, never look back, Jezebel decided, letting her eyes glaze over with salty wetness. She paid no attention to the sympathetic glances she sensed Lord Marksley was sending her way, unable to take his pity, unable even to be embarrassed that he had witnessed the full measure of her exposed feelings for his friend the duke tonight. There was no room left in her drained spirit for any emotion save mourning.

At last, the archaeologist's niece leaned her head wearily against the side of the coach, closing her eyes as the miles rolled by. Each bump and painful clatter was a welcome blow against the numbness that had invaded her soul.

## Chapter Thirty-one

$\mathscr{J}$t was just after daybreak when the gunshot rang out.

Gray light had barely begun to eat the dawn mists from the edges of the isolated post road upon which the coach carrying the dull-eyed but wakeful Miss Montclair and the peacefully sleeping marquis rode, when both were startled to alertness by the frighteningly loud report. An instant later they heard the sounds of their driver's alarmed yell, the thundering hoofbeats of a horse approaching at great speed from out of the fog, and the whinnying of their own horses as the coachman whipped them up in a vain attempt to elude the gunman.

"Halt!" a deep, resonating baritone called out, coming from behind them somewhere off to the left of the road, the edge nearest Jezebel's side of the vehicle. Though she had not been sleeping, her near-stuporous state of depression took time to shake off, and it was a minute before she realized what was happening. When she did, she gasped in shock.

Someone was holding up the coach! Her breath catching in her throat, her heart pounding suddenly, Jezebel glanced fearfully over at Damien, and was relieved to see that he was fully awake already, eyes bright and full of excitement. Why, he almost seemed to welcome the intrusion!

"Aren't you going to do something?" she asked incredulously. Lord Marksley had never struck her as the type to falter in the face of danger. "In case you hadn't noticed, we're being attacked!"

"Oh, all right," he sighed with jovial good nature. "If I must." Quite casually, he reached under the seat and removed a large carriage pistol from the plain wooden case stowed there. Despite his bizarrely unfazed attitude toward danger, she noticed he loaded the weapon from the accompanying bags of shot and powder with reassuring efficiency.

"Just keep low, Jezebel," he ordered calmly as he employed the ramrod to tamp the ball down the wide, threatening barrel. "And don't panic, dear girl. I suspect we've nothing to fear."

Nothing to fear, when a highwayman was bearing down on them with pistols blasting? Jezebel wondered incredulously. Was the man insane? But though the dark-haired marquis seemed unnaturally relaxed and his clear gray eyes were without even a hint of anxiety to cloud them, she guessed he was more confident than he was crazy. She must pray that confidence was not misplaced, she thought faintly, and found herself suddenly overwhelmed with the ironic wish that Rafe were here beside her now. Had she escaped the perils of remaining by his side, only to fall into the hands of an even greater danger without him?

She would find out very shortly, the archaeologist's niece thought nervously, for the hoofbeats were growing closer by the second. Their pursuer's lone horse was much faster than their coach-and-four, and Jezebel estimated that he would be upon them momentarily. Adrenaline raced through her veins.

"You don't happen to have an extra pistol in there for me, do you?" she asked Damien.

The question startled a laugh out of the devil-may-care marquis. "Afraid not, my dear. You'll have to let me do the shooting, should it come down to that, though something tells me we shan't have to engage in any duels this dawn. At least," he finished in a mutter too low for Miss Montclair's ears to catch, "I doubt *you* will. I can't swear the same for *me* after this little charade." A wide grin split his features, and he appeared to be finding the entire situation extremely hilarious.

Jezebel was in no mood for trying to figure out Lord Marksley's cryptic murmurings or inexplicable good humor, however. The marquis might be taking this whole thing far too casually, but she was not!

Another shot followed the first, and another command to stop the coach came bellowing forth from the man pursuing them. The gunman's voice echoed weirdly across the fog-shrouded rural valley through which they traveled, the sound distorted and frightening. If anything, Damien only seemed more amused at this dramatic turn of events. He began to chuckle softly, much to Jezebel's amazement. Only their hired coachman seemed to be reacting with appropriate seriousness, for he whipped up the horses once more and cursed the intruder vilely, damning him to hell. With each curse that spewed from the driver's lips, singeing the ears of the passengers below, the marquis seemed to laugh harder, the gun in his hand held loosely, forgotten by his side. Was he completely daft?

Abruptly, Jezebel decided to take matters into her own hands, since her escort seemed unwilling, or unable, to do so. She snatched the pistol from Damien's grasp, kicking open her door in the same motion.

"What?" he exclaimed. "Miss Montclair, wait! It's not what you—"

But Jezebel was already out the door. She twisted herself around to face the back of the coach, feet braced in the doorway and arm outstretched to grab hold of the luggage trap and steady her aim. Though her damnably cumbersome skirts and her loosened hair blowing everywhere impeded her sight, she managed to pick out the distant figure charging in their direction, riding atop a fearsome brute of a stallion. She couldn't see much through the mist and the skeins of her dark hair whipping every which way, but he looked to be a big fellow, cloaked and menacing, tearing up the space between them like a devil out of hell.

If only Rafe were here now! she thought again. But the duke would have no way of guessing where they were headed, or so Allison had assured her yesterday, promising to set his feet on the wrong path in the unlikely event he should still wish to come after his ward once the fateful concert was over. Jezebel could expect no help from him, even had she not so thoroughly embarrassed the man last night. She would have to save herself and the marquis both, it seemed, for the man inside the coach, now tugging frantically at her skirts to pull her back inside, had obviously lost his wits from fright. But despite all she had been through in the past twenty-four hours, her wits had not yet gone wandering. Heartbroken or whole, Jezebel was not about to let a highwayman become the death of her.

Suddenly, however, all became absolute chaos—as if the situation had not been bad enough already. The carriage lurched violently to the right, one wheel striking a deep rut in the middle of the muddy road and sending her smashing up against the side of the vehicle. Simultaneously, she heard the coachman's alarmed yell, and out of the corner of her eye saw him tumble from his high perch to land with a sickening thud upon the grassy bank at the far verge of the road. The horses, their reins let suddenly loose, slowed their pace, and she could see the horseman behind them gaining on the coach, his enveloping cloak billowing like the wings of a demon all about him.

The unrelenting rattling and shaking of the runaway vehicle, the encroaching attacker's thunderous approach, and Lord Marksley's shouts from inside the coach all combined to form a cacophonous din. On top of that, fear made it almost impossible to think. The wind knocked out of her, ribs sore from the painful crack they'd received upon hitting the side of the coach, Jezebel knew only that she had no more time to spare. Once the man was fully upon them, she would have no chance of fighting him off. It was now or never.

She took aim and fired.

"Jesus, Jezebel!" the highwayman howled indignantly, then tumbled from his horse all at once, hitting the road hard and rolling several times before jolting to a stop. A second later the hackney, its exhausted horses spent beyond their strength, also came to a halt. Inside it, Damien ceased his insistent yelling. Everything went quiet at the same time, the echoes of the gun's report ringing crazily in her ears.

Jezebel went cold with dread at the sound of the bandit's cry. How could he have known her name? All of a sudden, sick realization made her stomach churn with nausea, and for a moment she thought she might vomit.

She had just shot her guardian.

Screaming for Damien to come help her, she jumped

from the carriage and plunged back along the length of the road toward the place where the cloaked figure had come to rest, running just as fast as her feet would carry her.

Pray God her aim had been off!

# Chapter Thirty-two

*~*

*I* know I haven't been the best of protectors these last several months, sweetheart, but do you really think I deserved *that*?" asked the duke when Jezebel had fallen to her knees beside his bloodstained form, crying and begging his pardon all at once in a jumble of incoherent emotion. He smiled at her, raising himself up painfully on one arm, his clipped blond curls and bronzed cheeks speckled with mud. One shoulder of his evening jacket, which he had not had time to change out of before setting off on his wild chase last night, was slowly growing darker with an ominous red stain that spread from his collarbone to the middle of his chest.

"If I ever had any doubts about your ability to take care of yourself in dangerous situations, consider them allayed." He laughed, then groaned softly as the movement sent pain radiating all throughout his torso. "I think it's fair to say you have just won our wager, sweetheart, but I'll thank you very much to refrain from proving yourself quite so dramatically in future, if you don't mind."

As he talked, Jezebel's frantic hands were rushing over his body, trying to assess the damage she had done. She found herself laughing helplessly at his indignant tone, even as she wept with fear for his injury and remorse at the hasty, ill-considered action that had caused it. "What the blazes did you think were you doing, chasing after us like some crazed bandit?" she demanded through her tears. Not waiting for his answer, she yanked up her skirts, ignoring the duke's raised eyebrows, and ripped a long length of cloth from her muslin petticoats to form a bandage.

"I thought you liked adventurous men," he joked, then winced as she peeled back his jacket and shirt to explore

the wound she'd given him. Jezebel's touch was sure, un-
hesitating, though he noticed her fingers were icy cold
against his heated skin. He ignored the baleful glare she
gave in response to these flippant words. "In all seriousness,
my love, I didn't intend to frighten you like that. That
damned idiotic driver must have thought I was trying to
rob the coach, for he wouldn't let me get close when I tried
to hail him. I was only trying to pull him up when I dis-
charged the pistol. I wouldn't have followed in such haste
except that I needed to speak to you so urgently."

At that moment Damien ran up beside them, no longer
laughing but deadly serious. "R-Ravenhurst," he stuttered
in shock. "Dear God, man. Look what's happened to you!
I never meant—"

"Go check on the driver," Rafe ordered harshly, dis-
missing him with curt coldness. "He may be hurt worse
than I."

Despite Jezebel's frantic head-shake, the marquis, after
sending a swiftly assessing glance down at the damage to
his friend, did as he was ordered. He loped off in the direction of the fallen coachman, leaving Rafe and Jezebel
alone.

"Why did you do that?" she cried. "You're wounded!"

"I am well aware of that fact, thank you," the duke responded dryly.

"But we may need Damien's help," she protested, pressing the makeshift pad against the wound high on Rafe's
left shoulder, relieved to see that her bullet seemed to have
gone cleanly through the flesh, tearing no vital organs. But
good heavens, if she had aimed only inches lower or to the
left . . .

"Forget about Damien for one goddamned minute, will
you?" he swore. She might be tending to *him* with worry
and concern written all over her lovely features at the moment, but Rafe still hated to hear Jezebel speak his friend's
name. After all, he reminded himself acerbically, it was the
marquis with whom she had decided to race off, while
she'd chosen to run *away* from him. "I came here for a
reason, and, wounded or no, I intend to have my say, Jezebel. Let me finish."

"I'm sorry!" she cried, stung. She couldn't believe they were sitting here in the middle of the road, with mud and blood soaking both of them more thoroughly by the minute, and *bickering* with one another, of all things. It was insane. She was insane. Hell, even *he* was insane. The whole world had gone mad. She sniffled soggily and said once more, "I'm sorry, Rafe."

"Indeed, and so am I," he replied, more gently this time. His gaze softened as he searched her face. "I came to tell you—" Rafe broke off momentarily, grimacing with pain as he tried to sit up further. Jezebel quickly wrapped an arm about his waist, supporting him until he sat upright.

"What could you possibly have to say to me after the way I disgraced you last night?" she asked remorsefully. "And now look what I've gone and done to you. It is as I feared all along," she lamented. "I have brought you harm already, just as I knew I would someday. How can you even stand the sight of me?"

"The sight of you is what makes my life worth living, Jezebel," he replied softly. One large hand came up to cup the side of her tear-streaked face tenderly. "Listen, sweetheart. I have come here to ask you—nay, to *beg* you—not to marry Damien."

"Marry *Damien*?"

Rafe ignored her outburst, determined to get through the speech he had rehearsed throughout the long night's bruising ride before he lost his nerve. Stopping only to collect his stallion from the stables by his townhouse, the duke had set off along the north road for Gretna Green in total darkness, praying all the while that he would catch the eloping couple's coach in time. But would his words make a difference to his willful ward now that he had found her? He wasn't at all certain they would. He only knew that he must try.

"I shall not force you to desist from the marriage if it is your wish—I shall never force you to do anything against your will again, my sweet—but I beg that you will reconsider your choice. I know I am not an exciting man, Jezebel. I know I am not as adventurous as you might wish. . . ."

Rafe stopped, searching for words, looking for the courage to express what he wanted to say next.

*Not exciting?* Why, Rafe was the most thrilling, exhilarating man she'd ever known! No other man could take her breath away as he could, simply with a glance or a smile. No other man could make her heart turn over with a word, make her soul sing with a touch. She could love no other man, now or ever. How could he ever believe differently? And what was this nonsense about her marrying the marquis? She didn't know what he was talking about.

But Rafe was already continuing, and Jezebel gave up trying to understand anything that was happening on this crazy day, content just to listen to her beloved—who, miraculously, did not seem angry with her for any of what had occurred; not last night's disgrace, not her flight, not even this terrible accident that had left him wounded and bleeding in her arms. She stroked the muscles of his strong back reverently, thankful beyond words just for his simple presence, whatever he might have come to say. Yet his words were even better than the comforting solidity of his body next to hers.

"Jezebel," he said. "I know I am not everything that you might have wanted in a husband. I am not known for being lighthearted or gay. Indeed, I have often been told that I am overbearing—and I know that I was so with you. But I have seen now that I cannot hold you back. Nor do I *want* to hold you back. Not any longer. Wherever you go from now on, be it to the ends of the earth, I want to travel there with you. I want to be the man you choose, not Damien."

"But—the concert—how can you still say so, after everything . . . ?" He obviously thought there was something between herself and Lord Marksley. Yet even suspecting as much, she marveled, he still desired her enough to race through the night after them! Jezebel's eyes were welling with tears, disbelief and elation warring in her heart. Oh, it was dangerous to hope like this! Already, the heady madness of her feelings for him were swelling out of control, letting her dare to think, *perhaps* . . . But she must not.

"I know you think you have somehow caused me shame with your music, my darling, but I tell you, nothing could be further from the truth. I have never been so proud of anyone in my life as I was of you last night. I do not want you to change, whatever you believe, whatever I may have said in the past. I want you exactly as you are."

He swallowed, then went on softly. "I do not think I could bear it if you married Marksley. Not loving you as much as I do—and I *do* love you, so very, very much. Please," he finished humbly, all of his customary arrogance banished. "Do not do this just to punish me. If you truly love Damien, it is another matter, but—"

His last words were drowned out in a surge of joy so great Jezebel could barely breathe. Rafe loved her! Could it be possible? He'd just said as much, hadn't he? And the duke of Ravenhurst never lied—it was beneath him, too dishonorable an idea to consider. If he said he loved her, then against all reason, against all she'd believed, she must accept it as the truth. Yet now it seemed *he* believed she cared for his best friend more than she did for him. Oh, the fool! Giddy joy made her blurt out her thoughts without consideration.

"Love Damien?" she parroted incredulously. "Whatever gave you that idea, you foolish man? Have you been so blind you could not see, so deaf you could not hear what I have been trying to tell you all along, both with my music and with the very singing of my heart crying out to yours? It is *you* I love, you great, arrogant idiot. It has always been you, and always *will* be you. How could you think otherwise?" Her own hand traveled across the space between them to trace the beloved planes of his sculpted face with tender fingers, and her eyes were shining with sweet emotion despite the reproach of her words.

"How then do you explain the note Allison showed me only last night?" he demanded, not knowing whether to be angry still, or to allow the joy that was creeping through his veins to suffuse him completely.

"What note?"

"The note that said you were eloping to Gretna Green this morning with Marksley!"

"Eloping! With Damien? But that's ridiculous," she scoffed.

"Did I pick a bad time to return?" the subject of their conversation asked facetiously, strolling up to them with an air of innocence that somehow only made him look even more like a guilty schoolboy than usual. "The coachman will be all right, by the way. Just a sprained ankle and a nasty bump on the head. He's calming the horses at the moment."

Realization dawned abruptly within the duke's mind. Allison and the marquis, inveterate schemers both, had set up this entire situation! If he hadn't just been shot, he would have knocked that inane grin right off Lord Marksley's smug face. As it was, Rafe contented himself with a warning growl. "Damien . . ."

"What?" the other man huffed defensively. "It worked, didn't it? Nothing like the old best-friend-running-off-with-the-beloved trick to get the kinks worked out of a relationship, eh?" He saw that the duke was not smiling. "Come, now, old chap. You know I'm a prankster from way back. Just be glad I've got your best interests at heart. Think what I would do to my enemies! Now, if you're all right for the moment, I shall just pop over to the village yonder and fetch a surgeon for that shoulder of yours. No need to thank me!" he called over his shoulder, hightailing it down the road before Rafe could call him back.

"That bloody fiend!" Rafe seethed. "He stole you away just to get me to come after you. It's diabolical." He was grinning even as he fumed, however, unable to deny that his compatriots' plotting had indeed had the desired effect of reuniting him with the woman he loved more than his own life. The woman, he recalled, who had just told him she loved him every bit as much. Sheer bliss made him feel almost light-headed—though that could also have had something to do with the not-insubstantial blood loss he'd suffered before his ward had managed to stanch the wound, he reflected. No matter! He was happier than he'd ever been in all his years of searching, for he had finally caught hold of the woman of his dreams. He would give much more than blood to keep her by his side.

When he gazed up at this precious find, however, he saw that Jezebel's face had grown serious again, almost melancholy. "Lord Marksley did not precisely steal me away, my love," she confessed warily. "I did ask him and the baroness to help me leave you, though not in the manner they obviously led you to believe."

Rafe too grew solemn, sensing her mood. Something was yet troubling Jezebel. He dragged himself stiffly up to his knees, and then to his feet, pulling her up with him. He wrapped his arms about her tiny form, though he found that, with surprising strength, it was she who was supporting much of his weight. Looking down at her, he breathed the question that had plagued him ever since the musicale. "Why, Jezebel? Why did you run if you love me as you say?"

"It is *because* I love you that I had to leave you—and still must." She looked away, staring at her feet miserably, but the duke would have none of it. He lifted her chin with one forefinger, waiting until her shimmering sapphire eyes reluctantly met his own luminous aquamarine stare.

"What nonsense is this, Jezebel? Why leave now, when we have just found each other?"

"Because my love is cursed!" she cried suddenly, unable to keep the truth inside any longer. "Don't you understand? What I feel for you is madness! It is too strong, too pure and deep to be aught else. It will destroy us both!" She looked up at him, aching with sorrow.

But Rafe simply laughed. "If your love is mad, my sweet, then so is mine, for I assure you what I feel is no less powerful. But I have a cure for it, my love, one that does not require our separation."

"You—you do?" she quavered. Oh, how she wanted to believe. . . .

"Yes, sweetheart. I do. It is perfectly logical, I'll warrant. If our love is mad, then we shall simply be lunatics together," he answered triumphantly. "Live in our own private asylum, raise a dozen barmy children, keep a barnful of exotic pets. . . ." The duke broke off, grinning down at her so brightly that she was almost blinded, almost convinced he had the right of it. But she knew better.

Rafe thought it was so simple. But he did not understand the truth, the secret scandal buried in her family's past. He knew nothing of her mother's fatal illness, the imbalance that had driven her father away and taken the fragile Russian émigré's own life much too young. If he were to learn about Natalya, he would not be so confident of their idyllic future together.

"Be serious!" she pleaded. "It is no laughing matter, Rafe. I tell you, you will grow to hate me for my ways, soon or late!"

"But we lunatics are always laughing, my sweet," he teased. "We cannot help it. It is our nature." The duke ran his hand through the tangled waves of her glossy raven hair, the gentleness of his touch belying the lightness of his voice. He let the radiance of his smile fade to seriousness.

"I know what you fear," he confessed softly. "Allison told me some of it, and the rest I have guessed. You are afraid you will inherit the sickness of your mother, are you not?" he asked. "That the feelings and passions you harbor inside you will repulse me?" At her amazed nod, he went on soothingly. "But it will not happen, Jezebel. I swear it will not. You are not your mother, and I am not your father—nor my own, for that matter. We are only ourselves, and we may make of our futures anything we choose. It has taken me far too long to learn that simple fact, but I will never forget it henceforth.

"I will never take your gifts as a curse," he vowed, "never despise you for what you are. For what you are is everything to me, Jezebel. I know how you thought last night would end, that I would hate you for all you so bravely revealed with your music, but I tell you now, you need *never* fear that I will feel shamed in your company. I have seen what you have to show, heard what you have to tell, and I count myself blessed beyond all fortune to have done so. Indeed, I would wager all I own that no other man has ever felt as lucky to have found love with a woman as I do at finding it with you."

To her wonderment, Jezebel found that she believed the duke—believed him with all her heart. The fear that had clouded her mind evaporated like the morning mists, allowing the brilliant sunshine of his love to bathe her scarred soul with its healing balm.

"I would be your husband, Jezebel, if you will consent to be my wife. Will you marry me?"

The Honorable Miss Montclair—archaeologist, explorer, violinist, and high society's most shocking new bluestocking—found to her great surprise that she would.

In response to Rafe's question, she simply wrapped her strong fingers in his golden curls and pulled the duke's head down to hers for a kiss that contained all the answers he sought.

# Epilogue

$\mathcal{R}$inging out over the sounds of shovels and picks striking hard against unforgiving stone came the even more grating noise of a bow being drawn inexpertly across the strings of an antique violin.

Rafe looked up from the chart he was studying with a grin, mopping the sweat from his broad forehead with one dusty hand. He laid down his pen and sighed melodramatically. "She just couldn't have inherited any of *my* talents, could she?" he asked his wife, who had been leaning against his side, examining the chart over his shoulder.

Jezebel smiled up at him ruefully. She then shifted her gaze to watch their precocious four-year-old offspring as the little girl sat practicing her fledgling music. A beautiful child, little Allison Sunderland was a mingling of her two proud parents, with her mother's sparkling sapphire eyes and fair skin, and her father's high forehead and beautiful, luxurious blond ringlets. At the moment, the toddler was perched proudly upon the lap of the infamous Giovanni Belzoni, clearly unafraid of the engineer's fearsome mustachios or gleaming bald head, somehow knowing that she was as safe as any child could ever hope to be within his strong encircling arms.

Both parents were content to rest their fond looks upon their daughter as they stood in one another's embrace in the ancient Valley of the Kings; near, they hoped, to the very site where they had once made such furious, tender love during the fateful sandstorm that had altered their lives forever. Someday, if they were lucky, they would find that spot, and the tomb beside it, once again.

Until then, however, they were content merely to keep up the search during their frequent visits here from England—which, as Jezebel had reluctantly admitted recently under her husband's prodding, was not *all* bad. If Rafe could agree to let his underlings (the much-aggrieved Mr. Chumley foremost among them) take over some of the ducal responsibilities while they traveled and explored the world, well, then she could stand to live in London part of the time as well, as long as she had the opera houses and symphony halls to visit and plenty of blue bloods to scandalize. And, of course, there were little Allison's godparents to see, for the brazen baroness and the merry marquis demanded to spend time with their new charge quite regularly.

Perhaps, Jezebel thought with a secretive smile as she stroked her still-flat belly, Lord Marksley would soon have a namesake of his own. She snuggled back against Rafe's chest, warmed by the thought. And perhaps this child would also be lucky enough to inherit his father's strength, his fortitude, and his deep-rooted sense of honor, just as she knew her firstborn had done. When she looked at her daughter, it was not her own talent she was most grateful the toddler had received. No, she thought, it was Rafe's she thanked God for each day, for the duke had within him a rare gift of love, powerful enough to heal even a heart like hers.

Blissfully unaware of her parents' scrutiny, the blond, curly-headed little girl, whose tongue stuck out earnestly as she wriggled upon the knee of her gigantic playmate, continued struggling to pick out a simple tune from the instrument with her chubby fingers. Both winced sympathetically as Allison pulled the bow up too sharply, poking her indulgent, if unusual, nanny in the eye when he could not pull back in time. It was apparent that Belzoni was mastering the urge to swear only with difficulty, mumbling and chewing furiously on the ends of his mustachios as he rubbed his watering eye with one great meaty fist. Rafe chuckled softly into Jezebel's dark, unbound hair at the sight, and they relaxed in one another's embrace for a long moment.

At last, however, Jezebel succumbed to the inevitable urge to tease her tall husband. "Well," she commented, "I've been thinking, but I just can't figure it out. What is this great talent that you think you possess, Your Grace?"

"Why, the most difficult skill of all, my sweet—one that, I might add, only a veritable genius could achieve," he boasted, not at all put out by skeptical eyebrow she raised. Then Rafe, still grinning merrily, succumbed to an urge of his own.

After a long, deliciously drawn-out taste of her rosy, smiling lips, he ended the suspense.

"I, my dear, have mastered the art of marrying Jezebel."

# *Author's Note*

*~*

*E*gypt.

The very name conjures images of romance, adventure, and ancient mysteries beyond Western comprehension. The place itself will do far more to the visitor who travels along the Nile's banks with an open mind and heart.

I first discovered I was a writer while I was there, on a trip with my family when I was eleven years old. In the shadows of the great, silent monuments and exotic cavern hieroglyphs that loom over the modern society that now exists in its place, I discovered such power and intrigue in ancient Egypt that I knew I had to find a way to express it somehow, or I would burst.

Not wanting to spread a lot of eleven-year-old glop around the pyramids, I took up writing instead. I wrote my very first poem one day, sitting upon a granite block over-looking the Nile, and I have never stopped since. I've studied both the ancient Egyptian culture and its language, and I've read as much of its literature and seen as many museum exhibits as I could. But I doubt I will ever get enough of that fascinating civilization no matter how much I study it. Perhaps that is why Rafe and Jezebel's tale is so close to my heart now.

In writing their story, I have tried to stick as closely as I possibly could to the truth of that time. But it was surprisingly difficult to find out about the early period of the nineteenth century in Egypt. Much is written about ancient Egypt, and a good deal about modern Egypt as well. Even the latter part of the nineteenth century (Sir Richard Burton's well-documented explorations, for instance) is thoroughly covered. But of the beginnings of the Western exploration of Egypt, during and just after the Napoleonic conquest, less is written. However, a few very useful resources proved invaluable to me during the writing of this novel.

The two primary sources I wish to credit are *The Rape of the Nile: Tomb Robbers, Tourists, and Archaeologists in Egypt*, by Brian M. Fagan (Moyer Bell, 1992), and *The Genesis of British Egyptology 1549–1906*, by John David Wortham (University of Oklahoma Press, 1971). These two books were marvelous sources of information and inspiration for me as I put together Jezebel's story. As well, I have a small text by the name of *The Pharaohs of Ancient Egypt* by Elizabeth Payne (Random House, 1964), to thank for a key scene involving the discovery of Jezebel's secret tomb in the Valley of the Kings.

From these works, I learned of some fascinating real-life characters living at the time, and I've tried to include a few in my book so that my readers could enjoy them as well. For instance, there really was a Giovanni Belzoni, and he was one of the major Western figures in Egypt at the time, opening up the fledgling science of Egyptology with his sometimes brilliant, sometimes brutal methods of tomb raiding and engineering. And yes, he really did spend his early years upon the London stage as a carnival performer whose feats of strength delighted the groundlings!

As well, the tomb that Jezebel seeks in the story is completely real, though I've taken some definite liberties with her means of finding it and the timing of the find. This tomb, containing the mummies of thirty-six great pharaohs including Thutmose III and Rameses II, was found in 1871 by a couple of Arab tomb raiders who stumbled upon it in the Valley of the Kings and hid the secret of their find for as long as they could by claiming an evil *afrit*, or demon spirit, guarded the area, in order that they might secretly sell off the valuable artifacts within. It was another ten years before officials of the Cairo museum became aware of its existence when uncataloged artifacts began appearing on the black market, and by the time the tomb was explored, most of its untold wealth had already been plundered. Still, the mummies remained, safe in their ancient wrappers, and to scientists like Jezebel Montclair, I like to think that that was all that would have mattered.

I hope you have enjoyed reading the tale of Jezebel and her reluctant guardian. I know I enjoyed writing it!

Hillary Fields